BRIAR ROSE

Anna Barrie was born in 1946 and lives with her husband in a village near Bath. She trained as a painter and taught for a while, but now devotes all her time to writing. Her first novel, under the pseudonym Patricia Barrie, was published in 1986; her most recent novel is *Shadows in the Rain*, also available in paperback from Pan Books.

Also by Anna Barrie in Pan Books

Shadows in the Rain

ANNA BARRIE
BRIAR ROSE

PAN BOOKS

First published 1994 by Judy Piatkus (Publishers) Ltd

This edition published 1995 by Pan Books
an imprint of Macmillan General Books
25 Eccleston Place
London SW1W 9NF
and Basingstoke

Associated companies throughout the world

ISBN 0 330 33783 1

Copyright © Wendy Barber 1994

The right of Wendy Barber to be identified as the
author of this work has been asserted by her in accordance
with the Copyright, Designs and Patents Act 1988.

All rights reserved. No reproduction, copy or transmission
of this publication may be made without written permission.
No paragraph of this publication may be reproduced, copied or
transmitted save with written permission or in accordance with
the provisions of the Copyright Act 1956 (as amended). Any
person who does any unauthorized act in relation to
this publication may be liable to criminal prosecution
and civil claims for damages.

9 8 7 6 5 4 3 2 1

A CIP catalogue record for this book is available from
the British Library

Phototypeset by Intype, London
Printed in Great Britain

This book is sold subject to the condition that it shall not,
by way of trade or otherwise, be lent, re-sold, hired out,
or otherwise circulated without the publisher's prior consent
in any form of binding or cover other than that in which
it is published and without a similar condition including this
condition being imposed on the subsequent purchaser.

For Mandy Little, with love

Part One

Chapter One

When it was just the two of them they breakfasted in the morning room at a small, circular table near the window, where the sun streamed in through the purple falls of an ancient wisteria, through a tall gothic window, through the pale and dark gold of their hair.

Even with heads bent over toast, post and the morning papers, they were still very obviously a tall couple. Beautiful, too, although his face was marred by a broken nose and hers by a cleft between her brows which spoke of perennial anxiety. He was not yet forty, and although his hair – a soft mane of blond curls – was liberally streaked with grey, he looked scarcely a day older than his wife, who was ten years his junior.

Everyone said the Huntleys were a well-matched pair, that they'd been made for each other, and although Miles rarely doubted it, Bel often did. He was not an easy man. He was like an arrangement of pegs on a solitaire board, simple only until you tried to play the game. She had discovered long ago that the desire to win was not enough. One needed courage too, intelligence and patience, and she felt herself to be deficient in all three. Courage especially.

Her letters were mostly bills. She wasn't much good at mental arithmetic and drew the line at counting on her fingers before witnesses. So, working on the principle that the money one had was always half what one needed . . . No, she couldn't have overspent by that much, surely?

Pretending to inspect her rings, Bel counted it up on her fingers. Yes, she'd been right – more or less – the first time round. Those innocent-looking columns of shillings and pence really did add up to two whole pounds! That was more than a farm labourer's weekly wage!

'Don't do it, darling.'

Miles Huntley hadn't been looking at his wife. He'd been reading the newspaper, or so she'd thought. But he'd always seemed to have eyes in the back of his head.

'Don't do what?' She turned pink and hid her hands in her lap as if to rub out the answers to her furtive calculations.

Miles widened his eyes teasingly. 'Don't play the innocent with me. You're thinking of pawning your rings, I can tell.' He hid a smile behind his newspaper. 'Your face is an open book. That's why I married you.'

'For a good read, you mean? Turn the page, will you, Miles? Tell me what happens next.'

He lowered the newspaper and reached for the toast. The toast rack was Georgian. Solid silver. Bel hadn't been thinking of pawning her rings, but now she thought of pawning the toast rack. He'd never know. There were two others, very like it but plated, in the dining-room sideboard. Would a toast rack fetch two pounds, though?

Panicking slightly, she surveyed the rest of the room and realised with dismay that, at some time or another, Miles had expressed affection for virtually everything it contained. The candlesticks, the lamps, the paintings. Even that ghastly Chinese urn in the corner, with its writhing dragons and tangled lilies. Anyway, it weighed a ton. She'd never manage to sneak *that* out of the house, and even if she did, it would leave such an enormous gap.

'Confess,' Miles said mildly now. 'How much do you need?'

Bel swallowed a lump of humiliation which felt like a conker: spiny and bitter, tasting of failure. She rested her chin on her hands and gazed bleakly at the wisteria outside the window. He was nice. That was the whole trouble with Miles. A tease, a torment, even at times something of a bully; but when the chips were down, when one needed him, he was always there: as solid as a rock and built to match. He made one feel so pathetic.

'Bel?'

'Two pounds,' she murmured weakly.

'And?'

'I haven't quite added it up yet. This lot comes to eight pounds six and threepence. And there's six pounds...' She flapped her hands as if to chase off a persistent wasp. 'Oh, I don't know. Six pounds and *something* left in the kitty.'

Bel tossed her head, pretending to pout, wanting desperately to change the subject. 'You said you married me for my feet.'

He grinned. 'You'd have looked pretty silly without them.'

'You said you adore narrow feet.'

'Was that what I said? It's so long ago. I thought I said *big.*'

'My feet aren't big!'

'You're no good, then,' he said dryly. 'Go home to your mother.'

Bel laughed, and then almost wished she hadn't. They'd been married for eleven years. Eleven years, and not a single day of it had gone by without Miles making her laugh, often in the sort of crisis which should have made her cry. And this *was* a crisis. Since the stock market crash, last year, they'd had to economise quite drastically for the first time in their lives together, and Bel was making an absolute hash of it. She would have felt better if he'd torn her off a strip, made her take the blame. But he was too good. Too patient. Too generous by half. He treated her like a child.

'The housekeeping's my responsibility,' she said. 'You shouldn't keep bailing me out. It makes me feel rotten.'

'You'd feel worse if I didn't bail you out.'

'But there must be a way, Miles. Other people manage on a tenth of my allowance.'

'They don't have servants to feed or standards to maintain. They live at only one remove from cave-dwelling. I don't want to go back to being a troglodyte yet, thank you.'

Bel pretended surprise. 'Were you ever a troglodyte?'

She'd meant it as a joke. She hadn't expected to see his smile fade and a remote chill creep across his face. Something had reminded him of the war again, of the Somme, of the trenches. It had been over for twelve years and he'd never – not once – spoken about it; but it would change his face, like this, for as long as he lived. A memory, a fleeting agony from which – as from all his true feelings – Bel was excluded. It lasted just a moment. Miles never dwelt on his moods. He barely acknowledged them. They were like flies, settling on his nose for a second before he swept them away – and smiled again.

'Don't worry, darling. We can afford to live. We just can't afford not to think about it.'

'I do think about it, Miles.'

'Of course you do.' He folded the newspaper and set it neatly beside his plate. 'What are your plans for today?'

He was changing the subject, soothing her, distracting her; and although it was easier to be soothed, she wanted something else. Something more. She wasn't sure what it was. He had once accused her of wanting to be punished for her failures, and although she was certain he was wrong, she wasn't at all certain what she wanted instead. Perhaps just to be included. To fight his battles with him. Beside, not behind him.

'One of the things I think of,' she said wanly, 'is that when you bail me out you're using money you need elsewhere.'

He laughed. His mouth was wide and generous and he seemed to have more teeth than was normal, disposed in a straight white line. He always laughed at her struggles to be taken seriously, and every time he laughed she felt diminished, overpowered by his teeth. It was crazy, she knew. She'd fallen in love with his teeth, with the irrepressible laughter in his eyes, with his strength and his grace, the impression he gave that nothing would ever beat him.

'Let me worry about that,' he said. 'If it gets too serious, I'll let you know.'

She hadn't known, then, that she was one of the things that would never beat him. She hadn't realised that his laughter was a shield to keep the whole world at bay. He never lost his temper, never said a harsh word to anyone. When he was angry he snapped his teeth shut, turned white and walked out of the house; and when he returned, sometimes as much as a day later, he was smiling again.

He disciplined the boys with cheerful mockery, or with a playful clout which confused them into good behaviour simply because they weren't certain it had been *meant* to hurt. Sometimes she saw the same frustrated bewilderment in their eyes she so often felt burning in her own. He was a fine man, a good husband, a wonderful father. Bel *loved* him. And spent the best part of every day wanting to chop him up with a meat cleaver.

'Your plans?' he prompted now.

'Nothing much. Nanny's spring-cleaning the nursery, and I said I'd take Robin for a ride to keep him out of the way.'

'Not possible, I'm afraid. Lilliput's thrown a shoe.'

Bel sighed and inspected the wisteria again. 'Oh,' she said flatly. 'Oh, well, never mind. We'll go for a walk instead. What are your plans?'

'Nothing pleasant. The bank and the accountant this morning, Jack Carter this afternoon. In that order, because I suspect

Carter means to touch me for money. Something about a leaking roof.'

There was an edge of contempt in his voice which caught Bel on the raw and brought a faint, protesting flush of pink to her face. She'd never understood his antipathy to Jack, and Miles had never explained it. He certainly didn't feel the same about his other tenants. He'd break his neck to fix their buildings, mend their fences, loan men and equipment at hay-time or harvest; but Jack had to beg, every time.

'What roof?' she asked. 'Not the farmhouse?'

'I don't know. That's why I'm seeing Frank Tottle first. If it's the house I'll have to cough up, I suppose. Anything else and he can whistle.'

Bel frowned. 'You wouldn't say that about Solomon Hicks.'

'Say what?'

'That he can whistle.'

'They might all have to whistle before long, darling.' His eyes widened. 'Why are you blushing?'

'I'm not!' But she was. She covered her cheeks with her hands, searching for an excuse beyond his gaze, beyond the window. 'Guilt,' she informed the wisteria at last.

'Guilt?' Miles grinned mockingly. 'Not another confession, darling?'

'No. Same one. I overspend the housekeeping and everyone else has to whistle. Hardly fair, is it?'

'And hardly true.'

Bel's heart thumped uncomfortably. 'What do you mean?'

'That your housekeeping is only a small part of something far more important. The whole world is on its uppers, not just the little folk of Bishop Molton. Read the papers more often, darling. Keep in touch.'

He stood up, smiled, tweaked her nose. 'I must go. Cheer up.' He was halfway across the room before he turned again. 'I might invite Frank over for tennis tomorrow. You won't mind?'

'No, of course not,' Bel murmured. Then, as the door closed behind him, 'As if I'd dare.'

She felt a little better when he'd gone, but only a little. Eleven years of marriage to Miles Huntley was like being run over, very slowly, by a steam roller. She had bravely endured getting her feet and legs flattened, but it began to feel as if the roller was approaching something more vital: one of the bits which – so far – had kept her alive. Kept her hoping that someone would put the brakes on.

She had married too young. That was the trouble. At eighteen she hadn't been wise enough to choose a husband. Just vain enough to have loved being chosen when so many women, after that dreadful war, had been doomed to eternal spinsterhood. But it astonished her to recall how she'd compared Miles with her bumbling, disorganised, soft-hearted father and found her *father* wanting!

Even with the wisdom of hindsight, she knew she'd have gone crazy twice over if she'd married a man like her father. But at least she'd have known what to *do* with a bumbler! Organise him. Tell him. Let him *know* how much he needed her.

Miles didn't need her. He was sufficient unto himself. He didn't even *want* her any more, and that was hard, that was hurtful. He made her feel so lonely. A lonely, worm-like, worthless creature who couldn't even organise a budget.

Yet he'd been such a wonderful lover. At first. In that first year. It had been a honeymoon from start to finish. Then she'd had Andrew, and it was never the same afterwards. Miles hadn't wanted a boy. He'd wanted a girl, and Andrew's arrival had wiped the smile off his face as nothing, before or since, had ever done. It had been strange; it had seemed so unnatural, for Bel had understood that all men wanted sons. But Miles had grieved. Grieved for a daughter.

'I'm sorry, Miles. Better luck next time.'

'I doubt it. The Huntleys never have girls.'

'Nonsense. What about Aunt Hermione?'

'She,' Miles had said grimly, 'was the thirteenth child. Her mother died of exhaustion a week later.'

'We'll be luckier, darling. I know we will.'

But they hadn't been. She'd had twin boys next. Then Robin. And she wasn't at all sure how she'd managed it. One had to be extremely fertile to produce three more boys from only five more attempts! Not that she'd counted. It might have been more, but she was certain at this moment that he hadn't touched her since Christmas, on Boxing Day to be exact, and that was five months ago. But she wanted to do it again (and again and again) and have a girl next time. A girl, a friend, someone to talk to. One didn't send little girls away when they were only seven.

Andrew and the twins were at prep school now, and she missed them so much, so achingly, it was like having indigestion all the time. A constant, nagging pain under her heart.

She had cried herself sick when Andrew had gone, not just because he'd gone but because Miles hadn't understood – hadn't *wanted* to understand – why she was crying. He'd teased her, laughed at her, called her a sweet, sentimental little dope. Yet it had had almost nothing to do with sentimentality. It was something much deeper – and darker – than that, a profound awareness that, in surrendering her little boy to his 'good education', she had betrayed him, betrayed herself, betrayed everything she best loved and believed in. And it didn't get any better. With the twins now, as well as Andrew, it was the same agony, every time. The only difference was that she didn't cry any more. She'd learned not to. But Robin was five already! Two more years, and Miles would send him away, too! Then where would she be?

The clock on the mantel struck the half-hour and, remembering Nanny's spring-cleaning, Bel marched across the room to ring the bell. It was a relief to move, to remind herself that she was still in one piece: physically, if not emotionally. A long, brisk walk would do her the world of good. She'd take Robin to the river and let him fish for minnows.

'Suntley?'

Muriel, the maid, who was as English as anyone, had no respect for her native language. She condensed it to its basic essentials, giving her tongue as little work as could be contrived. She had reduced Bel to 'Suntley', Miles to 'Struntley' and poor little Ethel in the scullery who, at four foot ten in her boots could have done without further reduction, to a drab and undignified 'Eff'.

'Would you clear the breakfast things, Muriel?'

Bel had learned servant management from her mother who, having never had more than two at a time and those two never enough, had meant to get the very best out of them. 'Be firm, but *unfailingly* courteous, Bel. It may not always be apparent, but servants have feelings too.'

It had never become apparent with Muriel. Miles called her Mausoleum Muriel, the Walking Dead. Her eyes did as little work as her tongue, with no flash or flicker to indicate that anyone human dwelt behind them. It was possible to gaze into the eyes of a shorthorn cow and find more evidence of life, of love, of curiosity. There had been times in her life when Bel would not have understood why this should be: how anyone could get through a day without making some kind of personal statement, but she understood Muriel now. What use were personal statements, expressions of feeling, of thought, even of humour, when nothing one said or did made the slightest difference? Sometimes, at her worst, Bel could gaze into the glass and see no more life in her eyes than she saw in Muriel's. But she still had feelings. Oh, yes, too many.

'Thank you, Muriel,' she said now, very gently. 'You're a good girl. What would we do without you?'

Not a gleam. Not a glimmer.

'Virow, Suntley?'

'Yes, let the fire out. It's going to be warm today, I think.'

She gazed beyond Muriel's stooped shoulders to the garden and the park and the elm trees that bordered it, planning her walk with Robin. They would go to the river, fish for minnows, make ships out of sticks and race them under the bridge. Then, if there was time, they might call in to see Mrs Carter and her new baby. Another girl. And Jack had so much wanted a son this time.

Why was life so *unfair*?

Bel hurried from the room and up the main staircase to fetch Robin. For reasons she dared not investigate, she was blushing again.

There was never a moment of the day when Jean Carter was not conscious of being fat. She slept on her side with her back to her husband, and the first thing she became aware of, as she woke, was the flaccid heap of breasts and bellies which barred her entry to the day. She stood five foot two in her stockinged feet and was almost that big around. Jack had once called her a little fairy. Now he called her a fairy elephant.

She might have borne it if it hadn't been for fashion. Fashion had cast female flesh from grace just after the war and hurled it, screaming, into the raging hell of chest-flattening corsets. Why, in twelve years, it had not fought its way out again, Jean could not imagine. Corsets were agony. They were martyrdom. And for what? To defend Jack, and every other man-jack whose eyes rested upon her, from the wicked obscenity of *fat*. Damn them. Damn them.

She was still so beautiful inside. Frail, delicate, quivering and bejewelled, like an autumn cobweb. But who cared about cobwebs? And who could resist tearing them apart? Who cared about the poor little spider whose work they were? Not Jack. Nor any man-jack.

Jack said she ate too much, that she was a pig, rooting in corners for scraps even a pig would think beneath its notice.

As far as this went it was true enough, but only because in the face of his contempt she'd given up eating at table and was reduced to scavenging leftovers behind the scullery door. Cake, bacon, cabbage, the corpse-like remains of congealed suet puddings. They all went in together, jammed in by the heel of her hand and swallowed whole, before Jack could catch her at it. And, when he did catch her, with her mouth full to bursting and her chin smeared with gravy, who could blame him for calling her a pig?

She wasn't a pig. She was a spider, spinning nets out of nothing, trapping morsels of sweetness from thin air. And he hadn't taken everything. He'd given her a home and two lovely children who, because they were not boys, he'd said were hers alone. Hers to keep, hers to nurture, hers to love. She was full of love. Once – and not so long ago – it had all been for Jack.

She was cleaning the landing window, poking into the corners with a spent matchstick and a shred of soapy rag, seeing only the rippling glass and the gleaming, silvery leads. She was panting: partly with exertion and partly with lust for the shining corners of her home where no dirt had been left to settle since the day she'd moved into it, four years ago.

Jean had loved the farmhouse on sight, and her love had deepened to a passion in the moment she'd first crossed its threshold. It was too big: impossible to furnish adequately in less than a lifetime, but that was part of its charm – that it was almost beautiful enough to exist without furniture. Every wall was panelled in rich, golden oak, every ceiling beamed, every beam roughly carved with acorns, oak-leaves and strange, tulip-like flowers. The windows, which had once been tall rectangles, had been made smaller at some time in their history and transformed into leaded arches with tiny, blue-green lights. And there was a deep carved seat under almost every one, so that even the pleasurable business of window-cleaning became a triple pleasure, allowing Jean the unusual luxury of sitting down to view the world while she worked.

Save for the bedding and the rag rugs she had made under winter lamplight, there were few soft things in the house and fewer colours, for Jack had no use for comfort and refused to pay for it; but it was astonishing how much beauty could be created with soap and water, a jar of beeswax and a perennially aching elbow. Bare wood and stone, glass and iron: their colours were deep and subtle like the powers of ancient gods, surrendered only to the most fervent of worshippers. And Jean *was* the most fervent. With a polishing cloth in her hand she could slip into a trance a dervish might have envied, escaping to places beyond the world, where only the cries of her children could reach her.

'Mummy?'

Jean jumped. She widened her eyes. She blinked, turned, listened.

'Mummy, shall we be seeing the new baby?'

Visitors . . . Jean tip-toed into one of the spare, and still unfurnished, bedrooms to tidy her hair, to loosen the ties of her sacking apron. She peeped from the window, craning her neck. Mrs Huntley and Robin . . . And Jack.

Jean saw her husband every day, barely noticing him except to judge his mood. Whatever his mood, she deemed him ugly, even knowing that he was one of the most beautiful men she had ever seen. Tall, dark and handsome. A Valentino, minus greasepaint. They said that beauty was in the eye of the beholder, but Jean knew better. Beauty was in the *mind* of the beholder, in the knowledge – or lack of it – of what lay behind the face, the figure, the wolf's sheepskin disguise. Mrs Huntley had no such knowledge of Jack and, because Jean understood this, she now saw her husband as Mrs Huntley saw him: the perfect gentleman.

'Fool,' she hissed softly. 'Look closer! Use your eyes!'

But who was she to talk? One never looked close enough

until it was too late. He'd said he'd loved her . . . Liar. Filthy liar. And Mrs Huntley thought him a gentleman!

Well, maybe he was. Maybe Miles Huntley was the same. Who could tell? Jean had often wondered about the Huntleys' private lives, wondered what went on between them when the servants weren't watching. Miles, that most gentle of gentlemen, might well be a brute at heart. And Isobel Huntley – as sweet and innocent as a child to look at her – might just as easily be a whore.

Oh, yes. *Just* as easily! Jean crept nearer to the window, keeping to the shadows. She was smiling, biting her lip.

'Sweet and innocent, eh?' she murmured. 'Not with *that* look in your eyes, Madam.'

Something stabbed at her heart, making her moan, and it was not – not at all – the look in Mrs Huntley's eyes which had hurt so much. It was just that Jack had moved a little to one side, exposing to his wife's jealous gaze the straight, slender lines of their visitor's figure. Slim as a reed. Dainty as a fairy. And not the least sign of a corset to hold it all together!

She was wearing a soft blue skirt with pleats over the knees, a cream poplin tunic and a straw cloche hat, trimmed with blue. The hat, and the waving gold hair which peeped beneath it, set off the lean angle of her jaw, the swan-like curve of her throat, her narrow shoulders. And it was no wonder she had that look in her eyes! It was reflected from Jack's eyes; a deep, aching hunger for the taste of raw bones!

Jean chuckled to herself. 'Jack Sprat would eat no fat, his wife would eat no lean . . .'

The murmur of their voices drifted through the open window on the landing. They were talking about the weather and, as far as Jean could tell, had mentioned nothing else. But now Robin asked again about the baby, and Mrs Huntley turned her big blue eyes up to Jack's dark brown ones and said, 'I adore you.'

No. No, she didn't. She said, 'He adores babies. Is your wife at home?'

'Yes, yes. She'll be delighted to see you. Do, please, come in.'

Jack was mimicking her voice, her plummy accents; or, rather, her husband's voice, her husband's accents. He'd always wanted to be like Miles. He couldn't afford the handmade boots, the made-to-measure tweeds, but he spent half his income on cheap imitations. He'd even bought an imitation Bentley. It was called a Ford.

'Oh, please *do* come in,' Jean whispered bitterly. 'You'll take sherry? A glass of Madeira? And you simply *must* stay to luncheon!'

She heard the door in the hall creaking open. She heard Mrs Huntley laugh and Jack stride grittily over the polished boards to the foot of the gleaming stairs.

'Jean? Darling?'

Darling! Oh-ho! What had become of 'Pig-face'?

Jean thrust her knuckles between her teeth and bit until she tasted blood. Then, 'Coming, dear!' she called sweetly. But she was disappointed in herself. She'd been trying for 'dearest' – and choked on it.

Chapter Two

'I have no idea why it should be,' Bel's mother had confided to Miles before the wedding. 'She's certainly been *taught* the principles of economy. But she can't manage money, Captain Huntley. She's like her father in that respect. She thinks it comes from God, like the sparrows' raiment, and nothing I've ever said has convinced her otherwise.'

Miles had borne that in mind.

Bel's father, the Archdeacon, a dear, sweet old soul, had advised him, too. He'd said that Bel was a clement-weather plant, able to grow only when the sun shone. 'Try never to blow on her when the wind's in the east, Captain Huntley.'

Miles had borne that in mind, too. It hadn't always been easy, but he'd been helped by his own nature – or perhaps nurture – which had given him a deep antipathy to expressions of destructive emotion. Rage, sorrow and anxiety, the 'east winds' of his moods; if he couldn't laugh them off, he walked or worked them off, leaving Bel as safe as he could make her in her sunny corner.

But he couldn't walk off the cold winds of commerce. Property was falling, industry stagnating, agricultural land, rents, grain and fatstock prices at rock bottom. As a landowner and 'gentleman farmer' Miles could do nothing but lose,

lose and lose again. For himself, he didn't greatly care; but he had four sons to educate, to feed, house and nurture . . . And a clement-weather plant to keep safe from the frost.

He couldn't bear to think that Bel might suffer for any failure of his. It was bad enough to have to fail her in bed. He knew she didn't understand it, that she thought he was rejecting her in some way; but it was more than he could do to explain. It wasn't a thing one could easily discuss, and anyway, he barely understood it himself. He loved her. He wanted her. And there was nothing wrong with him physically. He could have made love under the breakfast table with no trouble at all! It was just in bed that it all went wrong. The desire left him, the strength departed, and he was filled with an inexplicable grief, 'too deep for tears'. Then . . . Then he wanted only to hold her and be held. To comfort her and take comfort . . .

But it didn't work that way. He had taught her too well, given her an appetite for . . . what was the word? Sex. Yes, sex, that was it. Funny how these things slipped one's mind . . .

Now, when he turned to her, kissed her, held her, she thought he was taking her on a journey to a certain destination. Paris. The Venice Lido. Capri. And he could see her point, for where's the sense in boarding a train which goes nowhere?

'The train now standing on platform three is the ten forty-five to platform three, stopping at platform three, platform three and platform three.'

No . . . no sense at all.

But it was playing on her nerves, on his conscience and his confidence. To a degree, he supposed, it was altering his behaviour towards her. He teased her more than he should, somehow needing to undermine *her* confidence, to make *her* feel as inadequate as he felt. He always regretted it before it went too far, but never enough to keep himself from doing it again. It was hurting them both, like the wretched economy, and Miles was helpless to change either of them.

He had driven home from Bristol the long way round, to

give himself time to think, approaching the Dray Valley from the soaring hill of Dundry. It was a beautiful day, but tomorrow it would rain, for the views were too clear, the air like polished crystal. He sighed and pulled the Bentley into an open gateway to light his first cigarette of the day. He'd been cutting down ever since the war, but had never quite managed to give it up. Smoking freed his mind, helped him to think. And anyway, he was devoted to the gold cigarette case which Bel had given him on their honeymoon. It summed her up, somehow. He'd given her twice as much money as she could possibly need to cover her private expenses during their honeyed month of bliss, and she'd spent every penny of it before the first week was over. Typical! Quite typical, for she'd spent it all on him. Solid gold . . .

Far below him, and disposed in a wide semicircle around the valley, were the three villages of Bishop Molton, Church Molton and Molton Draycott, the latter named for the River Dray which ran beside — and sometimes across — the High Street. Miles owned about half the properties in all three villages and, until now, he had maintained them with pride and some satisfaction. Some irritation, too, for he could do very little about the squalor in which some of his tenants lived. All he could do was keep the rain out.

But that might soon have to change. Christ, what an irony . . . Just as he'd begun to think they could all live cleaner, healthier, more civilised lives, he'd run out of bloody money! They already had electricity in Bishop Molton and the water main and mains drainage would be through before the end of the year. They'd have 'water, water, everywhere'! Through the blasted roof, as well as the bloody taps!

Miles groaned and threw back his head, shutting his eyes on his troubles. The sun warmed his face, a skylark soothed his ears and the air was heavy with the scent of wild hawthorn. *Peace.*

He sat up suddenly and laughed.

This was not the worst thing ever to have happened to him. He'd been in worse – far worse – pickles than this and survived. He was a lucky man. He was alive and – give or take the odd malfunctioning corner – whole and healthy, young and strong. He still had many blessings to count.

He'd start with his wife. He'd rush into the house, swing her off her feet, tell her he loved her and kiss her all to blazes!

And if that didn't get Mausoleum Muriel jumping out of her casket, he'd damn well kiss *her*, as well!

There were beef olives for lunch. Bel thought them rather good and was dismayed to see Miles turning one morsel over, as if inspecting it for gristle.

'Is yours tough, darling?'

'No. Why?'

'You don't seem terribly impressed.'

He shrugged. He chewed, gazing beyond her, to the garden.

'Miles?'

'Hmm?'

'Are you . . . Are you annoyed about anything?'

Suddenly their eyes met, and there was no mistaking it any more. He *was* annoyed. But now he grinned and reached for the mustard. 'What sort of thing?'

'How should I know?' Bel pursed her mouth irritably. 'You've got that look in your eyes, that's all.'

'Have I?' He laughed. 'Well, that makes two of us.'

Bel felt her face warming and, hoping to distract him she said crossly, 'If you want me to economise, you can hardly expect roast beef every day.'

'Quite. And I'm not complaining. Er – where were you when I came home?'

'Upstairs. Why?'

'Oh, no reason. I had something to tell you. It's slipped my mind now.'

'Oh, well. It couldn't have been important.'

'Either that, or it was a lie.' He scowled at his beef, prodded it suspiciously, wrinkled his nose.

'Still not complaining, darling?' Bel enquired acidly.

'I just think it could have done with less parsley. Dried parsley always seems to taste of socks.'

Bel breathed a sigh of relief. Parsley she could cope with. Cook had said the beef olives required rump steak, not braising, and with her budget in mind Bel had said, 'Nonsense. Stew them a bit longer. He'll never know.' It would have been embarrassing in the extreme to have to go back and confess, 'He knew.'

'I'd have thought,' Miles went on mildly, 'there'd be some parsley in the garden by this time. Shouldn't there be?'

'Yes, I suppose there should. Or – no, perhaps not. It was a late Easter, wasn't it?'

'Easter?'

'You have to sow parsley on Good Friday, and it takes an age to germinate.'

'What happens if you sow it any other day?'

'Nothing. Or, rather, the same as if you sow it on Good Friday. But it's no use my telling George that. He'd say I was "floyin' in the fyce o' Nychure".'

'How does Nature know when it's Good Friday?'

'Search me. Perhaps it reads the Parish News.' She was trying to amuse him, but Miles didn't want to be amused and Bel eyed him anxiously, wondering what was really bothering him.

Muriel brought in a rice shape with bottled pears, and they finished their meal in virtual silence. Several times, Bel almost managed to tell Miles about her visit to the Carters, but she couldn't find the right tone for it, couldn't decide on the right opening phrase. And he'd be going there himself straight after lunch. She'd have to tell him. Before Jack did.

Just as she opened her mouth to speak, Muriel arrived

again with the coffee, and before the door had closed on her departure Miles leaned across the table, his eyes bright with mischief.

'Now – ' he urged in a gossipy whisper, ' – tell me about your morning, darling. I hear you came home pregnant!'

'*What?*'

'Yes, I was surprised, too. Little pitchers have big ears, don't they?'

'Oh!' Bel laughed with relief. 'Brute! You've been talking to Robin! Yes, he was very taken with the Carter baby, and she's an absolute darling, Miles. They've called her Shirley. Isn't that pretty? And Robin was so gentle with her. He held her on his knee and positively *cooed*! He couldn't stop asking, on the way home, why we couldn't have one too! Is that what he asked you?'

'No, he told me it had all been arranged, that you'd discussed – with *Mr* Carter – the relative virtues of boy babies and girl babies and at last reached an amicable compromise. He'd give you a girl, and you'd give him a boy. Was that how it went?'

'Really, Miles!' Reddening, Bel laughed again. 'No, that was not how it went! You know what children are!'

'So how *did* it go?'

Bel shrugged helplessly. 'Well, he did say he was disappointed they hadn't had a son this time.'

'And you said?'

'I said . . . I said nothing's perfect. That I'd like a girl and he'd like a boy; but that really we ought to be grateful for the children we have and not – er – cry for the moon.'

'Ah.' He stirred his coffee. 'And what was his view of it?'

'He agreed, of course. But . . .'

'But?'

'But that they'd try again anyway and, if they had another girl, he'd give it to me. It was just a joke, darling. Not at all as Robin reported it. There's no need to be cross.'

'Am I cross?' He laughed, but Bel suddenly realised that even if he wasn't cross, she was. He'd engineered this entire conversation to embarrass her; and all because *he* didn't like Jack Carter!

Miles had never told her what she could or could not do; but it was as plain as the nose on his face that he'd like to tell her to keep away from the Carters. Well, she wouldn't keep away! Why should she? They were charming people.

True, Bel didn't quite know what to make of Mrs Carter. She *was* very nice. Very friendly and kind. But she was not at all of her husband's class. She rolled her 'r's. And she neglected her hands, which were plump and red and chewed at the nails. Jack had such beautiful hands . . . He was tall, slim and graceful . . . And his voice was not unlike Miles's voice: clear and crisp, with a soft, honeyed undernote . . .

She bit her lip.

'Now what are you thinking?' Miles demanded softly.

Bel jumped and then, to her horror, felt her eyes fill with tears. 'Nothing! Oh, for God's sake, Miles, leave me alone!'

'Bel!' He was with her, crouching beside her, holding her hands. 'What is it, sweetheart?'

'Nothing.' She looked beyond him, counting the blue and red squiggles in the carpet's border. 'I'm just . . .'

'Just what?' he asked gently.

'Oh, I don't know. Crying for the moon, I suppose. I *would* like another baby, Miles. A little girl . . .'

Miles sighed and patted her hand. 'Now come on, darling. We've been through all this before. My family doesn't *make* girls. *I* don't make girls.'

Bel gritted her teeth and swallowed. But her feelings had bubbled too close to the surface and wouldn't be kept down.

'Only because you won't *try*!' she cried furiously. 'You won't damn well *try*! And sometimes I hate you for it, Miles! I *hate* you for it!'

He dropped her hands and closed his eyes.

'Oh, I'm sorry,' Bel whispered drearily. 'I didn't mean . . .'
He stood up and turned away, making for the door.
'Miles, *please*!'
But he'd gone.

He slept on the narrow bed in his dressing room that night, claiming a headache which would keep him awake; and, in a distant voice which she immediately regretted, Bel said, 'I imagine you had too much to drink, darling.'

'Yes. Perhaps I did. Goodnight.'

It had never happened before. He'd slept in the dressing room before, of course, when she was too heavily pregnant to get comfortable, or when one of them had a streaming cold; but they'd never gone to separate beds on such bad terms. Bel remembered several nights, quite early in their marriage, when they'd stayed up arguing until four in the morning rather than 'let the sun go down on their wrath'.

But this wasn't the same. There was no passion in it – and that about summed up their entire situation. No passion. No direction. Always, before, their disagreements had felt like railway tunnels with a small spot of light at the end they could travel towards. But this wasn't a tunnel. It was a brick wall.

In a remote part of her mind, Bel felt a need to pull one of the bricks out, to poke her hand through and see if there was anything beyond it; but she was too tired to try. No, not too tired. Too afraid. Afraid that there was nothing at all beyond it. He didn't need her. He didn't want her. So what was the point of trying?

But they were married, for heaven's sake! Married, until death did them part! There had to be something more than this, surely? They had to find some way to satisfy each other!

Was it really all Bel's fault? Miles seemed to think so, or else why was he in that bed and she in this one, all alone? Was there something wrong with her, some dreadful flaw which only Miles had noticed? Most *other* people liked her. In fact, she couldn't think of a single one who didn't. People seemed to warm to her, to confide in her, to trust her in a way Miles had never done. She'd come to think that this was because other people didn't know her as Miles knew her, that he was right and they wrong. But perhaps . . . No, it couldn't be the other way around. He *did* know her. He'd lived with her for eleven years and knew . . .

No. No! What the hell *did* he know? She'd spent more than half her life with him wishing he'd look closer, wishing he'd listen, not just to the words she said but to their *meanings*. And she meant so much more than she could ever say; she thought so much more than she could ever explain! Perhaps she wasn't better than he thought her, but she was different, *different*. And he wouldn't look. He wouldn't listen. He made her feel so *worthless*.

Their bed was six feet wide. Sitting there all alone, pretending to read, Bel felt as small and exposed as a tick on a pig's back.

She sagged against her pillows. Sighing, she prised a brick from the wall.

'Did you take a powder, Miles?'

He didn't reply.

'Are you asleep?'

Bel sighed again and added, very softly, 'Some headache.'

Minutes passed. Bel returned to her book: a thin, rather depressing novel about the unemployed in Liverpool. Miles had suggested she read it. She wondered why.

'It would probably help,' Miles said suddenly, 'if you'd turn off the light, darling.'

'Oh!' Furious, Bel slammed the book shut. So he *had* been awake, damn him! She reached for the light switch and, at the last minute, withdrew her hand. They'd had the electric installed last year, and she'd grown accustomed to the wall switches, could flip them up and down without sparing more than a passing thought for sudden death by electrocution. But

25

the bedside light was another matter. The switch was so close to the bulb. It grew so hot, and sometimes made a faint, panicky buzzing sound, like a bee stuck in a foxglove blossom.

'Oh, what the hell?' she muttered. 'Who cares?'

Darkness fell with a loud clunk.

'Thank you,' Miles said frostily.

'My pleasure.'

It was horribly dark. Horribly quiet. The rich, honeyed perfume of wisteria drifted in at the open window, and Bel was suddenly possessed by a crazy urge to laugh.

'Think nothing of it,' she murmured wickedly. 'Anything for you, darling. I should hate you to suffer. Are you sure I can't fetch you a powder? A damp towel for your eyes? Some warm milk?'

Silence.

'How about a cheese sandwich?' Bel suggested flatly.

He didn't reply. Bel's tormenting urge to laugh became a leaden need to cry. She fought it off. She stared determinedly at the ceiling until her eyes began to ache, to droop with sleep.

Jack Carter loomed into view, his straight black hair slicked back from his brow, his dark eyes veiled with languor. When he smiled his mouth went up at one corner and down at the other. Wicked, but oh, so . . . His smile made Bel's knees itch. She drew them together, then stretched them apart, wriggling her toes. She reached out an arm, stroking the empty sheets to find . . .

– and, forsaking all other, keep thee only unto him, so long as ye both shall live.

She had almost been asleep. Now she was wide awake, her eyes wide, her heart thudding with horror. She didn't want Jack! She didn't, she didn't! And he didn't want her. Heavens, no, and why on earth should he? His wife was young, much younger than Bel. She was strong and capable (more capable than Bel by a long chalk) and really quite pretty . . .

She closed her eyes again and snuggled down under the

covers, trapping her hands between her knees. And – quite apart from all that – Mrs Carter was a wonderful mother. The way she'd looked into that baby's face had been enough to bring a lump to the throat of the strongest man. So much love . . .

Now Bel saw Jack taking his wife in his arms, smiling that beautiful crooked smile of his, whispering sweet, seductive nothings. He slid his fingers through the tight little bun at the back of her head (*most* unfashionable in this day and age) and withdrew all the pins one after another until her rich, russet-brown hair tumbled like a river about her shoulders and her green eyes danced with a bright, emerald light.

No, the green of her eyes wasn't at all like emeralds, more like over-boiled cabbage. She had a lovely complexion, though. Milk and honey and rose-petal pink, and not even a touch of rouge to enhance it.

Bel thought of her own complexion as it would look first thing in the morning. Parchment fine, parchment white, with tiny lines already crinkling at the corners of her eyes. Miles said that without her powder and paint she looked like a marble bust carved by a master; but that was just flannel. She looked like a corpse.

Jack Carter slid a softly caressing finger down his wife's smooth white throat. He stroked her shoulders, he weighed her milk-heavy breasts in the palms of his hands, and she sighed, she groaned . . .

'Ohh!' Bel drew her knees closer to her chin, rocking herself against the pillows.

'Bel?' It was Miles again. 'Are you all right?'

'What? Oh!' (Dear God, had she really groaned aloud?) 'Yes, fine. Touch of cramp, that's all.'

She was drenched in sweat. 'Oh, God,' she whispered. 'Oh, God, oh, God.'

She sat up again. 'Miles?'

'Yes?'

'Come in with me, will you, darling? Please? You know I didn't mean what I said. I understand. Really I do. We can't possibly afford to send *five* boys to Winchester.'

Again there was silence. Again Bel slumped against her pillows, but this time she wept, and her hand, stroking the empty sheets, searched for nothing more reprehensible than a handkerchief.

'Bel? Is that offer of a sandwich still going?'

She blew her nose. She laughed with relief. 'You weren't meant to hear that!'

'Well, I did, and I've been starving ever since.'

She heard his feet hit the floor, and jumped out of bed to meet him. He'd put on his dressing gown, but hadn't tied the cord, and she slid her arms around him, stroked his back, laid her cheek against the soft golden hairs on his chest. He smelled of sandalwood, brandy and Turkish tobacco.

'Oh, Miles, I do love you.'

Something moved against her belly. Something which hadn't moved there since Boxing Day. She smiled and kissed him.

'Bel?' he whispered.

'Mmm?'

'Now I come to think... It wasn't really a *sandwich* I wanted.'

A man wasn't a man until he'd had a son. Jack had confided this to his wife when she was expecting their first. She'd swollen up, by then, to the size of a charabanc, but he hadn't minded. She was going to have a boy.

She'd had a girl: a shrivelled, limp, grey little thing, with no hope of life in it. Jack wasn't there. The tortured screams of that dark, fruitless labour (she'd known it was wrong from the start) had scared him off and, long before he returned, the midwife had wrapped Jean's little girl in a newspaper and taken her away.

Wrapped her in a newspaper . . . Even now, four years on, the thought of it was an agony. Jean had borne that child for nine months, loved it for nine whole *months*, neither knowing nor caring about its sex or the colour of its eyes, knowing only that it was *hers*. It could have been born with two heads and she'd still have loved it. It had been born dead . . . and she loved it still.

But Jack hadn't cared. He'd stood at the foot of the bed, tapping his foot. 'Oh, well,' he'd said. 'Never mind.'

'I do mind! I do mind!'

'But it was only a girl.'

She had doubted him before, many times, but not enough to have warned herself of this. This breakage. She'd been too tired to weep, let alone scream, rage, or pluck out his eyes. But her grief had been all the greater for having no expression. It had collapsed inwards, somehow, like a spider's web, and shrouded her heart with hatred.

Her fault, perhaps. She'd expected too much of him. He was a just countryman, a farmer's son, and his flimsy Grammar School education had done no more than lay a veneer over the countryman's brutal acceptance of life and death, of nature in the raw. Maybe she'd asked too much when she'd asked him to care.

But no, no. No, it *wasn't* her fault, for he'd deliberately deceived her with that frost-thin veneer. He'd wanted her to believe him a gentleman, if only because he'd so wanted to believe it himself. Poor fool. Fools, fools, the pair of them.

A man wasn't a man until he'd had a son, and a woman was no good until she'd borne him one. Thus it was that, six weeks after the death of their first-born girl, the birth of their second, and now, the birth of their third, Jack must try for his manhood again.

She'd known it was coming. On the day of Mrs Huntley's visit, she knew it had come, because Jack was different afterwards, smiling and warm, glowing with lust and longing. That it was all for Mrs Huntley was neither here nor there. Mrs Huntley had another bed to lie in.

'She's a lovely woman though, isn't she, Jean? No side to her at all. Not like her husband. His manners are all right, on the surface, but you know what he thinks underneath. He thinks we're dirt.'

Even when Jack was trying to be nice, his eyes were as bitter as sloes, the curl of his lip an obscenity which turned Jean's stomach. But she never thwarted him. She never fought her corner. How could she, when behind her and dependent on her were the two little girls their father had disowned?

'But you do like her, don't you, Jean? It was nice, wasn't it, having another woman to talk to? You should ask her to come over more often. Get out of yourself a bit. Be sociable.'

It sounded good, almost reasonable, but Jean wanted to laugh at his foolishness. Who did he think he was? Did he really think himself good enough to dole out invitations to a woman like Isobel Huntley? As for her having no 'side'... Well, he was mad if he thought that. She was nice, yes, and so was her husband, but only until Jack was crass enough to take advantage of it. *His manners are all right, on the surface*... Fool!

Later still, when the geese were shut in their house and the soft dusk fading, Jack said brightly, 'I like the way she's had her hair done. You ought to have yours cut like that. Just because we live out in the wilds is no reason to let yourself go, you know. You're only twenty-five. I wonder how old she is... Thirty? Thirty-two, would you say? My kind of age? You'd never think she'd had four kids though, would you? Whew... Built like a greyhound.'

Jean smiled. Given time, and the run of his tongue, he reduced all women to animals. Pig, bitch, mare, cow. And he thought 'greyhound' was a compliment!

She went upstairs while the sky was still light, to check on the children and to wait – as he waited – for darkness to fall.

The imagination needed darkness to prime it. And tonight he'd be bedding a greyhound.

Jean could bear it. She could even *grin* and bear it, for she wanted a son almost as much as he did, if only for insurance purposes. He could not dismiss the mother of his son. He couldn't scorn her. And without his scorn perhaps Jean could be a woman again, not a pig, rooting in corners for treasures she could not find.

Yes, one day she might bear him a son. But there would *never* be a day when Jack Carter would come to manhood!

Chapter Three

It was Bel's birthday at the beginning of June. Her thirtieth. The big one. It was hard to know what to think about it. On the one hand she felt she'd grown up and come into her own at last. On the other she felt that a woman of thirty was beyond all hope of improving herself. Until now she'd been growing, learning, making mistakes. Making excuses. Now there were no excuses left. A woman of thirty should *always* know better.

Miles had said he would buy her anything she wanted for her birthday, meaning it only as far as he trusted her not to want a world cruise. She didn't, really, want anything at all, but he wouldn't hear of that, of course, and she wouldn't mention it. She didn't want anything . . . except to be eighteen again.

Would she still have married him? Yes, because she would still have loved him. But oh, dear God, she'd have done it so differently! For one thing she'd have known that marriage was just as much a question of politics as of love. At eighteen, Bel had been like the British Empire, like Africa, too innocent in the ways of the world to realise that Miles (the British Army), would take all that she had and give only glass beads in return. Glass beads and patronage and the noble rule of law.

Yet it wasn't really Miles's fault. It was no one's fault, except perhaps God's, for making eighteen-year-old girls such perfect fools. She'd been thrilled with glass beads. She'd had no notion that strength – a show of it at least – was more important. Now it was too late. The big guns had done their work before she'd even thought of sharpening her pathetic wooden spear, and now, however much she might flourish it, stamp her feet, chant her little war-cries, Miles barely noticed. 'A spot of trouble with the natives', that was all she was now.

'Hey,' Miles turned from the dressing chest to catch her chin, tipping her face to meet his smile. 'Thirty's not the end of the world, you know. I'm the proof of it, aren't I?'

'Men are different.'

'Nonsense. We have our vanities too.'

'It isn't a question of vanity!'

She shook him off. Always, always, he reduced her feelings to the most trivial he could imagine! Vanity! What the hell had *she* to be vain about? What had she achieved, what had she learned in thirty years, how had she grown, improved herself?

'Well, all right,' Miles said placidly. 'Look at my mother. Thirty wasn't the end of the world for her, was it? Nor sixty.' He smiled ruefully. 'I don't suppose even eighty will beat her.'

He couldn't have said anything worse, although he was not to have known it. His mother had never confided in him, deeming him 'too much a man to understand', but she'd told Bel that her marriage had been like a coffin, travelling to a distant graveyard in a slow-moving hearse. Not one to mince words, was Violet Huntley. She served them up whole, complete with their bones, and if you were at all inclined to choke on them, that was your misfortune.

Bel had choked on them. They'd sounded so familiar, yet at the same time made her feel such an ungrateful cur. Miles wasn't like his father: steeped for so long in the security of his ancient squiredom that (according to Violet) he'd thought even blowing his nose too much like hard work. 'But he sniffed with enormous *vigour*,' Violet had said acidly. 'It was the last thing he did before he died.'

He'd died of pneumonia in the December of 1914 and, before it had become even remotely decent to do so, Violet had shut up Bishop's Court and gone to London to drive an ambulance, to run a soldiers' canteen . . . to live. She'd learned who she really was, and the woman she was resembled the wife she had been only as much as a horseshoe resembled a cream bun.

In many ways, the real Violet was an atrocious woman. Miles could barely tolerate her and Bel was afraid of her. But Violet was afraid of nothing. She was real – and built of steel.

Not even by the wildest stretch of imagination could Bel imagine that *she* had any steel in her soul. But she was certain – almost certain – that there was more to it than sugared dough.

'Why,' she asked irritably now, 'do you never take me seriously?'

Miles was silent for a while, fixing his collar studs, selecting his tie. Then, 'I don't take anything very seriously, Bel. Not even myself. Why should you be different?'

'Would, "because I need to be," be a good reason?'

'Not really. *I* need a thousand a year more than I have, but what does it matter? My need makes me no different from anyone else. We none of us can have more than the system offers.'

'But money and feelings – '

'Aren't so very different, Bel. After all, why do I need money? To care for my family, my home, my employees, my tenants – in short, to protect my feelings. But my feelings don't matter. My needs can't change anything.'

He was still smiling, but his eyes were bleak. They often were. They'd been even bleaker when Bel had first known him, but she hadn't noticed. Her father had. He'd called Miles 'a poor, sad soul', and Bel hadn't even asked him to explain what he'd meant. She'd noticed only that Miles was handsome, wealthy, courteous and always smiling. He was the white knight: the sunlight glinting from his armour blinding the world to the man who dwelt inside it. Bel had never seen that man. Eleven years married, and she hadn't a clue who he was.

'Your feelings matter to *me*,' she said. 'At least, they would matter if I knew what they were. But you don't tell me. Obviously I can't give you the money you need – '

'But that's just my point. My needs can't change anything, so where's the sense in discussing them? And your needs can't change *me*, Bel. I wish they could, truly. But . . .'

He closed his eyes, and his face, reflected in his dressing glass, became for a moment very still. Bel knew him well enough to know that he was gathering his patience, changing his mood. She'd seen him do it so often – and resented it utterly.

Suddenly he whirled on his heel, laughing again. 'Oh, come on, Bel, it's your birthday! Let's enjoy it, shall we?' He caught her face in his hands. 'I do love you, you know.' He kissed her nose. 'I've always had a soft spot for old ladies.'

'What?' In spite of herself she laughed. He always made her laugh, damn him. And it *was* her birthday. One didn't stage insurrections on one's birthday. It wasn't done.

They lunched at the Grand Spa and then wandered through Clifton, searching for a birthday gift which wouldn't cost the earth. Miles hadn't, of course, stipulated a price. Mention of prices was strictly for the Home Farm accounts and the housekeeping budget. Beyond that, Miles was a gentleman who expected his wife to be a lady. When they were first married, being a lady had meant wanting only a *short* rope of pearls, so that he, the gentleman, could say, 'Aren't longer ones more the style, darling?' and generously cough up. Now it was more ladylike to keep the books balanced and their servants and farm people in employment.

The trouble was that Bel had expensive tastes. Always had had, even as a young girl, when having expensive tastes had been as futile as raking moonlight. She couldn't help it. It was some kind of instinct. Try all she might to pick the cheapest thing on offer, she always seemed to end up with the dearest. The cigarette case she'd bought for Miles on their honeymoon was a perfect example. She'd planned to spend a guinea on a humble memento and, with the humbleness in mind, had chosen the plainest, most unassuming case in the shop, thinking (almost guiltily), I'll have it engraved to make it seem more special. Miles had been using that case for the best part of five years before her heart had ceased to thud at the memory of those awful words: 'That will be eight guineas, madam.'

So she *had* learned *something* in thirty years. She'd learned to say 'How much?' before she said, 'Engrave it.'

They had searched the length of Blackboy Hill and Whiteladies Road before Miles took out his watch. 'If we're going to take the boys to tea, darling... Haven't you anything at all in mind?'

'Mm. A brooch, but for no good reason that I can think of. Oh, yes, I've just thought of it. My tweed jacket, the one we bought in Edinburgh. It always seems to need something. Something quite plain... and unassuming.'

'Oh, Lord,' Miles groaned comically. 'Now we're in trouble.'

But they found it at the very next shop: a dingy, run-down little place, its purple velvet display cases fading to brown. The brooch sat all alone in the window's top left-hand corner; and something about it attracted Bel immediately.

'That,' she said. 'The little briar rose.'

Inside, the shop had a smell of mothballs, dust and turpentine, and the old man who shuffled forward to greet them looked as if he'd been pickled in all three. But he was a charming old gentleman. Three of his front teeth were missing, yet still his smile managed to give an impression of courtliness and elegance, as if he was accustomed to much better things. The world was full of such people now: those maimed or disinherited by the war joined by the tens of thousands who'd been broken by the stockmarket crash. Terrifying . . . And it wasn't over yet. Not by a long chalk. Miles said it was almost certain to get worse before it would get better; yet here he was, spending his money on a birthday present for his wife! Fiddling while Rome burned? The thought made Bel feel slightly sick.

Close up, the brooch turned out to be rather different – and very much smaller – than first impressions had led her to expect. It was a briar rose on a twisted stem, barely an inch in length but quite cunningly and beautifully worked, with even the little boss of stamens in the eye of the rose marked out with an engraver's tool.

'Look, Miles. Even the pattern of the bark on the stem . . .' She laughed ruefully. 'I've got one of my feelings coming over me. It's too pretty, I'm afraid.'

As a lady should, Bel sat on the chair provided and examined her gloves while the shopkeeper wrote down the price on a notepad and slid it discreetly across the counter.

Miles snorted. The old man withdrew a pace, volunteering sadly, 'I'm sure we can come to some arrangement sir, since the lady – '

'Oh, that won't be necessary,' Miles said, but his voice was touched with a note of anxiety which sent Bel's heart sinking to her boots. She'd done it *again*.

'It is gold, is it?'

'Oh, yes, sir, very pure. There's a London hallmark, here, on the back. Quite tiny, of course. My eyeglass . . .'

Miles looked, and then gasped, 'Good Lord! Bel, look, it's a snake!'

'What's a snake?'

'The stem. Look! Isn't that wonderful?'

Bel looked. And indeed the stem (which really was a stem when viewed from the front) had twisted cunningly behind the tiny rose and transformed itself into a snake, its head the hinge of the pin. When the pin was opened, so was the snake's mouth, and even the pin, at the hinge end, was split into two, to look like a snake's forked tongue!

Bel's eyes widened with amazement at such fine workmanship. It was so cunning, so clever, so subtle – and all hidden away where no one could see! But it must cost the earth . . .

She sat down again, trying belatedly to look bored.

'Ah,' Miles said. 'I suppose that changes things. You wouldn't want a snake, would you?'

Bel frowned. 'Why? What's wrong with snakes?'

He grinned and raised his eyebrows. 'And you an Archdeacon's daughter? So, do you like it, Bel? Do you want it?'

She discovered that she was twisting her hands together and laid them hurriedly in her lap. 'Whatever suits you, darling,' she offered bravely, but she had a feeling she would sob like a thwarted child if he didn't buy it. The thought depressed her, made her think again of glass beads. She wanted to get up, walk out of the shop, say she didn't want the ridiculous brooch, but was stopped by the thought of the shopkeeper's disappointment when, within inches of making a sale – perhaps the first of the day – he lost it again and went home hungry.

Bel stroked her gloves, at the same time attempting to see from the corner of her eye how many notes were being exchanged. But Miles could be incredibly clever with his elbows and the old gentleman on the far side of the counter was just as clever with his hands. If only she could ask! But it wasn't done . . .

His money safely stowed in a drawer under the counter, the old man set the brooch in a small, satin-lined box which he wrapped with brown paper and string, chatting all the while.

'I believe you mentioned the symbolism of the snake, sir,' he said. 'I must tell the goldsmith who made it. He likes to give his work little meanings, but not everyone notices, of course.'

Remembering Miles's little taunt about her failure to notice, Bel said, 'I rather like snakes. Those little grass snakes we find in the paddock are so pretty.'

Miles laughed. 'You didn't say that the first time Andrew brought one into the nursery.'

'Well, at first sight I wasn't entirely sure it was just a grass snake. I've grown used to them now. And newts. And frogs. And beetles.'

'But not spiders.'

Bel shuddered. '*Revolting* things!' she said.

The Dray Valley was full of elm trees. They stood in towering groups in the middle of fields and in shady ranks along the hedgerows. They shadowed the farmyards, set clusters of cottages afloat in rippling seas of sunlight and shade, made playgrounds for children among their roots. They ruined the view. Unless one stood at the top of Dundry or on the highest ridge of the Mendips, ten miles distant, a comprehensive view of the Dray Valley was an impossibility. All one could see were the trees, with perhaps a glimpse of the river between.

In summer, Jean sometimes felt trapped by the trees, hemmed in, suffocated. Going out of doors wasn't much better. One could walk for miles and still see no further than the next bend in the road, the next tree, but at least one could breathe. As she walked the lanes, wrestling her heavy, boat-shaped perambulator through the grassy ruts, she sometimes pretended that she could keep going forever, around the next bend and the next, and never go home again. But life wasn't like that. Life tied you down. It hobbled you like a goat so that you could only travel the length of your tether. And with two babies in the pram and another in her belly (a son, this time, a son), Jean's tether was short indeed.

In April, when the leaves began to shut out the sky, she always thought with longing of September, when they would fall again and give her some air. And always, when September came, she was shocked to see the leaves as green as ever, denser and darker but still full of sap, with months still to wait before their fall. But the air was cooler, fresher, and her legs didn't ache quite as much as they had done in high summer. There were blackberries, nuts and rosehips in the hedgerows giving the illusion that, should she decide to keep on walking, she could feed herself and her family, at least until winter came.

But such thoughts were madness, and Jean wasn't mad – *yet*. Indeed, her September walks, for all that they filled her mind with fantasy, had a purely practical purpose. She was picking blackberries for jam, for bottling, for wine. The winter evenings dragged by more sweetly with the aid of a glass of blackberry wine, and while Jack sipped his by the fire, no doubt pretending it was an old crusted port, Jean could stare into the shadows and indulge in other pretences. That this shadow or that was a monster, tiptoeing from its lair under the oil-lamp and creeping across the floor on its belly until, like the wolf in the story book, it leapt at Jack's throat and . . . *ate him all up*.

Well, one had to do something to pass the time, and they didn't have a wireless.

'Babby, Mammy?'

Evelyn, who was two, could say 'Mammy', 'babby' and 'bed', and very little else, but she could convey a variety of different meanings just by waving her hands or widening her eyes, and in this case 'babby' meant 'blackberry'. Jean selected a large one, checked it for maggots, wiped it on her skirt and popped it into the already purple mouth which had opened to receive it. But she said nothing, had said virtually nothing all day. She communicated with her children with her eyes and her hands, knowing that she should talk more to them, but afraid that her tongue would run away with her, taking her into territories she dared not explore.

She never spoke to Jack if she could help it. She sometimes imagined that her mouth was like Pandora's box, seething with evils which, if given their freedom, could bring only ruin. She could endure a great many things in silence, ignore them, let them pass. But if once she said what she thought, expressed what she felt . . . There was nothing at all between saying 'Go to hell, you bastard,' and sending him there on the point of the breadknife. Keeping quiet was easier, safer. They couldn't hang you for it.

The best of the blackberries, she'd discovered in previous years, grew on the south side of the little stone bridge over the river, about half a mile from home. She had almost reached the bridge (hidden by yet another bend in the road, another stand of elm trees) when she stubbed her toe and took a painful litter of stones into her cheap, open-work sandals. But Jean welcomed the inconvenience. It was an excuse to sit on the bank at the roadside, an excuse to take the weight off her feet.

She went down by clumsy stages, supporting herself first on her arms, then her knees, before tilting her rear to one side and allowing gravity to pull it gently to earth. Evelyn had dozed off and looked like a little cat, the tip of her blackberry-blue tongue trapped between her teeth. At the other end of the pram, Shirley slept like a cherub, her tiny fist pushing her mouth out of shape.

The evening was sweet and peaceful, the sky overhead streaked with apricot and rose. In the hedge across the way, a robin sang, heralding winter.

Jean wriggled her behind between the roots of a tree. She leaned back, spread her legs wide and flapped her skirt to let in some air. Her veins throbbed. Her back ached. Relieved of the labour of walking, her heart struggled to steady itself, making her feel sick and dizzy. She could do anything, make any exertion, however difficult or painful, yet the minute she stopped it was as if she was dying. She felt like a wet sponge in a sieve, the strength pouring out of her like water. And she was only two months gone. Three months from now she would be hard-put to walk at all, and she scarcely dared think of the agony the last four months would bring. But it would all be worth it this time. This time she *knew* she was carrying Jack's son.

The robin flew away. Jean felt herself relaxing, her hands loosening at her sides, her head drooping. The world was silent. But, as always happened on the rare occasions when Jean discovered silence, she also discovered that silence was relative; in fact, that it didn't exist at all. Leaves rustled, flies buzzed, and beyond the bend in the lane the summer-depleted waters of the Dray made little whispering, gurgling murmurs.

Was it the river? Or something else?

Jean sat up, tilting her head to one side. No, not the river. Voices. She clapped her knees together and yanked down her skirt, blushing. If the owners of the voices were about to round the bend, she hadn't time to stand up and make herself respectable. She took off her sandal instead, shook out the gravel. But no one came, and still the voices murmured: humming and gurgling, like the river trickling over pebbles.

Jean put her sandal on again and heaved herself to her feet. Shirley and Evelyn were still sleeping and rather than risk disturbing them by jolting the pram into motion, Jean left them where they were and crept, craning her neck, towards the bend in the lane. It was no more than a few yards: three elms, an oak, a few spindle trees and a clump of goat-willows.

Jean's face had been bright with curiosity, sweet with the hopeful expectancy which is born out of loneliness. Save for the weekly shopping trip to Bishop Molton, she rarely met anyone, and smiled only for her children. To smile for someone else, to say, 'hello', or 'lovely evening', would have made a high-spot in her day, sent her home happy. But as she came in sight of the bridge her face froze, and she stepped sideways, hiding her bulk among the trees.

Mrs Huntley was not wearing a hat. She had a hat, but was holding it in her hand: a narrow, long-fingered hand, clustered with rings, which lay on the parapet of the bridge, within inches of Jack's hand. Their shoulders (Mrs Huntley's so thin they seemed almost to fold up, like a paper fan) were almost touching as they leaned over the parapet, gazing into the river. He said something – Jean didn't hear what – and Mrs Huntley laughed: a soft little gurgle, like water running over pebbles.

Although Jean had seen her many times, she'd never seen her without a hat, and now there seemed something almost indecent in the way she was displaying her lovely blonde hair. It was of the colour and sheen of new straw, cut just below the tips of her ears and rippling with soft waves. She was wearing a white frock printed with roses: the sort of thing one saw in Jolly's advertisements in *The Chronicle*, at five guineas a piece.

Jean wiped sweating palms over the slippery folds of her own frock, an art silk in navy blue: twelve shillings from the draper's in Bishop Molton.

' – might have to, before long,' Mrs Huntley said.

'No,' Jack turned his head as if to kiss her, and Jean's heart almost broke to see his smile. He had smiled for her, just like that. He had said he loved her . . .

Jean bowed her head and looked down at herself through a mist of tears, but all she could see were bulges. She didn't wear corsets when she was pregnant, and although the freedom was wonderful, the view certainly wasn't. Yet she was still so *beautiful* inside! Why couldn't he see that?

She couldn't hear everything Jack was saying, nor the whole of Mrs Huntley's responses, but it all seemed innocent enough. Something about the economic depression, and Miles Huntley's plans to work on the Home Farm, which Jack evidently thought highly amusing.

'He'll never be that hard up!' he laughed, and Mrs Huntley turned to face him.

'Oh,' she said. 'He's determined to weather this if he can.'

'And if he doesn't weather it?' Jack's smile changed, became strangely wistful. 'Would you still love him if he was poor?'

There was a long silence. Mrs Huntley bent her head in such a way that Jean, although she couldn't see her face, knew she was blushing. She murmured something. Then, ' – isn't a matter of money, is it?' Something else. Then, ' – trust, comfort and respect.'

Jean squeezed her eyes shut. Oh, yes . . . Trust, comfort and respect! That's what love was, and she didn't have any of it!

'And this?'

Jean recognised 'this' in the tone of his voice, and her eyes flew wide just as Jack bent his head and touched Mrs Huntley's mouth with his own. But she didn't see any more. Her face running with tears, she turned away and stumbled back to her babies.

At first, she had no idea why she felt such a terrible sense of loss. *She* didn't want him. *She* didn't care. Mrs Huntley was welcome to him, the bitch, the bitch! But as Jean shoved the pram out of the rut which had wedged it into safe immobility, Evelyn stirred in her sleep and, still sleeping, uttered a pained little whimper which pierced her mother's heart.

Two babies in the pram and one in her belly; and what the hell would become of them without Jack? It was one thing to dream about walking forever, quite another not to have any choice. He gave them so little, but the little he gave was precious beyond price: food and clothing and a roof over their heads. If Jack was playing around with Miles Huntley's wife (and he was) and if Miles ever found out (as he might), they'd have a roof over their heads no more. They'd have nothing.

Yet these weren't the only thoughts which crossed her

mind. There were others: frail, ghostly others, which flittered like flame-crazed moths just beyond the range of her understanding. Thoughts of love, of trust and comfort. Thoughts of rage and jealousy.

But they made no sense. She *hated* him!

Chapter Four

Violet Huntley had done something agonising to her back, quite early in the summer, and had cancelled her usual 'see the boys' visit to Bishop's Court. Bel had been delighted to hear it until she'd realised that a fortnight in London had been offered instead. Then, terrifying herself with an unprecedented show of rebellion, she'd dug her heels in and refused to go. She hadn't really expected to get away with it and when, instead of walking out in a thin-lipped rage, Miles had simply laughed and quoted 'The Wreck of the Hesperus' at her, 'God save us all from a death like this . . .' she'd had to sit down to get over the shock. Wonders would never cease, she'd actually *won*! And in the first round, too!

'You don't mind?' she'd asked faintly.

'Of course not. I'd be a hypocrite to mind, wouldn't I? And it gives me an excuse not to stay too long. I can't possibly leave you alone for two whole *weeks*, now can I, darling?'

The gleam of mischief in his eyes, the wicked curve of his smile had reminded Bel of the first time she'd seen him, before they'd even been introduced, when she'd thought he looked like an oversized elf, a Puck on a Midsummer rampage, hunting for devilry. She'd fallen in love with him then, and for the very quality which drove her halfway to madness now. Won? Damn fool. She'd played right into his hands!

'What will you tell her?' she'd asked frigidly.

'About what?'

'About my staying at home.'

His grin had widened. 'The truth, of course.'

'You can't tell her that!'

'Why not?'

'Because . . .' At that point, Bel had turned bright red and stammered stupidly, 'Because you don't know it!' and then turned even redder, because that was more true than he could guess. She didn't know it either, but she had some very nasty suspicions. Oh, why hadn't she kept quiet? Now he'd ask what the truth really was, and what the hell could she tell him?

But Miles hadn't asked. He'd just shrugged. 'All right, darling. I'll tell her exactly what I tell you when you ask impossible questions.'

'Oh? What *do* you tell me?'

'Nothing,' he'd said sweetly.

That had been almost a week ago, and the memory of it still made her writhe. Impossible questions . . .

Why won't you make love to me, Miles? Why won't you?

Nothing.

She had wondered, many times, if he might be having an affair with someone else, almost hoping he was, for at least that would give him a reason. But if he was . . . Well, it couldn't be much of an affair. He was rarely away from home more than a few hours at a time. He ate all his meals with his wife, spent all his evenings with her, and all his nights on the far side of the bed, hugging his pillow.

And now he was staying with his mother for five whole days, four whole blissfully peaceful nights. Bel had waved him off with a grin of pure relief and then, to her dismay, had begun to miss him about five minutes after he'd left. She'd had to coax herself to enjoy her solitude and even four days into his absence it still felt uncomfortable, as if she'd shed a layer of skin before the next layer was ready for exposure. Sore. Fragile. Vulnerable. And afraid.

She fought it, thought about it and admitted to herself that it hadn't been fear of Violet Huntley which had kept her at home. It had been a longing for freedom. A longing for privacy, to be alone for once and perhaps . . . if she was brave enough . . . to find out who she really was when she wasn't being Miles's wife.

But that hadn't happened. Try as she might, she couldn't decide *who* she was, except that she was someone with no more integrity than she'd learned at her mother's knee. You didn't lie, you didn't steal, you didn't shout or swear. You bathed regularly, kept your possessions in good order and went to church twice on Sundays.

A woman could put on a pretty good show with that kind of training behind her and, after a while, even convince herself that that was how she was. But it wasn't how Bel was. It was just how she wished she could be: simple, uncomplicated, *satisfied*.

And God knew she had plenty to be satisfied about! After all, where did love come on a decent woman's list of priorities? Above her children's happiness and welfare?

No.

Above her husband's loyalty, his decency and kindness?

No.

Above the beauty and security of her home, the money in the bank, the knowledge she had that, however tight things might get, she would never be a pauper?

No.

Love came far below all these things and a few dozen more; so why, in God's name, did it insist on floating to the top like the scum on a stew, obscuring her view of the good things? Because she was Bel. And Bel *wasn't* a decent woman. She was rotten clear through to the bone.

No, she wasn't! Heavens above, she'd never done anything really bad in her whole life, and wasn't intending to start now! No, she was just being silly (as usual), taking herself too seriously, as Miles was always telling her she did. And he was right. The best thing she could do was to forget it: enjoy life for the things it gave her, instead of constantly craving the things she could not have.

This decision made her laugh with relief, partly, she suspected, because it was the decision Miles would have reached had she dared to ask him (and had he deigned to reply). It was as though he had given his permission; and merely out of gratitude, merely to please him, she remembered his fondness for bramble jelly and took herself off, with a basket over her arm, to pick blackberries beside the river.

In previous years she'd found some marvellous brambles just beyond the bridge, not far from Drayfield Farm. Jack Carter's farm. There were even better ones in the hollow beyond Molton Farm, on Solomon Hicks's land. This was much closer to home, but not nearly as pretty a walk, and she adored being by the river, listening to its little splashes and murmurs. She might even catch sight of the kingfisher which nested in the bank by the bridge, and the thought of that kingfisher made her heart quicken with excitement, made her hurry, ignoring the plentiful blackberries which grew in the hedge along the way.

The strangest thing was that, even knowing she was lying to herself, it didn't seem to matter any more. She didn't feel bad about it. She felt wonderful: as young, as carefree and – yes! – as *innocent* as a child on her first visit to the fair. And why not? Where was the harm in it? After all, she might not even see him, for even when you knew where to look, kingfishers were maddeningly elusive birds. But a glimpse was all she wanted. Just a glimpse. After that, she'd go home and forget it, deeming her few days of freedom well spent. After that, she'd pull herself together and be *satisfied*.

She knew, of course, that she had chosen the right time of day to see him. Like most other farmers, he'd finish his milking at about six and then walk the cows back to pasture. It was going to be a matter of luck whether he walked them to the river meadows or to the fields beyond the farmhouse, but such things were always a matter of luck, like a game, a silly game, a game of no importance. It wouldn't matter *at all* if she missed him.

But her basket was almost half full of berries and her heart an aching lump of disappointment before – at last! – she saw him. He looked so tall! Taller than Miles, even though she'd seen the two men standing together and knew that Jack was an inch or two shorter. But Jack was more finely boned, narrower in the shoulder, and it made him look . . . so tall.

Her face flaming, her eyes blurred with panic, Bel turned away and gave herself to the blackberries, tearing at the red ones and green ones as well as the black without noticing the difference. The skin on her shoulders prickled and her spine turned to fire just to know that he was looking at her, walking towards her, coming closer, closer . . .

'Hull-ohh!'

'Oh!' Bel's pretence at being startled was a total failure. She'd jumped too soon – or too late, she wasn't sure which – and her smile had come too readily, before she could possibly have known (unless she'd already known) who had spoken to her. 'Oh!' she twittered stupidly. 'Hello – er – ' (She couldn't call him Jack. It wasn't done. But she'd have preferred to have her tongue cut out than call him Mr Carter.) 'You made me jump. I was miles away.'

'Is he?' Jack grinned.

'What?'

'Miles. Away.'

'Oh!' She laughed, blushed and patted her hat. She'd forgotten that the village gossips would have gone before her, telling everyone that Miles had gone away.

'Yes,' she said. 'Visiting his mother. Back tomorrow, thank goodness. The house seems so empty! He's taken the boys. To see their – er – grandmother.'

She was reversing into the side of the bridge, trying to get away. Not because she didn't want to be near him, but because she wanted it so much. She wanted to smell him, to inhale the warmth of his body. She wanted to touch him, to feel the muscled fibres under his skin. She wanted to see him, but could see only a Jack-shaped blur, for her eyes were full of steam, her mind like a soup, boiling over.

'Steady!' he reached out to grasp her elbow. 'Nettles,' he explained, and her stomach lurched at his touch, making her feel sick and faint.

'Thanks.' She laughed again, sidestepped the nettles and felt her hip brush against his thigh: the most fleeting contact, yet it felt as if she'd dashed herself against a boulder and would be cherishing the bruises for weeks to come.

'Look!' he said suddenly. 'Kingfisher!'

'Where? Oh, where?' She stared downriver, knowing – without caring – that she had missed it. Kingfishers were like that. Even if you saw them, you saw virtually nothing. Felt something, rather; a flash of blue light which pierced your mind like a dart, leaving you aching because you hadn't seen more.

'If we stand on the bridge,' he said. 'And keep our eyes skinned . . . I think it went into that willow, over there.'

They stood on the bridge, with their arms on the parapet, almost touching. It was a strange feeling, almost painful, as if the nerve-ends on Bel's arms and the tips of her fingers had forced through her skin and, like the tentacles of a sea anemone, were reaching out to touch him, searching the air for nourishment.

'Rather unusual isn't it?' he asked softly. 'For Miles to go away without you?'

'Mm. But it's just a duty visit. His mother wanted to see the boys, not me. I'm sure she won't mind.'

'And Miles?'

'Miles?' She knew what he meant and pretended she didn't. Seeming to be puzzled was an excuse to turn her gaze from the river to his face. But she couldn't bear to look at him for long. His beauty was like the kingfisher's, a brilliant flash of light which pierced her heart, leaving her bereft because she hadn't seen more.

Were his eyes really black, or just very dark brown? Was his smile really crooked, or did he tilt his head to make it seem so? Next time, even if she could do so only for a second, she must look harder, really *concentrate*, so that later, in the secret places of her memory, she could gaze at her leisure, learning all that she wanted to know.

'Didn't he mind your staying at home?'

'Not at all.' She was hot, perspiring. She took off her hat, shook her hair, letting the soft September air touch her scalp. 'Why should he mind?'

She dared another glance at his face (his nose *was* straight!) only to find him gazing, as if mesmerised, at her hair.

'If I was Miles,' he said softly, 'I'd never want to take my eyes off you.'

She felt drunk with pleasure at the compliment, but – strangely – not so drunk that she hadn't observed his error of speech. He should have said 'If I *were* Miles,' not 'if I was', because it was impossible for Jack to be Miles. Impossible. Yes, impossible. She ought to go home . . .

But she couldn't move. Not an inch, towards him or away. She began to pray that *he* would go, even knowing that it would be like being torn in half; and then, when he stayed, she thanked God for it, wanting him to stay for ever.

'I hear Archie Weaver's thinking of retiring.'

At the change of subject Bel felt the tension draining out

of her, a relief on a par with sliding into a warm bath after a long, exhausting day.

'Well, not exactly,' she said. 'He doesn't want to go, but he might have to before long. He's almost crippled with rheumatism, poor soul. It hurts me just to look at him.'

'Still, it'll be a job for someone else. I sometimes wish I could take on another man, just to feel I was doing something to help. But we're all in the same boat, I suppose – except for the ones who are already drowning. You don't dare reach out a helping hand in case you end up in the drink, too.' He chuckled softly. 'Has Miles anyone particular in mind?'

'For Archie's job? No. Like you, we can't really afford to take on someone else. It's sad, but as you say . . . We're all in the same boat. Quite frightening, really. There seems no end to it. I've often wished I understood about money, economics, that sort of thing, but I begin to think no one understands it. All those millions of people without jobs. And it's even worse in Germany, they say. So worrying . . .'

But she wasn't in the least worried. Didn't care two hoots. She had relaxed, and could look at Jack now without fearing she'd explode with excitement, look at him almost as she might have looked at Miles. But Jack was very different. He was as dark as Miles was fair, his thick black hair quite straight, smooth and glossy, shaping his head. He was younger than Miles: his skin smoother, fresher, his jaw firmer, the flesh clinging sleekly to his bones. And his eyes! The difference between blue eyes and black (or were they very dark brown?) was like the difference between white cambric and black satin: innocence and seduction, gentleness and brutality.

She swallowed and looked away again, searching the river for kingfishers. Brutality? Why had she thought of that, for heaven's sake? Jack wasn't brutal! No, not at all. But oh, God, she so wanted to be touched as if . . . as if she *mattered*, as if she was *alive*. She wanted to be grabbed, pushed and pulled, held until her bones cracked, lifted off her feet. And she wanted to give as good as she got, leave bruises on his mouth . . .

(*Miles's* mouth! She didn't mean Jack! She didn't!)

'Won't that leave Home Farm a bit short of labour?' Jack asked, and his voice seemed to come from a distance, breaking her panicky train of thought.

'I suppose it will,' she said hoarsely. 'But if he's needed, Miles will help.'

'Miles?' He smiled, raising a doubtful eyebrow, tilting his head to one side. 'Would he know how?'

Bel knew she should be offended, but wasn't. It was quite hard, in fact, to say the things a dutiful wife should say of her husband, true though they were. 'There's very little Miles doesn't know about farming. He was brought up to it, after all.'

'Yes, as a gentleman farmer. The practicalities – '

'He's practical.'

' – are tougher than they look.'

'Oh, Miles is very tough.' Against her wishes, frightening her, the thought crossed her mind: tougher than you are, Jack Carter. She shook it off, shivering slightly. 'And these are hard times. None of us can afford to rest on our laurels.'

She imagined resting with Jack on a soft bed of laurels, and then, ridiculously, wondered if a bed of laurels would be soft, or crisp and leathery and crawling with beetles. And wondered if she'd care . . .

After that, although they went on talking and seeming to make sense, she didn't know what he was saying, didn't hear her own replies. She knew, vaguely, that they were talking about Miles, but Miles was no longer important. He'd gone away.

'Would you still love him if he was poor?'

The husky undernote in Jack's voice caught Bel's attention, stopped her breath in her throat and made her tremble again.

Lord, how had they arrived at this? A man didn't say such things – such intimate things – to a woman, unless he . . .

She turned her gaze downriver again, smiling as if she'd noticed nothing, as if she was accustomed to discussing such things with her neighbours and could see nothing wrong with it. But there *was* something wrong. Something very wrong. She ought to go home!

But she couldn't.

'Love – ' She had meant to say it quite clearly, pretending it didn't matter, but only a whisper emerged, hoarse and thick, as if she were trying to speak underwater. She blushed and stared at her hat. 'It's nothing to do with money, surely?'

'What, then?'

'Trust.' But Miles didn't trust her with the least of his feelings. He couldn't trust her with money. He had never trusted her to know what was best for her sons. And now . . .

'And comfort . . .' she continued haltingly. 'Respect . . .'

Yes, that was what love was all about. Trust, comfort and respect, and she had none of it.

'And this?'

She was still looking at her hat, but something in his voice made her turn her face up to his. Something warm and treacherous which had been in her own mind for days, weeks, months, luring her to this. His mouth scarcely touched hers before he drew away again, but it seemed to Bel like an act of violence, like a blow which burns for hours afterwards, and leaves its mark for everyone to see.

'Oh . . .' She took a step backwards. 'Oh, Lord . . . You really shouldn't have done that.'

Jack averted his eyes. 'No,' he said quietly. 'I'm sorry. Forgive me, please. I don't know what . . . I don't know how I . . .'

He seemed utterly stricken by his error, grey-faced and grim, and Bel couldn't bear it. She couldn't let him blame himself. It had been her fault, not his. She'd come looking for him and found more . . . No, not more than she'd bargained for, not more than she'd wanted. Just more than she could bear.

'It's all right,' she said frantically. 'No harm done. And now . . .' She searched the bridge for her basket and stared into it, her eyes wide with shock and confusion. 'Goodness, I haven't picked many, have I? I'd better get on with it, before I . . .'

They were retreating from each other, one cautious step at a time, as if trying to make their parting seem as natural as if they'd merely been commenting on the weather, as neighbours do. But Bel couldn't meet his eyes. She was confused, not knowing whether to laugh or to cry, to stay – or run like a rabbit for home.

'Well,' she gasped breathlessly. 'Goodnight.'

'Goodnight, Mrs – er – '

She wanted to scream at him: 'Call me Bel!' but didn't dare. She turned away.

Oh, Bel, she thought bleakly. What have you done? What are you doing? What would your father think of you?

But her father had been dead for ten years and she couldn't remember what he looked like, let alone what he might think. She could only hear him, muttering distractedly, 'Where are my slippers? I had them just a moment ago. Agnes, where are my slippers?'

After walking only a few yards from the bridge, aware that she'd been rendered invisible by the trees which shadowed every bend in the lane, Bel stopped walking and closed her eyes, tipping her face up to the rosy, sunset sky. She sighed, then grinned, hugging herself until her basket tipped over, spilling its fruits at her feet.

Miles was angry. He sat on the terrace at Bishop's Court, twirling a tumbler of whisky (his third) between fingers which twitched for an occupation more violent than he could, at present, allow them. He had known men – his own father among them – who'd enjoyed being angry, but Miles hated it. It made him feel ill, weak and frightened. Frightened of himself. He hadn't lost his temper since the war, when he'd lost it more times than he could count, and always with the same result: that he'd killed someone. (Some one, or two, or twenty. Hundreds, probably . . .) But the war had been a case of kill or be killed, and when a man is faced with that sort of choice he has good reason to rage. He had no such reason now, and that was the most frightening thing about it: that it felt exactly the same, a violent fragmentation of mind, sense and memory, as if the civilised man he'd thought himself was no more than a carefully assembled jigsaw puzzle which someone had hurled to the ground.

He had no reason to be angry. He had not told Bel he would come home a day early, and could not blame her for not being here to welcome him. Neither could he blame her for giving Cook the evening off. Had he been in Bel's shoes he'd probably have done the same. But the sheer pandemonium of arriving home with four bored, hungry young sons, a travel-sick Nanny and only the slack-jawed Muriel to attend to them all . . .

No, that hadn't made him angry. Even Bel's absence hadn't made him angry. It had just hurt him a little: little enough not to matter. But he'd arrived home at half-past four, and now – he snatched his watch from his waistcoat pocket and glared at it accusingly – it was five past eight, and getting dark! Where the hell was she? Picking bloody blackberries? For four bloody hours? On her own? Which way had she gone, for the love of God? Via Moscow?

Yet if that had made him angry, he should be more ashamed of himself than he already was. He knew all about blackberries. Mushrooms, too. The damn things lured you on – (Let's try the next field. Remember those enormous ones we found last year?) – and it wasn't until the sun began to set that you realised home was now five miles distant.

No, it wasn't that. It was . . . It was loss of faith, loss of trust. He had failed her. He had failed her, and . . . And hadn't realised how much he'd failed her until she'd refused to go to London with him. That, not this, had been the beginning of his rage. A seed, no more; but he'd taken it with him and – irony of ironies – allowed his mother to water the bloody thing, make it grow.

His mother had lied to him. There'd been nothing wrong with her back. She'd dragged him to Town under false pretences, and he wouldn't have cared, would probably have made a joke of it had Bel been with him . . . instead of that little seed of rage. The rage and his mother's lies . . . They'd made him realise that Bel could lie too – if she was pushed far enough.

'I won't come with you, Miles.'

He frowned now, trying to remember what else she'd said, how she'd justified her decision, but he remembered only the look on her face, the way her eyes had blanked out, as if she'd closed down the shutters to her soul. She'd never done that before. He wouldn't have deemed her capable of it. But he'd guessed what it meant.

He'd spent most of his time in London trying to think things through, trying to find the words to tell her . . . Ask her . . . Trying to find a way to explain that he . . . He didn't know what was *wrong* with him! He loved her now as much as he'd ever loved her and needed her more – yes, more – than ever before. But he couldn't *do* anything about it! If only she could understand that, know that it was through no failing of hers and certainly through no change in his feelings towards her, perhaps she'd . . .

He swallowed another mouthful of whisky, his hand trembling. He'd had it all worked out. Every word, every smile, every mutually face-saving turn of phrase. But she wasn't here, and now . . . Now it had gone. His rage had consumed it. He couldn't say it now.

He felt as if he'd spent the past few days running to catch a train: not the one which went nowhere, but the one – the only one – which would take him, with his wife and their sons, safely into their future. He'd arrived out of breath and sweating from every pore, only to hear the stationmaster announce flatly, 'You missed it.'

'She'm gorn ah, Struntley. Blagbrin.'

'Blackberrying? Did she say when she'd be back?'

'Cuplahs.'

A couple of hours. Two, not four! Where the hell *was* she?

The sunset had been a glorious one which had turned the sky every shade of crimson, violet and gold, but now the colours had faded and the last, pink-streaked clouds had dispersed, leaving a clean, luminous vault of pale azure and jade. In another half-hour it would be dark.

Miles stood up. He paced across the terrace, his hands clenched in his pockets, and then plunged off down the drive to look for her.

But his search ended almost before it had begun. Bel was sitting in the little trellised summerhouse by the pool, barely a hundred yards from the house and sheltered from it by a thick screen of shrubs and crimson-tinted cherry trees. She was asleep.

Miles stared at her with his mouth open, his rage seeming to seep out through the soles of his shoes. She looked like a child: flushed, innocent and fragile. She'd taken her hat off, kicked off her shoes, and she'd been smiling as she'd fallen asleep, for the ghost of a smile was still there, peaceful and sweet. Lovely . . .

He crouched at her feet, biting his lip on tears. How long had she been here, while he'd waited and fumed? An hour? Two hours? God, she looked so young! So beautiful . . . He could make love to her now. He wanted her, *now*! And it was almost dark. The gardeners had gone. No one would know...

'Bel?' he whispered.

Her smile twitched, widened a little. But she didn't wake. Miles took her hand, shaking it gently. 'Bel?'

She woke then. Her manner of waking haunted Miles afterwards, although years were to pass before he understood what it meant.

Her eyes opened wide. She stared at him for a moment as though wondering who he was. Then, her face crumpling, she cried, 'Miles!' and jumped defensively to her feet as if, instead of gentling her awake, he'd slapped and shaken her, shocked her rigid.

'What are you doing here?' she demanded furiously.

It was as if she'd plunged a knife through his heart. But he laughed. As he always laughed. 'I live here, remember?'

The desire he had felt just a moment ago was already dead, and somewhere at the back of his mind he heard the clank and hiss of a steam train, moving out. Going away. Without him.

Chapter Five

Bel woke – as she always woke when she was worried about anything – at three o'clock in the morning, bang on the dot. She heard the faint, tinkling chimes of the clock in the hall, which always reminded her of the Anglican High Mass and of her father, whose face she now saw in the pale, silvery disc of a full harvest moon. He was still muttering about his slippers . . .

Bel heaved a sigh of regret. She'd actually hated him for those eternally lost slippers, for the soup he'd spilled in the lap of his cassock and the habit he'd had of running his fingers through his hair so that it stood up in little tufts, like stooks in a cornfield. Between the ages of twelve and eighteen, she had no recollection of saying anything to him which hadn't begun, 'Oh, *really*, Pappa, *must* you?'

But now she remembered something else. She couldn't recall the details – precisely what she'd done to occasion it – but it must have been something pretty bad because otherwise she'd never have lowered herself to admit, 'I didn't *mean* it, Pappa! I didn't *mean* it, really I didn't!'

She hadn't *meant* Jack to kiss her. She hadn't *meant* it, really she hadn't! She'd just been playing a game, like tennis or bridge, in which one's partner's knowledge of the rules was a thing one depended on, believed in, took completely for granted. But Jack hadn't known the rules. He'd trumped her master-card, hit the ball out of court. And she hadn't *meant* it to be like that! She'd just wanted to . . . play.

Her father looked down on her from the radiant vault of heaven, his moon-mouth thoughtfully pursed, his brow anxiously puckered.

'You know, m'dear,' he said sweetly, 'few of us really mean to do wrong. We simply miss our footing and fall, quite by accident, from the pavement to the gutter. And do you know why that happens, m'dear? Because we weren't entirely sure where we were going in the first place. We were just loitering. Hoping – but not really trying – to reach the right destination. If you travelled to China by that method, m'dear, you'd end up in Winnipeg. End up in Java. No good then to say you didn't mean it. Should have kept your mind on your destination, shouldn't you, m'dear?'

Bel knew now (too late) that her father had always kept his mind on his destination. That was why he was always losing his slippers: because they weren't essential to the journey. With or without them, barefoot and bleeding, he'd have kept to the road he had chosen. The good road.

'Well,' Bel conceded, although without much enthusiasm, 'that's the road for me, too, I suppose.' It sounded rather dull. The Christian life had always seemed to her to be rather dull: all the good works which earned no gratitude, all the prayers which received no answers. But that was the road she would take from now on. Dull wasn't fun, but it was a darn sight better than – she blushed and moaned – 'Disaster,' she whispered, and then held her breath as Miles stirred on the far side of the bed.

'Bel? S'marra?'

'Nothing. Moon woke me.'

'Mmph . . .' He turned away again and fell asleep as swiftly as a stone falling through water. Bel felt him go, knew him well enough to judge the exact moment when he'd ceased to be aware: and it had nothing to do with the rhythm of his breathing. Miles was a very quiet breather, although he made up for that more often than not by talking in his sleep: muttering away for minutes at a stretch, as if feverishly reciting the multiplication tables. In the eleven years of their marriage Bel had scarcely ever managed to make out what he was saying, although once, before she'd grown accustomed to it, he'd sat bolt upright in the bed and cried, 'Shit! Not *again*!' Another time he'd groaned, 'No, no! Oh no, I *can't*!' and begun to sob like a weary child.

It was the most eerie thing Bel had ever experienced. It was like lying in bed with a stranger: the 'poor, sad soul' her father had recognised and whom Bel had never seen. The Miles she knew *never* swore. He *never* wept. That he could do so in his sleep was proof enough, had she needed proof, that she knew him hardly at all, was excluded from all the things that mattered to him . . . The things that made him cry.

But he would never discuss those things. The war, the deaths (two of them within a space of six weeks) of his three brothers, the wounds he himself had suffered. Compared with many, his wounds had not been serious, but the scars were still there and one of them – a long, zig-zagging shrapnel wound on his shin – still made him limp in very cold weather. The first time she'd seen that scar (on their wedding night, she supposed) she'd asked, 'How did you do it?' to which he'd replied coolly, 'I didn't do it. It was done to me.'

She hadn't dared ask more, and it was his mother who'd eventually told her the wound had been caused by shrapnel.

But even his mother rarely mentioned Miles's brothers. Bel had never met them and knew virtually nothing about them save for their names and their ages. Alexander, nineteen. Thomas, twenty-one. Charles, twenty-four. Had Miles loved them? Bel didn't know. Did he miss them? Bel didn't know. He was a complete mystery to her, and he was her husband!

'This was the road you chose,' her father said suddenly. '*Chose*, m'dear. And why?'

Because she'd loved him. She still loved him.

But Jack . . . If Miles was the road she had chosen, where was Jack? In Winnipeg? Java? In the gutter? Oh, no . . .

Yes! In the gutter, damn it! He shouldn't have kissed her! Heavens, who did he think he *was*? And what did he think *she* was? *Desperate*?

With a soft gasp of outrage, Bel turned over, taking the blankets with her. She punched the pillow and then turned flat on her back again, sighing with frustration. On the far side of the bed, Miles began to twitch and whimper, like a dog chasing rabbits through its dreams. She reached out, patting the sheets in hope of finding his hand, and in the midst of his murmurings he said – quite clearly and with the utmost contempt – 'Bloody liar.'

Jack didn't know there was a tearoom behind the baker's shop in Bishop Molton, and he was unlikely ever to find out, because in the four years Jean had been frequenting it (every Thursday, after she'd paid the grocer) she had never once seen a man in there. She'd scarcely ever seen a man in the baker's shop at the front, either. Men didn't go to such places. They deemed domestic shopping beneath their dignity, and went only to the ironmonger's where, preening themselves on their eye for a bargain, they purchased half an ounce of cabbage seed or a bag of six-inch nails.

You could get a very nice threepenny bun in the tearoom, sticky and moist and crusted with sugar. The tea was pale and flavourless, but at sixpence the pot (and you could get three good cups out of that) Jean wasn't complaining. Her Thursday afternoon out was the star on her weekly horizon, the lure which led her from one day to the next. Yet she enjoyed it mostly in anticipation. The day itself was always marred by little twinges of grief that it had come at last, and therefore was almost over. And it would be a whole week before it came round again . . .

Even on the second Thursday in November there were still a few leaves on the trees and many more in the ruts of the lane, making a thick, deep carpet which clogged up the wheels of the pram. But the valley had opened up a little, and through the gaps between the trees it was possible to see deep, misty vistas of fields, hills and distant spires. Where the first hard frosts had bleached the corn-stubble the fields were the pale, glistening yellow of rich clotted cream. And, where the plough had been at work, the land was red: a deep, raw, juicy red which always made Jean think of battlefields.

Where she came from (barely ten miles from here), the earth had been dark brown and as dull as ditchwater. But she'd been happy there. She hadn't known it, of course. She hadn't known what happiness was until she'd discovered misery.

But misery, like silence, was relative. Just when she thought she'd fallen as low as she could get, a little spark of pleasure brightened the gloom, making her realise that misery, true misery, was still unknown to her. Misery was having no Thursday in the week, no tea and sticky buns, nothing to look forward to. Misery was having Jack find out there was a tearoom behind the baker's shop.

Bishop Molton was the largest of the three villages in the Dray valley and by far the prettiest, with a number of tall, Georgian buildings as well as the tortoise-like cottages which peeped out at the world from beneath sheltering thatches. The main part of the High Street straddled a star-shaped crossroads, ridiculously enough called The Square, from which point (given strength and inclination) you could travel to Bristol, Bath or Weston-super-Mare.

The Huntleys' house, Bishop's Court, was slap-bang on the High Street, within spitting distance of the shops, yet Jean had never clapped eyes on it. She could see the tops of its candy-twist chimneys, but everything else was hidden behind a high stone wall, which stretched as far as the eye could see, to the first sharp bend in the main Bristol Road. Jean had never had energy enough to walk that far, but Jack had been up the drive, seen it close-to. According to him (not that he could be believed), it made the Manor House look like a hovel.

The thought of it – and of Mrs Huntley – puzzled Jean half to death. How could a woman who lived in such a house, with such a husband, with servants at her beck and call and more money in the bank than most people could even imagine . . . How could she even spare the time of day for a man like Jack, let alone let him *kiss* her? She had to be crazy. Or worse.

Like Thursday itself, the half-hour Jean spent in the grocer's shop was a strange mingling of pleasures and griefs. She'd been brought up in a shop very like it: her granny's shop, where she'd been happy without knowing it, and knew it now too well. Just the smell of the place was a delight: perfumed tea and Cheddar cheese, honey, cocoa and sweet, spicy biscuits. But best of all were the people – even the miserable ones who looked her up and down as if she'd crept from an especially smelly mouse-hole. She said hello to them all, smiled her best smile, remarked on the weather, told them that she had once lived – yes, and worked! – in a shop just like this, her granny's shop, over at Winton.

She was aware that she overdid it a bit. She talked as if there was no tomorrow (which there wasn't; there was only next Thursday), barely pausing for a reply in fear that no reply would be forthcoming. But when it was her turn to be served and she became the centre of the grocer's attention, it was worth all the funny looks and stiff little smiles she'd received from everyone else.

'Mrs Carter! How very good to see you, this fine, sunny day! The little ones, too. Hello Evie! Hello Shirley! Dear little souls – good as gold, aren't they? Now! What can I do for you, Mrs Carter?'

The nicest Thursdays were the ones when Mrs Hicks and Jean arrived at the grocer's together. Mrs Hicks was small and round and cheerful and she smiled and chatted as though she and Jean were the best friends in the world. Jack always said that Solomon Hicks was an ignorant yokel, and for all Jean knew (although she doubted it) he was right; but Mrs Hicks was a lovely woman: kind and loving and strong, with eyes as brown and as wholesome as hot toast. They were wise, knowing eyes, the sort which didn't look at, but through you, to your soul. And she *knew*. It was as if when she said, 'Hello, my dear, how are you, today?' she reached into Jean's heart and found that it was small, grey and shrivelled, without even the hope of life in it. Then . . . then Jean wanted only to lay her head on Mrs Hicks's shoulder and cry, 'Help me, help me!'

But didn't, of course. Laughed instead. And, when the longing to confide became too strong, too painful, said brightly, 'Well, this won't pay the butcher, will it?' and hurried away. 'See you next Thursday, Mrs Hicks! Goodbye!'

The butcher was next door to the grocer, but the baker's shop and the Post Office were on the far side of the square, and it was difficult for Jean to get the pram on to the pavement while she was holding Evie's hand. She was still trying to achieve this without tipping Shirley out on her nose when Mrs Huntley, looking (as ever) immaculate in a fitted tweed jacket, emerged from the Post Office, just a few yards away.

Her face reddening with embarrassment, Jean pretended she hadn't seen her and was amazed when, instead of doing the same thing, Mrs Huntley gasped, 'Oh, Mrs Carter, you mustn't!' and darted forward to lift the pram over the kerb. She did it with one hand, gracefully bending her knees to grasp the middle of the back axle and flicking the entire weight up and over the kerb so that Shirley scarcely wobbled, let alone toppled over.

Then, directing an affectionate smile at the most prominent

of Jean's anterior bulges, Mrs Huntley said, 'We must take care of the little one, mustn't we?'

Jean's embarrassment changed to a strange, almost heart-wrenching gratitude. Had she misjudged the woman? Was she just . . . Just as she seemed at this moment: kind and good, thoughtful and sensitive? Perhaps even too sensitive to slap Jack's face when her kindness led him to think (as he would, the bastard!) that she'd *wanted* him to kiss her?

Mrs Huntley turned to speak to Evelyn, then to little Shirley and, still leaning over the pram, she glanced up at Jean, her blue eyes warm and dancing with pleasure. 'She's got your skin, hasn't she? Oh, *and* your smile!' She tickled Shirley's chin with a softly gloved finger. 'Just *look* at dat priddy liddle smile!'

She straightened up and burst out laughing. 'I'm an absolute fool for babies. They bring out the worst in me, I'm afraid. Oh, I'd so *love* a little girl . . .' She bent once more to talk to Evelyn, who blushed and hid her face in the voluminous folds of her mother's skirt. 'Ahh . . . isn't she adorable? They both are. You don't know how lucky you are, Mrs Carter.'

'No, I suppose not,' Jean said faintly.

'Oh!' Mrs Huntley clapped a hand to her mouth. 'Oh, Mrs Carter. I'm so sorry. That was the most tactless thing I've said since . . . Well, since yesterday, anyway. I'm an absolute idiot. I know how much you want a boy this time.' She reached out and gently grasped Jean's arm. 'And you will, my dear. I'm sure you will. You're carrying high. That's always a good sign, isn't it?'

Her smile was so kind, her words so completely devoid of 'side', and her voice . . . Like everything else about her, Mrs Huntley's voice was rich, smooth and curiously sweet, making Jean think of honey in a polished wooden bowl.

'Thank you,' she said. 'And,' she added shyly, 'we both

know how lucky we are, Mrs Huntley. It's just that we can't help wishing we'd been . . . Well, a bit luckier.'

Mrs Huntley laughed ruefully. 'True.' Again she squeezed Jean's arm, leaning towards her so that Jean was suddenly made aware of the golden brooch on her lapel: a little briar rose on a twisted stem.

'Oh, what a pretty brooch,' she said, and then blushed to hear the sharp spike of envy in her voice.

'You don't think it's too small?' Mrs Huntley peered down at it anxiously. 'I thought it would be just right for this jacket, but it just seems to disappear into the tweed.' Then, raising her eyebrows despairingly, she laughed again. 'I'll have to be careful, or they'll be carving, "Never satisfied" on my headstone, won't they?'

She went on her way, raising a friendly hand in farewell, and Jean watched her for a moment, her eyes blurred with tears, her heart at rest for the first time in months. No, there was nothing wrong with Mrs Huntley. Nothing wrong with her at all.

You're carrying high . . . What a lovely thing to say!

Yes, misery was relative. In fact, at times like these, it was virtually non-existent! She was going to have a son. (And tea and a sticky bun!)

Jack Carter aside, Miles thought of his farm tenants as his friends, and Solomon Hicks, who had once been the manager at Home Farm, was almost as dear to him as a brother. He was so dear, in fact, that it had become an embarrassment to accept the rent from him on Quarter Day, and Miles had taken to keeping a bottle of something in the office to ease the pain of the exchange.

'Yer 'tis then, moi dear zir, outa thy debt again, thanks be. Comes rewnd quick though, dun 'er? Lady Day awready. Be Midzummer again afore us can turn abewt. Ooh! Ah . . . Don't moind if I do, zir. Koind o' thee. Moighty koind.'

'Your good health, my dear sir.'

'*Thine* zir, an' all thy loved uns.'

Miles's father would not have approved. Charles Huntley wouldn't even have comprehended his son's willingness to drink whisky (or cider, depending on the season) with the likes of Solomon Hicks.

'Good God, Miles, the fella speaks the dialect!'

Yet Miles fully understood his father's point of view. Before the war, he'd shared it: believing the differences between 'the gentry' and 'the others' to be more a matter of species than of class. The gentry were hares, the others rabbits which, while looking very similar, were in fact entirely different: different at the core.

Miles was no longer of this opinion. At the Front, he'd met too many bone-headed louts who'd claimed to be gentlemen, and too many gentlemen who'd made no claims at all. Farmer, docker or peer of the realm: it made no difference who the hell you were when you were all in hell. All that mattered was how you conducted yourself there, and it was *that*, not your breeding, which declared what kind of man you really were.

By this principle alone, Solomon Hicks was a gentleman as, perhaps to a lesser degree, were Joss Radnor and Colin Sands. But Jack Carter was not. Miles couldn't have said why he was not. He couldn't have explained his antipathy to the man had his life depended on it, except to say that had his life depended on Jack Carter, he'd consider himself dead. And although the fella *didn't* speak the dialect (in fact he spoke like a prince) there was a barely discernible taint to his voice which somehow spoiled his every aspect.

It wasn't much. It was nothing Miles could put his finger on. He simply didn't like the man. He didn't like his eyes, didn't like his manner, didn't like his smile, and as much as Miles looked forward to his Quarter Day visits from the other farmers, he dreaded Jack Carter's.

But Jack didn't turn up on Lady Day, nor during the three

days afterwards, and when he did come he was not smiling as usual. That is, he *was* smiling, but not as usual.

'You've heard our news, I suppose, Miles?'

'Er – no. News? Nothing bad, I hope?'

The smile was wan, and the little laugh which followed cynical in the extreme. 'Depends how you look at it. But I'm surprised you haven't heard. Nurse Stokes isn't usually the type to keep such things to herself.'

'Ah . . .' Miles sat down, waving his visitor to do the same. 'Mrs Carter? She's – ?'

'Had another girl. Yesterday morning. A few weeks premature.' The smile disappeared entirely. Jack clenched his jaw and stared grimly into the corner as if fighting off tears.

Miles didn't know where to look. Had Bel not already told him how desperate the Carters were to have a son, he'd certainly have known it from the expression on Jack's face. Oh, dear. Poor chap. And poor Mrs Carter . . .

'How are you managing?' he asked quietly. 'Do you need any help? House, cooking, children – that sort of thing?'

'No. No, thank you, Miles. Becky Vale's helping out with all that. You know her, don't you? My cow-man's eldest girl. She's got a family of her own, of course, but her husband's out of work and they need the extra money. She'll stay a few weeks, I imagine.'

Miles stood up, waved the whisky bottle. 'Join me?' he enquired briskly. 'Soda with it?'

'Yes. Thanks.' Jack produced another little laugh. 'I hear you've joined the workforce, Miles. How do you like it?'

Miles felt the hairs on the back of his neck creeping erect. There it was again, that little taint which couldn't quite be identified. Malice? Mockery? It could even be sympathy . . . And he supposed it was an innocent enough question, although Miles had always worked on his own farm: never as much as he had since Archie Weaver's retirement, but enough to know what he was doing, damn it!

'I like it very well,' he murmured, 'thank you.' He passed Jack's glass, raised his own. 'A long life, health and happiness to your new daughter, Mr Carter. Do you have a name for her yet?'

Jack paused, stared and pressed his lips together, no doubt reflecting on Miles's determined use of his surname. 'No,' he said at last, and drank. 'At least... My wife sees to all that.'

Again Jack stared, this time into his glass, which was almost empty. Then, with another cynical huff of laughter, 'What is it about these women, Miles? Your wife produces boys with no trouble at all, yet Jean... God...'

Miles swallowed an overwhelming desire to show his visitor the door. *These women!* God, how dare he? How dare he use such a phrase to include Bel? *These women!* As if there was nothing to identify one from another, as if they were all the same! And all *Jack's*, to speak of as he chose!

No... No, that wasn't fair. Barring only that curious... whatever it was that Miles couldn't stomach about him, Jack had said absolutely nothing out of the ordinary. 'Women!' Solomon had said it, with a comic jerk of his eyebrows, a chuckle and shrug. Colin had said it, with a sigh. So what was the difference? Miles didn't know. He wished he did. Then, perhaps he'd know how to deal with it.

'Yes,' he said, attempting a word of comfort. 'It's a pity we can't choose our children. I would have liked a daughter – I'd have liked a sister, too, very much – but the Huntley men have never seemed able to father girls.'

Jack's eyes widened. 'Well, I've got two brothers, so it's certainly not *my* fault. God, you'd think after *four* attempts – !'

'Four?' Miles knew at once that he shouldn't have spoken, should have let it pass. The last thing he wanted was to prolong this wretched conversation. What the hell was the man whining about? He'd had a daughter, not a three-eyed monster!

'Mmm,' Jack said. 'Mind if I smoke? She lost the first one. Another girl, of course.'

'I'm so sorry. I had no idea.'

Jack was fumbling in his pockets for cigarettes. Sighing, Miles offered his own.

'Thanks. I seem to have left mine . . .'

He accepted the light Miles offered and drew smoke into his lungs, his dark eyes narrowed, his nostrils flared, his long, bronzed neck craning upwards as if to chase even the fine tendrils of smoke which had escaped into the air. Watching him, Miles was put in mind of the poet Coleridge, who'd probably inhaled his opium in much the same way. *He'd* been a handsome devil, too . . . *And* no gentleman.

'A man *needs* a son,' Jack continued with a sigh. '*Every* man needs a son, to follow in his footsteps, to do the things . . .' He shrugged. 'You know what I mean, I'm sure.'

'Yes, except that I should hate my sons to follow in my footsteps. I'd rather they walked another road entirely.'

'Oh?' Jack grinned suddenly and tilted his head to one side. 'Why?' Been somewhere interesting, have you, Miles?'

For sheer prurience neither the look nor the question could be surpassed, and Miles had great difficulty in not responding to it as it deserved. He flicked at his inkwell with his fingertips, longing to smash it over Jack's head, but it was a Coalport piece: quite valuable, with a spider and its web traced in gold filigree over the dark blue porcelain. It would be a shame to spoil it for a man like Jack Carter . . .

He said nothing. He smiled affectionately at the inkwell, whose gilded cobwebs were echoed in the heavy brass stand which contained it. Lovely piece of work . . .

'Oh!' Jack said at last. 'Oh, I see. You mean the war. Yes.' He shrugged again before adding defensively, 'I was too young, of course. Just missed it. But there won't be another, Miles. There'll never be another, and anyway – '

'You're wrong,' Miles said softly. 'There will be another, and sooner than I care to guess. I'm certain of it, as are most people who – er – keep their eyes on international affairs.' (He had almost called Jack a fool, and he wouldn't do that, however true it might be.)

'The signs are not good, anyway,' he went on briskly. 'But no matter. It's a lovely day out there, and I'm sure we both have work to do, war or no war.'

He stood up, holding out his hand to shake Jack's. 'Believe me,' he said kindly. 'And thank God for your daughters.' He was around the desk, opening the door.

Jack seemed astonished to find himself outside again so soon. 'Thank you, Miles. Er – my regards to Mrs Huntley, by the way. She's well, is she?'

'Very well, thank you.'

Jack laughed softly. 'Keeping busy with this free meals scheme for the unemployed, I hear. Nurse Stokes was full of it. Strange bedfellows, those two, though, eh, Miles? Beauty and the beast.' He slapped his forehead, faking shock. 'Phew, the language that woman uses! How does Mrs Huntley stand it?'

'I imagine she's too busy to notice.' Miles fished his watch from his waistcoat pocket and glanced at it rather more pointedly than good manners allowed.

'Well,' Jack said. 'I'd better be on my way.'

'Yes, of course. Give our kindest regards to your wife, won't you?'

When Jack had gone, Miles closed the door very gently and leaned against it, heaving a sigh. Suddenly he thought of the woman to whom he'd sent his regards, saw an image of her which bore virtually no resemblance to the Mrs Carter he actually knew. She was thin and very pale, propped against a vast heap of white pillows, with red hair tumbling in wild disarray around her shoulders. Her eyes were huge and sad, utterly defeated. She had given Jack another daughter.

Afterwards, as he walked home to lunch, Miles realised that the image had not been of Mrs Carter, but of a painting he'd once seen of a sick child. Yet somehow it made no difference. He pitied her with all his heart.

Chapter Six

Bel had resolved never again to go anywhere near Drayfield Farm. It hadn't been easy at first, but as the winter had progressed and she'd found other things to occupy her time, she'd found that whole days were going by without her thoughts straying to Jack Carter. Even when she did think of him it was without the same intensity, and she'd begun to hope she'd completely lost interest until Nurse Stokes called him 'an ignorant bloody numbskull'.

It wasn't possible to keep company with Nurse Stokes, even for five minutes, without also keeping company with her language, but until she'd spoken of Jack in such terms, Bel had thought she'd grown used to it. Now she discovered she hadn't. In fact, she discovered that she was furious.

'What a slanderous thing to say,' she remarked coolly, but she'd spoken only to relieve her feelings, without hope of influencing Nurse Stokes by even the smallest degree. The woman was a law unto herself. She swore like a trooper, smoked like a chimney, was unspeakably rude, loud, insensitive and overbearing. True, she didn't drink, consort with thieves or spit in the street but, these blessings aside, the only thing which made her halfway tolerable was the fact that she almost never ceased working, and had done more good during the five years of her 'reign' than any normal human being could have achieved in twenty.

'Slanderous? Bloody poppycock!' she snorted now. 'I wouldn't waste my time telling lies about *him*! I tell you the man's a bloody numbskull. Like it any better the second time round, do you?'

Bel took a deep breath, which she released very slowly, thinking how fortunate it was that they were in Nurse Stokes's house, rather than Bel's. Robin had reached the stage of trying out all the new words he heard, and he'd have had a feast-day with 'bloody poppycock'. Bel rather fancied trying it for herself, in fact . . .

'Oh, not now, darling. I'm tired.'

'*Tired*? Bloody poppycock!'

She wondered what Miles would say to that!

'No,' she said calmly now. 'I like it no better the second time round. But since you insist . . .'

'Oh, I do insist! On that point and a few more which I won't go into. Mind you, I barely know the man – '

'Then how on earth can you say – ?'

'But I know his wife, and when you've met as many wives as I have, you don't need to know their bloody husbands. One way or another, it all comes out. Out of their mouths, out of their eyes or out in bloody bruises. Oh, there's not much gets past *me*, Mrs Huntley!'

Bel felt her face turning red, but couldn't have said why for the life of her. It was partly anger. Only a small part, but that was the part she clung to. 'Are you saying he beats her?' she demanded indignantly.

'No. But there are worse things. And when a woman like that – good housewife, good mother – when she rejects her baby the way – '

'Rejects it? Oh, no!'

Nurse Stokes laughed shortly. 'Why does everyone argue with me, I wonder? You find one person who tells the truth, the whole truth and nothing but the bloody truth, and the first thing you do is call her a bloody liar! *He's* the same. And *that's* what I call being an ignorant bloody numbskull, Mrs Huntley.'

Bel blinked with shock and, when that didn't help, she closed her eyes. One did not, she had discovered, put one's nose in the air and walk away from Nurse Stokes's insults. She'd tried it before and found not only that the woman didn't care, but that it was impossible to proceed without her. Even the doctor, even the *rector* refused to make a move without Nurse Stokes's say-so.

Bel had first mooted the idea of a feeding centre for the unemployed at the beginning of October, but no one had raised a hand to help get it going until, in the second week of December, she'd at last learned to 'ride' Nurse Stokes. Riding a wild stallion would have been easier, but – as with most horses – the best thing to do with her was to stay in the saddle, for if once you let her throw you, you'd never summon the courage to get mounted again.

With this thought in mind, Bel fetched a calm little smile to her face and opened her eyes, only to find Nurse Stokes smirking at her knowledgeably through the wire-framed lenses of her spectacles.

'Better?' she demanded wryly.

'I'm very well, thank you,' Bel murmured innocently.

'So? Are you going to help me out, or sue for slander? Jean Carter needs more help than I have either time or talent to give her, Mrs Huntley, and you – unless I mistake you – have both.'

'You mistake me,' Bel said firmly. (She would not go to Drayfield again. She would not. She would *not*.) 'I've no talents at all, Nurse Stokes, and certainly not for –'

'Being tactful? That's what you call it, isn't it? I call it lying through your bloody teeth, telling the poor girl everything'll be all right in the end, even though it won't be because it damn well never is. Life's like the sailor's warning, I always say. Red sky in the morning, pissing down by lunchtime.'

'Oh, really!' Bel spluttered indignantly.

'Yes, really. And you needn't think *you'll* escape the rain either, Mrs Huntley. We all get caught out without a brolly at some time or another. The only difference is that some of us get wet, some get dripping wet and some get soaked to the bloody skin!'

Rather to her dismay, Bel burst out laughing. 'Well!' she gasped. 'No one could call *you* an optimist, Nurse Stokes!'

'I wouldn't want them to. "Optimist" is a polite way of saying "bloody idiot", and I'm no idiot.'

'You aren't entirely polite, either,' Bel remarked sweetly. 'And I'm sure you're quite wrong about Mrs Carter. She's not capable of rejecting her own baby. I know they're disappointed they didn't have a boy this time, but – '

'Huh, a bit of disappointment goes a long way, Mrs Huntley, especially when it's all you've got! It can turn your bloody brain, and don't tell *me* I'm wrong, because I know! I've been there!'

Bel closed her eyes again, not with temper this time but with shame. Nurse Stokes had lost four brothers and her fiancé to the war, her mother to the influenza epidemic which had followed it, and although these were the sort of things everyone wanted to forget, it was unforgivable of Bel to have forgotten them so completely.

'Oh, dear,' she murmured wretchedly. 'I'm so very sorry . . .'

'Well, good heavens above, *I* don't want your sympathy!' Nurse Stokes darted Bel a sideways look under dark, bristling eyebrows. 'You're good at it, though,' she added briskly. 'Trouble is, it takes so much bloody *time*, and I haven't got any. Bloody stupid arrangement, having only twenty-four hours in a day . . .'

She threw the end of a spent cigarette into the fire and

immediately lit another one, attaching it to her lip like a sticking plaster. She looked tired and old, the skin around her eyes as thin and as wrinkled as wet tissue. Yet Bel knew for a fact that she was still in her thirties. Younger than Miles, anyway, and not very much older than Bel.

'You're tired,' Bel said kindly. 'I'll put the kettle on, shall I?'

It was like setting light to a firecracker. 'No, you bloody well won't!' Nurse Stokes was on her feet, reaching behind the door for her gabardine. 'It may well be teatime for you, Mrs Huntley, but *some* of us have work to do!'

Bel swallowed and blinked, scarcely believing her ears. She'd been up since six o'clock this morning, had done the menus and the shopping lists with Cook, organised Muriel, given Robin his lessons and groomed the ponies. She'd spent three hours at the village hall, doling out soup, and another hour with Nurse Stokes organising yet more menus, shopping lists and budgets. And now the – the *bloody* woman was telling her she was lazy! Of all the odious, uncivilised, ill-mannered . . . Of all the contemptible . . .

Nurse Stokes was already standing astride her bicycle by the time Bel, twitching with fury, had donned her own coat and joined her outside in the lane. 'So how about it, Mrs Huntley? Will you see her?'

'Er – Mrs Carter?'

'Yes! Who else have we been talking about, for God's sake?' She bent her head suddenly. Bel thought she was looking for her bicycle pedal until she added hoarsely, 'Sorry. Best not to be nice to me, though, Mrs Huntley. Can't really take it. Makes me want to cry.'

Then she was scooting off down the lane, shouting back over her shoulder, 'And I haven't got bloody *time*!'

Jean lay slumped against a tumbled heap of pillows, staring mutely at the window. It hadn't been cleaned for weeks, and there were marks on the lower panes where Evelyn had drawn patterns in the frost. She was aware that Mrs Huntley was in the room and that she'd been there for some time, slowly freezing on a hard wooden chair beside the bed, but Jean had scarcely looked at her, scarcely spoken to her, didn't care.

It had been a cold spring: bright and dry, with a sharp, north-easterly wind which rattled the windows. People were dying of the cold. Old people, hungry people, the unemployed. They died in their beds under heaps of damp sacking. They died on the roads as they walked, searching for work. But Jean didn't care.

Count your blessings, Mrs Carter.
What blessings?
There are worse things than having three healthy daughters.
What things?

'How about Elizabeth?' Mrs Huntley offered softly now. She was holding the baby in her arms. Earlier, she'd changed her nappy, provoking in Jean a dull sense of amazement that she was capable of such things. 'Elizabeth Carter. That has a good, solid ring to it, hasn't it?'

Jean said nothing. She couldn't. Didn't want to. Didn't care.

'Mrs Carter, please. You can't help yourself by grieving like this. Even if you can't love this baby yet, you must think of Evelyn and Shirley, think of your husband. You love *them*, don't you?'

Jean almost laughed, but hadn't the energy for it. She smiled instead, knowing that it was not a pretty sight. Her lips were dry and cracked. They stuck to her teeth, turning her smile into a leer which scared her visitor half to death. And Jean was glad of that. She had a nasty feeling that Mrs Huntley was up to something, and that in spite of her sweet little smile, her soft, coaxing voice, she was determined to go through with it, however long it took.

The baby began to whimper. Mrs Huntley stood up and bent as though to lay it on the bed, and then straightened again, her mouth softening, her arms tenderly cradling the child, close to her chest. She turned her back on Jean and took a few steps across the room, and it was as if she'd gone away, withdrawn from Jean's agony into a world of her own, a place where Jean's baby was her baby, and nothing else in the world mattered to her – Jean least of all.

She rocked the child, smiled into its eyes, pursed her lips as though to drop kisses on its wrinkled little nose. She clucked her tongue, murmured, 'There, there . . .' and her voice came from deep in her throat, full of love.

'Take it!' Jean cried. 'Go on, take the little brat! I don't want it!' and was astonished when Mrs Huntley didn't react, but went on just as before, rocking the child in her arms.

Jean realised then that she hadn't spoken the words aloud, but screamed them in silence, inside herself, where all her screams were buried. But she'd meant it! She *didn't* want it! Didn't, didn't, didn't . . .

She looked at her hands. Oh, God, it was happening . . . The thing she hadn't wanted to happen, the thing she had feared more than anything else in the world. Feelings. Feelings. She'd been almost happy to think she'd never feel anything again, and now . . .

'Nurse Stokes says you've had a busy winter,' she said harshly, although she couldn't remember quite what Nurse Stokes had said, and was talking now only to distract herself.

'Oh . . .' There was a smile in Mrs Huntley's voice, a wry, gentle little smile which Jean felt rather than saw. 'If that's what Nurse Stokes said I'd be very surprised. "A *bloody* busy winter" is more her style, I think.'

Jean blinked and turned her head, only to find that Mrs Huntley was grinning proudly, like a mischievous little boy who had uttered his first swear-word and was thrilled to bits with himself.

Astonished, Jean burst out laughing, and almost at once began to cry, sobbing as she'd never in her life . . . Oh, yes.

Once before. But now she wept for the sheer irony of it, for the terrible bitterness which tore at her like a butcher's hook, ripping her heart from its roots. Oh, God, she didn't deserve this! It wasn't fair! How could a living child bring as much grief as a dead one? And how could she so loathe the living that it was all she could do not to drown it, smother it, beat its head against the wall? She didn't want it! She wanted a son, a son!

Mrs Huntley said nothing. While Jean sobbed and writhed and beat at the pillows, she sat very quietly, rocking the baby until the worst of the violence was spent. Then, patting Jean's shoulder, 'I'll organise some tea, shall I?' she offered briskly, and was gone, taking the baby with her. Jean heard her shoes clacking on the uncarpeted stairs and thought, 'Don't fall. Don't drop my baby . . .'

She smiled then, remembering precisely what it was that Nurse Stokes had said about Mrs Huntley. 'Huh, there's more to that woman than meets the bloody eye! Bloody nerve. Telling *me* I ought to get bloody organised!'

'Bloody nerve' about summed it up, too. *No* one, including the local doctor, ever told Nurse Stokes what to do, but Mrs Huntley had, and between them – eventually – they'd set up some kind of soup kitchen for the unemployed in the village, as well as a knitting circle to provide blankets for the old folk. Yes, there was more to Mrs Huntley than met the bloody eye . . .

Jean wept again, wept for a long time, and then lay on her side, staring bleakly at the wall. She didn't feel better. In many ways she felt worse, just because she felt so *much*, and all of it torture. But something very bad had flowed out of her with her tears, and she was glad to be rid of it, for the children's sake, if not her own. She had wanted to die. She'd wanted to kill *them*, to put them all out of their misery. She'd had it all planned. A pillow pressed to each little face . . .

She shuddered and blew her nose. With the tip of her finger

she traced the circumference of a tea-stain on the sheet which, no more than a week ago, would have transfixed her with shame to know that the gracious Mrs Huntley had seen it. But not any more. Credit where credit was due. Mrs Huntley was above such things. Anyone else would have tiptoed away after the first five minutes, but she'd sat in this freezing room for more than an hour without getting an ounce of encouragement. No smile, no welcome. No tea . . . But she'd stuck it out, coaxing and probing, gently picking away at Jean's reserve until the seams had split and the bad things . . .

Yes, they'd gone. She still didn't love the baby, but at least now she knew that it was safe, and that she wanted to keep it safe. But nothing else had changed. The world was more bleak and hopeless than it had ever been. She still had no blessings to count, still wished she was dead. And she still couldn't die . . .

Bel hadn't believed that Jean Carter was in as poor state as Nurse Stokes had claimed, and although she'd gone to Drayfield with the vague intention of helping in some way, she hadn't really expected to be needed. It would, she thought, be as it had been on previous occasions: a half-hour of polite conversation and home in time for tea.

But teatime had come and gone before she was ready to leave. The sun had set and a hard frost was beginning its glistering descent upon the world. Jack had not appeared at all, and Bel was both relieved and grieved that he hadn't been there to welcome her. She told herself that her grief was for Mrs Carter, who claimed not to have seen her husband all day, but in her heart she knew that she was grieving for herself. Just being in his house had been enough to awaken all the old longings, the awful need she had just to have him notice her. Well, he hadn't noticed, so perhaps Nurse Stokes had been right about that, too. The man was a numbskull.

No, she didn't believe that, either. His marriage was not

happy and perhaps had depended too much on the hopes he'd had of a son. Yet who could blame him for not being able to hide his disappointment? Miles hadn't been able to hide his at the time of Andrew's birth, and Miles was no numbskull. He had feelings, sensitivities. He was kind, sensible, tolerant . . . It was strange, now that she came to count them up, to realise how many virtues Miles possessed, and quite shaming to know that she usually hid most of them under the bushel of his one important fault. Was that the trouble with the Carters, too? Had they blinded themselves to each other's gifts just because the one they most wanted was denied them?

Bel had no doubt at all that Mrs Carter had been suffering the agonies of the damned during this past week. And she had no doubt that Jack's disappointment had been – at least partly – the cause of her agony. But Mrs Carter had been helped. Nurse Stokes, Becky Vale and now Bel had helped her. In the meantime, however, who was helping poor Jack?

Bel was ready to leave soon after six, yet stayed a little longer, helping Becky to get the children ready for bed, stoking the fire, laying out laundry on the fireguard to air.

'Oh, and you'll make sure to keep a fire in Mrs Carter's room, won't you, Becky? I almost froze in there this afternoon, and that can't be good for the baby, you know.'

'No, mum. I mean, yes, mum. Thank you, mum.'

'And you *must* keep everything properly aired, Becky. It's of the greatest importance with a new baby, especially when the weather's so cold.'

'Yes, mum.'

'Oh, goodness, I really must go . . .' She stopped to pick up the children's shoes, to straighten the tablecloth, draw the curtains.

She felt like crying. The kitchen was clean, neat and warm, with two bright yellow corners where the oil-lamps shone. There could be no excuse for staying a moment longer. She had her coat on. She'd said goodbye. But where was Jack?

He was waiting for her at the gate, his shoulders hunched against the cold, his hands thrust deep into the pockets of an old sheepskin coat. The very sight of him paralysed Bel, so that she stopped in her tracks for a moment, consuming him inch by inch with her eyes. He hadn't changed. He was still beautiful, even with the end of his nose chewed to scarlet by the frost, even with his shoulders hunched, even in that hoary old sheepskin which looked as if it had been attacked by maggots while it was still on the sheep. Beautiful . . . And frozen stiff.

'Mr Carter!' Bel's feet moved again, and suddenly she was running towards him. 'I've been here for hours. I thought –'

'Is everything all right?' he asked wanly. 'You've seen my wife?'

'Yes, yes.' He looked so worried, poor thing, it was impossible not to reach out, to take his arm, to comfort him. 'She'll be fine. Just needed someone to talk to. Another woman, you know.'

Jack averted his face. 'What did she say?'

Bel thought about it and realised with some astonishment that Mrs Carter had said very little that was worthy of repetition. Absolutely nothing, in fact. Yet Bel *had* understood her. Completely.

'Nothing,' she said gently now. 'Nothing disloyal, nothing unkind. Nothing that you wouldn't care about and share with her, if you could. She wanted a son as desperately as you did, and is disappointed, just as you are. But I think the worst is over now. She's just lonely, Mr Carter. She needs you.'

Jack smiled the smile of a man who is struggling against tears, turning his face to the sky. 'Did she say that?'

'She didn't need to. The birth of a child, whatever its sex, is the joy – or the sorrow – of the people who created it, and unless they can share their feelings with each other they *must* be lonely.'

Jack withdrew one of his hands from his coat and covered

his eyes with long, thin fingers which had turned purple with the cold. 'Thank you,' he murmured. 'You don't know . . . We've been so miserable . . .'

'Oh, my dear, I'm so very sorry. But . . . Well, she's on the mend. And she's thought of a name for your new daughter. Valerie Anne! Valerie Anne Carter! Isn't that splendid?'

Jack threw back his head and laughed. He looked down at her and smiled – so sweetly. 'Splendid,' he murmured. 'Valerie – what was it?'

'Valerie Anne.'

'Hmm. Yes, that will do very nicely. Do you have a middle name, Mrs Huntley?'

'Well, two, in fact. Isobel Catherine Louisa. Quite a mouthful, aren't I?' She'd meant to say, 'aren't they?' and the error brought a stinging colour to her cheeks which even the gathering darkness could not hide. 'Well, I must be on my way,' she murmured.

'It's almost dark. I'll take you home. Miles would kill me if you got lost on a night like this, wouldn't he? You'd freeze before midnight.'

It was impossible to get lost. The lane had no turnings one could take by mistake. It just went round and round and up and down until at last it arrived in the High Street at Bishop Molton. Bel knew that. Jack knew that. Neither of them mentioned it.

'But you're so cold,' Bel protested feebly.

'The walk will warm me up, won't it?'

She laughed with relief. 'Yes, I suppose it will.'

The vault of the sky had darkened to a rich, hyacinth blue where the thin rind of a new moon sailed among frail, silvery streaks of high cloud. But the western horizon was still light: a pale jade green against which the stark, wintry trees were picked out in black ink and the dark silhouette of a thrush suddenly opened its throat and burst into song. 'Ohh!' Bel whispered blissfully. 'Listen! It's spring!'

'Sounds like it, doesn't it? A few more weeks and we'll be up to the neck in bluebells, I suppose, but it's hard to believe just now. No matter how many times you see another spring, you still wonder, don't you? Will it come? Won't it?'

Bel laughed with delight. 'And then you hear a thrush singing and you *know*! Oh, Lord, won't it be wonderful to be warm again?'

'Mmm. Er – what else did you and Jean talk about?'

'Oh... Let me see... Nurse Stokes, of course, and her endearing little habits.'

'Endearing! Well, that's one way of putting it.'

'Probably the wisest way. She's a very complicated person, I've found. Every time I make a move to condemn her, she says something so unexpected it makes me feel an absolute heathen. The sort of heathen who burns saints at the stake.'

'Nurse *Stokes*? A *saint*? Never!'

Again Bel laughed. 'I think it's something we should be prepared for, if only on the "better safe than sorry" principle. Don't say you weren't warned. If you set light to her before I do, you'll save me from eternal damnation.'

There was a short, breathless silence. 'I'd do that willingly,' he said huskily, and although Bel knew what he meant, she pretended not to. 'What? Set her alight?'

'Save you from damnation. You're the sweetest, kindest, most beautiful woman I've ever had the good fortune to meet. I'd do anything – '

'Oh, please...' Bel wailed softly. She laughed again and wished she hadn't, for it came out all wrong: too loud and too bright, as if she'd already gone three parts crazy. 'We also,' she hurried on firmly, 'talked about your house.'

'Oh... Did you? Er – what about it? I suppose I have neglected it a bit. It's not as comfortable as it should be, but with money so short – '

'Neglect it? No, indeed. It's a beautiful house. That's what I was telling your wife. She loves it, you know.'

'Yes. I know.'

'The people who lived at Drayfield before you came – the Morrises? Did you meet them? They treated it abominably. Hammered nails into the panelling to hang up their pictures. Miles was livid. And they weren't even good pictures! No, you've made it quite perfect. You allow the bones of the house to show through, and they're such beautiful . . . bones.' Her voice trailed away. Her ankle turned in the ruts of the lane, causing her – or, rather, allowing her – to reach for Jack's arm again. She bit her lip, squeezed her eyes shut. She wanted him! Oh, God, she wanted him!

And she couldn't *have* him!

'You all right?'

'Yes, fine! Look, I can go the rest of the way on my own, Mr – er. You need your supper, and – '

'Nonsense. We're almost there.' He laughed suddenly. 'Listen, your teeth are chattering!' He slid his arm around her shoulder. 'You must be frozen!'

With a ferocious effort of will, Bel shrugged him off. 'Walk faster,' she urged. 'That's the best way to get warm. Oh, I was telling Mrs Carter about the lost room. She didn't know – '

'Lost room?'

'Oh! You haven't noticed it, either? How strange. We aren't quite certain it is a room, of course. The plans of the house, if there ever were any, were lost years ago. But there's certainly a missing space. Over the hallway, you know. The front part of your hall is about ten feet square, but there's no room overhead to correspond. And you must have noticed the bricked-up window over your front door?'

'There are several bricked-up windows.'

'Yes, we've got some too. But they have rooms behind them, don't they? Miles says his father once tried to find if there was a bricked-up doorway in your house somewhere, but the walls are two feet thick, all round. Quite intriguing, don't you think? Miles says it's probably just a dead space, full of rubble. But then, he has no romance in his soul. He likes sensible explanations. I prefer mysteries!'

A lamp glowed dimly at the end of the lane, heralding their arrival in the village. Jack stopped walking and turned to her, leaning close, so that she felt his breath on her face like a warm summer mist. 'I'll leave you now, Mrs Huntley. Thank you for all you've done for us today. I can't tell you how – '

'Oh, I've done nothing. Absolutely nothing. Thank you for bringing me home. It was so – It would have been a miserable walk on my own.'

'My pleasure, Mrs Huntley. My very great pleasure.'

He stooped suddenly to set a fleeting kiss on her cheek, and his lips were like ice, scorching her to the bone.

Five minutes later she was in the entrance hall at Bishop's Court, stamping white frost from her shoes and red-hot torment from her soul.

Miles came to meet her, his eyes glittering with cool disapproval. As was his custom he had changed for dinner, although tonight he was wearing a quilted smoking jacket which had the unfortunate effect of making him look bigger than usual: taller, broader . . . crosser.

'Welcome home,' he said aloofly.

Bel glared at him. 'Yes, I know I'm late, but – '

'Think nothing of it, darling. Nanny has put your son to bed, and I'm sure someone, somewhere, is attending to dinner.' He took her coat, produced a grin to taunt her. 'You've scarcely been missed, I assure you.'

'Mrs Carter needed me, Miles!'

'Of course. Which is why I'm so eager to convince you that we didn't. Can I get you a drink, darling?'

He opened the library door to show her through, and although Bel would have preferred to be alone for a few minutes, the sight of a blazing log fire changed her mind.

Miles caught her hand as she hurried past him. 'Lord, you're frozen. Come on, sit down.' He poured her a drink and pushed it into her hand, standing to survey her with smiling cynicism. 'You know, if you can't take better care of yourself, darling, I think we might have to put a stop to all these good works of yours. So much selflessness can go too far, you know.'

Bel tossed her head irritably, wondering how he could be so horribly sarcastic yet sound so *nice* at the same time.

'Oh, leave me alone, Miles! I'm tired!'

Miles sat opposite her, gazing sadly into the far corner of the room. 'Well,' he said at last. 'That makes two of us, doesn't it?'

Chapter Seven

The High Street ended where the boundary wall of Bishop's Court began. Beyond that, the narrow, winding strip of hedge-shadowed tarmac which trailed out into the countryside was known as the main Bristol Road and it was this road that divided Home Farm from Bishop's Court, a distance Miles usually measured with four long strides or, on his good days, a hop, a skip and a jump. On bad days, when the cold gnawed at the wound in his leg, his slight tendency to limp slowed the speed of his journey to the best part of half a minute, making him wonder wryly if he'd *ever* get home.

One evening early in April he slithered home on a sheet of black ice so sheer that, in resisting its efforts to floor him, he wrenched several muscles in his back, skinned his hand on the wall and, in spite of everything, still found himself sitting abruptly in the road. It was a deeply dispiriting moment: the literal bottom of a dark pit of a day, and he allowed himself the luxury of a quiet curse before he attempted to get up again. 'Oh, damn it to hell,' he whispered. 'When will this bloody winter ever end?'

Someone must have heard him, because when he got up the next morning, spring had arrived. They'd had intimations of it before this: the usual catkins and snowdrops in February and celandines in March, blackbirds singing in apple trees, all that. But the cold winds had never relented, the ground never completely thawed, and it seemed to Miles, looking back, that he hadn't been warm since the first sharp frosts in the middle of October.

Now he climbed out of bed as into a warm bath and stood at the window for several minutes, watching with wonderment the soft, amber dawn. The garden was alight with huge swathes of daffodils and the low stone walls edging the croquet lawn were a tapestry of golden thingummyjigs, purple whatsits and white stuff. He'd never been greatly interested in the names of flowers, although he'd always enjoyed looking at them. Now, touched to the heart by their beauty (which seemed to have sprung up overnight, and yet must have been there yesterday, unnoticed), he wanted to pay them the proper respect and call them by their names.

'Bel? Bel?' He leaned over the bed to shake her arm. 'Bel, what's the name of that purple stuff on the wall?'

She shrugged him off, turned over and buried her head under the pillow, muttering something which didn't sound at all like the name of a flower.

'Bel! Wake up, it's five past six!'

'Lea me *lone*, will you? Mibbla *night*!'

Miles laughed and crashed down beside her, lifting the pillow to tickle her neck, blow in her ear. 'Not mibbla night,' he growled teasingly. 'Mibbla morning. Nearly lunchtime.'

'Is not.'

'Is.'

'Liar.'

'Am not. Hey, Bel, it's spring! It's warm! Look, no dressing gown!' He rolled on to his back, waved his legs in the air, wriggled his toes and subjected them to a smiling inspection. They were all the same colour: a clear, healthy beige which made a very welcome change from the motley of stone white, pale grey and deep purple they had been for the past few months. He sometimes worried about his circulation. Now, unless the spring suffered a relapse (God forbid), he could forget about his toes for the next six months.

' "Oh, to be in England",' he quoted happily, ' "Now that April's there. And whoever wakes in England – " '

'Which seems to include me.' Bel sighed and turned over, rubbing her nose. 'What are your feet doing up there?'

'Defying gravity. It's incredibly difficult. Quite dangerous, too. If I were prepared to do this in public I'd make a fortune, you know.'

'What, wave your legs in the air?'

'*Sssh*! We don't want everyone doing it, do we? Think of the effect on poor Muriel if she latched on to an idea like this! It could be quite . . .' He grinned, imagining it. 'Ruinous,' he concluded in an awed voice. 'Topple the government, probably.'

Bel laughed and hit him with a pillow. 'You're horrid to that girl, you brute.'

'I know. It's one of my few remaining pleasures in life.'

Afterwards, while he shaved, he reflected drearily on the speed with which the human mind can work, for almost before he'd finished making that quite meaningless, light-hearted claim, he'd also called himself a bloody fool and offered up a prayer that Bel wouldn't have noticed it. But she had.

'Yes,' she'd murmured, and flicked him a glance under pale, glistening brows which, without even moving, had spoken every negative word in the dictionary. Contempt was one of them. The worst of them. It hung in the air between them like a cloud, making Miles shiver and reach for his dressing gown, the names of the flowers unlearned, the joys of spring all forgotten.

Becky Vale had departed Drayfield Farm on the day Jean departed her child-bed. Still weak and depressed, still apt to fall into death-like trances whenever she heard the new baby crying, Jean would have appreciated Becky's help for a few more days – a week, even a month – but Jack wouldn't pay for more. Money, he informed her, didn't grow on trees. He was damned if he'd pay someone else to do the work when Jean could do it for nothing.

But it was all so hard. So hopeless. The house was so big. So cold. She kept to the kitchen for a while, trying to forget that the rest of the house existed. She washed dishes, nappies, bottoms and faces. She threw food into pots, threw pots on to the table and then back into the sink to begin the cycle anew. Save for the few muscles, sinews and thought-processes which these activities forced into play, she was like someone dead: scarcely seeing, hearing or feeling anything. She didn't expect ever to change again; was certain that she'd spend the rest of her life like this, blind and deaf, insensate; and was shocked to the core when, on a sunny morning in late April, she did change. Her eyes and ears opened and her mind began to work as suddenly as if someone had flicked a switch to set it into motion.

That someone was Mrs Huntley.

She appeared at the foot of the garden path, wearing a frock printed all over with small flowers which almost exactly matched the colour of the buds on the lilac tree by the gate. She shone like the morning, was as clean and fresh as the sky, and the expression on her face was as sweet as the birdsong which echoed all around. Jean saw all that, heard all that, felt her heart slam against her breast, hot colour invade her cheeks – and she groaned aloud, 'Oh, no! Not *now*!'

She was still standing by the sink, up to the elbows in suds, but suddenly the whole house, every dusty, neglected corner of it, passed before her eyes, covering her with shame. She hadn't polished the hallway for weeks! She hadn't cleaned the windows! The bunch of early daffodils which Mrs Huntley had brought while she was still in bed had been brought down and abandoned – dead, brown and stinking – in a jug on the hall table.

In a wild flurry of activity, she dried her hands, raced out into the hall, opened the window seat and thrust the jug – complete with daffodils – inside it. She dusted the table with her apron, but there was no time for anything else. Scarlet to the roots of her hair, she opened the door.

'Oh, Mrs Huntley...'

'Isn't it a lovely morning, Mrs Carter? How are you, today? Feeling any brighter?'

Jean smiled wanly. 'Feeling ashamed of myself. I haven't lifted a hand since... The place is... I can't seem...' She stood aside to let her visitor in, knowing that there was no alternative except to slam the door in her face. 'Look at it.'

But Mrs Huntley didn't look. She peered into the basket on her arm. 'I've brought some cakes,' she confided wickedly. 'Chocolate, with butter icing. I brought them for the children, but I'm not sure I can resist stealing one or two. How about you?'

It was all Jean could do not to kiss her.

Jack had gone to market; so they sat in the front garden without fear of being observed in their sinful pleasures, drinking coffee and eating cakes, watching the children as they played on the path. The garden was a wilderness, still littered with the debris of winter yet already full of docks, nettles and dandelions. And even as she chatted with Mrs Huntley about other things, Jean found herself planning to do some weeding. Planning to clean the house and wash all the blankets. Planning to live again.

In the pram where she'd been sleeping, Valerie began to cry, and without even thinking about it, Jean went to pick her up, laid her over her shoulder and, for the first time, felt as if she and the baby were in tune, made of the same flesh, breathing the same air. It was a sweet, peaceful feeling which filled her with gratitude for Mrs Huntley's visit.

'I'm getting used to her, now,' she confided softly. 'Thank you for coming, Mrs Huntley. I know how busy you are.'

'Not as busy as I was. With the boys home for the holidays, I've had to leave the running of the soup kitchen to Mrs Shorecroft. She's better at it than I am.'

'Bossier, you mean?'

Mrs Huntley chuckled. 'Is that what I mean? Yes, I suppose I do, but I mean it enviously, not with censure. Bossy people seem able to get things done so easily, don't they? Their road is straight, their destination in clear view all the time. But I never seem to know where I'm going. I can't seem to decide . . .' She shook her head and laughed again. 'Enough of me. How about you? I don't suppose you've found our lost room, yet?'

'No, but I've found something else. I meant to tell you about it the last time you were here, but had . . . too many other things on my mind. Will you hold the . . . Will you hold Valerie for me? I'll go and get it.'

In fact she had found the papers only a few months after coming to Drayfield: three small, yellow, handwritten pages torn from a book. They'd been in one of the window seats on the rear landing, and were obviously very old: written in a tiny, old-fashioned script with strange letters, strange spellings, a kind of shorthand in which many of the words had been reduced to mere ciphers. She hadn't attempted to read it all. It seemed to be the remnant of someone's cookery book, with 'Rcpt fr Peafe Pudng' written on the first page, and 'Goose Forcmt' on the second. Except for its age, Jean had taken no interest in it and might never have thought of it again had Mrs Huntley not been so obviously intrigued by the history of the house.

Valerie was crying with some vigour by the time Jean returned, and she sat down to feed her while Mrs Huntley, her eyes bright with fascination, pored over the densely written pages. Every now and then, she breathed, 'Oh, gosh, oh, golly!' like a schoolgirl snatching through the pages of a cheap romantic novel.

Jean smiled and absently stroked the fuzzy patch of hair on Valerie's brow. How strange it all was . . . For the past six years she had lived in awe, envy and sometimes loathing of the beautiful Mrs Huntley, yet here they were . . . Not the best of friends, exactly – their social differences would always make friendship of *that* sort impossible – but Jean liked her, had grown fond of her: fond enough even to forget, for long minutes at a time, that they had any differences at all.

'Oh!' Mrs Huntley gasped suddenly. 'Have you seen this? It's a charm!'

'A what?'

'A charm! That's what it says! "A Charm to Sweeten Sour Milk"! And here's another – "A Charm to Cure Warts!"' Frowning, she read on, and then wrinkled her nose with disappointment. 'Same old one. Rub wart with meat, bury meat, and when it rots the wart's cured. What a bore. Absolutely *everyone* knows that one. Still, it's jolly interesting. Eighteenth century, I should imagine. One of my husband's great-greats was probably still living here then. You must show it to him the next time he calls.'

'Take it with you,' Jean offered.

'Oh, no . . . No, it's too precious. Keep it safe. Knowing me, I'd be almost bound to lose it on the way home.' She stood up and smiled. 'And I'd better get a move on, or I'll be missing lunch again. Miles is always complaining that I'm never where he left me!'

When she'd gone, Jean gave the children their lunch, put them down for their naps and, in better spirits than she'd been in for months, swept the landing, the stairs and the hall. She was almost ready to cover the same ground again – this time with a mop and a bucket of soapy water – when she remembered the 'cookery book', which she'd left on the garden seat outside the front door.

Mrs Huntley had carefully restored the pages to the old envelope Jean had always kept them in, and although she had no reason to take them out again, she did. The 'Chrm to Cr Wrts' was uppermost, and she smiled, and whispered in round, honeyed accents, 'What a bore. Absolutely *everyone* knows that one,' and flicked the page over, searching for the charm to sweeten milk, which might well come in handy during the hot days of summer.

But her gaze settled halfway down the page, at another heading which Mrs Huntley had missed. 'A Crse Agnst Thne Enemie'. Her eyes widening, Jean laid the page on the hall table and leaned over it, tracing each tiny word with her finger, but before she'd managed to decipher even the first line she became aware of a nasty smell issuing from the window seat and, remembering the daffodils, she retrieved them, laughed, and left the cheery business of cursing her enemies for a more convenient moment.

Bel walked home very slowly, picking little posies of primroses which she wrapped in dock-leaves to keep them fresh. The sky was the colour of periwinkles, the floor of the lane a shining maroon where dead winter leaves had rotted and been stained by the blood-red soil. She wished, idly, that she could paint well enough to express it all. She wished, far less idly, that Jack would come home from market before she reached the village, and stop and say hello. She'd forgotten it was market day. Miles would usually have reminded her, but with the boys home from school he'd stolen a holiday from work and taken them to Bath to get their hair cut.

She reached the village disappointed – and late for lunch. Miles, who had never been a *great* stickler for punctuality, had become increasingly so during the past few months. It seemed that virtually anything she did which was not strictly concerned with home and hearth annoyed him: although with Miles it was never easy to tell if he was really annoyed or just teasing.

Whatever it was, it irritated Bel out of all patience. If he wanted a dutiful wife, he should try being a dutiful husband! If he wanted her to dance on his every whim, he might try dancing on one or two of hers! Only one, in fact. But more often. Twice a week, not twice a year!

She let herself in through the scullery, which was quicker than walking all round the house to the front door, and washed her hands at Ethel's sink, which was already piled high with dirty pots. Then she hurried through to the dining room, having been warned by Cook that everyone was waiting for her.

'Gosh!' she said cheerfully as she took her place at the table. 'Are you early, or am I late?'

'You're late!' the boys replied in chorus, and she laughed and made a performance of unfolding her table napkin, studiously ignoring Miles.

'How was your morning?' She leaned towards Stephen who, with Simon, his twin, sat at her right. 'Oh, very smart, darling. It's lovely to see your ears again.'

'Horrid,' Stephen murmured crossly. 'I hate having my hair cut.'

'You'd hate it even more if people began calling you Susan,' Bel quipped lightly. 'As they would if you didn't have it cut. You have such beautiful curls. Just like Daddy's.'

'No one calls *him* Susan,' Simon muttered.

Irritated, Bel turned to Robin, who sat at her left. 'Don't play with your knife, darling. Sit up nicely, there's a good boy. Did you manage to get your new cricket flannels, Andrew?'

They were halfway through the soup before she dared look at her husband. He, too, had had his hair cut, and looked younger, more handsome than she remembered. It was partly because he was still dressed in suit and tie from the morning's excursion to Bath. She rarely saw him, these days, wearing anything smarter than an old tweed jacket, boots and cavalry twills. Since the onset of their money worries, they rarely entertained or went out together, and it was only now, seeing him as he used to be, that Bel understood how greatly their lives had changed.

The entire world had been through an earthquake of sorts in the aftermath of the Crash, and because – unlike many of his peers – Miles had not lost everything, Bel had thought they'd heard only the rumbles of the disaster, seen other desperate people falling into the vast chasms which had opened to receive them. But that wasn't true. They'd fallen too, but so slowly and subtly they'd scarcely noticed the difference. Or rather *Bel* hadn't noticed the difference. Miles had carried the whole wretched load of it, protecting her, as he had always protected her, from the worst.

And she'd been out this morning . . . Seeking the attentions of another man.

'You're looking very glamorous, Miles,' she said brightly.

'Am I? How kind of you to say so. Where've you been this morning? Checking up on Mrs Shorecroft?'

'No, darling. I'm quite sure she can manage without me. No, I just dashed over to Drayfield Farm. Nurse Stokes said Mrs Carter was still feeling low, so I thought I should make the effort.'

Miles was looking at her very steadily, and she blushed. To cover her confusion, she laughed and added excitedly, 'And guess what, Miles? She's found the most extraordinary little document in one of the window seats! Eighteenth century, I'd guess, early nineteenth perhaps . . .'

Having captured his interest, Bel described the papers in as much detail as she could recall, and then was dismayed to see him frowning at her with evident disapproval. 'Why the dickens didn't you bring them home?' he demanded crossly. 'They could be important – valuable even – and if Carter knows about them, he'll sell them without even asking himself whose property they are!'

'Nonsense. They aren't in the least interested in them, Miles.'

'Perhaps not, but now *you've* shown some interest –'

'All right.' Bel smiled and raised her hands in submission. 'I'll get them. Calm down, darling, do. Robin, wipe your hands on your napkin, please, not on your jersey. Simon, there's no need to scrape your plate like that. If you want more soup, you have only to ask for it.' She darted a swift glance in Miles's direction before adding, on a softly venomous note, 'You aren't at school now, you know.'

Bel knew that Thursday was Mrs Carter's shopping day, but pretended she'd forgotten. She knew that Mrs Carter usually arrived in the village just as the shops opened after lunch, and she set off for Drayfield ten minutes after that, taking a shortcut which allowed her to avoid the High Street entirely. She was not going to the farm specifically to see Jack. She was simply running a promised errand for her husband – what could *be* more virtuous? – to fetch the papers he so much wanted to see.

Andrew and the twins had gone back to school, and it had rained every day since then, making the May Day fair an absolute washout. Today was dry, but cloudy and chill, and Bel had abandoned her summer frocks for a light skirt and blouse and her favourite tweed jacket. She knew she looked very smart and businesslike, very much the lady of the manor, but she felt like a child: breathlessly shy of the adults, seriously scared of punishment, yet still determined on a course of mischief she could not, for the life of her, control.

She stopped, and almost turned back several times during her walk, her heart hammering with a combination of excitement and guilt. But excitement was always the greater. She couldn't control it. She couldn't turn back. And why on earth should she? She just wanted to see him, for heaven's sake, not to . . . No, no, she didn't want *that*. She just wanted to hear his voice, to have him say . . . What? Oh, *anything*. Anything at all! He could talk about the finer points of boiling up pig-swill for all she cared, just as long as she could be with him, look at him, take something home with her that belonged to him (the exact colour of his eyes, for instance) and keep that with her, like a charm, to warm the long, lonely nights.

But she loved Miles!

Did she? Still?

And Miles loved her!

No . . .

She knocked at the farmhouse door in half-hearted fashion, already turning away to seek Jack in the farmyard, and was appalled when she heard soft footsteps descending the uncarpeted stairs. Mrs Carter hadn't gone!

But it was Jack who answered the door. He had recently shaved and combed his hair, and was dressed very neatly in a checked shirt, green knitted tie and spotless fawn riding breeches. But he had no shoes on. He was wearing socks, yet somehow Bel felt as if she'd caught him with no clothes on at all, and backed away from the door, her face on fire.

'Mrs Huntley!'

'Oh . . . Oh, I'm so sorry, Mr – er. I thought your wife – '

'Oh, dear, I'm afraid you've missed her. It's her shopping day in the village.'

Bel pressed her fingers to her mouth. 'Oh no,' she groaned. 'Is it Thursday? Lord, what a perfect fool! I could have sworn it was Friday.'

It began to be clear that he wasn't going to ask her in, wasn't going to encourage her even to the extent of allowing her to cross his threshold. And Bel was glad of that. Relieved. Grateful. And, taking that she'd just walked two miles to get here, strangely eager to get away again.

'Well!' she said briskly. 'I'll say goodbye.'

'I suppose there's nothing I can do?'

'Do? Oh, no. I just came to pick up some . . . But it doesn't really . . . I'll call in another time.' She chuckled wryly. 'Some *other* Friday.'

'Pick up some – ?' he prompted curiously. 'Anything I could get for you? It seems a shame to walk all this way without getting what you came for.'

Bel blushed and bit her lip. She looked at her feet. 'It was just some papers,' she explained. 'Nothing – er – terribly important. Some old recipes, that's all.'

Jack grinned and held the door wide. 'Come in. I can't promise anything, but if I can put my hands on them . . .' He showed her into the parlour, a vast, cold room which had for its furnishings only a brown leather-cloth couch, two green plush armchairs and a small, rather moth-eaten, Indian carpet.

'Do, please, sit down,' Jack invited graciously. Then, 'Any clue where she might keep these recipes?'

'Er – well! Let me see now. I think she said one of the window seats on the landing. They were in a large manilla envelope as I recall. But you really mustn't trouble yourself . . .'

He smiled. 'No trouble, I assure you. I just hope I can find them.' He went out. 'Won't be a tick.'

He was more than a tick. Bel felt awful, putting him to so much trouble for something so trivial. He'd clearly been going out somewhere, obviously had better things to do than attend to *her* stupid whims. She felt such a fool!

She began to wring her hands, which were damp with sweat and trembling slightly. She stood up, walked to the window, sat down. She stood up again and hurried to the door to call the search off. But just as she reached to open it, it flew back in her face, with Jack, still padding about in his socks, close behind.

'Oh!' The edge of the door just skimmed Bel's temple, making her yelp and start back with shock.

Jack caught her arm. 'Oh, God, I'm so sorry! Did I hurt you? I didn't think! Here, let me see . . .'

He was stroking her hair back from her brow, holding her

very gently. Bel's breath caught in her throat. She closed her eyes to inhale the scent of him: carbolic soap, raw earth and brilliantine.

'Oh, my dear . . .' Jack whispered.

He cupped her face in his hands and gazed down at her with wide, wondering eyes. Bel stopped breathing.

'Nothing in the window seat,' Jack murmured dreamily.

'It doesn't matter . . .'

He kissed her very briefly, drawing away to observe her response, and although Bel knew she should do something, say something to defuse the situation, she couldn't move, couldn't say a word. She felt like a film heroine strapped to a railway line, too weak to break free and so petrified of the oncoming train that all she could do was hope it would hurry, hurry, put her out of her misery!

Jack smiled and sighed before kissing her again and at length: a fierce, hungry kiss which Bel returned with interest, standing on her toes so that their difference in height should rob her of nothing he had to offer.

Until now, she had managed to convince herself that her interest in Jack was purely romantic, like a schoolgirl crush which lives for a while and then dies of its own accord, with no harm done. But as he pulled her closer every thought of romance was driven from her mind, so that the only thing she was aware of was her body and its needs, Jack's body and its needs. They weren't even people any more. Bel didn't know who she was or where she was, let alone where she had come from. Every inch of her skin seemed to have been doused with spirit and set alight, and Jack's sole purpose in life was to put the fire out, in the only way he could contrive it.

He peeled off her jacket and threw it on the couch. Unbuttoned her blouse and slid it from her shoulders. He covered her neck and arms with biting kisses, walking her backwards until her knees hit the edge of the couch and she fell, reaching up to drag him with her. He came down very slowly, tantalising her, resting first on his knees to unbutton the front of his breeches. But all Bel could see were his eyes. They were brown.

'I thought they were black,' she murmured breathlessly, and then gasped as his hands dragged up her skirt, her petticoat, invaded the soft flesh on the inside of her thighs.

'Christ,' he muttered distractedly. 'How d'you get these things off?'

Bel helped him. She became aware, if only dimly, that there was something rather sordid about making love on a slippery leather-cloth sofa, with her petticoat around her throat, her knickers on the fender, her stockings in rumpled coils about her ankles. She also became aware that, just as she had wiped out Jack's personality, he had now wiped out hers, for his eyes were glazed, his mouth slack, his hands pushing and pulling, lifting and shoving, without acknowledging her as anything more sensitive than a large truss of hay. Yet somehow it didn't matter. In fact, it was a glorious feeling. She was getting what she wanted, after all: a man who wanted *her*!

He entered her with a sudden thrust of his hips which forced her head back against the arm of the sofa, and with each subsequent thrust she slid a little further back, ending up in an undignified sprawl – half lying, half seated – with one foot on the floor and the other on Jack's shoulder. And still it didn't matter. Nothing mattered at all until – it seemed scarcely minutes since he'd hit her with the door – Jack began to utter a rhythmic, choking, sobbing sound which ended with a yell, a final thrust, a shudder . . . And then nothing.

Bel couldn't believe it. She couldn't believe it. It was over, *over* and it hadn't even begun! She could have howled with disappointment. She could have wept with shame. Her knickers were still on the fender. She was naked except for the disgraceful tangle of underwear around her neck, and yet, save for his boots, Jack was still fully clothed. He still had his *tie* on, albeit slightly left of centre now. And he was already fastening the buttons of his breeches.

Suddenly Bel remembered who she was and where she had come from. She was Miles Huntley's wife, the mother of his sons! She was an Archdeacon's daughter!

She wished she was dead.

Chapter Eight

The Huntleys had dined. The evening was warm, the sun still some distance from the horizon, and they'd brought their coffee out to the terrace, where Miles now sat alone, watching his wife as she made a desultory inspection of the flower borders. Her dress – a clinging silk crepe with inlays of lace – was the exact pale, grey-blue of the tall flag-irises at the back of the border; but the irises stood as straight as guardsmen, while Bel was drooping: chin down, shoulders slumped, her feet trailing through the gravel as if handmade shoes came ten pairs to the pound. She looked like someone who'd been lost in a maze for a week and given up all hope of finding her way out again.

Miles knew why, of course. She'd turned to him every night this week, and he'd had nothing to offer but apologies, excuses, guilt and defensive irritation. If they'd made love more than twice during the past year, he'd forgotten the third time and Bel, it seemed, had abandoned all hope of the fourth. But what could he do? He'd taken his problem to a doctor (not the idiot in the village) and, as once or twice before, had planned his explanation down to the last word, smile and disparaging chuckle. Then he'd breezed through to the chap's office, said he had a pain in his chest and come home with a bottle of ipecac, 'to loosen the phlegm'. Miles was aware that this word had more than one meaning. The second was, 'not easily excited'.

Yet in spite of his cowardice in not asking the doctor's advice, he had a feeling that he didn't really need advice, that he knew what it was all about and that the answer to it was – like some chap's name – on the tip of his tongue. Whatsisname, thingummybob. Fella with a squint. Begins with an M. Masters! No . . . *Barton*, that's the chap!

Which just went to show that when it was right on the tip of your tongue it was no easier to find than the proverbial needle in a haystack. He could say (and frequently did) that he wanted to limit the size of his family, that he couldn't afford to educate another son. These things were true, but they were not the whole truth. These things were reasonable, but they were not the true *reason*.

Sighing, Miles finished his coffee and went indoors to write some letters. It was almost dark when he'd finished, and a moth was battering itself against the glowing bulb of his desk lamp. He closed the window, pausing to inhale the honeyed perfume of the wisteria which clothed the front wall of the house. As he strolled through to the drawing room, he found Muriel shutting the French windows, closing the curtains.

He smiled as he turned on the light. 'Thank you, Muriel. Mrs Huntley anywhere about?'

As usual when he spoke to her, Muriel moved her lips, apparently repeating his words as though to wring the last ounce of sense out of them. Then, after a brief, concentrated pause – during which she closed one eye and slewed her mouth sideways – she said, 'Seen 'er, Struntley,' which, even without an accompanying shake of her head to confirm it, meant, 'No, I haven't seen her.'

Miles wasn't sure how he knew this. Getting to know Muriel was rather like getting to know an intelligent dog: it didn't speak, exactly (and Muriel certainly didn't speak exactly), but somehow one knew *exactly* what it meant.

As he left the house in search of his wife he was surprised to find the evening still light: luminous, rather, as if the day, like an overtired child, was still refusing to admit that bedtime had come. The blue irises were quite grey now, and most of the greenery swallowed by twilight, but an enormous clump of white tulips shone like silver chalices against the boundary wall, their shapes picked out with perfect clarity. A blackbird hauled a worm from the lawn, and, as Miles walked by, flew off, screeching with irritation, to her nest in the wisteria.

'Bel?'

He knew he would find her. The garden was a large one: five acres in all, although before the war – with twelve gardeners to tend it – it had been more than twice that size. Nine of those twelve were now dead, and the flowers they'd grown had been ploughed up and laid to meadow-grass.

'Bel? Where are you?'

There was another wisteria – a white one – clothing the pergola, its long, pendant blooms glowing in the twilight like the candlelit crystals of a vast chandelier. The air was filled with its perfume.

Miles closed his eyes and inhaled deeply, thanking God that he was alive and in such a heavenly place, and then – curiously – wondering if perhaps he was dead and in heaven . . .

'Bel?'

'I'm here.' At the sound of her voice, Miles knew that he was not dead, and certainly not in heaven. She sounded utterly miserable. And it was all his fault . . .

She was sitting in the summerhouse, her shoulders hunched, her face averted, a balled-up handkerchief pressed to the end of her nose. Miles sat beside her and said nothing. Bel's tears always rendered him speechless. She only ever cried as a result of his actions – or the lack of them – and nearly always when, in spite of the blame he took upon himself, he could do nothing to help her.

The summerhouse overlooked the most formal part of the ornamental gardens: a rectangular stone pool with a row of pleached lime trees on either side. A tranquil spot. Bats flittered over the water. Under it, carp occasionally rose to the surface, making little plopping sounds as they snatched flies to their doom.

Miles reached out to find Bel's hand and, failing, patted her knee instead. 'I'm sorry, darling.'

'Sorry?' she repeated dismally. 'What for?'

'That you're so sad. That you're sad because of me, and that – '

'It's nothing to *do* with you! It's me! I'm . . .' The balled handkerchief moved from nose to eyes and back again. 'I'm sodden,' she whispered helplessly.

Miles groped in his pocket and silently handed over his own square of white linen. 'Have a good blow,' he advised, adding wryly, 'Clears the phlegm.'

Bel blew her nose. She mopped her tears. 'I've lost my brooch,' she confessed flatly.

'What?'

'The brooch you bought me last year. The briar rose with the snake. I've lost it! I've looked everywhere, but I can't – can't – ' Her voice rose to an anguished wail. She burst into tears again and sobbed as if her heart had broken.

His eyes widening, Miles stared at her, fighting certain emotions of his own. 'Is this?' he stammered incredulously, 'Is this why you're so . . . ? Is this why you're *crying*, Bel?'

'Yes! I – I – loved it, Miles! And I've lost it! Oh, Miles, I know it must have cost an absolute mint! The things I like always do, and I – ' She turned to stare at him, and even in what remained of the twilight, he could see the horror in her eyes, the appalling expression of loss. She hadn't been this distressed even when Andrew had first gone to school, and as

Miles made the comparison he lost his fight with his own emotions and exploded with laughter.

'You dope!' he howled. 'You crazy, ridiculous – !' He took her in his arms and rocked her back and forth. 'Eighteen bob, that's what it cost! Eighteen *shillings*, Bel! Not even a whole *pound*, for heaven's sake! You can have another. You can have six! It doesn't matter, sweetheart. Dear God, I can't *believe* . . . Oh, Bel, Bel, don't cry any more! It doesn't matter, believe me!'

Still she cried – with relief he supposed – although she didn't sound in the least relieved. Absently kissing her hair, Miles furrowed his brow in bewilderment, thinking how very *strange* women were. *What is it about these women, Miles?* Yes, what the hell was it? Jack Carter hadn't been insulting Bel, he'd just been expressing the age-old frustration of men through all the ages: that, for as long as they lived, they would never understand *women*!

'Hush,' he whispered. 'Hush now. Enough. I love you, Bel. And even if the brooch had cost five guineas, fifty guineas, I'd love you just the same.' He tried to tilt her face, to get some clue that her mood might be changing, but she cried even harder and tugged away from him, hiding her face in his handkerchief.

'You *shouldn't* love me!' she wailed. 'I'm no good, Miles! I'm . . . I'm wicked and selfish and ungrateful and . . . and utterly *stupid* – '

Miles gazed at her incredulously, guessing that something more than a lost brooch was at the root of this and that he was it. Wicked, selfish, ungrateful? Yes, with her religious background he supposed she might see it that way: putting sex first was not one of the things she had been taught at her father's knee. But the Archdeacon, bless him, had been next-door to a saint and Bel, bless her, was not. Miles didn't want her to be. He liked her the way she was, even if she did put him through the agonies of the damned for wanting what he could not give her. He knew – although he couldn't clearly remember – how it felt to be forever driven by the needs of one's body. And that wasn't wicked. Just natural.

'You should hate me,' Bel sobbed. 'I've taken everything from you, and spoiled it, and given you nothing!'

'That's *enough*!' Miles rarely used his voice as a weapon, having learned that, as a weapon, it took an unfair advantage, paralysing his opponent for the best part of ten seconds and rendering any kind of retaliation impossible. But there were times when no alternative would do; and this was one of them.

It worked like a charm. Bel stopped crying as suddenly as if she had been slapped, and then bit her lip and stared at him, her face as white as the moon.

'No one speaks of my wife like that and gets away with it,' he added softly. 'She is the light of my life, sir, and if you persist in calling her names I shall call you out at dawn. Do I make myself clear?'

'Oh, Miles, Miles . . .' Bel whispered despairingly.

'Come here.' He caught her hard against him and dried her face. He stooped to kiss her eyes and then lingered, licking salt from her lashes. 'You'll have eyes like golf balls in the morning, you silly girl.'

'I don't care.'

'You will in the morning.' He went on licking, finding a trail of salt which ran back into her ear. Bel lay against him like a rag doll, her eyes closed, her lips swollen, her cheeks radiating a feverish heat where her tears had burned.

'I love you,' he whispered, and knew suddenly that he meant it, even in the way that mattered most. He was strong with desire. Perhaps, he reflected wryly, it was because Bel was suddenly so weak and, for once in her life, desiring him hardly at all. Or perhaps it was just the place. He had wanted her here once before . . .

His fingers strayed to the little lace-covered buttons at the front of her dress. 'Do you love me, Bel?'

'Oh, yes! Yes, but – '

'Say it.'

'I love you, I love you! Oh, Miles, I *do* love you, but – '

'Hush, now . . .'

'No, Miles, I want – '

'More money? Certainly, darling. Now, be quiet, will you? I'm busy.'

Bel laughed at last. It was no more than a weary chuckle, but enough to be going on with. Better than nothing. Miles pulled her on to his knee and resumed his cat-like attentions, licking salt from her throat, her chest, drinking the tiny pool of tears which lay between her breasts.

She sighed, her breath quivering with the last vestige of a sob. 'Love me,' she begged. 'Please, Miles?'

'What d'you think I'm doing?' he growled softly. 'Be patient, woman. These things don't take five minutes, you know.'

He knelt at her feet to remove her stockings, and was so absorbed in the task that it was several minutes before he realised what he had said. 'Be patient.' Hardly the most tactful thing *he* had said this year!

Even with her interest in it reignited almost to fever-pitch, it still took Jean more than three weeks to return the whole house to its former pristine condition. She'd left the best parlour until last, because it was the room they used the least. It was too big to heat properly in winter, too gloomy to sit in on warm summer evenings, and they rarely had the sort of visitors who sat with their feet together, sipping afternoon tea.

To the best of Jean's recollection, even the Huntleys had never been shown into the parlour; and, when she came to look at it now, Jean was rather glad they hadn't. Drab was hardly the word for it. *Poor* was the word. The furniture and the carpet had come from her granny's home, over at Winton; but there they'd been jammed into a room scarcely big enough to contain them. Here they looked quite desolate, abandoned, like forgotten scarecrows in a windswept field.

When she'd first come to Drayfield, Jean had spent hours in this room, staring at the walls and dreaming dreams. Dreams of curtains and wallpaper, carpets and upholstery, tables and bookshelves and pretty little knick-knacks. She'd had a lot of *chintz*, a lot of *pinks*. Oh, and plenty of *brass* to reflect the little light there was and give an illusion of sunshine. She hadn't expected to acquire all of it. Not all at once. A little this year, a little next. A little sometime. A little . . . never.

Six years. Six long, dreary years, and none of it had materialised. None of it ever would. Until the day she died, her parlour would always look like this, and nothing she could do would ever change it. So she didn't dream any more. She just cleaned.

She took down the curtains and washed them. She rolled up the carpet and hung it over the privet hedge in the garden to be beaten clean. She took a stiff brush to the plush armchairs and a soft polishing rag to the sofa. More as a matter of superstition than of necessity, she thrust her hand between the sofa-back and the seat, searching for hairpins and half-crowns, and although she was certain no one had sat on the dratted thing since she'd last cleaned it, she in fact found one spent match, a 1920 farthing and a sixpenny bit dated 1904.

This had happened before and it never failed to puzzle her. Every time she dug behind the seat she found something which shouldn't be there. She'd begun to suspect that it had been swallowing things for the past thirty-odd years and was gradually giving them up again. A farthing here, a penny there . . . What would happen if she turned it upside down and jumped on it? A rain of gold sovereigns?

Had the sofa been in the least easy to upend, Jean would have done it years ago in the interests of cleanliness. Yet now that the idea of the sofa as a savings bank had crossed her mind, she was determined to do something to loosen its purse-strings. She sat on it: hurling herself backwards, bouncing up and down like a child on a haystack. When she'd got her breath back, she thrust her hand once more behind the seat, and came up with a florin, a penny, a bent nail, half a walnut and Mrs Huntley's brooch.

Mrs Huntley's brooch?

Oh, by the way, Mrs Huntley came when you were out.

She'd come for the old recipes – Jack had told her that much – but he hadn't known what she was talking about and had told her to come back another day.

Jean had thought at the time how odd it was that he hadn't asked her in. Even leaving out his obvious attraction to her, she was his landlord's wife, not just any 'bloody stupid woman', to be shooed from the door as of no account!

'Didn't you even offer her a cup of tea?' she'd asked wonderingly.

'No, I didn't! I was going to the bloody bank, wasn't I? I didn't have time!'

Since then, Jean had seen neither hide nor hair of Mrs Huntley, and although she was sure – almost sure – that the woman was too nice to take offence at Jack's churlish behaviour, she *had* begun to wonder. She'd wanted the recipes, so why hadn't she come back for them? Or waylaid Jean in the village? Or even sent a message?

Jean laid the brooch in the palm of her hand and gazed at it wonderingly. It was a dainty little thing: scarcely longer than the top joint of her thumb yet with every detail perfectly worked. A wild rose. You couldn't mistake it for anything else. The delicate curve of the petals was exactly right, the stamens, the sepals . . . She turned it over, her eyes widening with shock. A snake! Her fingers closed over it convulsively. A worm in the bud . . .

Jean racked her brains, trying to remember precisely what Jack had said, and what she had asked him. *Had* she asked, 'Did you invite her in?'

She wasn't certain. Inviting her in and offering her tea were two different things, and Jack had a nasty habit of giving only the information he was asked for. It was his special way of telling lies without actually lying, his way of being cruel without taking any blame to himself. Once, before she'd learned wisdom, she'd asked him to carry the laundry basket out to the line while she went upstairs to fetch the baby. (Evelyn, that would have been. She'd known better before she'd had Shirley.) When she'd come down, she'd found all her clean washing tipped over the dirty floor of the scullery. The empty basket was out by the line. 'Basket, you said,' Jack had said contemptuously. 'You didn't mention the washing. I did exactly as you asked.'

Had he invited Mrs Huntley in? It seemed unlikely. He'd been so impatient of the visit, impatient of the reason for it. 'How would I know where you keep your bloody recipes? I was going to the bank! I didn't have time!'

And what if he had asked her in? Playing the fine country gent as only Jack knew how, bowing and scraping, twinkling and smiling, 'Do come in! Do sit down.'

Then what? If he hadn't had time for tea, what had he had time for? 'Well, it's been good to see you, Mrs Huntley, but now I'm in a hurry, so you can damn well clear off again.'

Hmm. Pigs might fly. But the brooch was here. The brooch was *here*! Oh, dear God, had he asked her in and made another pass at the poor woman? Was that why she hadn't come again?

A dark flush invaded Jean's cheeks as she imagined yet another possibility, but she couldn't cope with that. Not that. Mrs Huntley had been so good to her, so kind. She'd been a friend in need – a friend of the highest order – and Jean couldn't, wouldn't believe *that* of her!

But neither could she ask for the truth. She couldn't ask Jack, she couldn't ask Mrs Huntley. All she could do was wait, and pray that soon, very soon, the question would be asked of her: 'I don't suppose you've seen my brooch, Mrs Carter? I'm almost certain I was wearing it the last time I called . . .'

And then everything would be all right again.

Everything would be all right.

Except for the mumps when she was three and the ubiquitous common cold, Bel had never had a day's illness in her life. She played tennis, rode, walked and gardened and, during the spring-cleaning, could shift beds and enormous wardrobes with an ease which left Muriel in a state of awe-struck wonderment. But she couldn't cope with morning sickness. Her body couldn't cope with it. She fainted dead away, every time. The first time, when she'd been expecting Andrew, she'd hit her jaw on the edge of the washstand as she'd fallen, and the resulting bruise had taken more than three months to fade. Since then, Miles had taken firm control of her pregnancy vapours, holding her while she was sick, carrying her, mopping her up and thanking God that this stage, at least, didn't last the full nine months.

But Miles didn't know about this pregnancy. She hadn't been able to tell him. *She didn't know whose baby it was!* And there was little chance of his discovering her secret by accident. The sickness didn't come until she got out of bed, and she made sure she didn't get up until he was safely occupied at Home Farm.

She took to throwing all the pillows out first, so that she'd have something soft to land on, but it was a frightening thing to endure all alone. She kept a metal pail hidden behind the curtains and crawled towards it like an animal, comforted only by the fact that if she passed out before she reached it, she wouldn't have far to fall.

She had never been more miserable in her life, and certainly never so scared. She might have borne it all had she not lost her brooch. Jack wouldn't have mattered, the baby wouldn't have mattered, *nothing* would have mattered as much if only she had not lost that brooch! But it was there, in that cold, gloomy parlour at Drayfield Farm. She knew it was there! Jack had thrown her jacket on the couch, and they'd made . . . No, they hadn't made love on her jacket. On Bel's side, at least, they'd made hatred and shame, rage and humiliation beyond bearing. And *he* might just as well have made water for all it had meant to him!

Oh, God, if she lived to be ninety and saw him again on her deathbed, she'd see him again too soon!

Mrs Carter would find that brooch and know whose brooch it was. And perhaps that wouldn't matter, except . . . Except that there was malice in Mrs Carter. Malice and hatred. Bel had seen it in her eyes. She'd seen it in other women, too: women who, on the surface, were as quiet and kind as Mrs Carter so often was – on the surface. Women who went to church, women who helped at the soup kitchen, women who'd spent every spare hour of the past winter working to help the poor. They'd been spoiled by the pain of their lives, by their griefs and disappointments, and although they denied it in their acts and their words, they were bitter to the core.

Bel wasn't certain how she could tell. She knew only that she could. She could tell when the bitterness was absent, too, and it was absent from Nurse Stokes. No matter what dreadful things she said (and she said plenty), she was as clean as a freshly scrubbed parsnip. She would never deliberately hurt a living soul. Even at her insulting worst she had only one object in mind: to nourish, to stimulate, to help and to heal; and it was a terrible, terrible irony that in her efforts to help Jean Carter she'd sent Bel – no, not sent her – given the silly fool permission to take herself to hell!

The sickness lasted about an hour every morning. Dizziness and vomiting giving way to a terrible weakness of mind and limb, during which she could only crouch on the floor, with her knees drawn up to her chin, her mind wiped clean of everything but despair and self-hatred.

She'd tried to tell Miles what she'd done. To rid herself of the weight of her guilt she'd tried to tell him, but the words wouldn't come. She couldn't do it to him.

No . . . It had been nothing so noble. She couldn't do it to herself. When he'd told her to be quiet she'd thanked God for saving her, for putting the words into his mouth. And when he'd made love to her . . .

Oh, God, if he hadn't . . . ! If she'd had to go through this without even a shred of hope that she was carrying his child . . . !

What would have happened to her? What would Miles have done? She didn't know, but she suspected the worst. She had no illusions about Miles. He had revealed himself too many times as he'd muttered in his sleep, and the man who merely clenched his teeth when he was angry was not the whole man, not the real man. There was someone else inside him, just as there was another woman inside Mrs Carter, and they were dangerous people. Between them, one way or another, they could kill her.

They still might . . .

Chapter Nine

According to Miles's calculations, his fifth son would be born in the second week of January. Bel had given him more than six months to get accustomed to the idea, yet even on Twelfth Night the thought of it still scared him rigid. He couldn't afford another son! He could barely afford the sons he already had. Oh, he could feed them, clothe them, even educate them by some means or another; but that wasn't good enough.

His sons had never, really, been children to him. From the day they'd been born he'd seen them as men, and for men the world was a hard and desperately cruel place in which only the best-equipped survived. He wanted his sons to *be* the best equipped: to have the deepest possible internal resources, the toughest possible exterior shells. You didn't give them that with second-rate schooling or with second-rate anything, yet it was beginning to look as if that was all Miles *could* give them, and the thought of it made him sick to his soul.

The economic state of the nation was growing worse by the day. Miles's own income had almost halved during the past two years. The markets were buying his cattle, grain, milk and potatoes at prices which brought tears to his eyes. And there was no way out. Even if the idea of asset-stripping had not been abhorrent to him, there was little point in it anyway, because no one wanted to buy his assets. Farm land was virtually worthless; property less than worthless. John Kemble had put the Manor House up for sale two years ago, and it was still for sale, for if Kemble could no longer afford to live in it, who else could?

Still, they were not yet in as bad a state as Germany where, to add to ruinous levels of unemployment, they had monetary inflation of nightmare proportions. Just to buy a loaf of bread the women were having to take their money to the baker's by the pram-load. It scarcely bore thinking about. It made Miles feel not so much sick as terrified, sending chills of foreboding up his spine, and God knew he was cold enough already!

Yet in spite of everything, he pinned a smile to his face as he went home for dinner. Bel didn't need to know his worries. She had enough worries of her own, bless her. For some reason – he supposed because she was carrying it – she'd taken the entire blame for the baby upon herself, regardless of the fact that Miles had put it there and, as he'd pointed out to her at least a dozen times, put it there of his own free will.

'But you didn't want another baby, Miles!'

'No. I wanted to make love to you.'

'You wouldn't have, if I hadn't pushed you into it! You only did it to comfort me!'

This wasn't true. He almost wished it had been. If he'd been capable of doing it to comfort her – or even to comfort himself – they might have weathered the past few years more happily. But then they'd be expecting their eighth son, and what was so happy about that?

He entered the house through the scullery where, since he'd become a 'man of the soil', he changed out of his boots and gaiters, hung up his hat and ulster, washed his hands and allowed his feet to warm by a few painful degrees. Ethel, the tiny scullery maid, was usually there to help him, but tonight she was not, and the kitchen – although it smelled as good as usual – was similarly deserted.

'Anyone home?' he murmured laconically as he strolled through to the passage. 'The master's returned from his labours. Anyone care?'

He regretted this last enquiry as he gained the main hall and heard the racket which was going on upstairs: Bel screaming, Nurse Stokes barking orders and everyone else running about like decapitated roosters. His son was making an entry into the world and, as Miles had predicted, bringing chaos and madness with him.

Bel had had her first four babies in a private nursing home, at an astronomical expense which she had refused to contemplate this time. The idea of Nurse Stokes officiating at the birth had appalled Miles, but Bel had expressed absolute faith in the woman, and he had been in no position to argue the point. Now, however, he was assailed by terror, and had to sit down on the stairs to get a grip on himself. If Bel died . . . ?

She screamed again. Miles felt his mind go blank for a moment, and knew that when it resumed its work he would be in control, would know what to do. It had always been like that. In the worst moments of his life, when survival was all, it was as if he switched from one kind of existence to another, from man to automaton, from feeling everything at once to feeling one thing at a time. It took no more than a second. Then he was on his feet and calmly climbing the stairs. Muriel sped past the end of his nose, carrying a pile of towels.

'Oh, Struntley, she'm – !'

'I know. Please tell her I'm here.'

But that was as much as he could do for her. Giving birth was exclusively women's work, as war was for men. And, just as mothers and wives wished that they might go to war with their men, to comfort them through its horrors, Miles wished with all his heart that he could go with Bel through this horror.

But it wasn't done. It wasn't allowed. All he could do now was wait. Listen. *Pray.*

Cook emerged from the bedroom just as he reached it, and through the open door he heard Bel cry out again: a wild, agonised scream which stopped him in his tracks, making him dizzy.

'Is she all right?' he hissed.

'I think so. I've never done this before, Mr Huntley, but Nurse Stokes seems happy enough, so . . .' She shrugged. 'She said you can go in if you like.'

Miles could only gawp at her. 'In?' he repeated hollowly. '*Me*? Is she mad?'

Cook had left the door ajar. Through the gap he heard Nurse Stokes utter a derisive bark of laughter. 'No, she's not bloody mad,' she said briskly. 'You put the little blighter in there, didn't you? Why shouldn't you help him come out? It's not much different from calving, you know!' Then, evidently addressing Bel, 'Bloody men. They're all the same.'

Miles sucked his cheeks and hooded his eyes, knowing to his sorrow that this was neither the time nor the place to throttle Nurse Stokes. She was a demon of a woman, an absolute anarchist. As no other person had ever done, she made him remember his station in life, simply because she afforded his station in life no respect or consideration at all. Landowner, gentleman, ancestral squire . . . It was all nothing to her. *Bloody men.* Hmm. As soon as she'd done her work for Bel, he'd throw her out by the scruff of the neck. Bloody woman!

Yet she was talking to Bel quite kindly, and seemed to know her job, which was all that mattered at a time like this, he supposed . . .

'Come on, my dearie, push! I can see the head. Not far to go now. Push!'

Bel seemed to push and pull at the same time for as she let out another yell Miles somehow found himself inside the room, trembling slightly and scarcely knowing how he'd got there.

'Blimey,' Nurse Stokes threw him a grin before turning back to her work at the foot of the bed. 'Wonders will never cease! Want to do something useful, or just stand there and gawp?'

He was all right after that. He told himself that it was no different from calving and managed to detach himself from his emotions to the extent that he really could be useful; but not so much that he wasn't acutely aware of Bel's feelings. Having always been on the wrong side of the door when his other sons were born, he'd imagined her in torment, lying helpless and humiliated on a torturer's rack. But it wasn't like that at all. Although she was in pain, Bel wasn't being tortured and she wasn't helpless. She was simply *working*, with all the strength she possessed, to bring their child into the world. In its way it was no different from watching a man digging a ditch, seeing the blood rush to his face, the sweat break from his brow, hearing him groan, 'Cor, Mr Huntley, me back's killin' I!'

Honest labour, proud labour. And oh, God, he was proud of Bel in this labour of hers! She was even – from time to time – managing to smile at him while she was doing it!

He held her hand, supported her shoulders while she pushed, mopped her brow. With tears pouring down his face, he told her he loved her.

'Nearly there,' Nurse Stokes said comfortingly. 'One more shove and we've got the head! Now, *push*!'

The rest happened very quickly, and Miles saw it all, his heart almost breaking with wonderment. The little head, the squashed little shoulders, the tiny, clenched little fists. This was his son! His very first son in a way, for although he had despaired at the thought of its coming, he knew that this son would mean more to him, be dearer to him than all the others.

'He's beautiful,' he croaked through his tears. 'Oh, Bel, he's so beautiful . . .'

The hips and thighs slithered forth without further exertion on Bel's part, but as Nurse Stokes caught the child in firm, expert hands, Miles held his breath, took a staggering step backwards and cried, 'Oh, my God!'

'What's wrong? *Miles?*'

He couldn't speak. He couldn't move.

'What's *wrong?*' Bel wailed.

'Nothing,' Nurse Stokes said flatly. 'But if you're still planning to call her Roderick, she'll have a bloody miserable life, I'm telling you.'

Miles burst out laughing. He leapt six feet in the air, yelling, 'It's a girl! It's a girl! Oh, my *God*, Bel! It's a *girl!*'

He was blinded by tears, crazy with joy. He didn't notice that Bel had closed her eyes and averted her face from him.

He'd never been happier in his life. He had a *daughter*!

The Huntleys' news had spread through the valley and beyond it before it was a day old, sped on its way by the proud father, who had run through the village like a lunatic, dispensing cigars, buying drinks, demanding that the church bells be rung to mark the event.

The irony of it had cut Jean to the heart, and Jack had turned white when he'd heard it, so that Jean, for a moment, had felt almost sorry for him. 'If it can happen for them . . .' she'd volunteered cautiously. 'Maybe we'll be lucky, too.'

'Oh, shut your stupid mouth! What the hell do you know?'

Miles Huntley arrived a week later, with the steam thresher. He was still grinning from ear to ear and looked ten years younger than when Jean had seen him last. She had still not seen Mrs Huntley again, and wondered now if she ever would. Her pregnancy had probably kept her away during the past nine months. Now, perhaps, she'd be afraid to come, afraid to show off her good fortune when she knew that Jean didn't share it.

But Jean was pregnant again, and still hoping. Hope had worn itself to a thread, but it was still there, shimmering like gossamer when the light caught it, invisible when the sun went in. But still there, even if nothing else was.

Jack had cut her housekeeping money twice during the past six months and sacked two of his labourers. But the farm had been undermanned to begin with, and he didn't seem to be working any harder to make up the difference. He still went to the pub twice a week, still smoked, still drove his car and still demanded four meals a day, the same as before. But Jean couldn't make eighteen shillings do the work of thirty. She and the children were living on next to nothing, and when Evelyn grew out of her shoes again . . .

'Do you think I'm made of bloody money? Don't you know what's going on in the world, you stupid bitch? We're broke, damn you! We'll be lucky if we have a roof over our heads this time next year, let alone bloody shoes on our feet!'

He was exaggerating, of course. He must be. It couldn't be as bad as that. He must be still paying the rent. Mr Huntley wouldn't be looking so cheerful otherwise, daughter or no daughter.

Cheerful? He looked wonderful. In fact, when she looked at him now, it was hard to imagine why she'd ever thought Jack in the least good-looking. Whatever else he might have done, Miles Huntley had never sulked! He did have lines on his face, but they were sun lines, wind lines, laughter lines. He looked pleasant even when he wasn't smiling, while Jack could laugh his head off and still look evil.

'Mrs Carter . . .' Miles doffed his hat. 'How are you?' His mouth twitched at the corners. 'And how are your little girls?'

The twitch was infectious, as Jean discovered when she tried, without success, to fight it off.

'How is *your* little girl?' she enquired mischievously.

'Oh, you've heard? She's . . .' He grinned, displaying what seemed an abnormal quantity of near-perfect white teeth. 'She's beautiful, Mrs Carter.'

'What have you called her?'

'Virginia. She's got red hair, you see, like Queen Elizabeth, the virgin queen. All our others were born bald, but she'd got this funny little crest of red hair.'

'The boys are all fair, aren't they?'

'They are, yes. They take after me, I suppose. My wife's hair has a touch of red, though she's always denied it until now. I can't imagine why. I think it's : . .'

'Beautiful?' Jean teased softly.

He laughed, but immediately cooled when Jack joined them. They went off to attend to the threshing, and Jean didn't think of him again until, several hours later, she saw the thresher trundling out of the rick yard, preparing to depart. It was then that she remembered the old recipes, and Mrs Huntley's abortive journey to fetch them.

She knew they weren't important, but for some reason she wanted to speak to Miles Huntley again, wanted . . . Oh, she supposed she just wanted to see a happy face, remind herself what happiness looked like, to steal just a small glimmer of it to keep for herself for a while. His eyes were so beautiful when he laughed. His mouth so wide and generous . . .

There wasn't time to fetch the recipes now. They were just an excuse to go out and speak to him, and she was glad she had when she saw his eyes light up with interest.

'Ah, yes!' he smiled. 'My wife told me you'd shown her them. I'd quite forgotten. Yes, I'd like to take a look, if it's no trouble.'

He glanced at her hands, as if expecting her to pass them over there and then, and Jean blushed, afraid that he might guess what she was up to.

Up to? Was it wrong to take pleasure from a man's smile?

To take comfort from the warmth of his voice? No, but to be in need of such comfort was shameful enough, and that it was Jack's shame to have brought his wife to such need was something Mr Huntley would never understand.

'Well,' she stammered, 'really I just wanted to ask . . . Ask if you'd mind if I copied them out before I . . . They are rightfully yours, and I . . .'

He laughed. 'Of course. No hurry at all. Perhaps your husband can bring them over when he next calls at the office.' He tipped his head to one side, surveying her with another smile. 'Your hair's red, too,' he remarked softly as he drove away, '*beautiful*.'

Even after the thresher had trundled beyond the bend in the lane, Jean could still hear it, still see its metal chimney belching out smoke and the lethal red sparks which made every cottager rush to the defence of his thatched roof as it went by. But the noise and the smoke were lost to her. Even Mr Huntley's delight in his new daughter was lost to her. He had looked at *her* hair, called *her* beautiful . . .

When she returned to the house she stood for some time in the hall, gazing at herself in the glass. It was a very small glass which, when she stood close enough to it, reflected only her head and shoulders, and even then left out the bulging swell of her upper arms. Her nose was red with the cold, but the rest of her face was as pale as milk with a faint flush of pink over her cheekbones. Her eyes were glowing, her hair shining (it always shone when she was pregnant), but red it was not. Brown. Plain brown with reddish tints where the light caught it. But it *was* beautiful. *She* was beautiful. Miles Huntley had said so.

After supper, she sat at the kitchen table with a sheet of paper, laboriously copying out the 'charm to sweeten milk' with an indelible pencil. She had never been fond of writing, and before she was halfway through she lost interest in the task and sat with her chin in her hands, weaving dreams. She dreamed of living at Bishop's Court, having servants, playing tennis. She dreamed that Miles Huntley had married her, and that every one of her daughters gave him the joy little Virginia had given him. She dreamed that she was thin, and that, when he came home at night, he swept her off her feet, cradled her in his arms and told her she was beautiful . . .

Sighing, she turned the pages over and again saw the cramped little heading, 'A crs agnst thine enemie'.

'I conjre thee, O serpnt of old . . .' The words made Jean's heart slam against her breast. Serpent of old . . . Was that the devil? Was this some kind of devil-worship? 'I conjure thee . . .'

She tiptoed out to the back parlour, where Jack lay snoozing by the fire, and took his old school dictionary from the shelf behind the door.

'Conjure: to call upon supernatural forces by spells and incantations.'

'Conjurer: a person who practises magic; a sorcerer.'

Her heart still racing with a strange kind of excitement, Jean went back to her copying exercise, translating the tiny, truncated words of the curse into her large, schoolgirlish longhand.

'I conjure thee, O serpent of old, servant of the wyse and begetter of all the wisdom of the earth, take my enemy from me, bind him in the coils of thy might and bring him ever unto darkness.'

It was horrible. Strange. A cold sweat broke out on her brow as she wrote the words, and a chill of delicious horror tingled down her spine. She wanted to giggle, like a child who, having been losing a quarrel, has suddenly seen a way to win it. The curse had been written for Jack! 'Bind him in the coils of thy might and bring him ever unto darkness.'

But the next line caused Jean to think again. 'Bring darkness unto his house, unto his children and his children's children, until his line is ended and nothing that is his endures upon the earth...'

Convulsively, she turned the pages face down on the table, slapping them into oblivion with the palm of her hand. She couldn't lay this curse on Jack without cursing herself, her house and her children. And she supposed there was some justice in that. Those who live by the sword, die by the sword. And those who live by sorcery...

She turned up the papers again, looking now for the charm to cure warts. Hmph! She couldn't have been much of a witch! Rub wart with meat, bury meat... Absolutely *everyone* knew that one! And absolutely everyone knew it damn well didn't work!

'We don't need another nanny, Miles. We can't afford another nanny, and with Robin going to school next month... Are you listening to me, Miles?'

Miles was lying with Virginia, on her rug on the lawn, helping her to take her 'sun and air bath', his face wreathed with adoring smiles as he bounced her up and down on his chest.

'Who's Daddy's liddle angel, den? Who's Daddy's precious?'

Bel grinned and raised her eyes to heaven. 'You're an absolute idiot,' she said. 'Virginia certainly doesn't need a nanny, with you dancing attendance on her every whim.'

'She doesn't have whims. You don't have whims, do you, sweetheart?'

At seven months, Virginia was able to sit up, fall over, roll over and laugh like a drain, and even Bel, who was almost certain her daughter was not a bona fide Huntley, was capable of being charmed out of all sense by her endearing little ways. She was as good as gold, had been so since birth, and when Nanny had announced her intention to join an American diplomat's family and see some of the world, Bel had been in no doubt that she could manage the baby on her own. But Miles, to her astonishment, was entertaining doubts. He wanted his little 'Jinny' to miss out on none of the boys' advantages. Only the thought of being saved a new nanny's salary had given him pause so far, but he still wasn't convinced.

'Where's her frock?' he asked anxiously now. 'Her shoulders are burning.'

They weren't: Bel had undressed her scarcely five minutes ago. But she knew better than to argue with Miles where Jinny was concerned. He adored her, worshipped her, couldn't get enough of her. When she cried, he thought the world had come to an end. When she was cutting a tooth, *he* felt the pain. He hadn't been at all like this when the boys were small. He'd virtually ignored them until they were walking and talking, and even then had kept at a discreet distance from the practicalities of their upbringing. Now he was reading books on the subject and claimed to know it all!

But he still couldn't dress her. The tiny buttons and laces of her clothes utterly defeated his large farmer's hands, and it was Bel who – to Jinny's furious protests – put her frock on again while Miles remained on the rug, scanning the local paper.

'Fry's are setting up an express air delivery service, Bel.'

'A what?'

'The first air delivery van in Britain, it says.'

'What? What'll it deliver? Where will it land?'

'*Oh*-ohh . . .'

'What?'

'Bristol Waterworks . . .' Miles frowned and went on reading, chewing his lip. Then, 'They're planning a new reservoir, darling.'

'What's that to do with air deliveries?'

'Nothing, you dope. I'm reading another article. They're

planning to build a new reservoir and one of the possible sites . . .'

'Yes?'

Miles rolled on his back, resting his arm on his brow to shelter his eyes from the sun. 'One of the sites is the Dray Valley,' he murmured thoughtfully.

'*What*?' Bel leapt to her feet, dumped Jinny in her father's lap and grabbed the newspaper. 'Where? Where, Miles? Oh, got it . . .' She read the tiny article, which was fitted into a space between two advertisements, one for Wolsey socks at two shillings a pair, and one for pipe tobacco, which read, 'Come on, Jack, cheer up, you old pessimist!'

Bel turned scarlet and it was some time before she managed to focus her eyes on the article about the reservoir. 'Oh,' she murmured at last. 'During the next ten years, it says, Miles. Anything can happen in ten years. Is it worth worrying about? Anyway, they can't just *do* that, can they? Take our land, I mean?'

'Yes, they can do that. And, no, it's not worth worrying about, if only because, should they decide on the Dray Valley, we can't do much to stop them. They'll probably decide on another site anyway. As you say, anything can happen in ten years.'

He prodded Jinny in the middle, making her shriek with laughter, and at the same moment Andrew yelled from the tennis court, 'Mummy, will you please come and umpire? Robin's cheating again!'

'I am *not* cheating! I *never* cheat! The ball was in! I saw the chalk, so there!'

Miles slanted Bel a despairing look. 'He's cheating,' he announced dryly. 'Honestly, darling, I don't know where he gets it from, do you?'

The joke was self-aimed: Miles was notorious for seeing puffs of chalk about three feet beyond the baseline; but as he tipped Jinny towards him and blew an adoring raspberry into her soft little neck, Bel turned cold with dread. Lord, how he worshipped that child . . .

Cheating? Yes, she knew exactly where Robin had got it from, and could only pray that Miles would never know. Never, please, God. Never.

Chapter Ten

Solomon Hicks's farm was the smallest and the best in the valley: neat and well-kept, with tidy hedges, clean ditches, spotless buildings, healthy stock. But Miles had noticed that even for Solomon the strain of the agricultural slump was beginning to tell. His ancient corduroy breeches, hoisted halfway to his chin by a set of scarlet braces, housed a good deal less of their wearer than had been their custom. It wasn't that he hadn't enough to eat – no farmer ever needed to starve – just that he and his wife were working themselves into the ground, running like rabbits to stay in the same place, and that place only a hair's breadth from ruin.

'Nay, zir,' Solomon said, when Miles expressed his concern. 'We'm not too bad off, considerin', and us 'ouldn't change places with anyone alive, would us, Prissie, m'dear? Better be zlaves to the land than to 'unger and cawld. Better drop from 'ard work than for lack of it, eh, me old lover?'

Mrs Hicks laughed. 'And we sleep well, Mr Huntley. We sleep very well. There's no worry in the world can keep *us* awake once our heads touch the pillow! Now, how's that little daughter of yours?'

Everyone in the valley knew that Miles was besotted with his daughter, and that the mere mention of her could divert his mind, in a twinkling, from more serious subjects. But Miles was not to be distracted this time. Joss Radnor had asked for a cut in his rent, and Miles had agreed. He intended to do likewise for Solomon, and perhaps for Colin, if he asked. But not for Jack Carter. Jack had fallen behind with his rent, making no apologies, just excuses, promises, arrogant assumptions that Miles would support his failures with no questions asked. Well, he could think again.

'Jinny's fine,' he smiled now. 'Walking, talking, reading the newspapers – '

'Well, well, ain't that summat! She'm only two!'

Miles laughed. 'Well, perhaps she doesn't quite *read* the papers yet, but she certainly knows how to tear them up! Now, my dear sir, about your rent – '

'Ah!' Solomon turned pink, shifted from one foot to the other and looked at the floor. 'Ah, well, zir, if you'm sure you can manage for a space. Just a space, mind. Just till things pick up a bit, like.'

He was a proud, independent man, and the words seemed to have been wrung out of him by torture. Miles knew how he felt. Cutting rents, at a time when he needed to increase them, felt as unnatural as cutting his right hand off, yet if he allowed his best tenants to go broke at a time like this, he'd be cutting off both hands, and he wasn't that stupid.

'Oh, that reminds me,' Solomon said when the discussion turned from rents in particular to farming in general. 'You've yeard mention of our Leonard, haven't 'ee, zir? Farms a piece over t'ward Frome; Prissie's brother's lad, ye recall? He've got his eye open for a piece acrawz this way, so if ye knows of anything, any time . . .'

Miles frowned. 'Is it a good time to move? If he's doing all right where he is – '

'Leonard does awright wheresoever he be, Mr Huntley. Got a bit of money behind 'un, see, and no . . . What d'you call them things, Prissie? What you're always saying our Leonard haven't got?'

Mrs Hicks giggled and smacked his arm. 'Aspirations, my dear. You haven't got any either!'

Solomon grinned. 'Ah, that'll be why I'm allus forgettin' what they'm called, then. Don't want to live fancy, that's what 'er means, zir. Just want to bide peaceful-like, with a bit of land to keep 'un outa mischief. It'd be good for 'un to be nearer his fambly, see, Mr Huntley, and he's got three young lads our Prissie'd like to see a lot more of. Lovely lads too, they be. Smart as paint, just like thy young 'uns. Readin' the papers when *they* wuz two, an' all!'

Miles promised to bear it in mind, but later that evening, while he struggled with the Home Farm accounts, he realised that he'd been thinking about Leonard Clare all day. He'd never met the man, but had heard of him often and had liked what he'd heard. He and Miles were of a similar age and had both survived the war relatively intact, although, according to Mrs Hicks, Leonard had had a bad case of shell-shock which he'd never fully recovered from. But he was a good farmer, an intelligent and honourable man – unlike some men who lived not too far from here . . .

Jack Carter had paid only a third of his rent for the past few quarters. And his land was not in good heart. His hedges had been left untended and his yards and buildings were beginning to look neglected. Miles doubted that Jack would pull through, and while this had worried him yesterday, today it didn't.

If Jack failed, perhaps Leonard Clare would take Drayfield Farm. He'd certainly make a better job of it. It would be hard on Mrs Carter and the children, of course, but that wasn't Miles's problem. It was Jack's problem, and if he couldn't handle it . . . ?

Miles pushed his accounts to one side and began to draft a letter to his erring tenant. A gentle reminder wouldn't go amiss. Perhaps even the hint of a warning. No one could afford to be too softhearted in these hard times . . .

By the time she was three and a half, little Virginia Huntley still couldn't read the newspapers, but she could read (after a fashion) some of the simpler words in her rag books, could say the alphabet, count to twenty, recognise colours and sing more than a dozen nursery rhymes. Her carrot-red hair had faded to a reddish gold, but her baby-grey eyes had never changed to blue. They were a smoky, mysterious grey which sometimes darkened almost to black. Her brows and lashes were dark too, giving her a wide-eyed charm which Miles found quite fascinating. Bel had said her grandmother had had grey eyes, so he supposed they'd missed a generation and popped up in Jinny especially to please him. And they did please him. They were beautiful eyes. *Beautiful* eyes.

But then, everything about her was beautiful. She was more finely boned than the boys had been at her age and as dainty in her movements as a fairy. She copied Bel a good deal. Miles sometimes watched them when they were together, and laughed with delight when Jinny (her eyes narrowed with concentration) matched Bel's steps or the movements of her head and hands so that they looked like dancers swaying to the same tune.

Miles had never been happier. He had been very much richer, but that didn't matter half as much now as it had once done. Jinny had changed everything. She had given him his heart's desire, and when a man has that, what can he lack?

Jinny was 'helping' him in the office when, more than a week after the Midsummer Quarter Day, Jack Carter came to pay his rent. In spite of two warning letters, he had not yet made up the deficit on his previous year's rent, and still had not had the courtesy to ask for some leeway. Miles understood his difficulties – he shared many of them, after all – but he was damned if he understood the man's manners. In effect, Jack was 'borrowing' money without asking for it which, in Miles's view, was tantamount to theft, whether he intended to repay it or not. Why the hell couldn't he have stated his case honestly, as Joss Radnor had done? Miles wasn't a hard man. He couldn't afford to be. But he was damned if he'd be taken advantage of like this!

Miles's office had originally been the 'best parlour' of the farmhouse at Home Farm. He'd given it an independent side entrance so that his comings and goings should not disturb his tenants – the farm's foreman and his wife – but Mrs Chard's kitchen was just the other side of the inner door, and as soon as Jack arrived, Miles shooed Jinny through, calling, 'Visitor for you, Mrs Chard!'

'Lovely little kid,' Jack remarked when the door had closed on her departure. 'Not a bit like the boys, though. They're the image of you, aren't they? I suppose she takes more after your wife?'

Miles smiled rather distantly at a point on the wall just east of his visitor's ear.

'Have you brought all your hay in, Mr Carter?'

'Not quite. I was wondering if you could loan me a tractor for a few days while the weather – '

'Loan?' Miles raised one eyebrow. He sat down.

'Things are a bit tight,' Jack murmured defensively.

'For us all, as I'm sure you realise. And there's still the question of your rent, although I imagine that's why you're here. You can make up the deficit now, I take it?'

Jack smiled. He sat down. 'Look,' he said. 'I've been a good tenant – '

'Have you, Mr Carter? Your calves were through to Mr Radnor's hay earlier this month, yet I recall giving you the wherewithal in *March* to repair those fences.'

'I haven't got the labour!' Jack's voice cracked a little and, just for a moment, Miles pitied him almost enough to relent, loan him the blasted tractor and a few men to complete his haymaking. But Jack's next words, and the rising tone of his voice, killed the thought almost before it was formed. 'I can't do everything, damn it! I can't afford ... Look, you've given the others discounts on their rents. Why not me? You loan *them* your bloody tractor, *and* extra men when they need help! So what's the difference?'

Miles gazed at the Coalport inkwell on his desk. He stroked the hair over his temple, wondering how best to respond. He didn't want to enter into any discussions about his neighbours, if only because, in Jack's present mood, it would be unwise to inform him that the difference between them was simply a matter of good manners. He did loan out his equipment and his men when he could spare them, but only because his other tenants always offered to pay for their use; and why not? Farmers were businessmen, now more than ever in competition for what little profits they could get in the market place. The only reason Miles was prepared to help any of them was because their rents were a part of *his* business. And Jack wasn't paying!

'Do you intend to pay your rent today, Mr Carter?' he asked calmly.

'I've got something towards it, yes!' Jack fumbled for his wallet and extracted a small sheaf of crumpled notes which he flung down on the table. At a glance, Miles estimated that he was still almost a year in arrears.

'Mr Carter,' he said quietly. 'I am not a charitable institution. If you are unable to pay your way at Drayfield, I'm sure I can find another tenant who'll find it less of a burden.'

'*What*? In this day and age?' Jack laughed bitterly. 'You'll be lucky! No one with any sense – '

'No one with any sense in *this* day and age, Mr Carter, would presume too heavily upon his landlord's goodwill. Even if I could afford to support you – '

'I'm not *asking* you to support me, for God's sake!'

'Yet you seem to be assuming that I will. You have taken

your living, rent-free, from Drayfield for the past nine months, Mr Carter.' He spread out the notes Jack had laid on the desk. 'This clears your debt only to Michaelmas of last year. You see that, don't you? Will you be able to pay a whole year's rent when this Michaelmas comes round?'

'No,' Jack responded sullenly. 'You know I won't. As for my taking a living from it, I'd like you to mention that to my wife! She can hardly afford to – '

'That is not my affair.'

'You mean you don't give a damn whether she and the kids starve, just as long as you get your bloody rent paid on the nail!'

'Hardly on the nail. Nine months leeway is leeway enough, I think.'

Jack stared at him in shock, his face paling under its bright, midsummer tan. 'Are you throwing me out?' he demanded incredulously.

Miles lifted the porcelain inkwell from its heavy brass stand and laid it on the blotter, gently tracing its fine gilt cobweb with the nail of his index finger. *Was* he throwing Jack out? No . . . No, he didn't really want to do that, but he did want the man to admit defeat and give notice before his neglect of the farm became too expensive to repair.

Had he been in Jack's position, with the threat of eviction a distinct possibility and his landlord still thinking it over, he'd have kept his peace and let the thinking process run its course. But Jack seemed to think that his silence represented some kind of assent – 'Yes, I am throwing you out,' – and before Miles had got any further with his thoughts, Jack stood up, leaned his fists on the desk and snarled, 'You . . . fucking bastard!'

Miles blinked. His heart thumped with rage. 'Please sit down, Mr Carter,' he said levelly, 'before you say something else you'll have cause to regret.'

'Oh, I won't regret anything,' Jack sneered softly. 'Not a

single bloody thing. Go on, throw me out! I don't care. I've had enough! Enough of your farm and enough of you, you stuck-up bastard. You think you're so much better than I am, don't you? Well, you're not.'

The sneering curl of his lip became a sly, triumphant grin. 'Ask your *wife*, Miles,' he said slowly. 'See which one of us *she* thinks is the better man.'

Miles was never able to remember what happened next. All he could recall was a heavy blow to his chest, although no one had struck him. The blow was rage: rage such as he had never – never in his life – experienced before. Then he was on his feet, holding Jack by his shirtfront, while his right hand, balled into a fist as hard as a lump-hammer, quivered in the air just inches from the man's nose.

'What did you say?' he whispered.

'You heard me. And while you're at it you might also ask her whose daughter you've given your name to. Not a bit like the boys, is she, Miles? And where, I wonder, did she get those big, dark eyes of hers? Not from you. The Huntleys never were any good at producing girls, were they?'

Miles's mistake was to have set his fist too close to Jack's face. As he drew back his arm to hit the man senseless, Jack moved too, grabbing the brass inkwell stand from the desk and dealing Miles a blow to the head which sent him staggering across the office, with blood in his eyes.

Miles heard Jack fall to the floor, but the punch which had been intended to silence him had only knocked him off his feet, and he was laughing when Billy Chard flew in from his wife's kitchen and led Miles to a chair.

'What the hell? What's going on, Mr Huntley? What's – ?'

'Nothing,' Miles said softly. 'Show Mr Carter out, will you, Bill? He'll be quitting Drayfield Farm at Michaelmas.'

The boys were due home tomorrow for the long summer holidays, and Bel, excited at the thought of seeing them again, was singing to herself as she checked that their rooms were ready. Muriel had dusted and made up the beds, but Bel, knowing the things the boys looked for, the things which meant 'home', had to be sure that everything was just so.

She didn't hear Miles come home, didn't hear his step on the stairs. The first thing she was aware of was Robin's bedroom door crashing back on its hinges, and her husband standing in the doorway with blood on his face.

'Miles! What's happened? Dear God, what have you done to yourself?'

But she knew, almost as she spoke, that whatever had happened to Miles scarcely mattered compared with what was about to happen. She had never seen him in a rage, yet the state he was in now made 'rage' seem something small boys felt when they were thwarted. What Miles was feeling was something very different. He was like a cat poised to pounce, so still, yet with every muscle tensed to its limit. His face was white, his eyes blazing and he was biting his upper lip, thrusting his bottom teeth forward like a wild dog. The only thing missing was the snarl from the back of the throat, but Bel had an idea that that would come.

'Miles?' she whispered, and then, rather to distract herself than to distract him, 'Where's Jinny?'

He took a deep, shuddering breath which swelled his chest until Bel began to think his lungs would burst with the strain. Her legs shaking, she sat at the edge of Robin's bed.

'Miles! What's wrong?'

'Who is Jinny's father?' he asked softly.

Bel closed her eyes. It had happened. She'd almost forgotten it, almost ceased to fear it, but it had happened, as all disasters happened, when one was least prepared to meet them. She had been happy. She had been singing . . .

'Tell me the truth,' Miles said. 'Or before God, Bel, I'll kill you.' He took another step into the room and slammed the door behind him. 'Bel!' he roared, and she jumped to her feet and faced him, knowing that she must lie, lie or die, lie *and* die if that was what it took, but never, never, never tell him the truth! He adored Jinny. She was his life! If she took Jinny from him . . .

'What on earth are you talking about?' she gasped frantically. *'You're* her father, Miles! Why should you think otherwise? For heaven's sake, what's happened to you?'

'You . . .' His face twisted into a mask of fury, and suddenly he had her by the arms and was shaking her. 'Bitch! Lying bitch!' He threw back his head and howled, 'I *knew*!' and still he shook her, his fingers biting into her arms until, desperate to escape him, she fell to her knees at his feet, sobbing with pain.

'Miles! Miles, please, stop! Let me go!'

'Let you go?' he roared. 'Let you go? Oh, I'll let you go! I'll throw you out in the street, throw you out with your lover and let you starve together as you deserve! A better man than I am, is he? Is he? *Is he?*'

'No!' Bel screamed. 'No, no, no!'

At last he released her, letting her fall to the floor where, frantic with pain, she attempted to rub the bruises from her arms.

Miles turned away. 'Who,' he murmured bitterly. 'You should have asked *who*! But I didn't expect it. I've known all along . . .' He shook his head as if amazed at his own stupidity. 'Dear God. You went to him when I was in London, didn't you? Was that the first time?'

'No!' Her voice choked to silence. Her teeth began to chatter with shock. There was no point in lying to him any more. He knew. 'There wasn't a first time,' she admitted sullenly. 'It happened once, and it was horrible. I've hated myself – and him – ever since, and if you believe nothing else you can believe that.'

'Horrible?' He turned to look at her, and his face was barely recognisable, twisted with bitterness and hatred. 'Don't tell me he raped you, because I'm *not* capable of believing that! You *wanted* him . . .' He ground the words out through his teeth. 'I saw it in your face every time his name was mentioned! And – and . . .' Again his voice rose to a howl of anguish. 'I told myself you weren't *capable of* it! Christ, what a *fool*!'

In spite of the warmth of the day Bel was shivering, and a curious dragging sensation on her skin informed her that her face was as white as chalk. She wished she was dead and felt as if she was dying, yet Miles's agony meant more to her than her own. She loved him. She had always loved him.

'You're not a fool,' she said dully. 'You always knew him for what he was, while I – '

Miles whirled around to face her again, his teeth bared with fury. 'I didn't know *you* though, did I? I didn't begin to suspect what *you* were! You and your – your *brat*! Do you have any idea what you've done to me? Do you *know*? Are you *proud*?'

Bel couldn't speak. Her *brat*! The love of his life . . .

She hid her face in her hands, wishing she could cry, but there were no tears, only a misery so heavy it seemed to be crushing her bones.

'Miles, I love you,' she whispered.

He laughed. It was the worst thing he had done yet: a dry, humourless little grunt which chilled Bel's blood and made her stare up at him in terror.

'What are you going to do? *Miles*?'

He slid his hands in his pockets and looked at her down the length of his nose, his lips quivering with contempt.

'I don't know,' he said. 'But don't allow yourself to hope I'll forgive you. Don't hope for anything. There's nothing left for either of us to hope for. *Nothing*!'

And he went out, slamming the door with a force which made the windows rattle.

Jack didn't come home for the midday meal. He didn't come

home to help the men with the milking. His supper was ready and waiting for him when he at last turned up, and Jean eyed him curiously as she set the food on the table, wondering what he'd been up to. He looked happy, almost smug, as if he'd won money on a horse and was not intending to share it. But she didn't ask. She never asked. Since he'd ceased to sleep with her, having given up hope of ever having a son, she felt, more than ever before, that she and the children were living on borrowed time.

He ate ravenously, shovelling the food into his mouth as if he hadn't eaten for a fortnight, and then, amazing her, he pushed away his empty plate, patted his stomach and said, 'Boy, that was good! I was starving.'

Jean's eyebrows went up of their own accord – he must have won an awful lot of money to be paying compliments about her cooking – and he looked up at her, grinning boyishly. 'I've had a busy day today. Been to see our noble landlord, got myself evicted, told him a few home truths about his dear wife . . .'

Jean stared at him, half-smiling. She blinked and frowned, wondering if perhaps he was drunk. Got himself evicted? *Evicted*? What the devil was the man talking about? It couldn't be true . . . He looked too happy for it to be true. And yet . . .

'What?' she murmured doubtfully. 'Are you all right?'

He laughed. He clapped his hands, throwing his head back to grin up at the ceiling. 'Hear that?' he called out pleasantly. 'At a time like this, she thinks of me! Homeless, destitute, ruined, and she asks if I'm all right! Was ever a woman more devoted?'

Jean found herself backing away from him, still half-smiling, yet half-believing him, too, her heart thumping with fear and confusion.

'Jack?' she whispered. 'You don't mean it, do you? You're joking, aren't you?'

'Joking?' He widened his eyes, the way a man might do

when he was teasing a small child. 'Joking? Over a thing like this? Now, *would* I?' He leaned back in his chair, letting his arms flop at his sides, and in a light, conversational tone continued cheerfully, 'No, I told him what he could do with his lousy farm.' He laughed again. 'Told him what he could do with his bitch of a wife, too, *and* his darling daughter.' He threw Jean a charming little wink. 'Another of mine, you know. Did you know? I've got daughters littered all over the valley, my dear. Isobel Huntley, Becky Vale, Jane Briggs the butcher's daughter, Annie Cope the blacksmith's wife. Hee! Happy families!' His face fell suddenly. 'And not a boy among 'em . . .' He shook his head. 'I thought it was your fault, love, but all those whores were the same. Not one of 'em could give me a son.'

It was when she saw the tears running down his face that Jean believed him. Believed him utterly, yet still believed nothing, for it was all beyond belief. Evicted? No . . .

She felt very strange: lightheaded, as if she'd been at the blackberry wine, and very sick, as if she'd drunk far too much of it. Everything was moving: her heart, her stomach, the windows and doors, making her feel dizzy and desperate, like a fox in a trap. She had been backing away from Jack, not realising where her feet were taking her until she felt the warm oaken surround of the kitchen range under her fingers. Then, just like Jack, she threw back her head and laughed.

A moment later she was screaming, racing towards him with the coal shovel in her hand. She hit him once and then fell backwards as with a roar of incredulous rage he punched her in the belly and knocked her to the ground.

'Cow!' He kicked her with the full weight of his boot. Then, stooping, he wrenched the shovel from her hand and brought it down across her shoulders. 'Fat, useless, ugly bloody cow! It's your fault! All your fault! If you'd been any good, none of it would have happened!'

He flung the shovel across the kitchen and took a handful

of her hair, hauling her into a sitting position and crouching over her, a malevolent grin on his face. 'Hit me, would you?' he demanded softly. 'Well, see how *you* like it, bitch!'

'Mammy, Mammy! Wake up! Oh, please!'

Jean had not been asleep. Just resting, lying on a cushion of grey mist, aware of everything but not caring enough to do anything about it. She had heard the children sobbing and Jack crashing around the kitchen, hurling chairs, smashing crockery, and then – after a weird silence – saying quietly, 'Look after your mother. I'm going out.' But it had all been so strange. So far away. Jean wasn't certain any of it had happened. He'd never hit her before . . . Had he?

'Mammy! Oh, please!'

She felt the balm of cool water on her face and opened her eyes.

'It's all right,' she muttered dreamily. 'It's all right, my lovely. Don't cry any more. It's all right now.'

And it was. She felt nothing – no pain, no anguish. She just felt tired, and longed to be alone for a while, if only to remember who she was and what had happened to her.

But the children must come first. They had all been in bed, and now they were all up, hiding in corners, trembling and crying. Even little Janet. She was only two, poor little duck . . . 'Come on, my lovely. All better now . . .'

It took a long time to settle them all down. Even longer to put the kitchen to rights. When it was done, she looked at her reflection in the glass over the hall table and gazed dispassionately at a face she barely recognised as her own. One of her eyes was half-closed, there were bruises on both cheekbones and one side of her lip was split and swollen so that it looked like an enormous blister, oozing blood.

She remembered that Miles Huntley had called her beautiful. She remembered that his wife *was* beautiful: a lovely, kind, generous woman whom Jean had trusted and admired. Isobel

Huntley, Becky Vale, Jane Briggs the butcher's daughter, Annie Cope . . .

The others didn't matter. But Mrs Huntley? Oh, dear God . . . It was beyond belief, rather like the fossils one found in the garden which one could know were a million years old without being able to comprehend what a million years really meant. Isobel Huntley! How could she have done it? With Jack! *Jack*!

She shuffled into the kitchen and opened the drawer under the table. After groping at the back for a while among the meat hooks and skewers, she found the small twist of muslin in which she'd wrapped Mrs Huntley's brooch.

She sat down, easing her bruised body into the armchair by the window. The sun was just setting, its rosy beams slanting through the bean-sticks, lighting the young, crimson-leaved beets so that they glowed like jewels. She gazed out over the flourishing rows of peas and beans, the potato trenches, the lettuces and radishes, gooseberries and currant bushes. Her work. All her own work.

She would dry . . . She *would have dried* most of the peas, salted the beans, stored the potatoes, bottled the fruits. She would have fed her children for yet another winter, kept them safe and warm.

Evicted! She couldn't believe it! What would become of them? Where would they go?

Tomorrow, if it was ready, she'd cut the lavender which edged the front path and lay it out to dry. Her house was full of lavender. She hung it in the linen cupboards and the wardrobes, laid it under the mattresses and in the drawers. There were lavender bags in all the window seats. They made the house smell like a palace, a temple, a church, lending all her hours of devoted labour an added dimension of beauty.

Evicted? No! She couldn't believe it!

She sat there for hours, until the light of the day had all but gone, taking with it the light of her life. She hadn't realised, until now, how much light there had been in her life: her beautiful home, her lovely children, her garden, her lavender...

Jack hadn't mattered all that much. Not really. He had died, somewhere along the way, and intruded on her thoughts – like the first of their children – only in fleeting moments of grief. She had allowed him that much power – to grieve her now and then – and had somehow forgotten that, unlike her dead baby, he could still make his mark elsewhere in the world.

'Got myself evicted... Told him a few home truths... His wife and his darling daughter. Told him a few home truths. Got myself evicted...'

Myself! Oh, that was typical of Jack! He'd got *himself* evicted, without even a thought for his wife and his children! And just to vent his spleen on a man who – rightly – despised him!

Suddenly Jean could believe it all. Her eyes burning with hatred, she opened her hand and stared malevolently at Mrs Huntley's brooch, which glittered strangely in the last of the twilight. Pure gold... Four years in the back of the kitchen drawer, and still as fresh and as clean...

Jean's swollen lip curled back over her teeth. 'Bitch,' she snarled. 'Dirty, traitorous bloody bitch!'

Her fingers clenched and unclenched, stretching and curling like claws, and the brooch turned in her hand, reminding her that it – like Isobel Huntley – had two sides to its nature. The wild rose and the snake. The serpent of old...

Jean smiled. Her eyes brightened with malice. She cupped the brooch in both hands and lifted it to her mouth, whispering softly, 'I conjure thee, O serpent of old...'

A great twist of fury tore through her: a huge, coiling snake rising from her guts to be spewed out with a venom of rage and cold hatred.

'I conjure thee,' she cried hoarsely, 'O serpent of old, servant of the wise and begetter of all the wisdom of the earth, take my enemy from me! Bind her in the coils of thy might and bring her ever unto darkness!'

The words came back to her as if she had copied them out only yesterday: dark, cruel, evil words which rang through the shadows and brought with them a wild thrill of power. Oh, she'd do for the bitch! She'd kill her! Her and her bastard! *Her children, and her children's children!* And while she was at it, she'd curse Jack, too! *And* his house! They couldn't throw her out and let some other woman live here! She loved it! It was her home, her *home*!

Some other woman live here? While Jean festered and pined in the Workhouse – or worse? Some *other* woman live here? *No . . . No, no!*

'Take my enemy from me,' she hissed. 'Bind her in the coils of thy might and bring her ever unto darkness! Bring darkness upon her house, upon her children and her children's children, until her line is ended, and nothing that is hers endures upon the earth!'

She spat on the brooch, and with a last shriek of rage hurled it at the wall. She saw it glinting against the plaster, heard it fall to the bare flagstones and roll away into the shadows.

Suddenly she felt empty and very calm. She huddled in her chair, hiding her face, and did not move again until, two hours later, in the pitch dark of a moonless midnight, Constable Rickman came hammering at the door.

Jack had been to every pub in the valley. He'd left The Boy and Badger in Molton Draycott with some difficulty, soon after closing time, and been helped as far as the bridge by two men who'd been almost as drunk as he was.

Nurse Stokes had found him on her way back from a confinement. He was lying face down in the river.

'Dead?' Jean whispered. 'He's . . . *dead?*'

'I'm very sorry, Mrs Carter.'

She could only stare, her eyes wide with horror. *Take my enemy from me* ...

'My God,' she breathed wonderingly. 'That was quick!'

Part Two

Chapter Eleven

The garden had been Bel's salvation. There was something about the business of growing things – her father had felt the same – which somehow put everything into perspective. No matter how you raged over slugs, frost and blight, no matter how you raced to beat the elements, gardening gave you peace: a strange kind of detachment which allowed your thoughts to move on, to grow and develop. In a garden, time passed without seeming to pass, although it could play different tricks elsewhere, turning minutes into days, nights into an eternity, making the very thought of a *whole year* enough to make you scream, 'No, no! I can't bear it! Let me die!'

But you didn't die. And time passed just the same. One year, two years, three . . . six.

The church clock, which Bel could just glimpse through the trees, informed her that it was almost ten to nine. The ache in her back fully concurred. But the sun was saying something else, and even after three years of war-imposed 'double summertime', Bel still found it hard to believe that the sun was wrong. Two hours of daylight left to go, and there was still all that ruddy chickweed to clear from between the carrots. Criminal to stop now, just as she was winning. Ten minutes more, and then she really *must* stop. Her mind ran over the rest of her evening's work. Get Jinny to bed, prepare tomorrow's breakfast, fix the hem on her best skirt . . .

Scarcely a minute seemed to have gone by when, with a muted wail, Jinny leapt off the garden wall, dived headfirst between two lines of bean-poles and failed to emerge again. Bel's heartbeat quickened. She paused, sighed and craned her neck to look once more at the church clock. Ten *past* nine. Damn it, she'd been hoeing for twenty minutes!

She marched down the garden until she came level with the beansticks. Then, without attempting to locate her fugitive daughter, she said wearily, 'Jinny, you are a confounded nuisance.'

'Oh, *please*, Mummy?'

'No. You haven't the ghost of an excuse, and I refuse to invent one for you. You can see the church clock from – '

'I *can't*, Mummy! The trees – !'

'That's not good enough, and you know it. If you played nearer to home the trees wouldn't *get* in the way. You have only yourself to blame.' This said, she felt her heart softening a little and added quietly, 'Are you sure Daddy saw you?'

'Yes. He was putting the horses in.'

'Then all I can suggest is that you sprint indoors, dive into the bath and . . . Well, say a prayer or three.' She swallowed. Her heart began to feel like a wound, prodded by a doctor's thumb.

('Does that hurt, Mrs Huntley?')

Yes, it hurt. But you couldn't die of torn loyalties. They were agony, but they didn't kill you.

'That's my last word, Jinny. Sorry, darling.'

She strolled away, poking at the fruit border with the toe of her gumboot, pretending not to care. A rustle of leaves in her wake, followed by a sharp hiss of gravel, indicated that Jinny had taken her advice and was sprinting for the sanctuary of her room. But the sound of running ceased almost before it had begun. Jinny gasped once and then was silent. Miles had caught her.

He had taken possession of the gate and was leaning casually against the archway, his hands in his pockets. Jinny, arrested in mid-flight, stood several yards distant from him, thoughtfully scratching her ear.

At nine, she was very tall for her age: tall enough to be mistaken for a twelve-year-old, although her hips were still narrow and her chest as flat as a plank. She regarded her height as a curse and with more than one good reason, for it was this (after years of pretending she didn't exist) which had at last persuaded Miles to 'take her in hand'. Jinny had Mrs Carter to blame for that. Dratted woman. One could never tell if she was being deliberately malicious or just passing the time of day . . .

'Goodness, isn't your Jinny growing up fast, Mr Huntley! Such a pretty girl, too. I expect you'll be fighting her boyfriends off before long, ho-ho!'

Boyfriends! She was nine, not fifteen! But it was of no earthly use to tell Miles that. The mere idea of Jinny as budding *femme fatale* had been enough to rake up all the troubles which Bel had thought long dead, or at worst rendered toothless with age. To have discovered that they were still wide awake and snarling would have been depressing enough, but having to stand helplessly by while Jinny took the backlash . . .

Still, in this matter as in every other, Miles never forgot his manners. Or his smile – although Jinny had long ago deduced how much comfort she could derive from that. Yet she loved him: loved him as Bel loved God, striving with every nerve she possessed to please and make amends and forever being led from the path of virtue by the sheer futility of the effort. Jinny could behave like a saint for three weeks at a stretch and never earn so much as a pat on the head to show that it was appreciated, yet the minute she fell from grace . . .

Miles had never given her anything beyond the basic means

of her survival: food and clothing, a roof over her head, his name. He'd said at the outset that there would be nothing more, and Bel had been in no position to argue the point: had been on her knees at the time, thanking him for not hurling them out, naked, into the street. And praying, of course, that he might one day relent . . .

Without moving from his leaning post in the archway, Miles smiled and beckoned. Jinny took two steps towards him and then stopped, evidently wondering what she should do with her hands. She clasped them behind her back, drew them up over her ribs, shrugged, tidied her hair and moved forward again. She seemed to get smaller and more frail with every step she took, Miles taller and infinitely more powerful, the contrast making Bel's heart ache with frustrated mother-love. He hated that child . . . None of it was Jinny's fault, and Miles knew that, he *knew* it! He'd said so several times in those first nightmare months after Jack's death: 'Keep her out of my way, Bel. I know it isn't her fault, but I can't trust myself to be near her!'

Bel had kept her out of his way. And, as soon as she was old enough, Jinny had learned to do herself the same service. She'd become virtually invisible for a while, roaming the valley like a gypsy during the summer months, disappearing into books or remote, dreamy trances when the winter kept her at home. No mother with the least smattering of sense could have said she'd been a happy child, but she'd been as happy as she *could* be. Like Bel, she'd created strategies, escape routes, found places of peace where she could relax and be herself. The Clares out at Drayfield, Solomon and Prissie, the beloved Nurse Stokes . . .

And now the benighted Jean Carter had ruined it all!

'Will you tell me the time, Jinny?'

'Umm . . .' Jinny made a cursory attempt to see the church clock, but from her position on the path the trees completely obscured her view. 'I can't see, Daddy, but I know I'm very late.'

'And what were you doing here? Hiding?'

Jinny bowed her head, letting a silky fall of straight, red-gold hair veil her eyes. 'Yes . . .'

'And what did that achieve?'

'Nothing.'

'On the contrary. It achieved a great deal, although none of it's to your credit. Being late – yet again – was bad enough, without your then adding cowardice and deceit to the score. And no doubt you asked Mummy to cover for you?'

Jinny nodded helplessly.

'Yes, quite an achievement. Four crimes for the price of one. Now, let's test your arithmetic, shall we? If you commit four crimes, how many punishments should you expect?'

Bel gritted her teeth and turned away. However he actually punished Jinny now hardly mattered. Asking her to condemn herself out of her own mouth was cruel enough to make even a beating seem mild by comparison. Not that he would beat her. He'd never laid a finger on her except, when she was still too small to understand that he could no longer stand the sight of her, to set her away from him, peeling her little hands from his arm as if her very touch was a contamination.

God, were ever so many tears shed for the love of one man? And there'd be more tonight.

'You'll stay in your room for the rest of the week,' Miles pronounced quietly at last. 'Go to bed now.'

Bel had returned to her battle with the chickweed, but was aware that, although Jinny had fled, Miles was still there. She heard his feet on the gravel, heard him pause just behind her on the path.

'The beans seem to be doing well,' he observed blandly. 'Do you pinch them out when they reach the tops of the poles?'

'Mm, usually.' She rested on the hoe, instructing her facial muscles to produce a cool, disinterested smile. 'I suppose you know it's only Wednesday, Miles?'

'Only Wednesday? What does that mean?'

'It means that Jinny's about to spend three days in her room, darling. A little hard, perhaps?'

He shrugged. 'A little hard, certainly.'

'A little *too* hard, Miles?'

'I don't think so. If it teaches her to be punctual it need never happen again.'

'And what if it doesn't?'

Again he shrugged. 'We'll have to try something else, won't we?'

Bel threw down her hoe and turned away, muttering, 'How about six months in the cellar? That should do it.'

He laughed softly. 'You're over-reacting.'

'So are you! Jinny's only *nine*, Miles. She's – '

'Yes, she's nine. Were you allowed to roam the countryside unchecked when you were nine? Were the boys ever given such freedom?'

'That was different! You cared about the boys!'

'Well, now I'm caring about Jinny. Is that something to complain of?'

His smile was as infuriatingly enigmatic as ever: disguising everything, revealing nothing but his teeth. But at least he was talking. Except before witnesses, there'd been a time when he hadn't spoken to her at all, even asking for the salt by a combination of sign-language and heavy breathing. It had been easier that way. For Miles, because speech had been inadequate to express the rage and hurt he'd felt. For Bel, simply because there was no point in saying what she wanted to say: that she loved him, honoured him, pitied him, and would do anything he asked to earn his forgiveness. But she'd known it was futile. It was rather like saying, 'Sorry I shot you through the head, darling.' Not only too late; not merely too little; just . . . stupid.

In the end, it had seemed wiser to behave as if she really had killed him, and that the silent man sitting opposite her at table was his ghost, come back to haunt her. She wouldn't be afraid of him. She'd pretend he wasn't there. She'd simply get on with her life, like a widow, with as much courage, independence and dignity as she could contrive.

The outbreak of war had changed that. With Andrew old enough to fight and the twins not far behind, Miles seemed suddenly to realise that, however much he had lost, he had a great deal left to lose, and that Bel was still a part of it: the mother of his sons. They'd talked about the boys then and had been talking – after a fashion – ever since, skittering politely over the surface of things, rarely exposing their feelings.

The sheer relief of simply communicating again had made Bel want to say everything which had been left unsaid for so long, but she'd controlled the urge with a restraint which had almost crucified her. It had become easier with time, but it wasn't easy now. She wanted to scream at him, hurl herself at him, fight like a cat in her child's defence. But ... she wouldn't. It could achieve nothing.

Caring about Jinny? Yes, perhaps he was. But it wasn't quite the same as caring *for* her!

'I'll go and tuck her in,' she said coolly. 'Any messages? A reprieve on Friday if she sticks it out like a trooper?'

His eyes crinkling with wry amusement, Miles turned away. 'No,' he said softly. 'No messages.'

Miles had confined all his children to their rooms at some stage in their lives. He considered it a sensible punishment, allowing them time to think about the error of their ways without causing them too much humiliation. They were allowed out for meals, and were visited at least once between times, if only to check that (as had once happened with

Andrew) they weren't busily engineering an escape down the drainpipe.

Andrew had earned himself an extra day in clink for that. For the others, one day had been enough, and Miles guessed it would be enough for Jinny, too. He'd made the threat of a longer term merely to make it seem worse in anticipation than it would be in fact, and was self-critical enough to be aware that he had an ulterior motive in this. Perhaps she'd be grateful. Perhaps she'd decide that he wasn't quite as black as she'd painted him.

He'd resented a thousand things about Jinny over the years, but nothing had hurt him more than the realisation that she was afraid of him. He hadn't intended that. If he'd intended anything where she was concerned it had been quite the opposite. He'd been conscious from the beginning that she was not at fault, that she could not be blamed for her mother's errors or her father's name. And yet, in that first nightmarish year 'after the fall', it had been more than his flesh could stand to be near her.

He had loved her so much! She'd been *his* little girl! More 'his', in a way, than any of the others, for he'd been there at her birth, had possessed her from the instant she'd taken her first breath of life.

To know, suddenly, that she was not his at all . . . To understand suddenly that her father was the man he most despised . . . He hadn't been able to bear it. So he'd set her aside. He'd known there was a danger that, in his need to punish Bel, he might punish the child instead, and he hadn't wanted that. It was not *her* fault!

Being late, however, was, and he was determined to cure her of it. Bel had allowed her too much freedom and people were beginning to talk. After doing his damnedest, six years ago, to nip in the bud any gossip about Bel and Jinny (he would *not* have his sons' lives tainted by scandal), it seemed crazy to let any murmurings start now. Oh, he knew that Jack had not departed the world in silence. He knew that at least half the inhabitants of the valley were still wondering, and that he couldn't stop them wondering. But he could at least see to it that they had nothing more to wonder about!

Since Cook and Ethel had departed 'for essential war-work', the family had tended to eat most of their meals in the kitchen with Muriel and the land girls. Miles's mother didn't approve, but Miles rather liked it, if only because it made life so much easier for Bel. She did most of the cooking now, as well as a good part of the housework and the gardening, not to mention running the Women's Institute. It was a mystery where she found all the energy, let alone the capability. But that was women for you. A mystery to the last . . .

There were fish cakes for breakfast. Bel was fond of remarking that, since rationing, bacon and sausages had not so much become a thing of the past as a thing of the moment: a few mouthfuls each and they were gone. Yet she could work miracles with the alternatives, and no one ever left the table hungry.

Miles was about to attack the second of the three fish cakes he'd been allocated when he noticed that Jinny was missing from the table. At first, he wasn't sure he should mention it. Bel must know what was going on, and she didn't seem more worried than usual. But Jinny had an appetite like a horse. She never missed breakfast!

'Where's Jinny?' he asked at last.

'In her room. Where else?'

'At the table?' Miles suggested mildly.

'She's not hungry.'

'She's always hungry.'

Bel darted him a look. It was accompanied by a bright, businesslike smile which – to the untrained eye – could have meant, 'Don't worry, darling, everything's under control,' but

Miles knew better. It meant, 'Shut up, you brute, and mind your own business!'

He wasn't quite certain how he knew this. Bel had never in her life said any such thing to him, yet where Jinny was concerned she seemed to be always saying it – with her eyes. And how, in all justice, could he complain of that? It was exactly what he'd wanted . . . at the beginning. *She's yours, not mine! I want nothing to do with her!*

But it couldn't continue like that. She was growing up, and no daughter of Miles Huntley's (no child who bore his name, at least) was going to grow up like a bloody gypsy!

He waited until everyone else had gone before he made further enquiries. 'Is Jinny all right, Bel?'

She sighed and turned away. 'She'll survive.'

There seemed no point in pressing her further, and Miles went off to inspect the War Ag's wheat fields, knowing that his vague feelings of guilt and disquiet were better worked off on his farm than on his wife. He didn't love her now, but it was impossible not to admire her. He hated having to admit it to himself (and he'd rather die than admit it to Bel), but in many ways he respected her far more now than he'd done before.

He respected her father a lot less, though. Clement weather plant, indeed! So were thistles! God, how could a man of the Archdeacon's sensibilities live with his own daughter for eighteen years and not know that she was as tough as leather? *Never blow on her when the wind's in the east, Captain Huntley.* Bloody fool!

'And how long did *you* live with her?' he asked himself wearily.

Bloody fool.

Jinny did not come down for lunch. Her absence did nothing for Miles's appetite and neither did Bel's vegetable curry, which was missing its most essential ingredient: the curry powder.

'Oh, I'm sorry,' she said when she'd tasted it and discovered why everyone was looking at her so strangely. 'Did I say curry? I meant stew, of course. Vegetable stew . . .'

'With rice?' Miles's mother demanded disdainfully.

Bel threw her one of her brightest 'shut up' smiles. 'Makes a change, doesn't it, Violet?'

'Hmm. It certainly does. The apples are a curious innovation, Bel. Aren't apples more suitable for curry, or am I just being old-fashioned?'

'Old-fashioned,' Bel said firmly. 'Apples in the stew are all the rage, Vio. Everyone's doing it. Helps you see in the dark, darling, like carrots.'

Miles suppressed a grin. Bel had learned her culinary skills in the single week she'd been allowed prior to Cook's patriotic departure, and she'd done very well – on the whole. She was always cutting out recipes from the *Evening Post* and had invented a few very good dishes of her own. But curry-without-the-curry wasn't one of them.

When everyone else had gone, Bel sat with her hand over her eyes, apparently waiting for Miles to speak. He wasn't sure what to say. 'Delicious lunch' was hardly suitable, and he was a little afraid to ask 'How's Jinny?'

In the end, just to set the ball rolling, he said, 'Well?'

'Well, what?'

'Jinny still not hungry, I take it.'

Bel turned her head and directed a smile at the wall. 'Probably best in the circumstances. I *did* forget the curry powder.'

'Ah, well. Perhaps you had something more pressing on your mind.'

'More pressing than what?'

'Curry powder.'

They stared at each other down the length of the table. Bel put her hands together as if in prayer and patted her lips with her fingertips. Then, her mouth trembling with the onset of tears, she dropped her hands to the table and began studiously to inspect her fingernails.

'She's devastated,' she whispered.

'*Devastated*? About what, for heaven's sake? She *is* in her room, I take it, not the cellar?'

'That's not the point! She feels . . . You've disgraced her, Miles, and she can't bear it!'

'Oh. Forgive me, darling, but I had the idea she'd disgraced herself. If she can't bear that – '

'She was *late*, Miles! Had you punished her for being late she'd have taken it on the chin. Even three days of it, although if there's any justice in that, I'm damned if I can see it!'

'I did punish her for being late. What else, for heaven's sake?'

'How about cowardice, deceit and coercion? Three of her brothers are out there, Miles – the sons you adore – all nobly, bravely and honourably fighting a war for Jinny's salvation, and now you've told her she's a coward!' Bel leaned forward suddenly, adding grimly, 'And she believes you.'

He shrugged. 'She was a coward last night.'

'She's a *little girl*, Miles, and she's – '

'And I wouldn't say it's especially brave of her to make such a fuss about being left in her room. Little girls and little boys alike have to learn to toe the line. If she can't bear being punished for her faults – '

'*What* faults? She's the sweetest, most amenable – '

'Least punctual – '

'*Buy her a watch!*'

Although she'd kept her voice down, this was the nearest Bel had ever come to screaming at him. She'd endured everything – his rage, his contempt, his sarcasm and neglect – with a restraint which would have split the corsets of a saint; and it was of no use to say that any of it had been easy to endure. He'd been a bastard to her.

'I've never cared what you did to me,' she said hoarsely

now. 'You could have taken a horsewhip to me and I'd still have told myself I deserved it. But Jinny *doesn't* deserve it, Miles!'

The tears overspilled and she covered her face, weeping quietly into a dishrag.

Miles sighed. He pushed himself up from the table. 'All right,' he said grimly. 'You win. I'll buy her a watch for Christmas, but if she's late just *once* in the meantime, Bel . . .'

He couldn't think what he would do if she was late in the meantime. He turned away, squeezing his eyes shut on a feeling very like despair. Christ, he'd lost this battle on every front, and all he'd meant was to make something right again!

'Can I tell her you've forgiven her, Miles?'

He looked at the ceiling. 'If that's what she wants,' he murmured hopelessly, 'I'd better do it myself, hadn't I?'

He'd half-expected Bel to stop him, had half-hoped that she would, for another interview with a crying female was the last thing he wanted just now. But Bel said nothing and he whirled from the room and ran upstairs before *his* courage could desert him.

He thought at first that he'd come too late, that Jinny had given up hope of a reprieve and decided to abscond through the window. She was not on her bed, in the chair or on the window seat. She was not lurking behind the door. The thought struck him that she might have heard his approach and taken refuge in the wardrobe and, colouring with embarrassment, he sighed and called softly, 'Jinny?'

He saw her then. She was sitting in the corner under the window and, until he'd called, had shrouded herself entirely with the lower drapes of the curtain. Now she stood up, clasped her hands behind her back and looked at his feet with a mild air of bafflement, as if wondering what they were and where they'd come from.

Rather to his surprise, he saw no signs on her face of recent tears, and nothing in her attitude to indicate that she'd made any fuss at all about her confinement. As ever, she was wearing shorts, sandals and a cardigan she'd grown out of while it was still being knitted. After her summer of freedom she was tanned, strong and healthy, yet she looked half-dead: stunned, like a sleepwalker who'd walked into a wall.

'Shall we call a truce?' he suggested softly.

Jinny raised her eyes – without quite meeting his – and lowered them again. She said nothing.

Miles sighed. 'I was your age once,' he said. 'So were the boys and I can assure you that none of us was perfect. We were often late, often cowardly and we told fibs by the cartload. Your faults are nothing special, Jinny, but if you aren't taught to overcome them while you are still young enough to learn, you'll grow up – as we would have grown had our parents not taught us – to be very much the wrong kind of person. Do you understand that?'

'Yes.'

Miles caught his breath at the lifelessness of her tone. It was odd . . . when she was smaller he'd hated her to call him Daddy. Now he felt sick because she hadn't.

'So . . .' he continued, 'this has been a lesson in growing up, Jinny. Nothing more. If you can tell me you've learned it, and that you won't be late home again, we can put it behind us and begin afresh. *Can* you tell me that?'

'Yes.' Still she didn't look at him. She didn't move.

'Then it's over,' he announced briskly. 'I forgive you. You can come downstairs.' He reversed towards the door, held it open and reached out his arm to shepherd her through, but Jinny still didn't move.

'Jinny?'

She looked at him then, but for days afterwards Miles wished she hadn't. Her face was stone-white, her mouth turned down at the corners, her eyes huge and filling with pools of tears.

'May I . . .' she whispered, 'stay here, please, Daddy . . . until I feel . . . better?'

Perverse little brat! All this bloody fuss to be let out of her room and now she was begging to stay in it! He'd never in her life seriously been tempted to strike her, but now it was all he could do not to take her by the hair and kick her downstairs. Instead, he blinked, swallowed and murmured frigidly, 'Of course. I hope you'll feel better soon.'

He stood outside her door for several minutes afterwards, listening for the sobs – of relief? – which he felt sure should follow. But nothing happened. For all he knew she was still standing exactly where he'd left her, still staring at the floor where his feet had been.

He wandered to the top of the stairs and waited a little longer before looking back into the shadowy depths of the landing.

Had he brought this upon himself? Had he had any choice? Could a saint have done better, acted more wisely, shown more restraint? There'd been times . . . There'd been times when he wished he'd killed the pair of them, or at least thrown them out to live or die as they saw fit. Why hadn't he? Why hadn't he?

He sat on the top step of the stairs and gazed bleakly through the tall gothic window which framed the main driveway. The gravel was seething with weeds. Before the war, George had had a 'drive-week' once a quarter, when he'd weeded the entire half-mile of it on his hands and knees and then flattened it all with a roller. Murderous work. Impossible now. It was all Bel could do to keep the kitchen garden going, although she did it – as she did everything else – far better than anyone could have imagined.

If he'd thrown her out, he'd have been lost . . .

But he hadn't known that at the time. He hadn't known (although he'd guessed) that another war would break upon them so soon. Why hadn't he thrown her out? Because he'd loved her. Even in his rage he'd loved her, and his rage... How much of that had been rage against himself and his failure to satisfy her? How much had arisen from the knowledge that he'd brought it all upon himself?

He didn't know. He hadn't known then and he didn't know now. But since Bel so clearly resented his interference in Jinny's upbringing, and since Jinny so clearly couldn't 'bear' it, the best thing he could do for everyone was simply to opt out again. Let them get on with it...

Wobbling a little on the unrolled gravel, a bicycle came into view, its rider swerving to avoid the branches of a holly tree which had overgrown the drive. Jean Carter was recognisable from any distance, even without her red bicycle and lumpy postwoman's uniform. She'd lost a great deal of weight over the years, but cycling had developed her muscles in a rather unfortunate way, making her legs look like china vases, her arms like hemp rope, full of knots.

Miles had been mildly fond of her before Jack's death. Now he liked her less. She'd seemed to him a very calm, patient woman when she'd lived out at Drayfield. Her eyes had been steady, her smile always kind. Now she talked too much and was always in a hurry, her eyes restless and evasive, her smile rather forced. The trouble was, he supposed, that they'd become embarrassed with each other, silently asking, 'Do you know that I know what you know?'

Sighing, Miles went downstairs to collect the post, hoping for a letter from one of the boys. It was a symptom of his depressed frame of mind that he made the descent with his hands in his pockets, so that when he lost his footing on the bottom step he had little hope of saving himself. His backside went down with such a thump it made his teeth rattle, and when he realised he'd tripped on Bel's abandoned dustpan, his temper finally broke.

'Damn and curse it all to hell!' he roared. 'Why does everything have to happen to *me*?'

Chapter Twelve

The sorting office behind the Post Office in Bishop Molton was almost exactly the same as the scullery at Drayfield Farm. It had the same rough plaster walls, the same tiny window overlooking a blank stone wall, the same enormous grey flagstones on the floor which, at five o'clock on a fine August morning, sent a chill floating up your spine which took a good ten minutes to work off.

Shivering aside, Jean was usually at her best early in the morning. Bert Tomkins, the sub-Postmaster, was not. He was an owl in a lark's job: a man who sat up reading until midnight and faced each new day bleary-eyed and fuzzy-jawed, a poor, shambling creature who came properly to life only when it was time to open up shop, four hours later. His wife had died ten years ago, and he did all his own cooking and cleaning, a state of affairs Jean thought much too good to be true. She didn't dare think what sort of muddle the poor man must live in, but he never invited anyone through to his living quarters and all you saw when he went through was a little vestibule with brown lino. Maddening . . .

'Uh . . . What's this say, Jean? My glasses are all fogged up.'

'Hicks.' She plucked the letter from his hand and lobbed it neatly into the appropriate pigeonhole.

'Huntley,' she said a moment later as she sorted through her own sack of mail. 'Ooh, it's from Andrew. He's got neater writing than the twins. His dad'll be pleased. I hope.'

'Mm? Why shouldn't he be?'

'Well,' she widened her eyes and pursed her mouth. 'I don't know, Bert. You haven't heard of anything going on down there, have you? Anything wrong? Or not quite right?'

Bert didn't reply. He didn't believe in gossip. He heard all that was going on, of course, but he kept it very strictly to himself.

Jean admired that in him. She respected it, and that was saying a lot because she had no respect at all for men, generally. Three years on the post had opened her eyes to men. She'd believed she'd been unlucky with Jack. She'd thought she'd found herself an especially nasty specimen whose like was not to be found in the length and breadth of England. But they were everywhere! All over the *valley*, leave alone England! Beasts, men were. You couldn't trust a one of them. Nasty, foul-mouthed, violent, ungrateful . . .

'Where's me bloody shirt, Agnes?'

'Shut thy bloody mouf, woman, afore I shuts it fer thee!'

'Damn and curse it all to hell! Why does everything have to happen to *me*?'

Oh, yes. Three years on the post could show up even the perfect gentleman in his true colours! It was a bit worrying, though . . . She'd always had a soft spot for Miles Huntley, and when you came down to it he'd been very good to her. Very good.

'Only,' she said anxiously, 'yesterday, this was, Bert: afternoon post, just before I knocked off. I was just putting his letters through – '

'Whose letters?'

'Mr Huntley's. And there was a terrible crash and Mr Huntley cussin' and swearing like nobody's business!' She giggled nervously. '*Ever* so savage. Not like him at all. Not what you'd expect, if you know what I mean. So I wondered, that's all. I wondered if you'd heard anything, Bert. Bad news, or anything. That's all.'

'They haven't had a telegram. I can tell you that much.'

'Oh, good! *That's* all right, then.'

She began to hum, pretending a satisfaction she did not feel. She hadn't been thinking of telegrams just at that moment, although the thought of them had worried her sick when Andrew Huntley had first gone into the Air Force. Bomber pilot. She'd thought his chances of survival were slim indeed, yet three years on he was still very much alive – if not exactly kicking. He'd spent his last forty-eight-hour leave fast asleep, Bel had said, and all the lovely meals and special treats she'd prepared had gone for naught. Such a disappointment. It must have been, although you'd never get a word of that out of *her*. According to her, his every snore had been a pleasure!

Dratted woman. You never saw her without a smile on her face, though how she managed it nobody knew. She was the only woman in the valley with three sons in the firing line, yet one was bad enough for most women! Mrs Yeoman had had a telegram about her Sydney, only last week. Taken prisoner, God help him. And Derek Bird had been fried to a crisp in a tank in North Africa two months ago. Penny Clare, out at Drayfield, had gone to pieces after that – their Alan was in North Africa – but Bel... Not a sausage. Oh, she'd been sympathetic, same as usual, but no *more* than usual. No tear in the eye, no tremor in the voice. Maddening. You just couldn't *tell*!

'He's ever so nice, usually, isn't he, Bert?'

'Who?'

'Mr Huntley.'

'Mm.'

'Not really the sort to lose his temper, is he?'

'No one's perfect, Jean.'

That was what worried her. No one was perfect. She'd *known* that, of course, right from the start. That was what had puzzled her so much about the whole thing, because if Jack had *really* said all that to Miles, even if the man was a *saint*, he couldn't have just ignored it!

Yet he'd come out to Drayfield the very next day, as sympathetic as you please. 'No,' he'd said gently, 'I didn't evict him, Mrs Carter. He told me he couldn't pay his rent and was tired of trying to make ends meet. But all the farmers in the valley are in the same position, you know, and I can't afford to evict them. New tenants are hard to find and, in economic terms, it's far better for me to keep the land in cultivation than let it go to wilderness. You see that, don't you?'

Yes, she'd seen it. She'd believed it. And yet . . .

'He said you'd evicted him!'

'He was a proud man, Mrs Carter. So am I. In his position, I think I'd have been more inclined to – er – lay the blame elsewhere. It amounts to the same thing in the end, but if a man can save his pride he usually will, Mrs Carter.'

He was right. Jack had never told the truth against himself if a brag or a boast would serve instead, and it would have been so *typical* of him to go out claiming not only that he'd had Isobel Huntley, but that he'd thrown it in her husband's face! Bloody liar. Of course he hadn't!

But nothing had been easy to believe that morning. She hadn't even believed that Jack was really dead, let alone known how she felt about it.

'How is Mrs Huntley?' she'd asked, knowing that, if there was a word of truth in it, Miles *must* react. And he had, but not . . . Not conclusively. Not to *tell* her anything.

'Very shocked,' he'd said stiffly. 'And very sorry not to be with you, but the boys are due home from school today, and we decided, in the circumstances, that I could be of more help to you just now. We have to think about your future, Mrs Carter. We have to think about your children.'

And he had. He'd been marvellous. Nothing had been too much trouble. He'd paid the men to keep the farm going, attended the inquest, arranged the funeral. And both the Huntleys had come to the funeral: Bel on her husband's arm, just as calm and kind as she'd ever been. No truth in it... All lies...

Yet she'd *cursed* them!

She'd tried to justify it a thousand times. Life had been so much easier without Jack; she hadn't mourned him for a moment. Yet how could you be happy, knowing you'd sent a man to the devil? How could you not have nightmares about it and wonder if worse was still to come? The Huntleys... The Clares out at Drayfield...

'Do you believe in curses, Bert?'

'Mm? What? No. Load of rubbish. Why?'

'Well... I was just thinking about what Mr Huntley said. "Damn and curse it all to hell," he said, Bert, and it was so *unlike* him. If it was anyone else, I wouldn't take any notice, but –'

'All men say that sort of thing.' Bert scratched his head over someone's illegible handwriting. 'Cor, I wish people'd change their pen nibs from time to time! Look at this. There's more blots than words on this envelope! Mrs Blotty, Blot Lane, Bishop Blotton, Somerblot. Makes you sick. How do they expect us to deliver *that*?'

'Give it here.' Jean took one look and threw it into the Church Molton slot. 'That's Ida Humphrey's mother. I'd recognise her writing anywhere. She puts tails on her 'n's.'

Bert gawped at her. 'How the dickens do you remember a thing like that?'

She laughed. It was lovely having a decent job, regular pay and a bit of security for her girls, but the satisfaction she derived from doing the job well made it twice as good and Bert had never been mean with his praise. She liked that in him. It was so surprising. It made her blush, every time! 'Oh,' she murmured smugly. 'You just have to keep your eyes open, Bert. Nothing to it, really.'

But no matter how she kept her eyes open, she couldn't guard the Huntleys from that dratted curse. Oh, the hours she'd lain awake, thinking of Andrew and the twins, thinking of those awful words, *her children and her children's children*. Not to mention Alan Clare! And Michael . . . Just three weeks the Clares had lived at Drayfield before that poor boy had fallen through the barn roof, and he hadn't walked straight ever since. Nothing had happened to young Felix, yet, but how could you stop worrying? She'd cursed them. She'd cursed the house. And after what had happened to Jack . . .

'Tell you a story about curses,' Bert said thoughtfully. 'Two uncles of mine – oh, years ago, this was – married Catholic girls in the Anglican church over at Keynsham, and the Catholic priest came along specially to curse them.'

'No! The *priest*? Why?'

'Well, it was a sin, wasn't it? The girls were marrying outside the faith, according to him, although I'm blowed if I can see it. Same God, same Mary and Joseph, same Jesus. We're all Christians, see, Jean, aren't we? But that priest didn't think so. He cursed them going into church and he cursed them coming out again, and there wasn't much they could do to stop him.'

'And what happened?' Jean breathed.

'Well! My Uncle Ted – he was the first to be married – had three sons and a daughter. Two of the boys died of their lungs, my Uncle Ted was killed on his motorbike and my Aunty Maud went barmy and ended her days in Barrow Asylum.'

Jean closed her eyes. She felt sick.

'The other one – my Uncle Alf – went into his father-in-law's business as a pork butcher and made himself a mint. He was happily married, had two healthy sons, a nice house, everything you could wish for. And he lived to be ninety-two, with never a day's illness till the month before he popped off.

So that's curses for you. If you didn't know about my Uncle Alf you'd say the curse on my Uncle Ted had worked, wouldn't you? But no. He was just unlucky. Some folk are, Jean, and that's all there is to it. So you leave poor Mr Huntley to say what he likes in his own house. If a Catholic priest can't do it, no one can.'

Jean took a deep, relieved breath and got on with her sorting. She didn't like men. Wouldn't touch another with a bargepole. But there was no getting away from it with Bert: he could be a real *comfort* at times!

Felix Clare's sixteenth birthday, in September, brought with it a creeping depression which Christmas did very little to dispel. He'd been looking forward to being sixteen ever since – at fourteen – he'd begun to take a sincere, but embarrassing, interest in girls. He'd been sure the embarrassment would wear off at the appropriate moment. He'd been convinced that, as soon as it all became legal and above board he'd suddenly acquire all the confidence and sophistication he needed to just walk up to a girl and say . . . What? He'd half-expected a romantic script to arrive with the birthday cards, but of course it hadn't. He'd had two new pairs of socks, a second-hand copy of *Bleak House*, and a 'new' belt which his father had made from an old harness. Apart from that, everything was exactly the same as it had been when he was fifteen, except that now he was disappointed as well.

The winter, until Christmas, had been very wet. Now, in the second week of January, it was dry and sunny, but the west winds had veered to the north and acquired a keen razor edge which seemed intent on slicing one's ears off. Felix had spent much of his Saturday hauling firewood from the woods above Drayfield and although, like most boys of his age, he'd have been happier doing nothing, if he *had* to help out he preferred to work at something which wasn't directly associated with farming.

He took after the elder of his two brothers in this: Alan had never liked farming, although Mike loved every moment of it and had never wanted anything else. Felix didn't actually dislike the work, but he wasn't in the least inclined to follow a career that was governed by so many variables. A farmer could never be certain of anything except the things that might happen in a perfect world and, since it was not a perfect world, he was forced to make the majority of his judgements by guesswork. Felix wanted something more predictable for himself: something he could learn as a matter of *fact*, without always having to add, 'If the rain holds off,' to the equation.

He had almost finished stacking the firewood in the yard beside the goose paddock when the geese began to hiss and yammer, craning their necks to indicate the approach of a visitor at the foot of the lane. Hoping it might be Robin Huntley, whose school holidays had two more days to run, Felix watched the gate and was not greatly disappointed to see that it was Jinny, not Robin, who emerged between the trees. He was fond of Jinny. He'd known her since she was four, and although she was very much taller now, in most other ways she'd scarcely changed at all. She had a solemn look about her which made her appear thoughtful and wise beyond her years, but she could also be very witty in a dry, self-denigrating fashion. Even Felix sometimes forgot that she was only nine, although at times like these . . .

'What have you been up to?' he grinned. 'You look – '

'Oh, I know.' She scraped a curtain of tangled hair from her eyes, then made another pass with the same hand to catch a drip from the end of her nose. She was blue with cold and looked like something a fox had dragged through a hedge, her coat done up on the wrong buttons, her socks in heaps around her ankles. Both knees were black with dirt, although one of them sported a rather bloody graze which needed urgent attention. 'I fell out of a tree.'

'Far?'

'I don't know. It didn't take very long.'

Felix laughed. 'Come on. I'll get Dad to clean it up for you.' He held out his hand to shepherd her indoors. Typically, she shrugged away, scratched her ear and said, 'I don't want to be a nuisance.'

'You won't be. I've finished here and Dad hasn't started milking yet.' He put his arm around her shoulders and she relaxed and butted her head against him, softly, like a cat. Felix laughed again, wishing all girls were as easy to manage.

'I'm ten now, Felix,' she confided as he pushed her into the scullery. 'Double figures!'

'Ten!' He widened his eyes, pretending amazement. 'How's it feel?'

'Exactly the same as nine. I felt very old when I woke up on my birthday, but it wore off before lunchtime. I think it's probably because I'm the youngest. Or . . .' She frowned and wrinkled her nose. 'Maybe it's because I'm a girl.'

Felix smiled doubtfully. 'What is?'

'Being unimportant.' She sat at the foot of the back stairs and, by force of habit, began taking off her shoes before venturing further into the house. She looked quite unconcerned with what she'd just said, but Felix knew better than to think it a casual remark. Except when she was in a giggly mood, Jinny wasn't the type to say anything she didn't mean and – like her parents – was tactful and loyal almost to a fault. Many times, when she was little, she'd arrived at Drayfield in tears, or so near to tears that it made no difference, but she'd never once said what had upset her. She was easily comforted though, and with that in mind, Felix laughed and said, 'Unimportant? Of course you aren't. You're important to me.'

'Am I?' She smiled wanly. 'You'd better not tell Evelyn Carter that. She wants to be your special girl.'

Felix blushed. 'Nonsense. She's not even fourteen yet! Who told you that?'

'Valerie. And Shirley told her, so it must be true, because

Shirley and Evelyn share a bedroom and they tell each other *everything*. Do you like her, Felix?'

He shrugged. 'She's all right, I suppose . . . If you like that sort of thing.'

Long legs the colour of ivory, long hair the colour of mahogany, rich brown eyes with flecks of gold in their depths and a well-developed bosom which Mrs Carter's clothing coupons had not yet managed to contain . . . Yes, he liked that sort of thing very well.

'But,' Jinny insisted gently, 'would you want her to be your *special* girl?'

Felix held his breath for a moment. This was precisely the chance he'd been looking for: someone to convey his feelings second-hand, so that, if anything went wrong, he could deny them outright. 'Jinny said *that*? Ho-ho. Well, she always did have a lively imagination, poor kid.'

But she was looking at him now, so wide-eyed and wistful, with the word 'unimportant' written all over her face. He couldn't do it to her. Not now.

'No,' he said softly. 'I've already got a special girl.'

'Who?' Her head went down suddenly and although she pulled up her socks and, quite uncharacteristically, straightened them and turned down the tops, Felix wasn't fooled.

'*You*, you dope,' he grinned. 'Who else?'

She laughed and widened her eyes: huge grey eyes, fringed with dark lashes, which contrasted strangely with silky, red-gold hair and skin the colour of honey. She should have had pale skin and freckles to match that hair of hers, but nothing about Jinny could be said to match anything else. In the arrangement of her nose, mouth and eyes you could see that she was Bel's daughter, but in all other respects she was unique, looking like no one but herself.

'Honest?' she breathed.

'Honest,' Felix said, and although he knew himself to be a

liar, he knew also that he was telling the absolute truth. There *was* something very special about Jinny Huntley.

She loved him.

It was gone four when Jinny left Drayfield at last, and even then she had to tear herself away, very painfully, as if she'd got her head stuck between the school railings and had either to leave her ears behind or stay there forever. But Drayfield was much nicer than the school railings. Everything about it was beautiful: the piles of dirty dishes heaped in the sink, the cat having kittens in the laundry basket, the cobwebs in the corners and the vase of petrified tulips which had stood on the windowsill since they'd been picked from the garden, last May.

Mrs Clare was famous for her housekeeping. When she spring-cleaned – which she did every year – the whole valley talked about it as if it was a miracle.

'She've washed every blanket in the house!'

'She've never!'

'And turned all the cupboards out!'

'No!'

'Had all the rugs up – '

'Gawd 'elp! She'll kill herself!'

Jinny was capable of recognising sarcasm when she heard it, yet the women were never as rude as they might have been about Penny Clare, and even when they were criticising, they said, 'Aw, bless her,' every now and then, to show that they weren't really cross.

It was impossible to blame Mrs Clare for anything. She was like an angel whom God had sent to earth to take all the pain away. She was warm and funny and thrilling and wise: a baronet's daughter who, before her marriage, had been a famous pianist with the world at her feet. Yet she'd given it all up for Leonard Clare. Jinny could see why. Felix was very like his father, and Jinny would have given up anything – had she had anything to give – for Felix.

She couldn't remember a time when she hadn't loved him. She'd been three, going on four, when he'd moved to Drayfield, and she had only one memory – a horrible one – before that time. In fact, it was just part of a memory, like a single scene from a play when you haven't seen the beginning and can't stay to see the end.

It had taken place in the hall at Bishop's Court. The front door had opened and Miles had come in, wearing a grey tweed overcoat and a grey hat, dripping with rain. Jinny was at the foot of the stairs and for some reason (which she couldn't now imagine) she'd run to him. There were no words or voices in her memory, but she was pretty sure she'd shouted, 'Daddy!'

But he'd bared his teeth and pushed her away: pushed her hard, so that she'd staggered against the wall. She remembered the feeling of that: a terrible pain in her chest and then the sensation of falling – as in a nightmare – from the pinnacle of a high mountain.

She'd never known what she'd done to deserve it and was certain that if she just racked her brains hard enough, 'Scene One' of the play would come back to her, and she'd know what she'd done and be able to make amends, ask him to forgive her . . . Not, of course, that that would achieve very much. He'd forgiven her for being late, last summer, and scarcely spoken to her since. Oh, he smiled; he said 'Good morning,' or – on rare occasions – 'How was school?' but his gaze always skimmed over the top of her head, as if she was a visitor he hadn't invited. Sometimes, when she went to bed, she imagined him creeping into the kitchen and asking Bel, very quietly, 'How long's she staying?' as he did sometimes with the ladies who came to speak at the WI.

He was always very polite to the WI ladies. He was always very polite to Jinny. But he made a little pain in her heart: half fear, half longing. She wanted to be near him, yet whenever he came near she wanted to run away.

She ran to Felix as often as she could. When Felix spoke to her he looked into her eyes and he watched her mouth when she spoke to him, as if every word she said really mattered. He listened. He answered. And he always, *always* touched her. Her father had touched her only twice that she could recall: once to push her away . . . and once to lay his hand on her forehead when she'd had tonsillitis, last winter. 'Hmm,' he'd said. 'You'll live.' She'd cried herself sick after that. He'd sounded so disappointed.

Since she'd arrived at Drayfield, almost three hours ago, the wind had strengthened and now seemed intent on freezing the skin from her bones, forcing her to take shelter between the trees every two or three hundred yards. Her grandmother had knitted her a hood for her birthday: a dreadful thing of scratchy grey wool which she'd privately sworn never to wear. It just went to prove that swearing was wicked. She wished now she'd worn the dratted thing . . .

About halfway along Drayfield Lane a gateway opened to the fields behind Home Farm. In summer, you could cut across that way and save ten minutes. In winter you were more likely to get bogged down in acres of mud and lose half an hour. But the ground had frozen yesterday, and there'd been no thaw since then. She decided to risk it. There'd be less shelter from the trees, but ten minutes was ten minutes . . .

The Clares had an old leather-cloth couch in the kitchen (Mrs Carter had left it behind when she'd moved to the village) and Felix had sat beside her and held her hand while Mr Clare dug bits of tree-bark from her knee and swabbed it with iodine. It hadn't hurt very much until then, but iodine was cruel stuff, endurable only because Felix was there, telling her how brave she was not to cry.

But even the iodine hadn't hurt as much as the wind, and

it was much harder to be brave when she was alone. She shouldn't have come out. Bel had told her it was too cold . . .

She'd been walking as fast as she could. Now, with the best part of a mile still to go, she began to run over the rough, frozen ground. The cows had been out until Christmas, and where their hooves had sunk into the mud were deep, ice-filled holes, as regularly spaced as the holes in a fishing net, so that the only path one could take was on the gridwork of frozen grass which lay between. It would have been a difficult walk, but running over it was a challenge which Jinny welcomed as a distraction from the cold. She had to keep her eyes on the ground, choose each footfall at speed and not allow herself to be lured into the occasional 'easy' path which would have lengthened the direct route to the stile at the top of the hill. Part of her enjoyment was in the knowledge that she could, at any moment, turn her ankle and fall down. Another was in knowing herself to be so quick on her feet that it wouldn't happen.

The last hundred yards of the hill were the steepest and most badly damaged by the cows. The grass had been trampled into oblivion where they'd crowded the gate, and although the hoof-pocks weren't so deep, neither were they as solidly frozen. Jinny slowed down to choose the least muddy route to the stile, confident now that in just five minutes more she'd be home.

She never knew what happened next. She thought at first she'd been shot, because the loud crack she heard and the pain in her leg happened in that order: the crack first, the pain a split second later. The pain was terrible. It went right through her, from her ankle to the roots of her teeth, making her scream.

She knew as soon as she fell that she would never get up, but as the pain subsided a little she tried to move and screamed again. She had built up a steam as she'd run up the hill. Now she turned cold all over and began to shudder with terror. She was lying in a wallow of half-frozen mud and dung, with the blank side wall of one of the outermost barns of Home Farm looming over her like a cliff. It was growing dark. It was freezing hard. In another hour, milking would be over and all the chores be finished for the night. Her father, the land girls and Mr Chard would go home . . .

No one would come this way now.

She was going to die.

Chapter Thirteen

Afternoon tea was virtually the only pre-war ritual Bel hadn't abandoned. She often wished she had. Rationing had made it one of the most difficult meals to organise, for although they produced much of their own food, neither the garden nor the farm could supply *cake*, and tea was never the same without it. Bel had never, before the war, been especially fond of sweet things. Now she felt fit to kill Hitler single-handed, just for a chocolate eclair. Or an Eccles cake, stuffed to bursting with currants and butter.

'Why on earth don't you make your own butter?' her mother-in-law demanded. 'All it takes – '

'Is time, Vio. And cream, of course. Tea, Miles?'

He had come in limping, and was now sitting by the library fire, curling his toes into the hearthrug, a look of concentrated agony on his face. For a man who spent so much time out of doors, he had about as much resistance to the cold as a plucked sparrow. Not that anyone could keep warm on a day like this: the wind went straight through you, no matter how many clothes you had on.

'Don't sit over the fire, Miles,' his mother ordered briskly. 'You'll get chilblains.'

'I've already got chilblains, Mother.'

She sniffed. 'Well, it's your own fault. I've told you not to sit over the fire. What's on this toast, Bel? It tastes like the fish pie we had at lunch.'

Bel shrugged. 'So much for clever disguises.'

She hadn't felt so depressed since this time last year. She hated January. All the excitement of Christmas was over and there was nothing to look forward to until spring came again – if it ever did. She couldn't bear to see Miles suffering and be able to do nothing to help him. She couldn't bear Violet's constant griping and be able to say nothing to shut her up – or make a swift escape to the garden. She couldn't bear having no cake for tea.

'That was a big sigh,' Miles observed laconically. 'What's up?'

She smiled weakly. 'January.'

'Oh.' He sighed too and held his palms to the fire, his mouth turning down at the corners, his face gaunt and sad. Bel wanted to kneel beside him, take his feet in her hands and rub some warmth into them, but she never touched him now. He'd been sleeping in the dressing room for the past six years. He made his own bed: a gentlemanly gesture intended to keep the knowledge of their estrangement from the servants. Barring Muriel, who didn't count, they no longer had servants. They had Violet, instead.

The silence stretched. Violet probed her teeth with her tongue, making spitty little noises which made Bel want to slap her.

'Where's Robin, Miles?' she asked, feigning brightness.

'Hmm? I think he said he was running over to Drayfield to say goodbye to Felix.'

'Ah. Good. He can walk home with Jinny.'

Violet widened her eyes. 'Has Jinny gone to Drayfield? Again? What on earth's the attraction for her there? Every chance she gets she's off to Drayfield!'

Bel glanced warily in her husband's direction, but he

seemed not to be listening. She could have said that Jinny had gone to the moon and it would make no difference to him. He didn't care. But it still wouldn't do to say that Jinny went to Drayfield in search of men! Men who teased her and ruffled her hair. Men who talked to her, listened to her, noticed her. Men who loved her for her own sake, without giving two hoots who her father was. Solomon Hicks was the same. He deemed the week empty if Jinny didn't call in to visit. He called her 'Pie-face,' and 'Juggins,' and 'Little Sally Slap-cabbage': and although she pretended to be insulted, she kept going back. If Miles had ever lowered himself to call her pie-face, she'd have been a happy child.

'Funny,' Violet continued thoughtfully. 'Drayfield has always had a peculiar fascination for this family. I think it's something about the house, you know. I've never walked past it without wanting to go inside. You used to go there a lot when you were a boy, didn't you, Miles?'

'Where?'

'Drayfield. I suppose you never found the lost room?'

'I've never looked, Mother.'

'Your father did. He was convinced someone had been walled up in there. That window over the front door – it's not a false one, you know, Bel. It's a real one, bricked up, but why should they put a window there, if there wasn't a room? *Quite* fascinating. Charles took a pickaxe to it once, you know. Ended up with a hole two feet deep, and still no sign of a room! But I'm sure there's nothing nasty there. You'd feel it, if there were. Mrs Clare would feel it. Women are sensitive to that sort of thing.'

Bel smiled stiffly. There *had* been something nasty there, by the name of Jack Carter, but Bel hadn't been in the least sensitive to it. She'd been as dense as the wall Miles's father had dug a hole in – three feet thick all round.

'It's curious, isn't it,' Violet went on thoughtfully, 'how history disappears? Take my great-grandmother. She came to

England to escape the French revolution, you know. I might have mentioned it before.'

She'd mentioned it a thousand times. Bel was tempted to say so, but instead widened her eyes and tried to look fascinated.

'She must have had such a *lot* of history to pass on,' Violet continued. 'But she died while my grandmother was still too young to understand, and all her history died with her. I don't even know what her name was before she married. It's the same with Drayfield. That house has been in our family for three hundred years, yet we know virtually nothing about it. When your father was a boy, Miles, there was a rumour that a witch had lived there. But who she was, or how she'd earned her reputation . . .'

'Mrs Carter found some papers,' Bel murmured. 'Did she ever give them to you, Miles?'

'Papers? Oh . . .' He frowned. 'Yes . . . I think she did send them over, but I never got around to looking at them. They're probably in the office somewhere.'

'Papers!' Violet echoed. 'What sort of papers?'

'Old recipes,' Bel supplied flatly. 'Eighteenth century, I think. There were a few charms as well, but nothing dramatic. Rub warts with meat, bury meat. That sort of thing. Hardly witchcraft, Vio.'

'Oh!' Violet was impressed. 'You must hunt them out, Miles!'

Miles rolled his eyes. 'Yes, Mother. I'll do it now, shall I? I'm sure the cows can milk themselves for once.'

He'd barely left the room when Violet said loudly, 'I hate sarcasm in a man. His father was the same, you know. Very cutting. I sometimes think the Huntley men have no feelings at all.'

'Or perhaps too many,' Bel suggested mildly.

Violet ignored that. 'I wouldn't have minded if he'd once lost his temper – Charles, I mean – it would at least have proved that he wasn't made entirely of rock.' She smirked suddenly. 'Should have left something on the stairs to trip him up, shouldn't I?'

Bel looked at her hands. It was odd how memorable that little incident had been. Violet had laughed until the tears ran down her face and she'd teased Miles about it for weeks afterwards. Every time he'd frowned she'd said, 'I hope you aren't going to throw another of your little *tantrums*, darling.' It was a wonder he hadn't strangled her . . . Or Bel, for leaving the dustpan there in the first place.

She eyed the tea trolley with a cynical smile. No one could call Miles a faddy eater, but he'd done rather well over Christmas – largely due to his efforts with a shotgun – and fish pie on toast, after jugged hare and roast pheasant, had evidently been a bit of a comedown.

'Well,' she said. 'Since my anchovy toast didn't suit – '

'Anchovy toast?' Violet scoffed merrily. 'Quick, darling, cross yourself, before God strikes you dead!'

It was well after five when Robin came home, his face scarlet and rather blue around the edges, his chest heaving with exertion. 'God,' he gasped. 'I ran most of the way, and I'm still freezing! What's for supper?'

Bel frowned and shunted the abandoned plate of 'anchovy toast' across the kitchen table. 'Where's Jinny?'

'Jinny? I don't know. Why?'

'Wasn't she at Drayfield?'

'No. She'd left before I got there. Isn't she home?'

'Didn't you pass her in the lane?'

He shrugged. 'You know Jinny. She probably went the long way round and called in on Solomon. He saves his sweets for her, you know. Brave man. I tried saving mine for her birthday, but the temptation was too much.'

He'd stuffed two squares of toast into his mouth before

he'd finished speaking, and now eyed the remaining two as if they were spread with caviare. 'Does no one else want any?'

Bel smiled wryly. 'They're queuing up for it, darling, but you go back to school tomorrow so I thought I'd spoil you.'

Of all her sons, Robin was the most like Miles and at sixteen was almost as tall. His hair wasn't as curly, but he had the same eyes, the same smile, the same square, determined jaw. But his character was Bel's: all good intentions and no willpower. To judge from the burden he'd brought home from Drayfield, he was still cheating, too.

'Isn't that Felix's handwriting, darling?'

'Mm. He did *The Winter's Tale* last term.'

'So you're copying his essay?'

'No! Just reading it. He's brilliant at English. He's brilliant at everything. Except farming, of course. He wants to be an engineer. Either that or – '

Bel frowned suddenly. 'Robin,' she said sharply. 'It's dark.'

'What?'

'It's dark!'

'Yes.' He produced a kindly smile. 'It happens most evenings at this time of year, Mother. The sun comes up in the morning, and sets in the – '

'Hush! What time did Jinny leave Drayfield?'

He shrugged. 'It was about ten-past four when I got there, and they said I'd just missed her.'

'Then she wouldn't have gone to Solomon's, would she? It was already getting dark then, and she hates walking the lanes in the dark.' She frowned and shrugged. 'Oh, well. Perhaps she's popped in on Nurse Stokes.'

She wandered to the sink, filled a saucepan with water, carried it to the stove. 'Er – what am I doing?'

'Cooking supper?'

'Mm?' Bel smiled and drummed her mouth with her fingers. 'Run along there, will you, darling? I'm a bit anxious. It's so odd for her to stay out after dark.'

'Mother! It's freezing out there! My ears haven't warmed up yet!'

'Who saved you the lion's share of the anchovy toast?'

He pulled a face. 'All right. I'm going. But if my ears drop off, you'll know who to blame!'

He was back in ten minutes to say that Nurse Stokes had gone out. Bel glanced around the kitchen, biting her lip. It was nearly six o'clock. She'd put the cottage pie in the oven, but nothing else was done, and if Miles and the land girls came home, frozen, to find that supper wasn't ready . . .

'Damn,' she muttered. 'I'll have to . . . Robin, ring everyone who has a telephone. I'll pop across to Briar Cottage and see if Mrs Carter . . .'

Except to grope her way to the monthly WI meeting, Bel rarely went out during blackout. On cloudy nights the darkness was total, rendering the familiar daytime landmarks as invisible as if they weren't there at all — until you fell over them. But tonight the sky was clear and a half moon, while giving insufficient light for one to actually see, at least gave a shadowy outline to the world. The land girls, four of whom walked out to Solomon's and Joss Radnor's farms in total darkness, had memorised the route down to its last stick and stone, but Bel, having lived in the village all her married life, still had to feel her way with hands and feet, counting her steps.

Briar Cottage was at the far end of the square, commanding a view — in daylight — of the entire centre of the village. Mrs Carter used that view to its fullest advantage and had become known, since her departure from Drayfield, as 'a woman who didn't miss much'. Her job as postwoman gave her an even deeper insight into people's lives, and she was not averse to telling what she knew. Even Miles's 'little tantrum' hadn't escaped her: she'd actually asked him if he was feeling better the next time she'd seen him. Damn cheek!

As Drayfield had once done, Briar Cottage smelled of lavender and beeswax, and the moon, as Mrs Carter opened the door, picked up a bright sheen of polish on the passage floor.

'Bel Huntley,' Bel announced briskly, knowing herself to be little more than a silhouette in the doorway. 'I seem to have mislaid Jinny, Mrs Carter. She's not here, is she?'

Until now, she'd been more cross than anxious, but as Jean gasped and clapped a hand to her mouth, the balance changed.

'Oh, my God! Where can she be, Mrs Huntley, at this time of night?'

Bel smiled nervously. 'Er – it's barely six o'clock. No need for panic, I'm sure. I thought she might be playing with Valerie. They do lose track of the time, don't they?'

'But they know when it's *dark*! Oh, dear, oh, dear, what can have happened to her? Wait, I'll get my coat and help you – '

'No, no.' Bel caught her arm. 'I wouldn't dream of it. She's probably gone home while I've been out. Good night, Mrs Carter, I'm sorry to have troubled you.'

'You could try the Holfords! Jinny sometimes plays with their Eileen. Oh, I do hope you find her!'

Frowning, Bel tried the Holfords. She tried the Rectory, her heart fluttering. She'd been all right until Mrs Carter had flown to panic-stations. Now she was scared.

Robin had come up with nothing from his telephone enquiries and, merely to give herself time to think, Bel washed the sprouts, chopped the carrots and laid the table for supper. She found that she was trembling and close to tears, although only a small part of that was a real fear for Jinny's safety. The rest was fear of what Miles would say when he came home and found no supper on the table and no Jinny . . .

Miles stood with sagging shoulders and listened in silence to his wife's garbled account of Jinny's disappearance. She was laughing nervously, wringing her hands, having to stop every few seconds to keep her teeth from chattering. 'Oh, I'm sure she's all right!' she gasped. 'She's probably called in on someone and forgotten the time, but – ' Her hands fluttered and she clenched them under her chin. 'But – but she hasn't . . . She doesn't usually . . . She hates being out in the dark, Miles!'

He closed his eyes. Robin had telephoned all the farms, but there were dozens of cottages all around the valley where Jinny could be 'hiding'. Unless she found her way home in the meantime, the search was likely to take hours. He thought he'd finally taught Jinny to tell the time. Well, he'd teach her now, once and for all!

He was so cold! He'd spent almost every hour of an endless day thinking of this moment: home, food, a chair by the fire and a chance to read the newspaper. And now this!

Bel's knees buckled, and she sat down very suddenly, jamming her knuckles between her teeth. It was only then that Miles realised how frightened she was, and his thoughts moved on a little, away from his own needs to hers and Jinny's. Why had Jinny not come home? There were many places she could have gone, many people who might be sheltering her . . .

But Jack Carter had fallen into the river, knocked himself out on a rock and drowned in three inches of water. The river hadn't even been deep enough to get him wet all over. Now, after months of rain . . .

Miles imagined Jinny dead. Drowned, like her father. There had never been any doubt in his mind that Jack was Jinny's father – her hair, her eyes, they had not come from the Huntley line – yet now, as he imagined her dead, he knew that none of it mattered. What was blood, after all? What did it mean? For more than three years, until he'd known about Jack, Miles had adored that child, adored her hair, her eyes, every single thing about her. Her blood hadn't counted for anything, then. She'd been such a wonderful kid: so bright and happy, so full of herself.

And what was she now? What had he made her? In many ways, she was his child now far more than she'd been before.

Everything she was, she was because *he* had made her so. Shy, gawky and uncertain, forever searching out the company and approval of others. Nurse Stokes, Solomon and Prissie, the Clares. She loved them all.

She loved Miles, too. He knew it, had always known it and, in spite of all his 'wisdom' to the contrary, had used her love against her, to punish her for . . . For not being *his*.

She was out there now because of him. No child of his would have been allowed out alone on a freezing day like this. Two miles to Drayfield and two miles back . . . Dear God, anything could have happened to her!

He laid his hand on Bel's shoulder and squeezed it firmly. 'All right,' he said wearily. 'Leave it to me. I'll find her.'

In all her life, Jinny had never once given a thought to how her body was made. For all she'd known or cared she was held together by cotton gussets, like a doll. Now she knew otherwise. She was joined together in such a way that when she moved her shoulders her leg hurt. When she shivered her leg hurt. When she yelled out for help her leg hurt. She was like something knitted from a single thread. When a stitch was dropped at one end, the whole thing began to unravel. She had never been so frightened in her life.

The pain was very bad, like a cold knife slowly paring the flesh from her bones. She was pretty sure now that she hadn't been shot, that the leg was merely broken. But it made no difference. She couldn't move and would certainly die – simply freeze to death – if someone didn't find her.

In spite of the pain, she shouted as loudly as she could, time after time: 'Daddy! Mr Chard! Daddy! Help me!' but she'd known all along that it was futile. The centre of Home Farm was barely a hundred yards from where she lay, but the wind was against her. The farm buildings lay between. The cows would be shuffling (and splattering), the land girls talking and laughing . . . No one would hear.

The cold had been almost unendurable even before she'd fallen. Now it became a maddening agony which made her head whirl with terror. At various times when she'd been very unhappy, she'd thought about killing herself and given up each time because she hadn't been able to think of anything painless enough. She'd never thought of lying down in a field and freezing to death, but now that she was doing it, cutting her throat seemed quite an easy alternative. Freezing was terrible. It was terrible. It was worse than having a broken leg.

People didn't die of broken legs. They died of cold, not of broken legs. Therefore, the leg didn't matter. The pain didn't matter. She must move.

She began to crawl towards the stile, dragging herself along with clawing hands and levering elbows. One inch. Two. Three. She screamed each time. After the third, she fainted.

It was pitch dark the next time she opened her eyes. She didn't feel as cold now and the leg didn't ache as much. She felt very tired. She had no idea how long she'd lain there. It could have been minutes. Or hours. Had everyone gone home?

'Daddy,' she whispered.

He didn't like her to be late. He'd be cross, he'd make such a fuss that everyone would put their coats on and come out to look . . .

No. That was last year. He'd made her promise never to be late again. He'd forgiven her. He'd said, 'We can begin afresh.' But they hadn't. He'd fallen downstairs and lost his temper, and afterwards it had been the same as before, when he hadn't cared if she was late or not. Oh, she'd been so *good*. She'd tried so *hard*. And he hadn't even noticed.

He wouldn't notice if she was late tonight. Bel would notice, but that didn't matter. Bel was powerless. Almost as powerless as Jinny was. She pretended to be strong, just as Jinny did. She pretended independence and made swift, firm decisions which declared to the world, 'I can manage alone.' But it didn't mean anything. When Miles spoke, Bel obeyed, just as Jinny did. They were like the puppets in one of Jinny's story books who, in the secret world of their cupboard in the attic, lived quite different lives from the lives the puppeteer gave them.

There was a wicked witch with blackened teeth and a wart on her nose who, when the puppeteer pulled her strings, shrieked and clawed her fingers and cast dreadful spells on everyone. But in the cupboard in the attic she was just a kind old granny. She was good and gentle and everyone loved her. She *wasn't* wicked really! If the puppeteer had only understood that, if he'd just once looked further than the wart on the end of her nose . . .

'Daddy!' Jinny wailed. 'Oh, Daddy, *please*!'

The silence was terrible and, as she listened to it, she felt something inside her die. It just sank away, and left an empty space. She was not too young, not at all too young, to know that its name was hope.

They had all, at one time or another, taken the short cut home from Drayfield. But it was Violet who remembered it. Just as they'd all put their coats on to search every other point of the compass, she'd said, 'Now wait a moment. It's freezing out there, and Jinny isn't fool enough to go wandering off just anywhere in weather like this. Since Robin didn't meet her in Drayfield Lane, she might have taken the short cut. Try that first.'

If they hadn't, she would have died.

At two o'clock in the morning Miles awoke, shivering, and knelt beside the hearth to place, with infinite care, a few more logs on the library fire. Behind him, on the sofa, Jinny mumbled, turned and cried out in pain.

'Ssh,' Miles glanced at her over his shoulder, and saw that her eyes were open, wide and bewildered. She'd forgotten where she was. 'Hush. Lie still, there's a good girl. Close your eyes. Go to sleep.'

'Where's Mummy?'

'Gone to bed for a few hours. It's all right. I won't leave you.'

Her face crumpled and she began to weep, very quietly. Miles had discovered, only last summer, that Jinny always did her weeping in silence. He'd stood outside her room waiting for it to happen, and she'd done it without a sound. He hadn't known a thing about it until she'd come down a few hours later, her eyes red and swollen, her nose all aglow. Yet when she was tiny she'd bawled her head off, knowing that the minute he heard her, he'd be there.

He was here now. He leaned over her and stroked her hair. 'Does your leg hurt?'

'No. Not when I keep still.'

He smiled. 'Keep still, then. Are you warm enough?'

She nodded, but the tears still flowed. 'I feel so strange! Can't I go to bed, Daddy?'

'The doctor advised against it, just for tonight. You got very cold, out there, and we aren't sure you won't be ill as a result. We have to keep an eye on you.'

'But my leg isn't broken?'

'No . . . You've torn the ligaments behind your knee, which is almost as bad, I'm afraid.'

'I don't know what linaments are.'

'Ligaments. They're the strings which hold your bones together. When they break . . . Well, your knee will be rather floppy for a while.'

'Like a puppet,' Jinny murmured.

'Hmm. Yes, I suppose so.' He patted her hand. 'Never mind. You're safe now, that's the important thing. Try to sleep.'

He'd put on his pyjamas and dressing gown and two pairs

of thick woolly socks. Now he wrapped his legs in a blanket and sat down again, staring into the fire.

'Aren't you cross?' Jinny whispered.

'No. Not at all.'

She'd closed her eyes again and her breathing was rhythmic enough almost to convince him that she was asleep, but she was frowning and her fist was clenched hard around her handkerchief. Her hands had been swollen like cats' paws and as purple as raw meat when they'd found her. Even now they looked bruised and stiff and it would be days before the ache of remembered cold would leave them. He knew about that ache but he'd never in his life wanted Jinny to share it. Poor little kid . . .

It would never happen again. Whoever her father had been didn't matter any more. In the world's eyes, in Jinny's eyes and, from now on, in Miles's eyes, she was *his* daughter.

He smiled ruefully. Easy to say. Not so easy to do. Six years of discord lay between them, and while six years meant little enough to him, they were the best part of Jinny's life. Could she remember a time when she'd sat on his knee, been rocked in his arms? Could she remember a time when they'd been all the world to each other?

No. She was frowning now, not just because she was shocked and injured, but because she was lying in the care of a stranger. Even when she'd been barely conscious, she'd stiffened at his touch and shrunk from the sound of his voice. She trusted him no more than a rabbit trusts a snake.

'Daddy?'

'Hmm?'

'Were you cross when I didn't come home?'

'No.' He slid off his chair and sat beside her, lifting tear-wet tendrils of hair from her face. 'It wasn't your fault, Jinny.'

He wanted to call her darling, but couldn't. He'd realised, tonight, that he had never stopped loving her, had only stopped wanting to love her, or to love anyone at all. He had lost too much, been hurt too much. There was something very hard in him, now, that would never be softened.

But he needed it. It was like his backbone. Without it, he'd have nothing to do but lie down and die.

Chapter Fourteen

It was early March before Jean saw Jinny again. She was walking to church with her parents, her grandmother and young Simon, who was home on a three-day leave and looking very handsome in his RAF blue. Jinny was still limping. So was Miles, but he always limped in the winter months: an old war-wound, nothing at all to do with Jean.

Not, of course, that Jinny's limp had anything to do with Jean! Of course it hadn't. It was the sort of thing that was always happening to kids. Ronnie Bey had fallen off the roof of his grandad's shed only a few weeks back and broken his arm, and Jean didn't feel in the least responsible for that, so why should she feel responsible for Jinny? She shouldn't. She didn't. She was just *interested*, that was all.

The lace curtains in Jean's front parlour were going ripe. They wouldn't take another wash, and replacements weren't to be found nowadays. The people who had once made lace curtains were now making aeroplane wings or some such, and Jean wasn't sure what she'd do without hers. They allowed you to stand so close to the window you could see the colour of people's eyes as they went by. Miles's eyes were as blue as the sky, his face wind-burned to a lovely hazelnut brown. He turned and smiled down at Jinny, taking her elbow to help her off the kerb. How he kept his teeth so nice had always been a mystery to Jean. He was no chicken – coming up to fifty, surely? – but they were all his own: you could see the fillings when he laughed.

'Jinny's got a new coat,' Evelyn remarked enviously. 'How many coupons do you think that took? It's ever so nice, Mum. I'd like a coat that colour.'

'You won't get one, then. That's one of Bel's old ones, made over. Look at the quality of the cloth! I've never seen Jinny look so nice. She's ever so pale, though, isn't she? I hope she's not sickening for something . . .'

'Made over? That's never! It's – '

'It is. Penny Clare told me. Mrs Huntley took it to that tailor chap over at Pensford. Phew, when I think of all the clothes she must have stowed away, she could probably keep us all dressed like that for the next ten years! You should have seen her in the old days, Evie. Never saw her in the same frock twice. Beautiful, she was . . .'

'Mm. Doesn't Simon look handsome? And Robin's *smashing*, Mum. He'll be home for Easter soon, won't he?'

'Oooh!' Jean laughed and nudged her with her elbow. 'I thought you were mad keen on Felix Clare!'

'I am.' Evelyn grinned. 'It's nice to have a choice, though, Mum.'

'You be careful, or people'll be calling you a flirt. Oh, here comes Bert Tomkins. He looks so different on Sundays, doesn't he? I wonder who does his collars. I used to think he wore paper ones, but I sat next to him in church last time I went, and they're proper starched linen! He never does that for himself. There's a knack with collars.' She turned from the window suddenly. 'Quick, where's my shoes? I think I'll go to church.'

Evelyn sniggered. 'He'll never tell you, Mum.'

'Tell me what?'

'Who does his collars. I bet it's Miss Bright. She goes in

for stamps every day, practically, and she always comes out with a smile on her face.'

'Puh!' Rather to her astonishment, Jean found her face reddening. 'She's ten years older than Bert! Anyway, how would she know how to do collars? She's never even been married!'

She piled into her shoes, jammed her hat on her head, grabbed her coat and was still putting it on when she went out through the front door. 'Peel the spuds for me while I'm gone, will you, love? And it's Janet's turn to lay the table. Aargh!' She dashed back into the passage again, scrabbling in her bag. 'No lipstick!'

Evelyn watched as her mother smeared an economical trace of carmine on her upper lip and wobbled both lips together to spread it evenly around. 'There! All shipshape and Bristol fashion!'

'You be careful!' Evelyn called mischievously as Jean fled down the garden path. 'You'll get called a flirt!'

Jean was astonished all over again. What on earth did the child mean – that *she* was chasing after Bert Tomkins? Never! Oh, he was nice enough, on the surface, but so had Jack been, on the surface. And you never got beneath the surface with a man until you'd married him and it was too damn late! No. Never again. Not that Jean hadn't thought about it. She had. But then she'd thought, What did his wife die of? and that was always enough to stop her in her tracks. Men were beasts, and that was all there was to it.

There were barely fifty yards between Briar Cottage and the church gate. Jean ran that far and then slowed to catch her breath, noticing with relief that not everyone had gone in. It was a lovely day: sunny and quite mild, although there was still a bit of a nip in the wind. Two of the Army officers from the Manor House were chatting to the Huntleys, and one of them must have said something to Jinny, because she shook her head and looked at her feet, too shy to answer. Miles put his arm around her shoulder and bent his head to whisper something in her ear, and she smiled and shrugged away, blushing.

There was something odd about that. Jean couldn't think what it was, but there was definitely something *odd* about it.

'Good morning!' Jean bustled among them, pretending surprise to see Jinny out and about at last. 'Well! Hello, Jinny! Aren't you looking fine, today! How's the poor leg?'

'Much better, thank you.'

'She's ever so pale, though!' Jean laid her hand on Bel's arm, and it wasn't until she felt it stiffen under her fingers that she realised she'd never touched her before: not even in the old days, when they'd been almost . . . friends. She hastily withdrew, laughed brightly and went into church, her eyes seeking frantically for Bert, not because she liked him so very much, but because she suddenly felt so terribly alone.

Bert was in the middle of a pew, with people wedging him in on either side, and Jean sat at the back, bowed her head in the appropriate manner and moved her lips, as if in prayer. But she wasn't praying. She was seething with a combination of hurt and disappointment out of all proportion to anything that had happened.

Why had Bel stiffened up like that? What had it meant? Miles could be a bit haughty if you overstepped the mark with him, but Bel had never seemed to be aware that any mark existed. Look at the way she'd set up that soup-kitchen in the Depression, the way she'd chummed up with Nurse Stokes (they were still as thick as thieves) and the way she mixed with everyone at the WI, high, low and middling, treating everyone the same. There was no side to her at all, and if Jack had been right about just one thing in his life, it had been that.

Jack . . .

No, Jean had gone over that a million times, but she'd never really believed it. How could she? Miles wasn't the type to put up with it. Give another man's kid his home, his name?

Support a woman who'd made a cuckoo of him? A proud man like that? Never!

They were just going into their pew. Old Mrs Huntley first, then Simon and Bel. Jinny was having trouble going in sideways and Miles slid his arm around her waist and bent his head to say something, bringing his face very close to hers, just as he'd done outside. It looked so... odd. So warm and protective...

Then it hit her. Since Jinny was just a little, tiny thing, scarcely more than a baby, Jean had never seen her father touch her and talk to her like this. And what had Jean said just before Bel had gone all stiff and remote? *She's ever so pale!*

Oh, dear God! Jinny was ill! She was dying! They'd *said* she could get pneumonia or something after lying out in that freezing wind half the night, but when the risk of pneumonia had passed, Jean had completely forgotten about the 'something'. Yet people died of it all the time! There were sanatoriums full of them, all over the country, dying like flies!

The Rector began the service, his voice booming softly through the quiet, sunlit church, but Jean heard not a word of it. She was on her knees and praying in earnest, 'Dear God, oh, please God, I'm sorry! I didn't mean it! Please, God, oh, please God, don't let Jinny die!'

The war had made Miles prosperous again. The country needed every ounce of food he and his tenants could produce and, as bombed-out families evacuated from the cities, he could have let every property he possessed ten times over. It seemed a terrible irony to Bel that, now there was enough money to go around, rationing prevented anyone from spending it. But she'd beaten budgeting long before the war began. It had been a matter of having to. Miles had given notice that unless she managed he'd disown her debts, and although she hadn't quite believed him (it would have meant publishing his intentions in the newspapers) she hadn't dared risk being wrong.

Since then, she'd asked him for nothing. She'd trained herself so thoroughly in the ways of independence that it had become almost an act of willpower to ask him the time of day. But when the blackout curtain on the landing window fell into holes, she was beaten. Muriel couldn't be persuaded to go that far up a ladder.

'Do you think you could do it, Miles? Would you have time?'

Logic informed her that asking him this was not the same as asking for money. It wasn't even the same as asking him to share the *Evening Post* when he'd spent all day foaming at the mouth to get at it. But it felt just as bad. It felt even worse when he raised one eyebrow and remarked dryly, 'You're not afraid of heights, darling.'

She swallowed. 'No . . . But that curtain's been there an awful long time, Miles. And it's . . . spring.'

'Spring?' Both eyebrows went up. She could have hit him. He knew precisely what she meant and was pretending not to. Spring and autumn were the times when the spiders came out. Bel had no idea where they came from, or why they insisted upon doing it on such a regular basis. All she knew was that she was terrified of the dratted things. In the old days, Bel had asked Miles to get rid of them. Now she usually asked Muriel, who claimed she 'wod'n scerra nuffin' – except ladders.

Bel drummed her fingers on the table, gritted her teeth, looked at the wall and said grimly, 'If I come face to face with – with a – with a spider when I'm perched at the top of a ladder, Miles . . . I'll – I'll – I'll fall straight off it and break my neck!'

'Good Lord, are you still afraid of spiders, darling?'

He looked genuinely surprised, and Bel supposed she could scarcely blame him for that. She'd beaten budgeting, cooking, housekeeping, gardening and – at a pinch – celibacy. She'd even learned to scream quietly when she saw a spider. But to take down handfuls of the damn things with the blackout curtain? *No.*

Miles went up the ladder. Muriel stood at the bottom, with a broom and dustpan at the ready. Bel dived into the morning room and slammed the door, resolving not to come out again until it was all over.

Violet was writing letters at the table by the window. She looked up as Bel came in and murmured cynically, 'And you a country girl, born and bred.'

'Hmph! You're afraid of bulls!'

'That's quite different, darling. Bulls are dangerous.'

'So are spiders if they make you fall off a ladder!'

She sat on the sofa and tucked up her feet, just in case any escapees should scuttle under the door.

'Is Jinny watching the proceedings?' Violet asked sweetly. 'Or have you infected *her* with this silly phobia of yours?'

Bel chose to ignore that. Jinny had gone down to the copse, looking for primroses, and Bel had been more than glad to let her go, if only in hope that the fresh air would put some colour in her cheeks and a smile on her face. She'd accepted more than two months of forced inactivity with brave resignation, but since her walk to church last Sunday she was getting restless again. A few more weeks, and she'd be wanting to take up her old wanderings. She didn't yet know that Miles had once more taken her 'in hand' and Bel predicted trouble when he broke the news . . .

'Oh, my God,' Violet gasped suddenly. 'It's that woman again! If she asks me just once more how Jinny is – ! What business is it of hers, for heaven's sake? What's she so worried about? Torn ligaments aren't infectious!'

Bel frowned and crept to the window. Jean Carter? Again? And she was on her bike, which meant . . .

Her heart thumped suddenly. 'We've had the afternoon post, haven't we, Vio?'

Violet's eyes widened. 'Well, yes . . . I'm just answering – '
Their eyes met. Bel turned cold.

'She probably . . . just . . . wants a recipe for . . . something.'

'Get Miles off that ladder,' Violet said.

The spiders didn't matter any more. Bel wasn't afraid of them. They could have crawled over her by the hundred and she wouldn't have cared. Jean Carter was crying, and the small buff envelope she held in her hand was a telegram. Mr Tomkins would have told her the news it contained, but still Bel could have slapped her to Kingdom Come for exhibiting such grief for sons not her own.

'I'm so sorry, Mrs Huntley! Oh, Mr Huntley, I'm so sorry!'

Miles said nothing. His hands didn't even shake. He opened the envelope, read the short message it contained, handed it to Bel and then walked away.

Andrew Huntley was missing, presumed dead.

Bel felt nothing at all, at first. The terror she'd felt a moment ago had gone, leaving only a faint, tingling sensation in the pit of her stomach. But as Jean Carter continued to sob, apologise and – as was her duty – demand broken-heartedly, 'Any reply?' it all began to seem rather funny. Bel had lived in dread of this since the war had begun. Her son . . . Her eldest son was dead. The son she'd loved for twenty-two years . . . was dead.

She couldn't even believe it, let alone shed a tear. Yet here was Jean Carter – the bloody *postwoman*! – bawling her eyes out for a boy she'd barely known.

Muriel came behind her and pulled her clear of the door.

Then, 'Fanks,' she muttered. 'There ain't no answer,' and slammed the door in Mrs Carter's face.

Bel giggled. She pulled her face straight. She giggled again. The floor of the hall was littered with cobwebbed blackout material, the landing window smeared with the dust and dirt of three years' neglect. It would all have to be cleaned and the new curtain be put in place before darkness fell . . .

Violet was staring at her as if into the mouth of a volcano that would presently erupt. But Bel didn't feel in the least like a volcano. She felt like a flower which had cast its seed upon stone: weak and useless, wasted, empty. She wondered how Miles was feeling. She wondered where he was and what he was thinking. Then, rather strangely, she saw in her mind's eye the white silk nightgown she'd worn on her wedding night, and felt Miles's hands, stroking her thighs. She'd wept, then... She'd been so scared and excited, so awed... So in love.

She loved him still. She *loved* him. How could she grieve alone – how could Miles grieve alone – for the son they had made together? 'Miles,' she whispered. 'Where's Miles, Vio?'

'He's gone out, darling. He... He needs to be alone, I suppose.'

Bel swallowed. She nodded. Yes, damn him, he needed to be alone. He always had, so why should this be any different? Why should he care about her feelings, now, when he'd never cared before?

'Oh, well,' she said flatly. 'Pass the bucket, Muriel. We'd better get this dratted window finished, hadn't we?'

A freak summer storm had flattened the summerhouse last year, but its foundations were still there, as was a short flight of wooden steps which were almost as good as a garden seat. It was still too cold to be sitting out of doors, but this was the only place Miles knew where he wouldn't be disturbed. No one came here now. The ornamental gardens had gone to rack and ruin, but the pool was still intact and at least some of the carp had survived the winter.

They didn't know there was a war on. They didn't know Andrew was dead. Missing, *presumed* dead. But one didn't allow oneself to hope. One wasn't stupid enough. Hope was a scourge in situations like this... Best not to have any.

Andrew was dead.

God, how hard it was to believe! Yet he'd looked like death the last time he'd been home: so gaunt, so tired, so *empty*. Save for his desperate need for sleep, Miles had known that, after three years of war, Andrew had gone far beyond feeling anything. He was punch-drunk, so accustomed to living in terror for his life that he wasn't even terrified any more. Miles knew about that. Beyond a certain point you became an automaton, doing everything – even kissing your own mother – just because that was what was expected of you. You smiled, you laughed, you complained of the cold or of the food, you even mourned your dead, because *that was what was expected of you*.

A golden shadow passed under the surface of the pool and was gone. Miles smiled and stared at his hands. He felt nothing. His son was dead and he felt nothing except . . . Yes, relief that it had happened and he needn't fear it any more.

Miles didn't believe in God. His faith had left him many years ago, and he went to church now in much the same spirit as fishermen drop anchor in a safe port. The Christian church and Christian civilisation were as closely knit as a man's flesh to his bones: lose one, lose the other. If Miles worshipped anything it was the idea of civilisation: law, respect, decency and honour. But God? No.

Yet now he turned his face up to the sky and spoke, very softly. 'I never wanted sons, you see. I wanted a daughter.'

He'd always said, 'a daughter' in the singular because he'd had little hope of having one, let alone two or three. But ten wouldn't have been too many. He could have given himself to a family of girls, trusted them – as far as one could trust anyone – to survive. He had never trusted the boys that far. On the day Andrew was born, Miles had seen him lying dead in a trench, and had known from that moment that even if his death was not inevitable it must be anticipated, prepared for, guarded against . . .

Miles had guarded himself from loving his sons too much,

just as he'd guarded them from being loved. Nannies, prep school and public school were all an accepted part of the class they'd been born into, but Miles had had all that and hated it. Given a guarantee of peace he would have been far gentler with them, but as one who had been hardened by the traditions of his class he'd known that the best thing he could do for his sons was to harden them in the same way.

He'd recognised, during the last war, how well he'd been trained for it. Pain, loneliness, bad food, harsh discipline and comfortless conditions... The Army was not very different from a first-class public school and Miles had not been hurt by it as some men – Leonard Clare for example – had been hurt. Raised in a warm and loving home, never separated from his family until he'd joined up, Leonard had been as soft as a snail without its shell, and although he'd survived, he'd returned from that war a gibbering wreck.

Miles had returned empty: stripped of virtually everything he considered human. He'd had no sentiments left, no feelings. His father had died, his brothers and every friend he'd ever had had been killed, his mother had changed almost beyond his recognition. Yet none of it had mattered, except... The only thing which had mattered was that nothing really mattered.

Andrew was dead.

Andrew was dead, and the most grievous thing about it was that Miles could feel no grief. He was like a light that had been switched off at the mains, knowing his function, yet having no means to fulfil it. He had loved Andrew. He *had* loved Andrew. Andrew, his first-born, the flesh of his flesh... was dead.

Miles shook his head. He wondered what Bel was doing now, how she was feeling, where she was. He imagined her in her room, alone on their marriage bed, sobbing her heart out for their lost child, her baby. He envied her. He wished he could be with her now, not only in person, but in spirit: feeling the same grief, shedding the same tears for the boy they had made together.

But how could he go to her like this: stone-cold and empty? He had nothing to offer, nothing to say. Even holding her in his arms would seem unnatural, and would perhaps be distasteful to her after their long years of estrangement.

She had wept so many tears alone. She had become harder too, and so independent that, save for the allowance he gave her, he'd begun to feel rather less necessary to her existence than the pattern on the wallpaper. He had rejected her and now felt rejected, lonely, left out in the cold.

The business with the spiders had come as a curiously pleasant surprise, making him feel needed again . . . God, he'd left that job half-done and the bloody ARP warden wouldn't accept mere bereavement as an excuse!

He stood up, and wandered along the edge of the pool, seeing glimpses of his own reflection between the scummy clots of blanket-weed that floated on the surface. He had worried himself to death about this pool when the children were still small enough and daft enough to have drowned in it . . .

He thought blandly, now there's one less to worry about, and suddenly it hit him: a great, twisting agony which almost knocked him off his feet.

Andrew was dead!

He turned, his hand pressed to his heart. The world, which had been so quiet a few moments ago, now seemed hectic and noisy. Everything was moving, everything was wrong! He must sit down again, pull his thoughts into order, reclaim a part of himself from the ruin of his life. He wished . . . ! He wanted . . . ! Oh, God, he wanted Bel! He couldn't bear another minute of this without her!

Suddenly he was running, and didn't slow his steps until he came in sight of the front door and saw the foot of the ladder he'd left in the hall. He must finish that job... But not yet, not until he'd found Bel, touched her, held her.

He halted, closing his eyes, remembering the first time he'd held her in his arms. She'd been so young and strong, so untouched by suffering. He'd had no thoughts in his mind beyond his natural passions, yet the solace she'd given him had had nothing to do with lust, love, or romance. She'd taken his pain away. She'd taken it *away*!

Save for the dusty tumble of old curtains he had left on the floor, everything was precisely as he'd left it. Muriel was still there with her broom, Violet still seated at the hall table, her hands clenched firmly in her lap. She met his eyes, searching his face for a sign of grief; but he'd mastered it for the moment. He wouldn't let her see.

'Where's Bel?' he asked quietly, and was amazed when his mother shrugged and directed her gaze to the top of the ladder.

'There,' Bel said flatly. 'That should do it. Try the curtain pole, Muriel, see if it runs.'

Miles was speechless. He could only stare. Muriel tried the curtain pole. Bel gave the window frame a last, housewifely flick with her duster and came nimbly down the ladder. She didn't look at Miles. She didn't look at anyone. Her face was very calm, very white and still, but her eyes were blazing with a rage Miles had never imagined her capable of.

For a brief, bewildered moment he thought she was angry because he'd left the blackout unfinished. He caught her arm and began helplessly, 'I would have done it – ' and then staggered against the wall as she threw him off.

'Leave me alone.' Her voice was hushed, deep, pulsing with quiet venom. 'I don't need you for *anything* any more.'

Chapter Fifteen

It was going on half-past eight. The young ones had gone to bed but were still larking about, bouncing on each other's beds, telling the latest jokes and 'dying' laughing. Jean supposed she should be grateful to have such happy kids, but just at this moment she wanted to run upstairs and knock their cruel, insensitive heads together. How could they laugh? Andrew Huntley was dead!

She'd left the leather-cloth couch at Drayfield: it had been too big to fit into the parlour at Briar Cottage, and anyway, Jean had hated it. Ever since she'd found Bel's brooch down the back she'd hated it. But she'd kept the armchairs. She'd covered them with a nice cretonne: pink and blue on a beige ground with maroon piping. She'd worried about the maroon. She'd thought it might run in the wash and been very careful the first time: best soap flakes, no washing soda, water just tepid, same as for woollies.

Andrew Huntley was dead.

She huddled against the back of the armchair, nursing a cushion to her chest. She rocked it in her arms, like a baby. She knew what it was to lose a child. She had lost a child she had never known: yet still the grief of it tormented her. But to have known him, loved him, to have heard his voice and shared his laughter . . . Oh, God, how could Bel bear it? How could Miles bear it? Pilots burned to death and fell out of the sky screaming, in flames. Everyone knew that. Bad enough to have your baby carried off in a newspaper, but to have him carried off in flames?

It was almost dark. She stood up and went to the window to keep an eye on Evelyn as she said goodnight to Felix Clare. No kissing. She'd told Evie that. And no walking beyond the outskirts of the village. At fourteen, she was too young for that sort of thing: roaming about with boys where no one could see what she got up to. Village busybodies had their uses. If Felix took Evelyn even a yard too far down one of the lanes, Jean would hear of it, double sharp, and send him off with a flea in his ear which would itch for a month of Sundays!

But oh, he was such a nice-looking boy! He'd taken after his father in everything but the nose, and while Penny Clare's enormous hooked beak looked positively outlandish on her, Felix carried it rather well. Not that looks mattered . . . She kept telling Evie that: 'Looks don't matter, Evie! Handsome is as handsome does! People can be beautiful on the outside and as ugly as sin in their souls!' She always wanted to say, 'Like your father,' but didn't like to. It wasn't respectable. Never speak ill of the dead.

Evie didn't listen, of course. She was too proud of her good looks to think of her own soul, let alone anyone else's. She had her mother's complexion and her father's long, slender limbs, but her hair was her own: a long, rippling fall of dark auburn which, when it was washed on a sunny morning, had the bright, coppery gleam of a new-minted farthing.

She made most people look drab by comparison, but Felix, although his hair was an undistinguished shade of brown, was more than a match for her, in exactly the way Jean had meant when she said that looks aren't everything. Felix had something inside him which glowed just as brightly as Evie's hair. Intelligence, warmth, a passion for life which animated his face even when he was just standing there, listening to Evie prattling on about nothing. They made a handsome pair. Too young yet, of course, but childhood sweethearts so often became . . .

Their children and their children's children, until their line is ended and nothing that is theirs endures upon the earth.

With a gasp of horror, Jean rapped her knuckles against the window, flung the casement wide and snapped, 'Evie, get in here this minute! It's nearly dark, you wicked girl!'

It was not so dark that she couldn't see the look of astonished fury her daughter sent her and not so dark that she couldn't see Felix colour up like a beetroot before he turned swiftly away, but Jean didn't care. She'd cursed the Huntleys and Andrew was dead! She'd cursed Drayfield and all who lived there! She couldn't let Evie play with that kind of fire!

'Oh, Mum!' Evie stormed through to the parlour, almost in tears. 'You're always telling me to mind my manners and be nice to people, and then you go and – '

'Half-past eight, I said, Evie, and what time is it now?'

'We were back at half-past eight! You saw we were, and you needn't say you didn't, because I saw you poking your nose through the nets!'

'Lace,' Jean corrected sniffily. 'Lace, not nets.' She was proud of her lace, ripe though it was. She was proud of her home. She'd filled it with frills and pretty colours, bits of nice china, bits of brass – everything she had always longed for. *Lace*, not nets! 'And you're too young to be hanging about with boys, leaning on gates, making a spectacle of yourself. I won't have it, Evie, and if he comes calling for you again – '

'He didn't come calling for me! He was just passing! He had to bring Jinny home from Drayfield, and – '

'Jinny? What on earth was Jinny doing down there? She can scarcely walk! And at a time like this – !'

Suddenly she burst into tears. It was too much. Bert was right – of course he was right – curses didn't work. But what was the point of knowing he was right, when all the time you kept thinking, thinking . . . Thinking of Jack! He'd died – he must have done – within half an hour of her uttering those words! But of course Bert was right; he was, he was! Some people were just unlucky . . .

'Mum? Mum, what's wrong?' Evelyn was a good three inches taller than her mother, and when she reached out to touch Jean's arm, the collar of her coat was just at eye-level, glinting with gold. Jean shrieked and clapped a hand to her mouth.

'What's that?'

It was almost dark, and she couldn't switch on the light because she hadn't drawn the blackout. But it was the same size, the same shape, she was certain!

'Evie! What's that on your collar?'

'What? Oh, this. It's a little brooch. Felix found it. It's broken, but – *Mum*! What's *wrong* with you?'

Jean pushed Evelyn backwards into the passage and then into the little kitchen, where – thankfully – the blackout was in place, and she was able to turn the light on. One glance at the brooch and she was sobbing again, although whether with relief or disappointment she couldn't have said. The 'brooch' was just a cheap bit of brass, roughly stamped in the shape of a daisy. A daisy, not a rose . . .

'Mum?'

'Oh . . .' Jean sat down and reached for her hanky. 'I thought . . .'

'What?'

'I had a brooch once, a little gold brooch. Pure gold, it was. I lost it when we lived out at Drayfield. I turned the place upside down after your father died, but I never found it.'

She'd even tried to get the flagstones up, but they were six inches thick in places and each one weighed the best part of a ton. Yet she'd been so desperate to find it! She'd whispered to the snake on the back: 'I conjure thee, oh serpent of old, servant of the wise and begetter of all the wisdom of the earth, take my enemy from me . . .'

She'd whispered to it, spat on it and hurled it away, and she'd never seen the damn . . . the dratted thing again! If she could have found it, she'd have taken it to church, had it blessed, anything to get the curse out of it. Anything to ease her conscience.

She could see it now, hear the little 'ping' as it hit the wall, and then a last glint of gold as it bounced away and fell to the floor. It must have gone down one of the cracks between the flags, but she'd dug between each one with a carving knife, hour after hour on her hands and knees . . .

Miles spent his nights in the twins' room and his days, grey-faced and grim, working every hour God sent. He ate almost nothing. He avoided being alone with his wife and refused to meet her eyes.

Bel had never regretted anything – not even her three-minute affair with Jack Carter – as much as that utterly meaningless rejection of her husband. Immediately the words were out she'd regretted them, but it was too late then. 'I don't need you for anything!' What had possessed her? What in the devil's name had prompted her to say such a thing – then, at the moment when she'd needed him more than ever before in her life? She didn't know. All she knew was that it wasn't true. She needed him for everything. He *was* everything. Without him, although she wept and writhed and beat her pillow until the very feathers ached, she couldn't even mourn her own son. She wept for Andrew and then discovered that she was weeping for Miles. She wept for Miles and then discovered that, in rejecting him, she'd rejected Andrew, too.

There was no sense in any of it. She had lived more than six years without Miles, feeling that they were as remote from one another as they could possibly be without actually living in different countries, divided by the sea. Yet now she realised that they had been much closer than they'd seemed. They'd been tied together by hope – her hope – that one day, if she worked, thought and prayed hard enough, their hurts would be healed and all would be made right again. Yet now, without trying, thinking or praying, she had destroyed it all with a single angry retort.

Angry? Yes. She'd gone up that ladder in a state verging on trance, not feeling anything at all. But she'd come down it in a fury, knowing not only that Andrew was dead but that, thanks to Miles, she'd scarcely known him – her own son! He'd been cared for by a succession of nannies, school masters and house-matrons since the day he was born, and now, twenty-two years later, his own mother wasn't even certain who had died. She could list his childhood diseases, his likes and dislikes, his interests and hobbies. But what had he thought, hoped and feared? Whom had he loved? Bel didn't *know*!

When you sent your son away to school you relinquished such a large part of his life that you could never again say, 'I know him'. And because you knew . . . Because you knew that he would suffer homesickness, loneliness, bullying and beatings . . . Because you knew all that and more – and worse – you almost ceased wanting to know, lest knowing drove you mad. You ceased to have sons. You had visitors for the holidays: people you loved with all your heart, yet dreaded to love because you knew the holidays would end and your heart be broken again. And the boys felt the same, she knew. They had never talked much about school, never confided more than the barest details and only the best of those. Jokes, japes, friends, sporting triumphs . . .

It had been exactly the same with the war: jokes, japes, friends and parties, a girl named Louisa, a girl named Mary. Nothing of fear, grief and danger. They came home exhausted (Simon had fallen asleep face down in his 'welcome home' dinner the last time he'd had leave) and said they were 'a little tired'. Bel had always wanted to ask how they took a pee in an aeroplane – down the bomb-chute? – and had never dared – it was too intimate, too trivial a question to ask of young men you scarcely . . . knew. But Miles would know. They'd talked to him. They'd always talked to him, not – Bel told herself – because they loved him more, but because he'd been through so much of it himself and could be expected to understand. Miles would know. Miles would know . . .

She'd been in bed since nine-thirty and now it was one in the morning. She hadn't slept. She'd been on the edges of sleep once or twice, but nothing restful, nothing which gave her any peace. She kept seeing Andrew's face, but it was always a small boy's face, innocent and shining, never the haggard young man who had died for his country. How had he died? She couldn't bear to think about it, yet did think, trying to envisage the quickest, least painful alternative – a bullet through the head – yet somehow always seeing him burning, screaming, falling to the merciless earth in a rain of flames and ashes.

Missing, presumed dead. Missing . . . But that dreadful little shred of hope was far worse than utter hopelessness, for if he was not dead, perhaps he would be better dead. Alive, but disfigured, crippled, in agony? No, no! In agony, and in the hands of the enemy? *No!* She sat up, sobbing, praying, 'Oh, dear God, let him be dead!'

She jumped out of bed, and dragged on her dressing gown, a smoky pink wool challis (eaten into holes by moth) with an enormous sash she could never find the ends of. She didn't try to find them, just ran down the landing to Andrew's deserted bedroom. She might find him there, tonight. She might just find some part of him there which would tell her, 'This is your son. These are the things you never knew about him. This is the boy you've lost for ever.'

But she didn't find Andrew. She found Miles, sitting in the dark by the uncurtained window, his face eerily lit by the moon.

'Ohh . . .' She swallowed and sniffed, wiped her face with her sleeve. He didn't move and for a moment – until he sighed – she thought he had died, too.

Her heart was thumping. Her breath had stopped in her throat. This moment meant everything. The whole of their lives seemed to be encapsulated in it: all that had passed and all that was still to come. As in the moment she had learned of Andrew's death, she felt like a flower casting its seed, utterly powerless, knowing that only God could say where it might fall.

'Oh, Miles.' Her head went back, her chest heaved with the agony of controlling the grief of years, but the time for control had long gone. The time for pride had gone. 'I didn't mean what I said the other day! I need you, Miles! I need you so much! Please! *Please*, help me!'

He said nothing, just stroked his face with his hand as if to wipe away his own tears.

'Miles?' Bel whispered.

But he said nothing at all.

On her wedding day, according to the photograph, Penny Clare had been a very beautiful woman. She wasn't, now. When Jinny looked at her objectively – which was very hard to do – she saw a woman who was ugly in every particular save for her hands, which were long, white and slender, with skin so translucent you could see all the little blue veins which traced across their backs. Her hair was very thin and mousey with large tracts of pink scalp shining between the artificial curls, her nose was hooked and her protuberant pale blue eyes were magnified by thick, pebble-lensed spectacles, without which she was as good as blind.

It was perhaps due to this failure of vision that much of her ugliness arose, for Penny Clare was not the sort of woman to let herself go. She wore powder and lipstick and, for special occasions, rouge, but the powder, which came from a large, pre-war tub, had turned orange over the years and, since she couldn't see where she was putting it, produced an effect which looked like the latter stages of jungle fever. She had the same trouble with lipstick. Her mouth was evidently not where she'd last seen it and she drew it in, in brilliant carmine, sometimes as much as an inch adrift in every direction.

'There!' she'd say, when she'd finished plastering it all on. 'Now I'm ready to face the world!'

No one had been unkind enough to tell her that the world was killing itself laughing.

Yet everyone loved her. There was something about her which shone through the livid streaks of orange, crimson and candy-floss pink so that, after the first hysterical glance, you became as blind as she was and knew that she was beautiful.

Except for her great talent as a pianist she wasn't clever at all and the number of things she couldn't do were legion. She'd never been to school, and although she'd had a few governesses, none had managed to teach her to add up, spell, or read a map. She'd taught herself to play the piano when she was two and had played it for six hours a day ever after, which was one of the reasons she so rarely did any housework.

But in spite of her ignorance of so many things, she was wise: deeply knowledgeable in the ways of humanity and able to understand its many evils as well as its virtues. She said that music had taught her everything she knew: darkness and light, love and hatred, tenderness and cruelty, happiness and sorrow.

'Summer and winter,' she said gently as Jinny wept salt into her second cup of Bovril. 'You were born in winter, my darling, which means that spring's still to come.'

Jinny sniffed mightily and searched the leg of her knickers for a handkerchief. 'When were you born, Mrs Clare?'

'November, and I had a rotten childhood, too. Spring didn't come for me until I met His Nibs.'

Jinny's tears flowed again. Penny nearly always referred to Leonard as 'His Nibs'. It was a habit she'd developed when she'd first married him and wanted the world to know that, although he couldn't say a single thing without stammering, and although he burst into tears when he heard a loud noise, he was still a man, still important, a hero who had endured worse than death for his King and Country.

Miles had endured the same war and although Jinny had sometimes been irritated by Mr Clare's stammer and been glad that Miles didn't have one, she wished now that he did, if only to show that he had some feelings. Mr Clare had never – not even to his wife – talked about the Great War, but his stammer *proved* that he had suffered and gave his family a clue to the kind of comfort they could give him. He invited them into the dark places of his soul and allowed them to light candles there. Miles – if he suffered – suffered alone and made everyone else suffer alone, too.

'I'm afraid he'll die,' Jinny whispered now.

'Your father? No!'

'Yes. Mummy's worried, too. She cries, you know, all by herself in the kitchen, and it isn't just about Andrew. Daddy eats hardly anything, you see. Sometimes he doesn't even come in for lunch and when he doesn't ... She cries. But she won't *talk* to me the way you do, Mrs Clare! And Daddy doesn't talk to anyone. After supper, last night, he went into the library, Grandma went into the morning room and Mummy went upstairs. And do you know what Muriel said? She said we were like a lot of rabbits in separate hutches. Well, *I* know why rabbits are kept in separate hutches, Mrs Clare. It's to stop them killing each other!'

'But you aren't rabbits, Jinny.' Mrs Clare leaned forward and took Jinny's hand, cradling it, stroking it with her long, pearl-white fingers. 'Did you ever hear your father telling Andrew how much he loved him?'

'No, but – '

'Or the twins? Or Robin?'

'No, but it's different for them! They're men!'

'Yes, it's different for them – not just because your brothers are men but because your father is. Men are inarticulate, Jinny, even when they don't stammer. Their feelings go so deep that they . . . They become like music. Think of a tune – any tune you like – and try to make me hear it without actually singing it or tapping out a rhythm.'

Jinny tried, but it couldn't be done. 'Four slow notes with a high one in the middle,' didn't sound a bit like the opening phrase to *The White Cliffs of Dover*.

'There,' Mrs Clare said gently. 'And that's how it is for your father and His Nibs. They know the music – it plays over and over in their minds, it fills their hearts – but they can't describe it, because words aren't enough. Your father could say he loves you, Jinny. He could say he loved Andrew. But it would be like saying "four slow notes with a high one in the middle"; it wouldn't scratch the surface of what he really feels. The only way anyone can make music is to make *music*. If you can't play an instrument you sing, and if you can't sing, you whistle, and if you can't whistle – ? What then?'

'No music,' Jinny whispered.

'No music unless someone else plays it for you, Jinny. That's what your father needs, someone to play his music for him, as I play – and the boys play – for His Nibs. Have you ever told Miles how much you love him?'

'No . . .'

'Why?'

Jinny shrugged and looked at her feet. 'Because I'm afraid.'

'Have you ever thought that he might be afraid, too? You said you hated it when your leg was so bad he had to carry you up and down stairs. You were shy and embarrassed. You didn't know what to say. Yet he was good to you, gentle and kind, Jinny. Perhaps he didn't know what to say, either. Perhaps *he* was shy.'

'Of me?'

The idea of Miles being shy – and of *her*, of all people –

was more than Jinny could comprehend. But Mrs Clare had talked about music many times before and the idea of its being an expression of feeling wasn't so new that Jinny couldn't – with a little effort – put it into reverse. 'Feelings as music' made sense and made even more sense as, at the end of her walk home from Drayfield, she saw her father in the yard at Home Farm and stood in the gateway watching him, her heart drumming a tune of such fear and pity, such love and longing that she couldn't have put a single part of it into words.

Miles had always been a neat, upright man, quick and graceful in his movements and, even when he was quite cross, pleasant of face. But in the three weeks since Andrew's death he had changed. He was gaunt and tired with stooping shoulders, shuffling feet. But the biggest change was in the expression on his face. He looked like a wild man caught in a cage, enraged and bewildered, frantic to be free.

Yet he was talking quite softly to Mr Chard, who – as usual at this time of year – had brought out all the haymaking machinery to check it over for repair. Mr Chard noticed Jinny and smiled. But Miles just flicked an irritated glance over his shoulder, which was more than enough to make Jinny turn away, defeated. His music was too complicated, too loud and frightening for her to sing. She couldn't catch the tune.

'Jinny!'

Her eyes widening, she turned again. Miles was hurrying across the yard, holding out his hand to her – a commanding hand, which forbade her to move – while still pursuing his conversation with Mr Chard. 'And don't pay him. Tell him to send me the bill at the end of the month. That'll fix his tricks!'

His head snapped around suddenly, his eyes blazing. 'And where have you been, madam?'

Jinny was shocked rigid. Madam? In all her life, Miles had never addressed her in such a way, so harshly and with such contempt. She swallowed and looked at her feet, remembering too late that, although he hadn't forbidden her to go to Drayfield again, he had advised her to keep her wanderings closer to home. But that had been before Andrew had died, when he was being kind and seeming to care that she didn't do too much before her leg was properly mended. Jinny knew that her leg wasn't what mattered now. He was angry about something else.

'Well?'

'I've been . . . to see . . . Mrs Clare.'

'Right.' He took her elbow and hustled her into the office, kicking the door to open it, kicking it closed again. Terrified and trembling, Jinny kept her eyes on the ground and didn't see her father take his riding crop from behind the door. She didn't see it until he held it under her nose and demanded icily, 'Know what this is for, Jinny? It's for teaching nappy horses and disobedient children the error of their ways. *My* children don't disobey me.'

Jinny's face became very cold and she knew she'd turned white with shock. Miles was not the type of man to whip either his horses or his children. He'd struck Robin once – a careless back-handed slap, accompanied by a laughing reminder to 'Mind your manners,' and although it had hurt, Robin had laughed too, and dodged swiftly away, saying only, 'Whoops! Sorry, Dad. Slip of the tongue.'

Miles was not the type of man to whip his children . . . But he had changed. The dark music he'd buried inside him for so long had come too close to the surface. Anything could happen now.

'Well? What have you to say for yourself?'

It was a difficult question, having too many answers, none of which Jinny felt capable of articulating and too few of which, in his present mood, Miles would want to hear. 'For herself' she wanted to say that her brother was dead, her mother in tears, her grandmother a stranger and her father . . .

worse than a stranger. She wanted to say that, needing comfort, understanding and advice and finding none of them at home, she'd had to go elsewhere or go mad with loneliness. She wanted to say that she was not crass enough to trouble her parents with her grief when theirs was so much worse, and that she would have done anything to comfort them had they just once recognised that she needed comfort, too. She wanted to say . . .

Miles tapped the loop of the whip against his boot and Jinny caught her breath and whispered, 'I'm sorry, Daddy.'

'Sorry isn't enough!'

Jinny flinched and stopped breathing, listening to the echo of his voice in her mind. *Sorry isn't enough.* It was the sort of thing grown-up people said all the time, the sort of thing she'd heard her teacher say when she wanted explanations, not apologies. But Miles didn't sound like a teacher. He sounded like a child, spiteful and triumphant, warming up for a fight in the corner of the school playground, *wanting* to fight!

She knew then that he would beat her and that nothing she could say or do would stop him. He hated her. He always had, and now there was nothing left except to hate him in return. It would be easy enough to do. All her life he'd been hurting her, rejecting and humiliating her, and this was not really so much different except . . . Except that now, instead of feeling sorry for herself, she felt sorry for *him*, for letting her go. She had loved him so much!

She raised her head, looked him straight in the eye and said in a hushed, trembling voice which contained all the passion of a scream, 'Shall I tell you *what* I'm sorry for, Daddy? I'm sorry I wasn't Andrew! I'm sorry *I* didn't die!'

She fully expected him to hit her then, and when instead he took a faltering step backwards, she snatched the whip from his hand and raised it above her head to lash at his face.

But instead of dodging, or shielding his face with his hands,

Miles simply closed his eyes, standing quite still, almost as if he wanted her to hit him.

'Oh, Jinny,' he whispered. 'For the love of God, forgive me.'

And then he wept.

Chapter Sixteen

Bel sat hunched over the fire in Nurse Stokes's kitchen, her head bowed, her fingers idly twirling her wedding ring. She noticed a blob of dried porridge on the front of her cardigan which must have been there since yesterday: they'd had Force Flakes today . . .

'Look at this,' she said wonderingly. 'Porridge. Sums everything up, somehow, doesn't it?'

Nurse Stokes chuckled. 'Oh, shut up,' she said. 'If you cry any more I'll sue you for a new hearthrug. You're making the bloody colours run. Have a fag. That'll cure you. Like a kipper.'

'Hmm. Do kippers have feelings, Stokesy?'

'Dunno. I've never managed to engage one in conversation. Not that I haven't tried, of course. I'll talk to anyone.'

'Thank God. Oh, Stokesy, what would I do without you?'

'Does it matter? If it wasn't me, it would be someone else. There's always someone, Bel. God litters us about on the sidelines of life especially to fill in the gaps.'

She lit a cigarette, inhaled deeply, pursed her lips and blew a series of smoke-rings at the ceiling. 'Seen Jean Carter lately – to talk to?'

'No.' Bel shuddered. 'I can't stand that woman. It's like seeing all my nightmares whizzing by on a bicycle.'

'She's going nuts; I'm sure of it. Heard her nattering away in her garden the other day; looked over the hedge and she was all by herself, racing up and down the path, explaining something to someone who wasn't there.'

Bel smiled drearily. 'Anyone we know?'

'Sorry, Bel. I thought I was changing the subject.'

'I don't think you can, Stokesy. It's like Rome. All roads lead to it.' She twirled her ring again. 'I'm . . . I'm thinking of leaving.' She shrugged. 'Probably a good time to do it. There's plenty of war work to be had. I won't starve as I would have done if he'd thrown me out after . . . Jinny.' She closed her eyes. 'Dear God, how is it possible to wreck so many lives in a few short minutes?'

'It's possible to wreck lives in a second. Compared with bombs and bullets you were a mite slow off the mark.'

'Mm . . . But I did just as much harm as . . . as Hitler, in my way. I was selfish, stupid, greedy, cruel and . . . Oh, I was resigned to be punished, Stokesy, but I don't think I can bear it any more! Everything I've done, tried to do or pretended to do . . . It's all . . . *gone*. Do you know, I can't even cook any more? And I was so proud of learning to cook!'

She began to weep again, snatching a rag from the sodden heap of rags in her lap to blow her nose, which was as red and shiny as a radish. 'And then I think . . . Then I think of Jinny, living in lodgings with an outcast for a mother. I think . . . I think of Robin and the twins, hating me for leaving Miles at a time like this. But if I have to go on seeing him, looking the way he does, knowing that I'm to blame for all of it, I'll go mad. I know I shall. And of what use will I be then, to any of them?'

Nurse Stokes fished in the drawer of the kitchen table and slung a clean pudding cloth into Bel's lap. 'There, blow on that and dry up, for God's sake. This isn't getting us anywhere.'

'There's nowhere to *get*, Stokesy! I might as well be walled up in that bloody room at Drayfield! There's no way out!'

'But you're still alive. And while you're still alive, there's hope that someone will *dig* you out. Do you still love him?'

Bel averted her face and stared for a long time at the wall. 'Yes,' she said at last. 'But I hate him, too! He's . . .' She closed her eyes, held her breath. 'He's *pitiless*.'

'Hmm. I've had my thoughts about that, you know, and he's not a pitiless man, generally speaking. He's good to his workers, tolerant and generous with his tenants. He thinks about people's needs and does what he can to supply them, within reason. But I think . . .'

'What?'

'I think he's as much at the mercy of nature as you were, when you went with Jack. What's the difference between male and female in nature? She's got a womb and milk, he's got balls and a John-Thomas and, all being well, nature drives the pair of 'em to put that equipment to good use. *That's* what drove you to Jack. Not his charms, for if you hadn't been so driven you'd have seen that the little bastard didn't have any.' She smirked wickedly. 'God rest his soul in the warmest corner.'

'Oh!' Bel laughed in protest and then, shrugging her submission, 'Amen.'

'But Miles had a little problem with his equipment, didn't he? Something had halted his natural drive, which made yours all the more urgent. Now he's no fool, Bel. He *knows* the part he played in your infidelity and he'll have blamed himself for it just as much as he blamed you. And what about Andrew? After years of rejecting you and shutting you out, Andrew's death suddenly puts him in need of you, and – lo and behold – you shut *him* out. Whether you meant it or you didn't doesn't matter, Bel. He'll have seen the justice in it. He'll have recognised – if only at the back of his mind – that he was to blame. You say he's not eating, not sleeping, not even keeping himself tidy any more. Well, I could be wrong, but it seems to me that from the start to the finish – in *his* eyes – he's brought the whole bloody lot of it on himself. So who's he being pitiless towards? You or himself?'

Bel stared, trying to see if she could find hope in this idea. But she couldn't. 'No! I went to him! I begged him! He didn't even answer me!'

'Maybe he couldn't. A man's emotions go deep, Bel, especially for men like Miles, who went through hell ten times over in the last war. Some things are not to be spoken of, love. And some men – men like Leonard Clare, for example – have never learned to speak since then – not of anything which really touches them. If it touches their hearts, you see, it opens their wounds, makes them bleed all over again. And what do you do with a bleeding wound? Press a cloth to it. Clamp it down. And don't let it go until a good, solid clot has formed over the gash. Miles was bleeding when you went to him, Bel. He couldn't involve himself in your emotions because he could barely cope with his own. That's my opinion, anyway, for what it's worth.'

'And now?'

'Now he knows he's let you down again, doesn't he? You went to him in agony. You begged him to help you. And the poor sod couldn't. But I could be wrong. and you could be right. All you can do now is wait and pray. Be kind to him when you can. And when you can't . . .' She smiled. 'Kick some other bugger.'

Andrew was dead, but hope was alive again as Bel hurried home to prepare the supper. Alive, but small and very frightened, like a newly metamorphosed frog when the heron flies in for breakfast. Would it live, would it grow, would it mate and spawn a thousand more little frogs? Or would it die on the very threshold of life as so many of its kind had done?

Oh, hope. Oh, torture . . . For the heron flew in every day!

Cheese and onion pie. That was easy. She couldn't burn that. She must remember the mustard. It was no good at all without the mustard. And Jinny's spare knickers needed new elastic. She must remember that. People were already whispering about the Huntleys' miseries, and Bel couldn't bear their whispers, their mawkish questions, their sweet, sympathetic smiles. She'd always, before, managed to put a good 'front' on things, to keep smiling, keep busy. Even when she went home to cry her eyes out, no one had known. Now she had swollen eyes, a scarlet nose and a blob of porridge on her cardigan, plain for all to see, and when Jinny's knickers fell down in the middle of the High Street, everyone would *know* they'd hit rock bottom.

She giggled at the unintended pun, blushed and covered her mouth with her hand. Dear God, never mind about Jinny's knickers! When a woman giggled, all by herself in a public place, she wasn't at rock bottom so much as in cloud-cuckoo-land!

Jean Carter, racing up and down the garden path . . . talking to someone who wasn't there. Jack? Bel dreamed of him sometimes or, rather, had nightmares about him. But he never looked as he had done in life. He was gross and stinking, with a limp yellow phallus dangling to his knees like a bull's wasted pizzle. Ugh! It was like dreaming of the devil. But how did Jean dream of him? How did she remember him? Did she miss him, ache for him, pity him? Was she so lonely for him that she conjured him out of his darkness, just as Bel so longed to conjure Miles?

Cheese and onion pie. If you put a slice of bread on the saucepan lid, it soaked up the smell of boiling onions. Or so it said in the book. In fact it didn't work, but Bel always did it. It made her feel like a proper cook, with lots of clever little tricks up her sleeve: efficient, capable, knowledgeable, *useful*. 'I may be a rotten wife, but at least I can feed you . . .' Yesterday she'd burned the cabbage. This morning she'd run out of porridge oats. Oats! Virtually the only thing you could buy just for the asking, and she'd run out of the bloody stuff!

She had to pull herself together. It was already April, and she hadn't been near the garden, hadn't even prepared the ground, let alone sown any seed. They'd starve if she didn't soon make a move.

She stopped outside the garden door and closed her eyes, her heart pounding with misery. How could one's heart *pound* with misery? Surely it should plod, whisper, wheeze with misery, not *pound* like this, as if misery were something exciting, frightening...

But oh, God, it was frightening! Like a beating which just went on and on, until the pain ceased to matter and you began to think of being mutilated: scarred for life, damaged beyond even your own recognition.

No... She'd survived before. She'd survive again. She would. Because she must. Because... Well, really, just because she was too cowardly to kill herself. And when you're too scared to die, what else is there to do but live as best you can? Concentration, that was the trick. Do just one thing at a time and really *concentrate*, do a good job (remember the mustard), so that when it was done you could feel you'd achieved something, however insignificant it might seem. The world was wrecked, but it could be rebuilt. One brick at a time. One brick at a time.

She was concentrating on grating the cheese when she heard Jinny come in at the scullery door, talking to someone.

'I didn't really know what she meant about playing the music. She sometimes forgets I'm only ten, and it was a bit difficult to understand.'

'But you managed it, didn't you?'

Miles... Bel frowned and stared at the door, unconsciously letting her hands move so that the cheese she was grating began to fall into the sink. *Music?* What the hell was going on now?

The door opened. Miles's arm was on Jinny's shoulder, Jinny's face red and swollen with tears.

'What's wrong?' Bel gasped. 'What on earth's happened, Miles?'

He smiled, very stiffly, but there was a warmth in his eyes which hadn't been there for years. 'We had a little tiff.' He heaved a sigh and drew Jinny close to his side, closing his arms around her. 'But it's all right now, isn't it, Jinny?'

Bel could only stare, mesmerised, for although when her leg had been injured Miles had touched Jinny, if only to carry her up and down stairs, Jinny had responded to his touch like a cat, painfully immobilised by a hand at the scruff of its neck. Now she leaned her head against his chest, laid her hand over his heart, closed her eyes – and smiled.

Miles stroked her hair. He stooped to whisper something in her ear and she nodded and hurried away, leaving Bel with her husband, alone with her husband, gazing at him amazed, as if for the very first time.

Hope ... It leached the blood from her face and the strength from her legs. It burned in her eyes, making her blind to everything – save the slow sweep of his arms, opening wide, calling her home.

Miles thought of knocking on the door. He stood outside on the landing for several seconds, thinking about it. He hadn't entered his wife's room since they'd had that wretched telegram, almost a month ago ... But the evening had been a busy one. There had been no time to talk, and if they let it go now ... No, he mustn't knock. He must make it seem quite natural, even if it felt no more natural than red grass growing out of green earth. A dream.

He opened the door. Bel was sitting at the dressing table, brushing her hair. She'd been growing it and usually wore it in a pleat at the back of her head. Now it was loose, thick and glossy, reaching to her shoulder blades and softly curled at the ends. But she wasn't looking in the mirror, she wasn't thinking at all about what she was doing. In her striped flannel pyjamas she could have been a young girl, dreaming of her lover . . .

She was forty-two, and might have been eighteen again: so neat, so slim, so *delicately* pretty. Yes . . . That had been his first mistake: to marry a girl of eighteen and believe her to be as fragile as she looked, like a rose which, having come into its glory, has nothing left to do but cast its petals, cast its seed. He hadn't spared a thought for its roots, its stem, its thorns. He hadn't once considered that a rose is just a small part of a greater, stronger, more noble plant, with many branches, moods and seasons.

Suddenly Bel looked into the mirror, saw him and bent her head to study the pattern on the back of her hair brush. He came behind her, set his hands on her shoulders, breathed the scent of her – like a rose.

'Here,' he murmured. 'Let me do it.'

Her hair crackled as he brushed it. The air crackled too: their long-held fears, loves and hatreds striking sparks from each other like clouds in a summer storm. Yet only a few hours ago he had held her in his arms and felt none of this – just love, relief and comfort, beyond the power of words to express. They'd been playing each other's music, then. Now they were playing different tunes and perhaps only words could bring them back to harmony.

'Did Jinny talk to you, Bel?'

'About your tiff? No . . . She was too happy that it was over, I think. Or perhaps . . .'

'What?'

'Too aware of the rules of the house. We don't discuss such things, do we? We sit on them. Try to suffocate them . . .'

Miles nodded. 'And then are surprised when they jump up and bite us in the fundament. The rules of the house could do with a little revision, Bel. Jinny taught me something today. It's a thing I've always known . . . In my heart . . . Yet never had the courage to prove. It's something your little chum up the road had been proving all her life, and although I've admired her for it, it's rather like admiring men who climb mountains, wondering why – with all the seemingly *unnecessary* risks involved – they should bother to do it.'

'Do . . . what?'

'Tell the truth.'

He put the hairbrush down. He turned his wife to face him and crouched at her feet, holding her hands. 'This is the truth, Bel. I've been testing it for twenty-four years and done . . . many things to prove it untrue. I've sat on it, tried to smother it, but it's jumped up and bitten me and I can no longer deny it. I love you. I've always loved you. I loved you when you were young, when you were . . . foolish. I loved you when you were strong and brave. I loved you when you were broken.' He bowed his head, stared at her hands. 'I love you now,' he whispered.

The star-burst of a tear splashed his hand. 'Oh, Miles, I've hurt you so much!'

He smiled wearily. 'And I, of course, have never hurt you.'

Bel was silent. She pulled her hands away and mopped her tears, whispering, 'If I cry any more I'll dissolve.'

She blew her nose, squared her shoulders, smiled – and then, with a wail of despair, burst into tears again and threw herself into his arms. 'Oh, Miles, hold me! Hold me!'

No . . . Words couldn't sing the tune. Only tears and more tears until they were exhausted and fell asleep, lying crosswise on the bed just as they had fallen.

They woke soon after midnight – Miles with frozen feet (they'd been hanging over the edge of the bed) and Bel with a crashing headache. As he limped through to the bathroom to mix her a powder, Miles saw both their faces reflected in the mirror and winced with dismay. What the hell had they done to one another? Bel's face was as bruised and swollen as if she'd done fifteen rounds with a fairground pugilist. He was gaunt, grey, red-eyed and shambling, like one of the tramps who'd walked the land during the Depression, begging alms, food and shelter from the cold.

He laughed.

'What?' Bel murmured drowsily.

He turned, ruefully stroking the stubbly growth of beard on his chin. 'Oh,' he smiled. 'I was wondering if even Churchill would guess that this was our finest hour.'

Bel was soon sleeping again, but Miles lay awake until dawn, thinking things through. They had talked hardly at all. No long-belated apologies. No explanations. No pleas for forgiveness. And yet, for the first time in their lives, everything between them was understood. They were together at last, singing the same tune.

And they owed it all to Jinny... He'd been on the very brink of telling her that she was not his child. Telling her that she was the cause of all his grief, the thorn in his flesh which had festered and oozed until everything he owned, everything he loved, was rendered worthless and empty. And he'd *planned* it: that was the astonishing thing! Not in cold blood, thank God, but in moments of such rage and bewilderment that only the thought of 'eye-for-an-eye' vengeance could give him relief.

An eye for an eye... But it had been Jack Carter's eye he'd been after. That was why he'd taken Jinny to the office, to replay the old scene and this time win it, beat him, break the bastard, once and for all. He'd set Jinny up, poor child, only to knock her down, quite forgetting that he'd already done that and that she – in her own estimation, at least – had no further to fall. Poor little Jinny...

He'd been watching her, for two thirds of her life, for a single clue that she was truly Jack Carter's child: the obscene curl of his lip, the sneer in his voice, his arrogance, his insolence, his laziness and cruelty. But Jinny had none of it. She was Bel all through: in the way she spoke, the way she smiled, the way she walked and turned her head. Even in the way she so passively allowed him to diminish her she was Bel. It was as if Jack had been no more than a shade, a wraith, an incubus, impregnating Bel while she slept, leaving nothing of himself to prove that he'd been there. Even Jinny's eyes were not his. Even her hair.

Yet Miles had been certain (in his madness) that if he just pushed her far enough... He hadn't intended to hit her – even half crazy he hadn't been capable of that – but he'd thought the threat, not to mention the sheer injustice of the threat, would be enough to bring out the evil in her and justify...

Ha! Justify what? That he'd wished... wished... That he had wished Jinny could have died, instead of Andrew!

And she'd known it, poor child. Known it and wished it too, not for herself, but for him. Oh, the shame of that... If she'd whipped him halfway to hell for it, she'd have let him off too lightly.

But there was nothing of Jack in Jinny. She hadn't hit him. She'd wept, held his hand and talked... about music.

It had made no sense at the time. He'd been too shattered to listen, she too shattered to explain it. Yet the mere mention of music in a moment so dark had somehow redeemed him.

'Music, Jinny? What do you mean?'

And she'd told him. Yes, she'd sung his music when she said she wished she'd died for Andrew. She'd understood. She'd heard the tune. And, in singing it for him, she'd transformed it, 'made it better'. He was no less sad that he'd lost his son – the music of sorrow is always slow to reach its end – but he knew it now for what it was: sorrow, not rage; sorrow, not hatred. Sorrow, not bitterness for betrayals long gone... and now, blessedly, forgiven.

How had Jinny understood that? Because she'd known his tune all along; he'd made her dance to it, all her life. But today was the first time he'd allowed her – the first time he'd forced her – to sing.

Beyond the eternal night of the blackout curtains a thrush sang its first song to the dawn. Miles turned to his wife and stroked her hair, kissed her eyes. He nibbled her ear and, as she woke, he gathered her in his arms and rocked her – to the deep, slow music of love.

June, and all the farmers of the valley had looked at their grass, looked at the sky, listened to the song of the birds and the music of the river and muttered, narrow-eyed, 'Looks like it'll hold.'

Then all hell (otherwise known as haymaking) had broken loose. Jean hated it. Well, it was *dangerous*! She'd fallen off her bike three times in a week, just trying to avoid being flattened by yet another tractor. It hadn't been like this in the old days. Horses couldn't do twenty miles an hour round the bends (or on the straight, for that matter) and they hadn't been driven by crazy-idiot land girls! Land *Army*. Huh, that was true enough! If they'd been let loose in tanks instead of tractors they'd have flattened Rommel in half the time Monty took to do it!

'Have tractors got brakes, Bert?'

''Course they got brakes.'

'Well, why won't someone *tell* them they've got brakes? That Avril Robbins. I'll kill her, so help me. She must have seen me coming, Bert. But did she slow down? And her language! Ooh, if there's anything I hate, Bert, it's language! "Don't you know there's a something-something war on?" Well, of course I know there's a something-something war on! And she's the something-something enemy!'

'Oh . . . Avril's all right.' Bert was locking up the Post Office for the dinner hour, his movements slow, calm and thoughtful, like his voice. His calmness, on the too-frequent occasions when Jean was blowing her top about something, always made her feel a bit ashamed of herself, made her worry, just a bit, that he might think less of her. She blushed, laughed and – with difficulty – ate her words.

'Oh, I know they're doing a hard job, doing their best – '

'And there's rain in the forecast, see, Jean. That'll be why they're rushing it.'

'Oh.' Her blush deepened. 'I didn't know.'

The telephone rang and as Bert went to answer it she tiptoed away to get the children's dinner, feeling awful. She was always doing that: going off 'half-cocked' as Bert called it; getting herself excited about things before she knew all the facts. Jinny Huntley was an example of that. Why Jean had been so certain the kid had TB she couldn't now say, but oh, the worry of it while it lasted! She'd been the same with Penny Clare, a few weeks back, when Penny had tipped boiling water over her hand. It hadn't turned out too bad in the end, but in Jean's imagination (within minutes of her hearing about it) it had festered, turned black and dropped off, bringing Penny's days as a pianist to a rapid and cruel end. Mad, that's what she was. She was going mad . . .

'Jean! Hey, Jean!'

She turned at the back gate to see Bert at the sorting office door, waving a small buff envelope.

'Could you? Huntleys. It'll only take a minute on your bike.'

Jean's mouth dropped open. Her flesh crawled with dread.

Bert grinned. ''S all right. Not bad news, and you might catch him at Home Farm if you get your skates on.'

Jean swallowed. 'N-not bad news?'

He'd come down the path to hand the telegram over, but instead of doing that, he put his hand on her shoulder and squeezed it comfortingly. 'Come on,' he said. 'Switch it off, love. You're a good girl, but if you take everyone else's troubles on your shoulders, you won't be able to call your soul your own.' He flapped the little envelope under her nose. 'And this isn't trouble, so give us a little smile, eh?'

Jean could have kissed him. Instead, she let out a rather wild (rather embarrassing) shout of laughter, jumped on her bike and pedalled away, her face burning with a mixture of elation and shame. She never used to be so excitable . . . She'd sounded a bit weird when she'd laughed like that, but if it wasn't bad news, and if Bert really did like her . . . Then, to her dismay, she laughed again. Curses didn't work!

She did catch Miles at Home Farm. He was just going home to his dinner (except that he called it lunch), and Bel had evidently come to fetch him, for she was hanging on his arm as they left the yard, turning her face up to tell him something. They smiled. Then, as Jean skidded to a halt beside them, they huddled together, their faces suddenly ashen with fear.

'It's not-bad news!' Jean gasped.

An Army truck, closely followed by two American jeeps, came hurtling round the bend in the road, and with a howl of outrage (why was everyone trying to *kill* her?) Jean scooted her bike into the safety of the farmyard before putting the telegram into Miles's hand.

He opened it, he read it. He blinked and read it again, a look of utter bafflement on his face.

'Miles?' Bel whispered hollowly.

Frowning, he read it again. Then he squeezed his eyes shut, bared his teeth and hunched his shoulders as though taking a rain of blows from an invisible cudgel.

Bert had lied!

But before Jean could burst into tears, Miles Huntley let out a wild, yodelling shout, leapt six feet in the air and came down again, laughing, 'He's *alive*! Andrew's *alive*!'

He scooped Bel off her feet, swung her around, covered her face with kisses. Then, to Jean's utter amazement, he did the same to her! 'Mrs Carter, I love you, you blessed, blessed woman!'

Bel was on her knees, trying to read the telegram through

a rain of tears. 'Taken prisoner!' she wailed happily. 'And he's all right! Oh, Miles, Miles, he's safe!'

Cycling had made Jean Carter fit and strong, but when Miles returned her to solid ground, she staggered like a drunk and fell against the wall, joyfully sobbing, 'Any reply?'

Curses didn't work! They didn't work!

She had never been happier in her life, and, as she pedalled slowly home, she realised that she hadn't felt so peaceful for years – not since Jack had died . . . bless him. He hadn't been up to much, poor soul. All he'd had were good looks, and they don't last, so what had he got, after all? A man who hates everyone hates himself, and perhaps that's what had killed him, in the end – not Jean's hatred, but his own.

She was humming as she parked her bike against her garden fence, not realising that it was a hymn-tune until the words came.

> *'All people that on earth do dwell,*
> *Sing to the Lord with cheerful voice,*
> La, la, de-da, *His praise forth tell,*
> *Come ye before him and rejoice.'*

Just as she was about to close her front door, Nurse Stokes turned into the lane on her own bicycle, looking old and tired, fed up to the back teeth with the war and life in general.

Jean ran down the path again, her face alight with smiles. 'Nurse Stokes!' she cried. 'Quick, over here!' She flapped her hand. 'You'll never guess what's just happened!'

Nurse Stokes braked and set her foot to the ground, her head drooping wearily. 'No,' she said. 'And neither will you. I've just come back from Drayfield. Michael Clare – ' She covered her mouth with her hand as though to quell a rising sickness. 'He turned the bloody tractor over,' she announced flatly. 'He's dead.'

Chapter Seventeen

It was almost ten o'clock and still broad daylight. They lay naked on the bed, Bel half asleep, Miles propped against the pillows, smugly smiling.

'Mmm . . .' he said.

'Mmmm . . .' She turned over and stroked her fingers through the silky hairs at the base of his throat. 'Aren't people good?' she murmured contentedly.

'Mm . . .' Then, after a short pause, 'Are they?'

'Do you suppose they knew?'

'Hmm? Knew what?'

'Well,' she breathed, 'that we'd want to . . . you know. Be together. To celebrate, like . . . this.'

'Lord, I hope not. How will I face anyone tomorrow? Oh, goodness, Bel – ' He burrowed down and hid his face between her breasts, squealing comically, 'I'm *shy*!'

She giggled like a child, and Miles, still hiding, bit back a sob which seemed to have risen from the soles of his feet. Ah, God, this was so beautiful he was afraid he might die of it. They'd been in bed for scarcely two hours, had made love twice and the third . . . was already threatening. He was insatiable: not merely for love but for the sheer fun of it, the blissful luxury of being together – mind, body and soul – without fearing anything at all.

'She must have *told*, Miles. Even when she's asked to be discreet, she can never quite manage it.' Bel wriggled clear of his embrace, pushed the hair from her eyes and thumped her pillow. 'Remember when Ivy Shilling ran away with that fellow who came to do the drains? Mrs Shilling begged her not to tell anyone, and she spent the day saying, 'I know something *you* don't know,' and getting everyone to wring it out of her! The whole valley knew by teatime. So she *must* have told, Miles. Mustn't she?'

'Who? Told what?'

'Mrs Carter, you fool! About Andrew!'

'Oh, I see . . . But we don't want to keep it secret, do we, darling? It's wonderful news. Everyone will be glad for us, surely?'

'Yes!' She wrinkled her nose, calling him an idiot. 'That's the whole point! If everyone's glad for us, why hasn't anyone called? Solomon! The Clares! Stokesy! *Anyone*!'

Miles grinned and narrowed his eyes, walking his fingers along her naked flank. 'Maybe they do know,' he whispered lecherously. 'Perhaps they're all out there now, imagining it, envying us . . .'

'Ooooh!' She blushed and hid her face in her hands, then splayed her fingers to peep out at him, her eyes bright with mischief. 'What a disgraceful thing to say,' she murmured throatily.

'Mmm,' Miles groaned. 'Mm-*mmm* . . .'

The third time proved to be Bel's swan-song. The satisfied smirk had barely faded from her lips before she was asleep, curled at his side like a cat after a successful raid on the game larder.

Miles sat up and smoked a cigarette, watching a warm, purple dusk fall upon the garden. God, he was so happy, he could scarcely bear it, let alone believe it! A few months ago he'd been ready to kill himself, and now . . . Now he was glad he hadn't.

He heard the slow (unusually slow) rumble of a tractor coming in from the hayfields and thought dryly, 'Avril must be tired . . .'

The times he'd told that girl to slow down! But it was like telling a bird not to fly; if she wasn't going flat-out she withered and pined. Nothing would convince her that a speeding tractor was a lethal weapon, as liable to tip up and flatten her as to mow down any poor idiot who stood in her way. Youth. It was a wonder anyone survived it.

Andrew had survived. Later, perhaps, Miles would begin to worry about the kind of privations his son would suffer as a prisoner of war, but at the moment . . . no. The worst his imagination could conjure, at the moment, was a flower-strewn Austrian valley: a gentian sky overhead and snow-capped mountains all around, with cowbells and birdsong taking the place of ack-ack fire. As he allowed his mind to dwell on this image, he realised that, in a way, he was envisaging the heaven of the Resurrection. Andrew had been dead and was alive again. He'd been lost and now was found.

But Andrew wasn't the only one to have been resurrected. The two experiences were so closely linked as to be virtually the same thing, but that somehow made each of them all the more wonderful.

Miles closed his eyes and smiled. And smiled. And went on smiling until his jaw ached.

Resurrection . . . The truth and the life. The truth had been on the tip of his tongue since the day Andrew was born, yet in all his ponderings, all his wonderings and worries, he had never once managed to identify what was wrong with him. Yet it was so *easy*, so *obvious*! He'd lost his brothers to a war he'd been certain wasn't over and had felt that in producing sons he was simply filling the ranks with yet more human sacrifices. Young men, beautiful men, beloved men . . . doomed to die.

For a while he'd managed to convince himself that their deaths weren't inevitable and thus had managed to father three more sons, but after that . . .

Oh, God, it was so *simple*! He hadn't been able to explain to himself how he felt, but now he could: he'd felt that to make love with his wife was to murder his sons. Until today.

But Andrew hadn't died! Andrew was safe! His death had not been inevitable. It had never been inevitable! After all, Miles had survived, Leonard Clare had survived, perhaps a million men had survived for every ten thousand who had died, and it had been just an unlucky stroke of fate that Miles's brothers had been, like the Shulamite's lover, 'chief among ten thousand'.

Good old King Solomon . . . The wisdom of Solomon had escaped Miles for far too long. *The Song of Solomon* likewise, although he'd learned every word of it at the Front, quoting its mysterious, love-impassioned verses as a hedge against madness. He hadn't guessed that it was foretelling the tale of his own love. And of Bel's . . .

I opened to my beloved; but my beloved had withdrawn himself and was gone. My soul failed when he spake. I sought him, but I could not find him. I called him, but he gave me no answer.

His eyes drooping with sleep, Miles turned to his wife and with a gentle finger stroked the hair from her eyes, traced the bony line of her jaw and the swollen mount of her lips.

He kissed her and lay back against his pillows, reaching for her hand to lead him into sleep. ' "Thou art all fair, my love," ' he whispered. ' "There is no spot in thee." '

Through all that long, dreary summer, Felix led his father by the hand, working with and for him, talking to – and for him. Mike's death had brought Leonard's stammer back in force so that he could barely pronounce his own name, let alone do any of the normal business at market and with his neighbours. Mike had taken over most of the business side of the farm anyway – he'd had the right turn of mind for it – and Leonard was lost without him.

Felix was lost, too, although he didn't know quite how lost until, with the feverish work of harvesting over, he realised that the new school year was due to begin and that he would not be a part of it. It was not a difficult decision to make. He had no choice. Leonard couldn't manage without him. But it was the hardest decision he'd ever made, if only because it made him understand that Mike was truly dead and could not come back, ever again.

Strange . . . He'd always understood that death was final – as painfully irreversible as throwing a banknote into the heart of a fire – and yet when Mike was killed it seemed that only the top layer of Felix's mind had recognised the truth of it. Beyond that, in the buried places where memories, habits and long-held affections did their work, it was as if Mike had simply gone away for a while and might be expected to return.

It was this unconscious expectation which had carried Felix through, given him strength to fill the gaps his brother had left. Then – it was on the last day of harvesting, when he was tired and dirty, thirsty and aching – Felix had lost patience with the whole lot of it and thought, Right, that's enough! Wherever you've gone, Mike, you can damn well come back!

Come back to soothe his father and comfort his mother. Come back to send his brother to school for just one more year. Come back to sort out the Inland Revenue and all the piles of red-tape that went with producing food for a nation at war. Felix had been saying, 'All right, Dad, I'll see to it as soon as the harvest's in,' and he'd meant it, but in the buried place of his mind he'd always added, As soon as Mike comes back and shows me how to do it.

He wasn't coming back. Not ever. Felix had been a fool to believe that he could and when at last he gave in to his grief, more than two months after the event, the tears he shed were partly for his own foolishness, his own selfishness and ingratitude . . . His youth.

He had wanted so much to get away! It wasn't that he didn't love his parents; he loved them dearly, but . . . Well, they required so much tolerance, so much care and thought. The trouble was, he supposed, that he was too much like them: deeper than he either wanted or needed to be, so sensitive to their feelings that he suffered theirs almost more than he suffered his own.

Mike hadn't been like that. Mike had been a plain, honest farmer: hard-edged, practical and objective almost to a fault. His character had come from Leonard's side of the family — the solid, plain-living yeomanry which Aunt Prissie and Uncle Sol represented so well. Felix and Alan had come more from Penny's side, and although Felix had never known his mother's people (who had abandoned her on her marriage), he'd heard enough to guess that they were mostly nutcases: poets, painters, inventors, travellers. People who achieved things, who did precisely as they liked and to hell with the consequences; people who would rather die than end up as small tenant farmers!

Not that Leonard had had a whit more choice in the matter than his son had now. He'd been virtually mute at the end of the last war and farming had been one of the few options open to a man who could barely speak. Cows, pigs and horses don't demand much by way of conversation, and grass, grain and weather can get by with the occasional swearword, complete or in part. As long as you get the tone of voice right, the b-b-bl-bloody rain still f-f-falls just when it's least c-c-con, con-v-v-venient.

There was no point in railing against rain. You swore at it just to relieve your feelings and after that accepted it and adapted it, as best you could, to suit your own purposes. You could chew your nails down to the knuckles because your hay or your grain was spoiling, but that could only add insult to injury: spoilt crops, short fingers. Better to whitewash the byres, repair broken tools or do the accounts. *Get* something out of it, not let it rob you of everything.

Penny always said that Nature had everything worked out and that, if you trusted it, a perfect balance would always result. Good would be returned for evil, wealth for poverty, happiness for sorrow. She said that life, like each turning year, was seasonal, having its times of cold, famine and hardship, its times of warmth and plenty. You endure one to enjoy the other, for spring always comes again.

It was easy enough to say, especially in a bitter March, with spring just around the corner; but in November (and, in terms of grieving for Mike, it *was* November) they had a hell of a lot of shivering still to do. But Penny was right: unless you died of cold in the meantime, spring *would* come again, and if you wanted to get the best out of it you had to be prepared. Plough the land, sow the grain, clear the ditches. If Felix was going to spend the rest of his life as a farmer, he'd be a damn *good* one!

He took his jumbled piles of red-tape to Miles Huntley who, having produced sense out of them in the space of half an hour, laid his hand on Felix's shoulder and murmured, 'Are you sure this is a good idea, Felix?'

Felix blushed. 'What?'

'Taking on Drayfield. It's not at all what you wanted from life, is it?'

'No... Losing Mike wasn't what I wanted, either, but I wasn't given a choice, Mr Huntley. You can do what you want only when you're given a choice, and how many can say they have a choice, in wartime? Your boys don't have any.'

'No... But when the war's over... If, God willing they survive, and if, God willing, we win, they'll have every choice. They completed their education, Felix, and although I shouldn't say it,' he smiled ruefully, 'none of my boys is as clever as you seem to be. You're giving up your life for something which might prove unworthy of the sacrifice.'

'My father?' Felix asked softly.

'No, no. Your father's worthy of everything you can give him. I'm speaking of Drayfield. Have you forgotten the reservoir scheme?'

Felix laughed nervously. 'Oh, that'll never happen! The bill didn't even get through Parliament!'

'Only because the war intervened. But the war won't last for ever, and Bristol's need for water certainly will. Go back to school, Felix. Let me help your father. All it will take – '

Felix stood up, close to tears. 'No,' he said hoarsely. 'Thank you, Mr Huntley, but I've thought of all that. No one can help Dad, except . . . Except people who understand what he's saying! Without understanding him, you see, you'd have to make your own decisions, do as *you* thought best, and before you knew it he'd have lost his authority, his control over . . . He'd have lost all *his* choices, Mr Huntley, and he's already done that once in his life! Now it's my turn.'

Miles nodded sadly, understanding; and although Felix had wanted him to understand, he found now that he had hoped for something else. *Anything* that would let him return to school and clear his conscience at the same time. But it would take a miracle to do that, and miracles . . . didn't happen.

'There's something else,' he murmured. 'Farming's a protected occupation, and while that seems . . . ironic at the moment, it won't help my parents if I have to join up next year, will it? It's been bad enough worrying about Alan, but now, with Mike gone . . .'

'Now that the Americans and Russians are in on our side, the war might soon be over, God willing.'

'Do you believe in God, Mr Huntley?'

Miles hesitated, but before he could answer, Felix laughed. 'Neither do I, but I believe there is a power – not unlike electricity, I suppose – which we can find for ourselves and use to make our own light.'

He collected up his papers, preparing to leave. 'And that's what I'm going to do, now, Mr Huntley. With Drayfield.'

Miles smiled and shook his hand. 'Then you'll be a happy man, Felix. Good luck – ' His smile changed to a warm, mischievous grin. 'And don't forget to pay your electricity bill.'

Bert Tomkins put a large mug of tea into Jean's right hand and a large clean handkerchief into her left. 'Now,' he said gently. 'Pull yourself together. I've told you before, Jean, there's no sense – '

'I know! Oh, Bert, I know! But it's not just me! Everyone's upset about it, not just me!'

Bert took a step backwards and leaned against the sorting office door to blow thoughtfully on his tea. 'Well, let's put it this way,' he said dryly, 'you're the only one I've seen crying about it. We all shed a tear for poor Mike – we'd have been less than human if we hadn't: he was a fine boy, Jean, and so's young Felix, but – '

'He's brilliant!' Jean sobbed. 'He could've done anything with his life and now it's all ruined! Ruined!'

'Rubbish. What's it say in the Bible, Jean? "Honour thy father and thy mother," it says. It doesn't say anything about getting your exams and going to college, does it? And you can bet that if those things mattered a hang, they'd be there. "Thou shalt study," it'd say. "Thou shalt hunger and thirst for trigonometry's sake." But it doesn't, Jean. "Honour thy father and mother," it says, and that's exactly what the boy's doing. So what's there to cry about?'

Jean shook her head, blew her nose and stared forlornly into her tea. 'He never wanted to be a farmer, Bert. He told our Evie that. He wanted – '

'Now, hang on,' Bert interrupted softly. 'Who gets what

they want? Did you? Did I? Did anyone you've ever heard of get what they wanted from life? Look around you. Think, Jean. It doesn't work like that, does it? We get what we're given, and make the best of it and, after a while, we come to be grateful for not getting what we wanted. Look at me, for instance. I wanted to be a ruddy admiral when I was a kid!'

Jean giggled tearfully.

'But what kind of life would I be having now if I'd got it, eh? Worrying myself sick over every poor sailor in the Fleet, never getting a wink, breaking my heart every time a ship went down! No, being a village postmaster suits me. I'm happy with it, grateful for it. And I thank the Lord for giving me this instead of what I wanted, fool that I was. That's what young Felix'll do, too, eventually. You see if he doesn't.'

Bert was right. Jean knew he was right. But he didn't know what she'd done! And he was such a good man, such a fine, upstanding, decent man. Oh, dear God, if he knew what she'd done, he'd hate her for evermore!

'You don't understand,' she whispered.

Bert was silent save for the creaking of his throat as he swallowed great gulps of hot tea. Then, 'I think I do,' he murmured. 'Do you know what I think, Jean? I think you're lonely. I mean to say, you do your rounds on your own, go home to clean and cook on your own. Do the garden on your own . . . I know you've got the kiddies, but kiddies aren't the same, are they?'

'No, but – ' Jean took a deep breath, bit her lip and decided, once and for all, to tell him everything. 'The thing is . . . The thing is . . . Well the thing is that . . . Well, I've sometimes thought Drayfield . . .' Her courage failed her. 'Oh, nothing! I'm just being stupid!'

'Doesn't matter if you are, Jean. That's what I'm saying. We're all stupid at times, and that's when we need someone to talk to, someone to put things in perspective a bit. What about Drayfield? Think there's something bad down there, do you?'

Jean caught her breath and stared at him with wide, astonished eyes. He knew!

Bert laughed. 'They been saying that, off and on, for time out of mind, love! Old Mrs Huntley said something about it the week Mike died – said there was a witch there who'd put a curse on the place, or somesuch silly nonsense. Well, you know my opinion of curses, Jean. Load of rubbish. You ever heard there's a curse on Manor Lodge?'

'No! Is there?'

'No, but that's just my point. There was a whole family wiped out there about forty years ago – typhoid or somesuch. Then . . .' He began to count on his fingers. 'Two of the Miller boys killed in the last war and the sister died of flu right after, and how many kiddies did the Shepherds have altogether? Fourteen! How many survived? Five! And what do they put that down to – curses or the damp?'

'It wasn't the damp killed Jack, though, was it?'

Bert smiled teasingly. 'Wasn't it?'

'Well . . .' She laughed her defeat, laughed her gratitude. He'd done it again: talked her out of it, bless him. 'Oh, Bert, what would I do without you? You're such a comfort!'

'Ah. Well.' He coughed and turned away to take the empty mugs back to his secret haunt behind the sorting office and Jean, sighing, put on her cap and her bicycle clips for the morning delivery.

The morning was wet and, save for a few streaks of grey on the eastern horizon, still dark, but except in snowy weather, which she loathed, Jean enjoyed her first round of the day. It was peaceful, and quiet. It gave her a chance to think, although just lately, since Michael Clare's death, she hadn't *thought* so much as . . . She couldn't really put a name to it. Her mind hadn't been her own. It was as if it was a bicycle chain, going round and round on the same set of cogs, with someone else – or something else – pushing the pedals.

She'd thought, until this morning, that it was that wretched curse pushing the pedals, driving her to the brink of madness so that she hardly knew what she was saying or doing. Now, with just a few words, Bert had put it all straight again. 'Know what I think, Jean? I think you're lonely.'

God, it was so obvious, so *ordinary*! So true. When you were lonely your thoughts did go round in circles, just because there was no one to divert or develop them, 'to put things in perspective'. Bert had just done that, bless his heart, and not for the first time. She'd have gone loopy years ago if it hadn't been for him.

Lonely. Oh, yes, she'd been lonely, and for so long! And she'd been wrong about men; she knew it now. The only real trouble with men was that none of them was perfect which, when you came down to it, was the only real trouble with women, too. But *some* men ... Well, take Solomon Hicks, for example. *He* was a good man. Miles Huntley ... He was a good man, too. Leonard Clare ... Leonard Clare ... Leonard Clare was a lovely man, say what you like about his stammer. And then there was Bert.

Was Bert lonely, too? He seemed contented enough, and (Jean had been keeping her eyes open since she'd noticed his collars) he obviously wasn't starving, he didn't smell or have dandruff and he never had any female visitors outside of office hours, so he must be looking after himself. But why did he stay up all night, reading? That wasn't natural. That wasn't healthy. If he'd had someone to cuddle up to, round about ten o'clock at night, perhaps he wouldn't want to read so much ...

Jean blushed. Someone to cuddle up to. Someone to laugh with and talk to and 'get things in perspective' before the light went off. And ... And other things. Jean had never liked the other things when she was married to Jack: he'd done it so selfishly, so brutally, like a bull in a farmyard. But Bert wouldn't be like that. Bert wasn't that sort of man. He was warm, kind, gentle . . .

Jean imagined warm, gentle hands stroking her body, warm lips kissing hers . . . and, even knowing she had six letters and an electricity bill to deliver to the Radnors, she pedalled straight past their gate and had to turn round and pedal back again.

'Lovely morning, Mr Radnor!'

Joss Radnor had not come into Jean's list of 'good' men: she'd always thought him a mite cynical. Very polite, but with hard eyes and no sense of humour. Now, looking at her sideways under the dripping brim of a battered felt hat, he grinned and said, 'Well, it is, now. Had some good news, have you?'

'What?' Jean blushed. 'Oh! No . . . Just feeling . . . happy.' She laughed, handed over the post, turned her bike and pedalled away again, her cheeks burning like fire.

At the top of the little rise which led down to Molton Draycott, she braked, stood astride her bicycle and leaned on the handlebars, trying to calm herself. She was in love, heaven help her, and had probably been so for years without realising it. Without wanting it. Without wanting to take the risk.

Yet she'd known Bert ever since she'd first come to the valley and had never heard him speak a harsh word to anyone, never heard anyone speak a harsh word about him. So what kind of risk was it? It wasn't the same as falling in love with Jack, being swept off her feet by a man she scarcely knew. But Bert . . . Well, so far as everyone belonged to everyone else in a community like this, Bert was practically *family*!

And she wanted him. She *needed* him.

Now all she had to do was persuade him that he felt the same . . .

Chapter Eighteen

Felix had fallen in love with Miriam Winterson at entirely the wrong time. Mike had been dead barely a week and Miriam had sung at his funeral: her voice so strong, her diction so pure, her expression so lovely that Felix, temporarily blinded by his grief, had been well-nigh convinced that she'd sprouted wings and a halo.

About ten months later he discovered that *Miriam* thought she'd sprouted wings and a halo, too. No, it was worse than that: she thought she'd been born with them. But she wasn't proud. No, indeed. If anything, the peculiar honour of having been born perfect had made her feel more humble than most – ashamed of herself, in fact. Well, goodness, what had she ever done to deserve so many blessings? She hadn't intended to be wonderful, really she hadn't. She just couldn't *help* it.

'It's Daddy, I suppose,' she confessed ruefully. 'When your father's the Rector, you have to *try* to be good, don't you?'

'Most people try to be good,' Felix said irritably. 'But there's no need to take it to extremes. Did you ever hear about the Boy Scout who took the blind man across the road?'

'What Boy Scout?'

Felix sighed.

Miriam smiled warily. 'Is this a joke, Fee?'

'No, it's a parable: the point being that the blind man didn't *want* to cross the road. You've heard the phrase, "being cruel to be kind"?'

'Yes . . .'

'Well, it works the other way, too.'

'Felix!' Miriam laughed uncomfortably. 'What are you *saying*?'

'I'm saying you don't think, either about other people's needs or your own.'

Miriam pretended to look ashamed of herself. 'I know I don't think about my own needs much,' she began humbly, 'but – '

'That wasn't what I meant.'

Their walk had brought them to Draycott Bridge and Felix leaned on the parapet and gazed down river, hoping for a glimpse of the kingfisher.

'What *did* you mean, Fee?'

He sighed again. It was no good. He didn't love her any more and knew that he would hurt her if they went on like this. His fault. Entirely his fault. He'd been in need of comfort after Mike's death and, although he'd *thought* he'd fallen for Miriam by accident, he knew now that it had been a very calculated choice. Miriam was a good, kind, gentle girl: exactly the sort to give comfort without taking much in return. And if all she took was food for her ego, who was he to criticise?

'I do think about other people's needs, Felix.'

She was a small, dark girl, with glossy black hair and big brown eyes which looked up at him now very soulfully.

'It's all I *ever* think about. What's wrong with that?'

He laughed and put his arm around her shoulders. 'Nothing,' he lied. 'As long as there's nothing else worth thinking about.'

'Do you mean intellectually? I thought you meant morally.'

'That's – ' He swallowed, having almost said, 'That's what's wrong with you,' which was the last thing he wanted to say.

'That's one of the differences between you and me, Miriam. You keep your morals and your mind in separate compartments. Is that because you're too convinced by Christianity to ask it any questions?'

Miriam smiled and wound her arm possessively through his. 'Perhaps. But that's what faith is, Felix.'

'Your faith,' he said, 'is another, very important, difference between us. You know I don't share it.'

'It doesn't matter. Christ loves sinners, too.'

(Too! As if she were a *saint*!) 'Oh, good,' Felix said dryly.

'But I'm no more a sinner than you are. No less, either.'

He closed his eyes. He hadn't meant to say that. 'What I mean is . . .'

'Oh, look! A kingfisher!' Laughing, she broke away from him and ran to the far end of the bridge to get a better view. Felix didn't even look. The kingfisher was something you saw if you were lucky. Finishing with your girlfriend was something you did because you'd decided to *do* it. Even if it killed you.

And as Miriam smiled, craned her neck and attempted, not very convincingly, to climb up on the parapet, Felix saw that she knew what he was doing. She hadn't seen the kingfisher at all. She was creating a diversion, putting on a show. The smile was to remind him how pretty she was and the climb to make him fear for her safety.

He wasn't afraid for her safety. He might have been, when he'd thought her an angel, but now he couldn't help thinking that a sudden dunking in the Dray might do her the world of good. She was smug, sanctimonious, narrow-minded and shallow. Nothing bad had ever happened to her, and although in her determination to be 'good', she did think about other people, she didn't think deeply enough, didn't understand, didn't even try.

Felix hadn't understood how wrong this was until, just a few weeks ago, he'd seen her race across the square to help poor old Archie Weaver with his shopping basket. Felix hadn't been able to get it out of his mind ever since: the look on the old chap's face, the look on Miriam's. Archie was going on eighty, and so doubled up with rheumatism that he never saw anything above the level of his knees, but he was a proud, independent old countryman and a gentleman in his way: the sort of man who, in spite of his infirmities, felt that it was *his* place to carry a woman's shopping, not let her carry his!

'No, no, m'dear! Thank 'ee most kindly, m'dear, but no, I can manage 'un fine!'

'Oh, Mr Weaver, please! It's no trouble!'

They'd virtually come to blows over it, but of course Miriam had won. She was young and strong. Determined to be . . . kind.

The shopping basket *had* been heavy. And Archie lived a long step away from the square. On the surface of it, one knew that to help him would be a kindness; but why hadn't Miriam looked beyond the surface, seen the hurt in his eyes, heard the wounded desperation of his protests? Because she didn't care. She'd been putting on a show, just as she was now.

Look, God, how good I am! Look, Felix, how pretty I am! Don't you just *love* me?

Felix sighed, wondering – if there was a God – what He felt about it. Sad, of course. He wouldn't be angry, just sad. And perhaps, if God was as good as Miriam claimed, He'd be a little amused, too, and very forgiving.

Don't be so hard on her, Felix. She's young yet. She'll learn.

Felix smiled and lifted her down from her perch. 'Come on,' he said. 'Time to go home.'

Jean began wearing lipstick to work. Bert didn't notice. She had her hair cut and spent hours every night putting it in curling rags. Bert didn't notice. She went on a diet – it nearly killed her, too – rationing was a diet in its own right and she was already slimmer than she'd ever been. But Bert didn't notice.

Everyone else noticed. It got so that she couldn't put her nose out of doors without someone stopping to say, 'Oh, you do look nice!' or, 'You'm looking very smart, m'dear,' or even, on one very embarrassing occasion, actually *wolf-whistling* at her!

But the Rector had been very good about it. 'Take it as a compliment, my dear,' he said, as the Army lorry sped away down the Bristol road. 'After all, Mrs Carter, you *are* looking very charming today.'

So even *he'd* noticed.

And then something awful happened. Arnold Fudge noticed, and because Arnold Fudge was the last man on earth Jean would have wanted to notice, she didn't even notice he'd noticed until people started to talk.

Like Miles Huntley, Arnold Fudge was famous for his teeth, which were as strong and as white when he was fifty-six as when he was fifteen. But there was one important difference. Where Mr Huntley's teeth emerged from his gums in a firm, straight line, Arnold's fanned out over his bottom lip like a porch over a doorway, making him lisp, making him spit. No one ever stayed long in conversation with Arnold Fudge for fear of being drowned in his drool, although in most other respects he was a fine figure of a man: kind-hearted and sensible and not badly off, for of course he'd never married.

He lived all alone in a galvanised bungalow out towards Molton Draycott. Before the war, he'd kept a twenty-acre smallholding, with a few cows, a few steers, a few chickens, a few pigs. Now he'd gone into market gardening and had done very well for himself, although everyone knew he was lonely.

Jean had known it and pitied him. She'd made it a point, every time she delivered his post, to smile and wave and shout good morning. She'd also made a point of pedalling away again, very fast, before he had a chance to reply and soak her in spit.

Now, shy and polite, touching his cap, he brought her a sack of forked carrots: 'No good for market, shee, Mishish Carter, but I reckoned, shinsh I was passhing, 'ee might appreshiate 'em in a shtew or shummat.'

'Oh! Oh, well, if you're sure, Mr Fudge . . . How kind.'

She thought he was just being kind. Even when he came again with a brace of big-hearted cabbage (full of shlugsh he said, though they weren't), she didn't suspect that *his* heart was involved. He was a good bit older than she was, more the fatherly type than . . . Well, it just never crossed her mind!

It was soon after he'd brought the raspberries that Mrs Moon in the draper's remarked slyly, 'I see Arnold Fudge got his courting cap on then, Mrs Carter,' and *still* Jean didn't see it; she didn't even *suspect*!

'Never!' she gasped. 'Who? Not shomeone in the village, ish it?'

She did notice that Mrs Moon looked at her a bit 'comical', but thought it was just because she'd been cruel about his teeth. She worried about it afterwards and wished she'd been kinder. His teeth weren't his fault, after all.

'So,' Bert said a couple of days later when they were sorting the post at the crack of dawn. 'What d'you make of old Arnold, then?'

'What?'

'Decent sort of chap, of course. And they say he've got a nice bit put by. The war's set him up very tidy, I should think. Pity about that old bungalow of his, though. It may be all right; I'm not saying otherwise, but I can't say I've ever liked the idea of metal. Not to live in. And think of the noise the rain'd make on that roof.' He shrugged. 'Still, I suppose you'd get used to it.'

Jean giggled. 'It's never true, is it, Bert? Is he really going courting? Mrs Moon said he was, but – '

The penny dropped just as Bert's jaw did.

'Bert!' she shrieked. 'It's never – ! It's not – ! You can't mean – ! *Me*?'

They stared at each other, Jean's eyes popping with amazement, Bert's steady and thoughtful and then slowly warming, crinkling at the corners as he tried to suppress a grin.

They burst out laughing in the same instant. In the three years she'd been working with him Jean had never seen Bert laugh. He'd smiled a lot; he'd chuckled now and then; but really laugh, really let himself go, never. And it was the most wonderful thing to see. It was wonderful to hear him, whooping and roaring, howling and giggling until the tears ran down his face and he was as helpless as Jean was.

For Jean, it was like being let out of a cage, like being told, 'Go free, fly away, enjoy yourself,' and it wasn't until her ribs began to ache with the effort of flying that she realised *she'd* never really laughed either. Not for years and years. Not since she'd married Jack.

'Oh,' Bert gasped at last. 'Oh, Jean, I haven't laughed like that since – '

'Nor me! Oh, Bert, oh, Bert, I never heard anything so funny! Me and Arnold Fudge! Oh Lord! Oh, my Lord!'

They mopped their faces. Bert blew his nose, laughed again and sagged against the wall.

'You're lovely when you laugh,' he said.

Jean blushed and laid her hands on her cheeks to cool them. 'You don't look so bad yourself, Bert,' she murmured.

He pushed himself off the wall and held out his arms to her, so naturally, so easily, it was as if they began every day like this, knowing each other, loving each other. And Jean stepped into his arms, naturally, easily, tipping up her face to smile into his eyes.

'I haven't even shaved,' he said.

'Neither have I, Bert.'

'I'll rub your lipstick off.'

'That's what it's there for.'

He smiled. He sighed. He cupped her damp, burning cheeks with gentle hands. 'That's all right, then,' he said.

Felix could not say that he regretted it. He could say that he regretted hurting Miriam, he could say that he regretted – deeply regretted – his own dependence on her company, for even at her sanctimonious worst her company had been better . . .

No. No, it hadn't been better than loneliness, for at least loneliness didn't make him feel as angry as Miriam had done. Looking at it objectively he realised that he'd been more angry with himself than with her, because he'd done precisely the thing he'd accused her of. He'd been 'good' for all the wrong reasons and made himself downright bad in the process.

His father needed him no more than Archie Weaver (and a few dozen other poor souls) needed Miriam. True, Felix was helping to carry Leonard's burden, but the truth was that he'd have been better left to carry it alone. The man had his pride. Stammer or no stammer, with or without Mike, he'd have won through. He'd done it before. He could have done it again.

Now that it was too late (much too late) to change his mind, Felix knew he'd been a fool to give up his own life for something . . . something as cheap as public approval, and yet that was all it had been when you came down to it. Yes, he'd cared about his father, but not as much as he'd wanted to be seen to be doing the right thing for him. And he had no excuse. People much wiser than he had advised him against it. Even a year later it made him blush to think of how he'd turned down Miles Huntley's offer of salvation.

'There's a power, like electricity . . .' He might just as well have simpered, 'Christ loves sinners too,' for all the wisdom that had lain behind it.

He was wiser now. He'd begun to learn his limitations and to understand that the power he'd spoken so carelessly about was the power . . . of love. Not the love of a man for a woman, or of a son for his father – and most certainly not the love one bore oneself – but simply a love of *farming*. The kind of love that Mike had had for the land, for the elements that governed it, for the tools that worked it, the animals that grazed it, the very shit that fed it and brought it – safely or otherwise – out of winter to seedtime and harvest.

Felix might never have known a thing about this power, this love, had he not, during the past year, felt it for himself and thought – oh, for such brief, tantalising moments – 'I've got it! I understand it! I know!' before being plunged once again into a state of near desperation when he realised that he had nothing at all. He would never make a farmer. He had deliberately – and almost literally – harnessed himself to a plough he had neither the strength nor the inclination to pull. And he was stuck with it for the rest of his life.

'Hello, Felix. Everything all right, is it?'

He snapped himself out of his thoughts and smiled automatically, before he quite realised who had spoken to him. But it was only Mrs Carter with the afternoon post. He didn't greatly like Mrs Carter. Good looks aside, Evelyn had meant very little to him, but he'd never quite forgiven her mother for protecting her so fiercely. 'Fierce' wasn't quite the word for it. Hysterical was the word. He could, if he tried very hard, see her point of view. Evelyn had been too young for any 'playing around'. Felix had known that and – within certain limits – respected it. But what the hell was the point of having a girlfriend if you couldn't even kiss her? That was all he'd wanted at the time and it had been rather disgusting – not to say embarrassing – to be suspected of something far worse.

'Yes, thanks,' he lied pleasantly. 'Everything's fine. And with you, I hope?'

She blushed and he remembered hearing something about her and Mr Tomkins from the Post Office. He hadn't given it more than a fleeting thought at the time, but now . . . She did look a little different than usual: calmer, softer, prettier. Younger! He'd always thought of her as one of his parents' generation: 'somewhere between forty and sixty', even knowing that she must come near the bottom of the scale, but today she looked scarcely old enough to have a daughter of five, let alone one of fifteen.

'I suppose you've heard my news?' she laughed shyly.

'No. Good news?'

'I'm getting married.' Even as she spoke, another five years were stripped away and she was eighteen again. Felix sighed mightily, smiled bravely, congratulated her and asked all the right questions, but he felt close to tears. The power of love – whether it sprang from the land or from the Bishop Molton sub-Post Office – was a hell of a lot stronger than electricity!

He'd been going to fetch the cows in for milking, but as Mrs Carter pedalled girlishly away, he leafed through the pile of letters she'd given him, found one addressed to him in Alan's hand, and dropped the rest on to the hall table before tearing the letter open. Alan had never written especially to Felix before, and it was an honour he felt very keenly. The war had already lasted almost five years, long enough for even Felix to have only vague memories of peace, and in that time Alan had been home only twice. The objective part of Felix's mind kept reminding him that his brother was still a human being, with as many faults and failings as everyone else; but in spite of this he still saw him as a kind of superman whose every trivial mention of his 'little brother' in letters to the family felt like a special blessing. To have a letter written exclusively for him was almost too good to believe.

He did not, at first, believe it. He read it twice. He read it three times and then sat on the garden wall, staring thoughtfully into space. 'I've seen enough of the world,' Alan had said. 'My first and last thoughts are always of Drayfield and I know I'll never want to leave it again. Hold the fort for me until the end of the war, and then we'll both be free: you to go if you still want to, and me to stay, which I want now more than anything else.'

Felix had never been so happy or so at peace with himself. Alan was the last person on earth he would have expected to save him from the error of his ways, and simply because he had communicated none of his discontent either to his parents or to Alan, he felt sure that the offer was genuine. Alan wasn't doing as Felix had done: 'the right thing for the wrong reasons'. He wasn't making a sacrifice. He wanted to come home for his own sake, which meant that Felix could now go away for *his* own sake and with a clear conscience.

Without for a moment suspecting that he was making yet another mistake, Felix put all his mistakes behind him and began to enjoy the freedom of simply *anticipating* freedom. The most curious thing was that now he no longer felt bound to it, even farming became a pleasure. He saw it through different eyes, as a means to an end rather than as an end in its own right. Although he'd never been unconscious of farming's importance in pursuing a victorious conclusion to the war, he now began to see it as a passport to his own personal victory and put his heart into the work for the first time in his life.

Much to their surprise, his parents, with the equally surprised Huntleys, were invited to Jean Carter's wedding on the third of June: a quiet affair at which the only other guests were Mr Tomkins' grown-up son and daughter-in-law who'd come over from Bristol. But in the evening there was a party at the church hall, and it seemed that everyone in the valley turned out for that. Felix didn't really want to go – Miriam was sure to be there – but if only to do the polite thing, he called in 'for five minutes', stayed for another five and finally left with everyone else, just before blackout.

It was a wonderful party. At first, Felix thought most of the guests had come to honour Bert Tomkins, who was universally liked and respected, but from odd snippets of talk he heard during the evening it seemed that Mrs Carter – Mrs Tomkins

– was far more popular in the valley than Felix had realised. People said she'd had a hard time, come through it like a trooper and deserved some happiness at last. They muttered and shrugged about her late husband – a bounder, apparently – who'd treated her like dirt and left her with nothing. They talked about her wonderful housekeeping, her beautiful daughters, the fact that she'd never, for all that she was a bit high-strung, complained of her lot or done anyone a bad turn. And they looked at her and smiled and talked of ugly ducklings turning into swans.

Felix had never thought her an ugly duckling. She'd always, since he'd known her, been a nice-looking sort of woman: short and plump and pretty, albeit in a quite ordinary, motherly sort of way. But now she was radiant, so glowing with happiness and goodwill that Felix forgave her everything and wished her joy with all his heart.

Another guest at the party was almost equally surprising. He hadn't seen Jinny Huntley for months. She'd been attending a private day school in Bath for the past year and had no time, any more, for her old wanderings. But the change in her – ! She could be only twelve, if that, but she was no longer a child. She'd always looked like Bel, but – in Felix's eyes at least – the resemblance had been just a matter of features, height, tone of voice. Now, her features were much less like Bel's and everything else far more. She had Bel's grace, her way of smiling which seemed, paradoxically, both to embrace its recipients and hold them at arm's length. Penny had once described that smile as saying, 'I shall love you with all my heart, but you can love *me* from ten miles off'.

It was the smile of a woman who knew her place in the world, had confidence in it and was proud of it; the smile of a *woman*, not of the kid whose tears Felix had mopped, whose knickers and socks he'd pulled up, the kid he'd known since she was scarcely out of her pram!

'Hello, Jinny. You're looking very grown-up tonight.' (He meant beautiful, but was damned if he'd say so!)

'Oh,' she said, 'well, that's a comfort.' It was the sort of thing he might have expected her to say: dry and rueful, mildly self-denigrating, and yet there was something so different about her! Felix felt quite awed and bewildered, wondering how, in so short a time, she could have changed so much without really changing at all.

He thought about it, on and off, for the next few days and each time he felt a little sadder. Everything was changing. It had been changing ever since the war had begun: big changes, small changes, bad changes, good changes; but somehow he'd taken them all in his stride, seen each one as a separate entity, not as a whole. Now, just because Jinny was growing up, he was able to look back and realise that he'd lived not just through a war but a major revolution. When he'd first met Jinny there'd been no electricity at Drayfield, no telephone, no tractors, not even an indoor lavatory. On long summer evenings, the village kids had played football in the square, and if they'd had to stop once to let a car go by they'd regarded it as an event. Now they didn't dare cross the street without praying they wouldn't be mown down by an Army truck! When he'd first met Jinny, he could have counted the number of aeroplanes he'd seen on the fingers of one hand. The world had been so quiet, so still, you could almost hear the grass grow . . .

No, life wasn't changing; it had *changed*, and now seemed balanced on a cusp between two worlds, the old and the new. Life for everyone must surely be better from now on. The war was proceeding well, the Allies increasing in strength on every front. It would soon be over. Alan would come home. Then the new world could begin in earnest, with Felix playing his part in it, just as he'd always planned.

So why did he feel so *sad*?

Chapter Nineteen

'Four thousand ships, eleven thousand Allied planes in assault on France.' Miles read the headlines to his wife in a voice which strained between laughter and tears. This was it: the day they'd all waited for, prayed for, dreaded. Eleven thousand planes! Yet he could think of only two of them and pray that even if all else went down, those two, just those two, would come home.

Bel sat opposite him at the kitchen table, her hand over her eyes. 'Thank God for haymaking,' she murmured wearily.

'What?'

'Take our minds off it . . .'

He smiled. She was right, of course. It seemed impossible that the twins could suffer even a moment of mortal danger without their parents worrying about them, yet – if one included their months of training – they'd been in mortal danger for the best part of four years, and Miles, for one, hadn't spent even a quarter of that time in a state of terror for their safety. Except when he knew there was a big push going on, he thought of them by a measure of seconds, not hours. The fear was too great to sustain for longer. A single thought set one's stomach churning, stretched one's nerves almost to snapping point. Then there was nothing left except to say,

'I can do nothing to help them. Work, read, go to sleep, forget it.'

In another month, Robin would be joining up too, but even he would add only another few seconds to the score. It was easier to worry about Andrew. The misery and frustration of his imprisonment, even the thought of his being cold, hungry and comfortless, were things one could contemplate *without* going quite mad.

'When this war's over,' Bel said drearily, 'we'll all go barmy, and I don't mean with excitement. I don't know about you, but I'm beginning to feel like a barrage balloon, so full of gas – '

'Take some bicarb, darling. That'll shift it.'

She laughed softly. 'I meant tension, you fool. While it seems necessary I can go on and on, stretching myself out just a little bit more and a little bit more. But when, please God, it's all over, I think I'll just go pop. The relief will finish me off. I'm sure of it.'

He patted her hand. 'Let's hope for that then, shall we? Relief enough to finish us off.'

'Oh, yes!' She wept, her face twisting as she struggled for control. Then she straightened her spine, brushed the tears from her lashes (there hadn't been enough to wet her cheeks), blew her nose and was calm again.

'I told Jinny you'd help her with her geometry, Miles. Think you can bear it?'

'Mm.' He sighed and stood up, preparing to depart. 'Think *she* can?'

Jinny, poor child, had inherited her mother's mathematical talents. She'd been fine with the basic precepts, which were as much as the village school had asked of her, but it seemed she'd prefer to fight the Nazi hordes single-handed than tackle a page of geometry without aid. The trouble was that his help was scarcely better, in Jinny's view, than no help at all. In spite of all he could do to reassure her, she still trusted him no further than she could throw him and, oddly, trusted her mother now scarcely more. What had seemed so wonderful to *him* about his reconciliation with Bel had had quite the opposite effect on Jinny, who seemed to think they'd all changed sides, leaving her out in no-man's-land, even more isolated than before.

But she'd changed a good deal during the past year: the new school had worked wonders for her confidence, and the onset of puberty had given her a startling beauty which scared Miles half to death, for she sometimes looked nearer eighteen than twelve. Still, she seemed to have stopped growing. That was something. Bel had feared that if she held off maturity until her fourteenth year she'd shoot out through the roof. Five foot nine would make an elegant woman of her: six foot four would have been a disaster!

She was meant to be attending to her schoolwork on the terrace. In fact, even though she was surrounded by books, ink, rulers, pencils and blotting paper, she was sitting with her chin in her hands, staring dreamily into space, her long legs outstretched to catch the still-powerful rays of the evening sun.

'I do hope you're thinking about something educational,' Miles quipped lightly.

'Hmm,' she said. 'No, I was thinking about honeymoons.'

'Good Lord. Why?'

'Well, really I was thinking about the twins, and all the mess they're making in France.'

Miles bit his lip on a smile. When she was still very young – seven or eight – Jinny had seen an appalling road accident on the outskirts of Bristol. She and Bel had both come home in tears: Bel describing the swift and bloody deaths of a young motorcyclist and his girlfriend; Jinny sobbing, 'And the lamppost was all bent!'

Miles hadn't understood it at the time. Now he knew that, unable to confront such carnage in her mind, she'd deflected her thoughts to the least bloody – yet most symbolic – part of it. Had there been no lamp-post, there'd have been no accident. Had there been no France for her brothers to make a mess of, there'd have been no France to make a mess of her brothers.

'You had your honeymoon in France, didn't you, Daddy?'

'Yes, but not that part of it.'

'Still, it'll be ages before anyone can have a honeymoon again, won't it? I think that's sad. Mrs Car . . . Tomkins was only married one and a half days before she went back to work.'

'I shouldn't worry,' he smiled. 'She doesn't seem too sad about it. And Mr Tomkins isn't really the sort to contemplate Cannes for a honeymoon. Weston-super-Mare, perhaps.'

'They will be all right, won't they, Daddy?'

'Mr and Mrs Tomkins? Yes, why shouldn't they be?'

'I meant the twins. Alan Clare. Everyone.'

His stomach lurched. He closed his eyes and sent a short but fervent prayer to the God he didn't believe in. Then, extracting a dog-eared geometry textbook from the heap, 'Work,' he said firmly. 'It's all we can do, Jinny.'

He began haymaking the next day and for the next few weeks, with virtually everyone else in the valley, he worked until he dropped, slept like a stone and then worked until he dropped again. By the eighth day they'd heard from both the twins, and, simply because they'd survived the first push, Miles's level of anxiety went back to 'business as usual'. They could still be killed. But since it didn't bear thinking about any more, he pushed it to the back of his mind, let it simmer, and merely stirred it now and then to keep it from burning.

He was actually thinking about rabbits when Felix arrived at Home Farm one evening during the last week of June. (Rabbits seemed to multiply about ten times faster than anyone could shoot them and the damage they did was by no means compensated for by a glut of rabbit stew.) At first he saw Felix from the corner of his eye and, since such sightings rely as much on memory as on true perception, he saw him as he'd seen him last: a tall, slender, sweet-faced boy, still glorying in the tireless strength of his eighteenth year.

'Hello, Felix. Hay all in?' He turned his head as he finished speaking and saw not the sweet-faced boy he remembered but a man, new-forged, the steel in his eyes still hot from the fire. Only one thing could have changed him so much, so swiftly. Men weren't made overnight, unless . . .

Miles turned away, bowing his head. 'Alan?' he asked softly.

'We heard this afternoon.' Even Felix's voice had changed, become cold, hard and clipped. 'Wounded on D-Day. Died a week later.'

'I'm very sorry.' Miles spoke to the barn door, addressing it with all the dignity he could muster while he fought against tears. He had known Alan only slightly and could scarcely remember him. He couldn't, therefore, mourn him for his own sake, but for Felix, for Leonard and Penny . . .

'I won't ask how you are, Felix. I see, I know how you are. But your parents?'

'My mother will survive it. My father . . .' He paused, sucked a breath through his teeth and went on quietly, 'I think this might be the straw that breaks the camel's back, Mr Huntley. He's borne too much. I'm on my own.'

Miles sighed and turned to address Felix's boots. 'I shan't tell you otherwise,' he said gently. 'The only comfort I can offer is to say – truly – that we are all of us alone. No one can do our suffering for us. No one can give us strength to endure it. The best any of us can hope is that we may be alone among friends and, for what it's worth at a time like this, you *are* among friends, Felix.'

'I know it. Thank you, sir.'

They shook hands without meeting each other's eyes. Michael Clare had been dead only a year. Now Alan. Tomorrow Leonard?

Miles couldn't bear to see such grief.

Felix couldn't bear it to be seen.

For Jean, marrying Bert Tomkins was like dying and going to heaven. Not just because of *him*. Appreciate him as she did, love and admire him as she did, *he* was only half of it. The other half (she sometimes thought it was the better half) was his house, his home, that mysterious place beyond the vestibule which he'd kept secret for so long. She'd imagined it as being as cold, as dark and as poky as the vestibule itself. She'd imagined it strewn with odd socks, dogeared books, cobwebs and cigarette ash. Had Jack been left to live even a year on his own he'd have been up to his ears in muck, but Bert . . . Oh, Bert! Bert lived in a palace!

What had deceived her, what she'd never known (or even imagined) was that he didn't just live behind the Post Office. His home stretched behind the butcher's, the newsagent's and the Methodist chapel. It was huge! It had five bedrooms, a lovely big bathroom with hot and cold water, a parlour, a dining room, a . . . A library!

'Oh, Bert!'

'Like it, Jean?'

'Oh, Bert! Oh, Bert!'

'Not what you expected, then?'

'Oh, *Bert*!'

It wasn't spotless. No good to say it was, because it wasn't. There was fluff under the sideboard, dust on the wardrobes and a pile of unwiped dishes on the draining board. But that didn't matter. Spotless or not, it was a palace. He had such lovely things! A rich man's things. Things she'd never have thought he could want or even know about! Rugs and paintings, brass and silver, china and crystal and books by the thousand.

'Most of it belonged to my wife's people, see, Jean. I'd never seen anything like it until I met her, but then I made a bit of a study of it, bought a few bits myself, got a taste for it. It's not something I could have afforded to start from scratch, but it's nice to add to, just a little bit, here and there.'

When he'd finished showing her the house, he'd shown her the garden and she could scarcely believe her eyes there, either! Oh, she'd known he *had* a garden, because they'd talked about it, many a time, while they were sorting the post. The best time to sow broad beans, the best way to deal with slugs and blackfly. But never in her wildest dreams . . . It was better than Bishop's Court!

'No, no; not as big, see, Jean. They got too much at Bishop's Court; that's their trouble. They got no time to keep it nice; not like I can.'

'But why have I never seen it, Bert? I only live just up the road, and I've never – Oh, it's like a dream! It's like magic! Oh, who'd ever have *guessed*?'

No one could have guessed who wasn't sitting on a roof somewhere, for Bert's garden was completely enclosed by the blank back walls of other people's houses, shops, barns and, of course, the Methodist Chapel. But it was the size of it that was so bewildering. It was like a little park, with lawns and trees, shrubs and flowers as well as vegetables; and all of it slap-bang in the middle of the village, like an oasis in a desert!

'Oh, Bert, Bert! I've never seen anything so beautiful in all my life!'

'I have,' he said. But he was looking at her at the time, and she blushed and dithered and didn't know where to put herself. For he'd changed. He wasn't just Bert any more. He was a prince. He lived in a palace!

They gave it a good clean-down-through the Sunday before the wedding. Bert didn't really approve of labouring on the Sabbath, even in wartime. He said the Sabbath was meant for worship, not for work. Jean said that if they worked and worshipped at the same time it would probably be all right, so while Bert shifted the furniture and she cleaned behind it, they sang hymns at the tops of their voices: 'All Things Bright and Beautiful' and 'Jesus Bids me Shine'.

Jean had never been so happy. She realised too that she had never before been in love; or, rather, that if she had been in love with Jack, she was not now in love with Bert. This was so different, so easy and warm. They laughed – really *laughed* – over the silliest, most ordinary little things: things Jack would never have noticed except to sneer at or complain of; and they talked about serious and important things: feelings, beliefs, principles. Principles! Jack had never had any of those! And had *he* been marrying a woman with four children not his own, it would never have crossed his mind to ask, as Bert did, 'Think they'll take to me, love? Think they'll be happy?'

If Jean hadn't loved him before, for so many reasons, she'd have loved him then, just for that.

The wedding night was a bit of a disappointment. Bert was no drinker and he'd had one too many at the party. It didn't make him tiddly, just tired, and after one rather embarrassing attempt – more anxious than ardent – he fell asleep and left Jean wondering . . . What *had* his first wife died of? Frustration?

But Bert woke up again a few hours later. And a few hours after that. And again. And it was all Jean had hoped for: gentle, generous and sweet; making *love*.

So it definitely wasn't frustration.

A couple of weeks later, when Bert broke the news to her about Alan Clare, she clapped her hand to her mouth, cried, 'Oh, no!' and fell into his arms, sobbing like a child. 'There,' he said. 'There, there. Don't take on about it, love. These things happen. Bound to, in wartime.'

He was right. They did. It wasn't her fault.

And anyway, when you came right down to it, she was really too happy to care any more. Oh, she cared about Alan and the grief he'd left his family to bear, but curses? Load of rubbish!

* *

Two pails of water are easier to carry than one. One will pull the body aslant, destroying the balance and creating muscular tensions which can't long be sustained. Two maintain their bearer's centre of gravity, keep him straight on his path and upright in his stance, so that, even though he is carrying twice the burden, he can carry it ten times as far.

For Felix, Mike's death had been one pail of water. It had bent his back and made him stagger. Alan's death, although it doubled the burden, set him straight again. He had no options left and therefore no confusion of mind. He was a farmer now, and whether he liked it or not was no longer a matter of consequence. He didn't even consider it. Happiness? What was happiness? Whether at Drayfield, at Oxford, in France or beyond the furthest reaches of the Amazon jungle, happiness didn't exist and was no longer to be looked for.

When Bert Tomkins had brought the telegram, when Felix had read it, he'd felt that his soul had been seared by a fire so hot that when it cooled there was nothing left of him. He was burned hollow. He was as light as air. He could think very clearly, could see with greater clarity than ever before, but feelings – he had none. He cared as tenderly as he could for his parents, he worked as hard as he could on the farm. But it meant nothing. He could see that certain things were expected of him or, if not expected, hoped for; and he performed them all with the ease and detachment of an automaton, feeling no pain. Even when he knew that what he was doing should have been agonising, he felt no pain.

Leonard hid under the stairs. He crouched there and wept, rocking himself. Felix sat with him, talked with him, held his hand, and when – after four hours – his father at last agreed to come out, Felix helped him upstairs, washed his face, undressed him and put him to bed.

Penny's expressions of grief were even worse. She cleaned the house, cleaned every inch of it; and, when it was cleaner than it had ever been before, she cleaned it again. Before the war, in fact for the whole of her life before the war, she had never used her hands for anything that might hurt or harden them against her music. Even when her devoted 'help' had been swallowed up by the war-effort, she'd done just enough (as she'd been fond of saying) 'to keep the cholera at bay'. Felix had thought he'd never grow accustomed to living with so much dirt and disorder. Now he found that he'd loved every minute of it, for there was something almost obscene in a house which shone for such a reason, a house rendered silent for such a reason. He'd have faced cholera ten times over just to hear his mother play again; but, except to dust it, she never went near the piano now.

Yet for all that he did and said to relieve his parents' grief, for all that he could observe and understand what they were suffering, he didn't really care. It was as if he'd read about them in a newspaper: 'Pianist and War-Hero Lose Son on D-Day'. How sad. What a tragedy. But what could one do? What could one say? Life went on . . .

Remembering the delay his emotions had suffered after Mike's death, Felix suspected that the same thing would happen again, that the devastation would suddenly sneak up on him, knock him down and leave him as near-dead as his father was, or as half-alive as his mother. The thought of it terrified him, for if *he* lost his grip they'd all be lost. Miles Huntley – as ever – was bending over backwards to help, encourage and advise, but even Miles had his limits. He couldn't run Drayfield for them and if they failed . . . If Felix failed . . . No, he couldn't afford to go under.

The war was nearing its end, Hitler was dead and the newest of Drayfield's two tractors had broken down. Felix was very tired. His father had recovered enough to want to get back to work, but not enough to do very much and his presence on the farm was more a hindrance than a help, if only because he needed to be handled with tact, respect and, above all things, patience. Felix hadn't much patience left. Just this evening, when he'd bodged a temporary repair of the tractor and still ended up in need of spare parts, Leonard had said, 'I d-d-duh – duh-don't . . . thuh-th-thuh-think . . .'

It was like being stretched on a rack; standing there smiling, waiting, guessing. He'd guessed that Leonard was going to say, 'I don't think that's necessary,' and – eventually – come up with the answer Felix needed. But he hadn't. After another tortuous wait, he'd finally managed to say, 'I don't think we've had this trouble before. Ask Miles if he's got some spares,' which was precisely what Felix had been meaning to do in the first place.

Intending to catch Miles on his last 'tidying up' round of duty at Home Farm, Felix set off soon after supper, taking his gun and walking through the woods behind Drayfield, hoping to bag a few rabbits. If you could kill five rabbits in May, you saved yourself the depredations of fifty in July; but no matter how many you shot there were always too many. The wheat, oats, mangle and barley yields would have been as much as thirty per cent higher had God not invented rabbits.

There was a huge warren of them just to the north of the woods and Felix was still tiptoeing towards it when he saw Jinny, sitting in the sun on the very banks of the warren. His mouth thinning with annoyance (they wouldn't show their noses while she was there) he took a deep breath, closed his eyes and scraped the back of his mind for yet more patience. It didn't matter that he couldn't shoot rabbits now, this minute. He could just as easily – in fact, more easily – do it on his way back. And it was good to see Jinny again. She hadn't been to Drayfield at all since Alan's death and in that time Felix had caught only the occasional glimpse of her: busy, distracted glimpses which, if they'd prompted any thoughts at all, were only that she was growing into a fine-looking girl.

She looked neither very fine nor very grown-up at the moment. In fact she looked very much the forlorn little waif he remembered from the past. Her knees were clean; but the grey flannel shorts and the tattered blouse, the red-blonde hair in a tangled veil over her eyes . . . Yes, that was the Jinny he knew.

Patience restored, he stepped out from the shelter of the trees and called out cheerfully, 'Hello, stranger!'

Thanks to the veil of hair, he hadn't seen her face. Now, as she glanced briefly up at him he saw that she'd been crying and was about to do so again.

'What's up with you?' Even to his own ears his voice sounded cold, hard and weary. He'd witnessed enough tears, dealt out enough sympathy during the past couple of years to last him a lifetime; he hadn't the energy for more. But as Jinny scrambled to her feet and made to depart, he was stricken with guilt and self-hatred. Poor kid; she'd always come to him when she was in trouble and although she'd learned to do without him just lately, he couldn't let her go uncomforted now. 'Hey, Jin? Hey!' He ran across the clearing, caught her by the elbow and turned her gently into his arms. 'Jinny! What's wrong?'

'Simon,' she whispered, and then laying her head on his shoulder, she soaked his shirt with tears. It didn't take very long – Jinny had never been a great one for indulging herself – but it took long enough. Simon was dead? No, he couldn't be! The war was as good as over! He couldn't be!

He set her away from him, shook her gently. 'Quick,' he whispered urgently. 'Tell me, Jinny. What's happened to Simon?'

'Engine failure,' she sobbed. 'He came down in the sea.'

Then it happened. The pain hit him like a soft-nosed shell, penetrating his heart and then exploding, tearing him apart. Even then, at that moment, he was aware of the strangeness of it: that Simon – a man he scarcely knew – should be killed before he could realise that Alan, the brother he'd worshipped, had been lost for ever.

It was some time before Jinny realised that she was being shaken by sobs not her own. When she did realise it, and drew away from him, Felix tightened his arms about her and cried, 'Stay! Please! For God's sake, Jinny, hold me!'

Any other kid of Jinny's age would have been scared rigid by his sudden collapse, but if Jinny was scared, he knew nothing of it. She held him with arms as strong as iron, soothed him with murmurs as soft as milk. She led him to the warren bank, sat him down and rocked him in her arms until he was quiet: stunned to silence.

'All right now, Felix?'

He raised his red, swollen eyes to her red, swollen eyes, and chuckled wryly. 'Thanks,' he said. 'I've been a great comfort to you, haven't I?'

'It wasn't Simon, was it?'

'No. I'm ... I'm sorry. It just ... I just ...' He began to weep again. 'Oh, God, now I've started I don't think I'll ever stop!'

Time and time again he wept. And recovered, laughed, apologised and tried to help Jinny as she had helped him. But his mind was filled with strange images which, however hard he fought them, undermined his every attempt at self-control.

'I keep thinking of old Nipper,' he whispered. 'Remember Nipper? He was the best dog in the world, Jinny, but I didn't even cry for him. Now I seem to be crying for everyone, everything!'

'Nipper was old,' Jinny said gently. 'And in pain, Felix. That's why you didn't cry.'

'Alan wasn't old! Mike wasn't old! Simon ...'

'Know what I think, Felix? I think maybe it doesn't matter. I know Simon would laugh if he could see me now. Crying for him, just because he's dead. If it were possible for a dead person to feel anything about being dead, I should think he'd be quite relieved.'

This made so much sense that Felix was surprised into thinking about it. Yes, she was right. It was life, not death, that hurt so much. Only the living could suffer. The dead – ?'

'I suppose you believe in heaven, Jinny.'

'No. I know I should, but I'd much rather not. When we thought Andrew was dead... I believed in it then, and it worried me so much I decided not to believe in it any more. Everlasting life sounds so exhausting, doesn't it? I'm sure they wouldn't want it. They were always so tired.'

'Yes...' Felix smiled and closed his eyes. Jinny was still holding him. His head had slumped to her breast, and she was stroking his hair, the soft, repetitive caress of a mother soothing a fractious child. 'I'm tired too,' he whispered.

'Mm. I know.'

'It isn't the work. I could work for ever without getting tired. It's everything else. The worry, the sheer hopelessness of it all. Oh, Jin! All the years we've hoped and prayed for this bloody war to be over and now... Now it almost is and it means nothing! We've lost too much, Jinny. All the reasons we wanted to win... They're gone! Fighting for freedom! Huh!'

'But being dead is being free, Felix. Alan and Mike and... Simon.' She swallowed tears, her throat creaking against Felix's ear. 'They're free. I'm sure they are.'

'Yes. That's something.'

'*I* wanted to die, you know, when I was small. There didn't seem to be any sense in being alive and I still think... I still wonder.'

'Wonder?'

She shrugged. 'Well... I don't imagine the world would be much poorer if I wasn't in it.'

'I'd be poorer.' He spoke with feeling, for had anyone else told him of Simon's death, had anyone else unmanned him like this... But perhaps no one else could have. Jinny had done it because she was Jinny: so well-known, so loved and trusted she was almost a part of him. 'You don't want to die now, do you, Jin?'

'Not at this moment, no.' There was a smile in her voice; a woman's smile: sad and warm. Loving. She sighed and her breasts rose and fell, causing Felix to press a little closer for fear of losing his pillow. A soft pillow, lightly scented with Castile soap, warm grass and . . . rabbits.

He opened his eyes. Jinny had drawn up her knees to support him and her shorts had slipped into her groin, exposing silky brown thighs. Half-mesmerised he stared at them, thinking back over everything she'd said, the way she'd spoken. There'd been nothing childish about any of it, nothing silly, nothing selfish or ill-considered. She hadn't been appalled when he'd broken down. Now he came to think of it, she hadn't even worked very hard to comfort him. She'd just accepted him, known him . . .

Slowly he turned his head to look up at her only to find that she was looking down at him, her mouth barely an inch from the end of his nose. He had only to tilt his head back a little . . .

It was all so natural, so easy, so right. He sat up, laid her on her back and kissed her again, glorying in the swollen heat of her lips, the taste of salt on her skin where her tears had dried. God, she was beautiful! Oh, God, this was so good! He was nearly twenty. He'd be twenty in September and had never yet made love to any woman. He'd never felt like this before: not merely wanting, but knowing that it was *right* to want, to take, to give, to share . . . *everything*.

His mind still wasn't functioning as normal. The strange images kept coming and going: Alan lying wounded on a Normandy beach, Nipper with a bullet through his head on the floor of the barn. And Dr Clarence Bindy, master of mathematics at Felix's prep school, passionately intoning, 'Never think of a number, boys, without thinking of another!'

Felix was nearly twenty. He was more than six years older than Jinny, which meant . . .

Oh, Christ! Oh, holy jumping Jesus! Jinny was only thirteen years old!

He froze.

Chapter Twenty

Jinny knew a great deal about being hurt, and although the hurts she knew most about were emotional, each of them caused some kind of physical pain: heartache, headache, stomach ache. But when Felix stopped kissing her, when he pushed her away and said, 'I must be out of my mind!' there was a different pain, one she'd never felt before and never wanted to feel again. It was like . . . dying. It was as if he'd ripped the soul out of her body and stamped on it, like a beetle.

'Don't look at me like that, Jinny!'

She looked away.

'I'm *sorry*!'

He didn't sound sorry. He sounded furious. 'Look, I was just . . . I was confused, Jinny. I forgot . . . I forgot who you were! Oh, damn it! Damn every bloody thing! Just forget it, will you? It was a *mistake*, Jinny!'

She'd loved him all her life. She'd never thought that he could love her; a few little dreams were all she'd allowed herself and she'd lived on those, even knowing they were dreams which could never come true. She'd seen him with Evelyn Carter, with Miriam Winterson and with one or two other girls since then; but they'd all been so much older than Jinny:

so much more suitable and right for him. She'd acknowledged that. She hadn't even been jealous. Just sad.

Being sad was easy. She'd been sad for as long as she could remember; she'd grown accustomed to it; she'd never expected it to change. But when Felix had kissed her, when he'd held her, when he'd stroked her body with hot, searching hands . . . It had been like flying away. Flying away from herself, the self she so hated and despised that to believe anyone could truly love her had been impossible. But *he* loved her. *He* loved her.

No . . . She'd been right the first time.

She supposed she'd learn how to cope with it, but even three days later it still hurt just as much. She couldn't think about anything else. Even the death of her own brother was important to her only because other people kept assuming it was. She felt terrible about not feeling terrible about Simon. Last night, when she'd gone to bed, Miles had stroked her hair and said, 'Don't cry for him any more, Jinny. It's the last thing he'd want, you know.'

Just as well.

As for the V-E Day celebrations . . . She wasn't sure how she'd get through the day without screaming. She wanted nothing to do with it. She didn't care. Had she thought there was the slightest hope of getting away with it, she'd have stayed in bed all day and missed the whole show.

Miles was passing the foot of the stairs when she finally came down. He said, 'Good morning, Jinny,' very kindly, and she stretched a faint smile to her lips, and turned away.

'Jinny,' Miles caught her elbow. 'Try to cheer up, will you? I know it's asking a great deal, but we are all going to try, just for today. Simon died for this, you know. For victory. For peace. So . . . just for today, we must do our best to . . . be thankful.' He sighed heavily. 'Rather like Easter, isn't it?'

'Easter?'

'Mourning on Friday, rejoicing on Sunday . . . We've got the days wrong, that's all.'

Jinny stared at her feet. 'But Jesus rose from the dead,' she murmured. 'That's why – '

'Yes, I know.' He spoke through gritted teeth. 'I was just . . . Oh, never mind.'

She glanced into his face and saw that he was suffering, not just because of Simon, but because of her. That he'd been making more effort to like her had become very clear during the past few years: painfully clear, because he wasn't making much progress. She was always mistaking his meaning, saying the wrong things, not realising what he'd really meant until she'd disappointed him and it was too late. He'd been hoping, of course, that Simon, like Andrew, would 'rise from the dead', and her mention of Jesus hadn't helped.

'I'll be cheerful,' she promised bleakly.

He smiled. 'Good. Now, go and help Mummy, will you? It'll be easier if we can all keep busy.'

It was half-past six in the morning. Bel was festooning the outer walls of Bishop's Court with red, white and blue bunting. She'd been up since four, making jellies and milk shapes for the party of a lifetime. But she looked like a ghost, her eyes swollen with tears, shadowed with purple. She looked old.

'Shall I do that for you?' Jinny offered.

'*No.*' Bel shrugged with annoyance. 'Leave me *alone*. I'm perfectly *all right*.'

'Daddy said – '

'I wish Daddy would mind his own business! How the hell am I supposed to get on, while everyone keeps hounding me? I'm all *right*, I tell you!'

Jinny hadn't supposed otherwise. Of course Bel was all right. She was grieving for Simon, but she was surrounded by people who loved and cared for her, her own husband not least of them.

Until very recently, Jinny had never thought – never even imagined – that her parents might love each other. She'd sometimes thought they hated each other, but she'd been quite wrong. Even now, even though she *said* she wanted him to mind his own business, Bel meant something else. She'd always meant something else. It was just a game she played. Had always played.

Jinny supposed she'd been too young to realise it before. Too young, and perhaps too much in need of an ally against Miles. She'd wanted to believe that she and Bel were partners in crime and Miles a watchful village bobby, quietly patrolling the perimeters of their lives in hope of catching them out. But it hadn't been like that. *They'd* been the partners, Jinny the outsider; and she'd known it, deep down. She just hadn't wanted to believe it.

She believed it now. She didn't belong to them, didn't understand them, didn't even want to any more. She couldn't even share their grief for Simon. She'd cried for him not because he was lost but because she hadn't even known *who'd* been lost.

Simon? Who was he?

She'd been eight years old when he'd gone away to war and even before that she'd seen him only during the school holidays. Since then... If she'd seen him ten times it was as much as she'd seen him and – like the others – he'd spent no time with her, had told her nothing about himself that he hadn't told everyone else. That he was tired. That he adored roast potatoes (or perhaps that was Stephen) and that he'd had three punctures on the drive down. Oh, she'd loved him, she supposed. But he hadn't loved her. He'd barely known her. He'd called her 'Little Sister' so habitually that she'd sometimes wondered if he even remembered her name.

Felix hadn't forgotten her name. He'd just forgotten who she was.

I must be out of my mind!

She sat on the low stone wall outside the scullery door, staring at her feet in a trance of misery. People had recently begun to say that she was pretty, and when Jinny looked in the mirror she could see what they meant, even if it was hard to appreciate their taste. She hated her hair, her eyes, the shape of her nose. She hated being tall. Yet she knew she wasn't really ugly. If she'd been ugly, people would have said something (the girls at school would certainly have said something). Felix couldn't have kissed her if she'd been *ugly*.

It all seemed to point to something she'd known all along: that there was something bad about her deep inside, something that had been there since she was very young. Miles had pushed her away then, just as Felix had pushed her away now.

But what had she *done*?

I forgot who you were!

So who the hell was she?

The Dray Valley Women's Institute – led, as usual, by the redoubtable Mrs Huntley – had been preparing for the victory celebrations for weeks on end. Bel had found the bunting, the Union Jacks and the party hats, charmed the grocer into giving up his entire stock of jelly and custard, dug up fifty trestle tables from God only knew where and organised the catering with a strict, military precision which even Monty might have envied. There were teams of cake-bakers, sandwich-makers, tea-brewers and jelly-setters. There were table-layers and chair-collectors, a choir (chosen for volume, not sweetness of voice) to lead the sing-song and a team to pick up all the litter when the day was over.

Jean was impressed. 'She's thought of everything, Bert! We're even having buckets under the tables for when the kids start throwing up!'

When the news of Simon's death came through, everyone supposed Bel would step down, shut the doors of Bishop's Court and let the celebrations go on without her. There were some who'd been more pleased than sorry about this unexpected development. Maud Shorecroft, for one. Mary Winterson for another. They liked to *say* they believed in democracy, but really they were as power-mad as old Hitler. Both of them had put up for President, supposedly 'nominated' by their cronies, but while Bel was still willing to take the job on, no one else stood a snowflake's chance in a bread oven.

'Well, why not? That's what I say, Bert. If it hadn't been for Mrs Huntley, we'd never have had a WI in the first place!'

And she was good at it, that was the thing. She was diplomatic, fair-minded, generous and good-humoured. In Jean's opinion, the best thing about Bel was that, with better cause than anyone to be a bit above herself, she never was and never would be. She treated everyone the same: slummocky little chits from the back end of Goosefeather Lane, daft old spinsters (not that Jean had anything *against* Miss Bright) and interfering busybodies like Bossy-boots Shorecroft.

What Bel always said was that no woman was like any other; every single one was unique, she said, which meant *special*, and therefore entitled to as much respect and consideration as any other woman. But when first Mary Winterson and then Bossy Shorecroft went round to Bishop's Court to offer to take over the V-E Day arrangements, they'd both come away much smaller in the head than when they'd gone in. Bel had given the pair of them what for and, if the look on their faces was any indication, she hadn't been all that tactful about it, either! Now, if only to save their dignity, they were telling everyone how brave she was to carry on, for to have lost her son within days of the victory was too cruel for flesh and blood to stand.

It was too cruel for Jean to even think about. She refused to think about it. Thinking about that sort of thing made her panic, and she'd given up panicking. Bert didn't like it. Although he was sympathetic, she sensed that he disapproved of any train of thought that wasn't governed by plain common sense and even plainer Christianity. He was a good Christian, Bert was. He reckoned that if everyone was *just* good enough to get on quietly with his neighbours and do nobody a bad turn, that was sufficient. In fact, he said, if everyone was only *that* good (which wasn't much to ask, after all) there'd be no need for saints, and no need for 'all these perishing do-gooders who think they're so much better than everyone else'.

He'd never said so, but Jean had an idea that Bert thought Jean was getting above herself when she (as he saw it) 'took other people's troubles on her shoulders'. That wasn't really what she was doing, of course; but it was the same in a way. To think that a few words she'd said in a temper could have any effect at all (except on her own conscience) was mere self-importance and as far from common sense as anyone could get!

No. Simon Huntley was none of her business, and if Bel wanted to do the V-E Day party in his honour, the kindest, most sensible thing anyone could do for her was to enjoy every minute of it.

Bert, with a few other holidaying tradesmen, had made a lovely job of decorating the square. It was red, white and blue all over: not just flags and bunting, but pots of red tulips, blue hyacinths and white arabis arranged in circles around all the lamp-posts and telegraph poles. The flowers had been Bert's idea and all his own work and, in fear that they'd 'go over' before the victory was made official, he'd come nearer to panic-stations than Jean had ever known him.

Bless him. Oh, bless him. He'd made her so happy. They'd been married almost a year now, and the only thing she could *seriously* find to complain of was his occasional habit of blowing raspberries in bed. Phew! But at least she knew now what his first wife had died of. 'Heart,' Bert had said it was, but Jean knew better: the poor dear had been gassed!

The party began at three with a lively peal of church bells, a prayer of thanksgiving and a speech from Miles Huntley in his capacity as Squire. While he spoke, a pair of magpies sitting on the bakery roof screeched incessantly, but no one else, not even the smallest child, made a murmur. He looked wonderful, too. Tall, upright and smiling and beautifully turned out in a suit of heather-mix tweed which must have been lying in mothballs since the start of the war.

'We might all be very sad today,' he said, 'if we chose. But we don't choose. We won't choose. Those who have died, been injured or imprisoned, might well deem their agonies wasted if, instead of rejoicing in their victory, we can do nothing but weep. Yet why should we weep? Thanks to our sons, our brothers, our lovers and husbands, we've lost nothing that would not have been lost had defeat been our inheritance today. Slavery, plunder and barbarism have been turned from our door. Now we shall turn away sorrow and for this day – for their sakes – be happy. Three cheers for Victory!'

He would have been forgiven had he then gone straight home and cried his eyes out; but Miles Huntley had never been a man to say one thing and do another. He stayed, he talked with everyone, and not once did Jean look at him without seeing a smile on his face. Bel was the same. A stranger, coming in on that party without knowing anything about her, would have said she'd never known a day's grief in her life.

Jinny looked a bit sad, bless her. And although Jean admired the other two with all her heart, she couldn't help liking Jinny better for looking – just a bit – sad.

'If *they* can do it, Leonard, *we* can do it!'

For only the second time that Felix could remember, Penny Clare was riding her high horse, her bulging blue eyes almost popping out of her head, her chin twitching with indignation. 'You should have seen him, Leonard! You should have heard him! I was *proud* of him; proud to know him and to know he meant every word he said! And he's *right*! Why should we weep? We've lost nothing that Hitler wouldn't have taken from us anyway! But he'd have taken Felix, too! He'd have left us with nothing!'

Her voice softened to its usual tone as she went on sternly.

'Alan left us something very precious, Leonard. He left us . . . peace. This is *his* victory, and if we can't celebrate it for him, then he died for a pair of ingrates. Do you hear me?'

Leonard blinked, licked his lips and cried angrily, 'Yes! I-I-I'm n-n-nuh-nuh . . . not *deaf*!'

'Good! Get your glad-rags on.' She grinned suddenly. 'And don't damn well argue!'

Leonard slouched from the room, muttering, 'Ch-ch-chuh . . . chance'd b-be a fuh-fuh-fine th-th-thuh . . .'

Felix met his mother's eyes across the kitchen table. 'Secret of a happy marriage,' she murmured. 'Always give a man the last word, even if he can't quite spit it out. How's my hair?'

'Pretty,' Felix lied.

'How's my face?'

He tipped his head to one side, pretending to think it over. They were all going to Bishop's Court for the adults' victory party. Very select. Only the Huntleys' tenants had been invited, which probably left out about two dozen people in the entire valley. Penny had put on the same plum-coloured taffeta gown she'd worn at every formal 'do' for the past fifteen years and it was strikingly evident that, at one of those long-ago functions, fried-egg sandwiches had been on the menu. Still . . . One thing at a time . . .

'Your face . . .' he said, teetering at the brink of honesty before falling (not without regret) into the lap of love. He couldn't do it. He couldn't say she had one eyebrow higher than the other. He couldn't say her lipstick had dived up her left nostril. He couldn't say she looked like a clown after a hard night at the circus, because . . . He loved her. 'Your face is as always, Mother. Beautiful, with or without the warpaint.'

She smiled. She blew a kiss from the tips of her fingers. 'You'll make someone a wonderful husband, darling. Do you have anyone in mind?'

Felix smiled and turned away, his stomach churning with

thoughts of Jinny. 'I'll go and help Dad with his collar studs, shall I?'

As usual when he was dragged within stuttering range of the public ear, Leonard approached Bishop's Court with every appearance of trying to run off in the opposite direction – which he would have done had Penny not held on to him so hard. He'd lived in the valley ten years now. Everyone knew him, liked and respected him. No one bothered him with deep, philosophical questions and most were very patient in waiting for the one or two words he was obliged to utter. It seemed crazy, then, to be so shy and Felix had often been less tolerant of his shyness than he felt he should have been. Not tonight, however. Tonight he understood.

He hadn't seen Jinny again. He didn't want to see her. He scarcely knew how he could face her without making a bloody fool of himself again. Oh, and *what* a fool! Give or take six months or so, he'd always known how old she was, if only because she'd kept reminding him of it. Thirteen! And he'd very nearly ravaged the poor kid! She'd been scared of him; and who the hell could blame her? When he'd controlled himself enough to look at her, her face had been as white as a sheet. He hated himself for that and if Jinny ever forgave him, he would never forgive himself. She was the last person on earth he'd wanted to hurt!

But he'd never felt like that before. He'd thought he had, but the feelings he'd had before, with other girls, hadn't been anything like it. They'd been the equivalent of wanting to scratch an itch: a need he'd been acutely *conscious* of because, like an itch, it affected only a part of himself, not the whole. He hadn't been conscious of wanting Jinny, of wanting sex, of wanting any damn thing, except . . .

No, he hadn't wanted *anything* because, just at that moment, he'd had everything he wanted. He'd been lying there with his head on her breast, weak and content, warm . . . And, in a quite extraordinary way, *alone*. It hadn't been that he'd disregarded Jinny – she'd been everything – only that he knew her and trusted her so well that she was already a part of him. He hadn't thought then what a beautiful feeling it was. He hadn't thought anything. He'd just known it, felt it, wanted to go on feeling it; to hold her against him for ever and never let go.

But she was thirteen! A man shouldn't feel that way about a . . . *child*!

'Oh, look!' Penny gasped when – more than an hour late – they at last reached their destination. 'They've switched all the lights on, and it isn't even dark yet! Look, Leonard, no blackout!'

Leonard managed a quavering smile. 'D-duh-don't you kn-know . . . th-thuh-there's n-n-no wuh-wuh-war on?'

It was the first joke he'd made since Mike had died, almost two years ago, and although Felix noticed it, and was grateful for it, other, more urgent, thoughts were possessing him. Something he'd never thought of before: something terrible! If Jinny had told Miles . . . Oh, shit! If Jinny had told Miles, Felix was as good as dead!

The house was heaving with people, the most noticeable of whom – at first – was dear old Muriel who, having spent the entire war in a wrapover pinny, plaid woolly slippers and ankle socks, had found herself a new uniform.

'Suntley meddun fry,' she muttered shyly when Penny complimented her on her style. 'Zo blagut curn unna taycloff. Sorigh dough inner?'

'What?' Penny whispered as they left Muriel in the hall. 'An old blackout curtain and a tablecloth, and *what* else?'

'It's all right though, isn't it?' Felix supplied abstractedly. He was looking for Miles, and found him in the same instant, charging towards them through the throng with a furious scowl on his face. Even scowling, he looked marvellous, dressed as Felix had never seen him before, in an elegant black dinner jacket which, on closer inspection, proved to be full of moth-holes. But before that close inspection became possible, Felix felt his face draining of colour, his knees beginning to shake. Although he hadn't appreciated it until now, he loved Miles almost more than he loved his own father: respected him, depended on him, *needed* him. To fall from that man's grace would be a disaster to beat all, a shame he could see no way of surviving.

Then, as he edged his way through the crowd, Miles smiled at last, paused for a moment and cried, 'Welcome! Welcome!' before he reached out to shake Leonard's hand, to kiss Penny's cheek and then . . . 'Felix, my dear boy!'

She hadn't told . . .

For the next half hour, Felix wandered about in a dream, just looking and listening – and wondering. During the war years the Huntleys had closed up the dining room and drawing room at Bishop's Court, locked all their valuables away and lived as everyone else had lived – mostly in the kitchen. Now everything had been opened up, the lovely old carpets unrolled, the furniture and silver polished to a glow. It was a feast for the eye and a solace for the heart, a return to peace, order and beauty which no one could hold as anything less than precious.

Yet as these thoughts crossed his mind Felix was filled with a feeling that he was living inside a fading memory, an illusion, a vision of times past. Everywhere he turned he heard people talking of going back, of doing such-and-such things again, if it was only to eat chocolate until it oozed from their ears. He heard people saying, 'Isn't it wonderful to have these rooms open again!' as if, in the thirties, they'd attended parties here every night. They hadn't.

Most of them had never even entered this *house* before the war, let alone the drawing room! Before the war, they wouldn't have been invited beyond the tradesmen's entrance. The butcher, grocer and baker, the blacksmith, the Postmaster: during the past six years they'd proved themselves the equals of the

Squire and his lady, if only in usefulness, courage and endurance, in danger, grief and deprivation. But to hear them talk you'd think it had always been so. And it hadn't.

Perhaps, when the euphoria of this day was over, people would slip back into their proper places, but surely it could never be the same again? Too much water (most of it tears) had flown under the bridge and somehow changed the course of the river. 'Before the war' had been a different world where Alan and Mike and Simon – and perhaps half a million other young men – had lived in health and hope, making plans for a future . . . a future which no longer existed, not just for them, but for everyone who had known them.

'Felix,' the warm, honeyed voice at his ear was Bel Huntley's. '*Don't* look so sad. Have you found a drink? Something to eat?' She took his arm and led him into the crowded dining room where an enormous buffet had been set. Bel laughed. 'Now, what will you have? Bloater-paste canapés, bloater-paste sandwiches, bloater-paste pinwheels or bloater-paste tarts?'

It wasn't that bad. No one family could possibly cater for a party this size and each of the guests had brought a contribution, either from the daily ration or from secret hoards which had only needed an occasion like this to bring them to light. There was corned beef, American Pork, Canadian salmon, several cold chickens (one had been killed only yesterday, at Drayfield) and an enormous smoked ham, courtesy of the Army and probably 'borrowed' from the Yanks.

Felix was still trying to fight his way through to the spread when he met Jinny trying to fight her way in the opposite direction with a large plate of sandwiches held aloft like a brolly. She was smiling, laughing, turning her head this way and that to speak to everyone who jostled her or stepped on her foot. She looked so calm and self-assured that Felix had again to remind himself she was only thirteen. A child.

But in spite of the reminder, he blushed.

'Hello, Jinny.'

Although she kept smiling her face seemed to freeze, as if the wind had changed, turning her smile to stone, fixing her gaze on the knot of his tie. 'Oh, hello. Want a sandwich? Essence of salmon. You don't eat them; just inhale very deeply.'

He laughed and tipped his head to one side, trying to make her meet his eyes. But she looked away. 'Oh, hello, Mr Brindle. Would you like a sandwich? They're essence of salmon . . .

The jostling crowd closed around her and although she kept talking, joking, laughing, she never once looked back.

Felix felt sick. She'd done it as only a Huntley could: with grace, with charm, with tact and generosity. But there'd been no mistaking her intention.

She'd cut him dead.

Part Three

Chapter Twenty-One

The darkest secrets of the war were revealed to the people of the Dray by slow degrees. Some heard the news on the wireless, some read of it in the newspapers. Bert Tomkins took his wife to the pictures in Bristol and brought her straight home again, having seen only the cartoon and the Pathé News. They hadn't the stomach to stay and enjoy themselves after that.

Jean cried half the night, managing to stop herself only when she saw that Bert was almost as upset as she was. He wasn't crying, but he looked grey and cold. Angry. Was he angry with her? She supposed he had reason to be: it was two o'clock in the morning and they had to be up again at five to sort the post.

'Oh, I'm sorry, love,' she wailed. 'I've been so selfish, keeping you awake all this time! Go to sleep, love. I'm all right now, really. Go to sleep.'

'I wish I could,' he muttered. 'Bastards. Bloody bastards.'

'*Bert*!'

'I'm sorry. I know you can't stand bad language. But there are times when nothing else will do. I hope they hang 'em. Every one of 'em. Slowly.'

Jean was speechless. She'd never heard him say anything so harsh and unforgiving. Not that you could forgive such things.

However hard you tried, you couldn't forgive that. But Bert... It was so *unlike* him.

Andrew Huntley had come home from prison camp half-starved, and although Jean and many others had been angry about it, Bert had been as reasonable as ever. 'Always look at it from the other chap's point of view,' was his motto, even if the other chap was the enemy. 'You've got to be reasonable, see, Jean. The *Germans* have been starving these past few months. How could they feed prisoners of war, when they couldn't even feed themselves? You can't give what you haven't got, Jean, can you?'

But concentration camps were different, and Bert wasn't the only one who thought so. A lot of people – good, regular churchgoers, like Bert – lost their faith overnight. They said there couldn't be a God if such things could happen. Others blamed God for *letting* it happen. Jean had a feeling that Bert felt the same and only went to church now because he knew she'd be upset if he didn't. It wasn't that she was especially religious. She'd always believed in God – after a fashion – but if she was frank (which she wasn't, except in the privacy of her own thoughts) she believed in Him just to be on the safe side. If He *was* there, it was best to keep in His good books; and if He wasn't... Well, it didn't really matter, did it?

But the reason she wanted Bert to go to church had very little to do with religion. She wanted him to go because going to church was a part of his character: one of the best parts, the part she loved most. It was steady, gentle, virtuous and safe. She hadn't married the sort of man who used language and wished to see people hanged. She didn't want Bert to be like that, for however just his reasons, it seemed all wrong. It wasn't *Bert*!

She was rather glad when the Rector took up the theme of forgiveness in his next sermon. She smiled forgivingly and held Bert's hand, squeezing it gently at the bits she thought he should listen to most carefully. But his face remained stony, and all he did at the important bits was to shake his head, as if listening to the excuses of a naughty child.

John Winterson had never been the sort of speaker who could inspire his flock. Except on very rare occasions, when he'd got a bee in his bonnet about something, he was much more inclined to send them to sleep. There was nothing of the actor in him and not much of the teacher. His voice, although clear enough, was flat and expressionless, conveying rather less excitement than the wheels of a train as it shunts drearily into a siding: da-da-de-da, da-da-de-dum. There was a tendency in his listeners to long for a change of pace: a sudden diddle-diddle or dumpty-dum to give the idea that he might be getting somewhere.

But the theme of forgiveness rattled on the same as ever and after the first five minutes even Jean began thinking of other things: the Sunday dinner, the hole she'd burned with the iron in Janet's best cardigan, and how to stretch out the sugar ration until Tuesday.

Then, very suddenly, the Rector stopped speaking. No one noticed at first. But as the silence went on, drooping heads were raised and glazed eyes focused and it suddenly became clear that something quite interesting was about to happen.

'Tetanus,' he said at last, and that was interesting enough to make everyone sit up and listen. *Tetanus*? What had that to do with anything?

'Tetanus is a germ which lies in the soil,' he explained flatly. 'It is capable of infecting us only through wounds: little cuts, grazes, scratches, the kind of wounds we barely notice and can scarcely see. We can't see tetanus either, but it is everywhere, awaiting only its chance to enter our bloodstreams and bring us to ruin. Most of us know it is there. Most of us know that it can kill us. But as we tend our gardens and plough our fields, how many of us even acknowledge its existence, let alone allow ourselves to dread it? We view the land not for the infection which lurks in it but for the harvest it will yield when our labours are over. Because we cannot see the evil, we pretend it is not there.'

He paused, gazed steadily into a few puzzled faces and then, bringing his fist down on the edge of the pulpit, he roared, 'But it is *there*! It is *always* there! Why do you *forget* it?'

Jean covered her mouth with her fingers, wondering if the poor man had gone mad.

'Our lives,' the Rector went on wearily, 'are the soil upon which we expend our thoughts, hopes and energies, and Heaven is the harvest we, as Christians, work towards. But evil, like the tetanus germ, always lurks, awaiting only the smallest breach in our defences to make its entry into our souls and bring us to ruin. *Why* do you forget?'

Because I want to, Jean thought crossly; but at that moment Bert leaned forward in his seat and stared intently at the Rector, his eyes alive with interest.

'If you believe in God,' the Rector went on, 'you must also believe in the devil. Evil works are the devil's works and the men who help him in that work are his victims, his slaves, more to be pitied than blamed for falling under his dominion. They are brought to ruin not by their own will but by their own folly – they forget that the devil is there.

'We have won a war – in Europe and the Far East – against the servants of Satan. But the war against Satan himself must go on. Here! Here in England, in Somerset, in the green valley of the Dray.' He sighed as one who is depressed beyond words. 'Even here,' he said. 'In the house of God.'

He turned his head and seemed about to announce the next hymn when, almost as an afterthought, he added softly, 'If we forgive our enemies we will do God's work. Curse them and we conjure the devil. Into our hearts, our minds and our acts, until there is nothing to choose between us and the enemy we have so recently vanquished.'

Then he announced the next hymn. But Jean didn't sing it

and she only dimly heard Bert, singing like billyo into her benumbed and ringing ears.

Conjure the devil! Conjure the devil!

I conjure thee, O serpent of old, take my enemy from me . . .

No . . . No, it was all rubbish! Just a load of silly rubbish. Bert had said so! And Bert was *always* right!

'Huh,' she said shakily as they walked home down the lane. 'What on earth got into him today, Bert?'

'I don't know.' There was a happy note in Bert's voice which hadn't been there for weeks. 'But he's set me right, I'll tell you that much. Between you and me, Jean, I've always thought old Winterson a bit of a hypocrite, but it takes real faith to give a sermon like that. He'd thought it all through. And he *meant* it, that's the thing. He really meant it!'

'Meant it? But it was all a load of rubbish, Bert! All that about curses! You've said it yourself: load of rubbish, you've always said!'

'Ah,' he said sweetly, 'but I was wrong, love.'

Jean nearly fainted.

The end of the war resembled not so much the sudden 'pop' Bel had predicted as a slow puncture. She was pedalling as hard as ever – harder, in fact – but no longer seemed to be getting anywhere. The sheer grind of working for victory had been eased simply because there'd been a victory to strive towards. Well, the victory had been won. So what? The grind still continued, but now it seemed to have no purpose, no end in view. Hope had failed without quite failing. She had dreaded to lose *all* her sons, yet could barely stir herself to be grateful that she'd lost only one. Only one! It was like saying she'd lost only one arm! She was mutilated, out of balance. She would never be the same again.

But Andrew was home again and, as far as Bel could make out, he intended to stay. It was a strange feeling. For the first few weeks, while she'd fussed and fretted to feed him up, keep him warm, to make up to him for all the years of suffering he'd endured, the realisation that he need never go away again had filled her with a bright, possessive joy. He was hers at last! Hers to hold, love and protect. Hers to keep for ever, safe under her wing.

Miles, of course, was no less happy, although he'd never expected Andrew to take up farming. Like the others, Andrew had spent most of his school holidays helping out and learning the ropes, but he'd done it less out of interest than to earn a little more pocket money. Even now . . . But it was too soon. He said he intended to stay and that he had no plans to do anything else, but it was too soon to ask more of him than that. In September, perhaps, when Billy Chard was due to retire. That would be soon enough for Andrew to think – just begin to think – of taking up the reins.

Miles wasn't old. But he was no longer young and the grind of the war had wearied him. He didn't want to retire, he didn't want to rest; but he wanted to share the burden of his responsibilities with someone he loved and trusted. His son. But when September came round, Andrew made no move. He didn't seem to care. Even when Miles complained of the new manager's inadequacies and hinted, very gently, that he needed more help, Andrew merely listened and made no comment.

'Give him time,' Miles said. 'He'll come around to it.'

But he didn't. He wasn't interested in anything, it seemed, beyond the confines of his own skin.

'He needs rest,' Bel kept saying. 'He needs time to get the soul back in his body.' But after more than four months at home he was still staying in bed until noon and then sleeping off his lunch on the couch in the library. He looked pale and, in spite of being very lean, slack and soft as he'd never been before. The only thing he'd ever told them about prison-camp was that it had been tedious, that he'd been bored beyond words to express. But what could be more boring than the life he was leading now?

Bel couldn't bear it. Whatever their excuses for being so, she'd never been able to understand sluggards. Even in the golden years of their marriage she and Miles had always been early risers, energetic and organised, rarely permitting a day to go by without doing *something* useful. But even then there'd been more to it than that, some kind of moral commitment to make the best of each day they were given lest (perhaps) it should be their last.

As she thought about it now, Bel supposed that she'd been motivated by her Christian upbringing and Miles by his close-hand experiences of sudden death. To die, on a day that had been utterly wasted, had been more than either of them could contemplate.

It was more than Bel could contemplate for Andrew. She began, very gradually, to be angry with him. Even more gradually, she began to show it.

'I'm sure it can't be healthy for you to sleep so much, darling. How about a nice walk? The fresh air will do you the world of good.'

'Mm. Yes, perhaps it will. Later.'

'The forecast seems good for tomorrow, Andrew. Why don't you go to market with Daddy?'

'Mm. Yes, perhaps I will. What time does he leave?'

'Just after breakfast.'

'Mm. Well . . . Perhaps I won't.' He smiled, shrugged and had the grace to look – just a little – ashamed of himself, but Bel had the feeling that he was not so much the victim of his indolence as its architect. He had *decided* to live like this and would hold to it for as long as it remained easier than the alternatives.

Bel was all for making the alternatives less easy. Miles advised leaving Andrew alone to work it out. He was a grown man who could be expected to know what was best for himself

– or at least to discover it sooner or later. He'd endured six years in several kinds of hell. They couldn't expect him to recover his balance in a matter of a few months.

Bel knew Miles was right. She told herself, time after time, that he was right. But it was hard. And it became even harder as the winter closed in. She got up in the freezing dark to carry coal, light fires, to cook and clean and get to the shops to queue for their rations. The fact that Andrew was sleeping snugly throughout, and would get up only to eat what she had laboured to provide, irritated her beyond reason. Why had he survived if only for this? What had been done to him that he actually *wanted* to lay waste all that he'd been given? He'd been home almost six months! Six months was *enough*!

For reasons she'd never been quite sure of, Bel had always been inclined to nag the boys. She'd never done it to Jinny. This was partly because Jinny had spent so much of her life in terror of Miles that any further discipline had been unnecessary. Tell Jinny to tidy her room or polish her shoes and it was as good as done. Tell the boys, and you could still be telling them the same thing a week later. Bel had sometimes feared that they held her in contempt (if Miles put his foot down they obeyed him at once) and were testing her to see how far they could go. She had the feeling that that was what Andrew was doing now, using her love for him as a scourge, using her as a slave to his comfort. The thought enraged her. It pricked at her mind like the hot pitchforks of so many little devils, urging her to confront him and put him in his place, once and for all.

She managed to restrain herself. Christmas was almost upon them and although Robin was stuck in some ghastly training base on the east coast, Stephen had hopes of getting leave and Bel wanted, more than anything else in the world, to give him a good Christmas. He had lost his twin brother. They hadn't been identical: both in looks and character Stephen had always borne a closer resemblance to Andrew than to Simon, but they'd loved each other as only twins can. If Bel felt she'd lost an arm, Stephen must think he'd lost half his soul, poor boy.

But Andrew almost ruined Christmas, too. Just when it would have been a blessing to have him out of the way, leaving Bel free to give all her care and attention to Stephen, Andrew suddenly burst into life and the two brothers spent most of the holiday out and about, driving into Bristol to drink and dance every night; walking, riding and shooting by day. Bel scarcely saw Stephen, let alone found a chance to talk to him. But as soon as his leave was over, Andrew went back to bed, complaining that the house was too cold to make getting up worthwhile.

The house *was* cold. In spite of fuel shortages they'd managed better than most to keep warm during the war. Miles had expended much of his energies every summer clearing the woods of underbrush and dead trees and there'd always been firewood enough to keep at least two fires going. But last summer, with the last of the land girls returning to their pre-war occupations, there'd been neither the time nor the labour to spare. Now they were short of both wood and coal and it was hard to keep even the kitchen warm. Bel usually lit a fire in the library after tea, but that barely took the chill off. The rest of the house was so cold, Bel and Muriel had taken to wearing coats even to make the beds.

Miles had always suffered from the cold, but never as much as he did now, and Bel worked like a demon to give him as much comfort as she could, even going to the woods, like a witch with a sack on her back, to bring home enough fuel to warm him. But she didn't know how much he was suffering until one evening, when she went through to the scullery to fetch the coal scuttle, she found him doubled up in a corner, as white as a ghost, with his knuckles jammed between his teeth to keep him from screaming.

He couldn't get his boots off, and when Bel eventually managed the task, he did scream: a terrible howl of pain which brought tears of rage and pity gushing in a flood from Bel's eyes. Gently she peeled off his socks. His feet were swollen like marrows and from the instep to the roots of his toes his skin was the colour of raw meat. The big toe of his left foot was black.

'Miles, Miles! There's something wrong here, darling! You must see the doctor. Tonight! Please!'

Andrew had been huddled over the kitchen fire for most of the afternoon and had gone to his room only to find an extra jersey. Now, shivering like a leaf in a gale, he came back, raised one eyebrow and enquired off-handedly, 'What's all the row about?'

Something seemed to snap in the region of Bel's heart. She turned and stared at him, knowing – if only for that moment – that she hated him utterly. 'Look at your father,' she said softly. 'Look at his feet, my noble little war-hero! *You've* brought him to this!'

'Bel!' Miles couldn't move from his chair, but his hand flashed out to catch her wrist. 'Don't – !'

It was too late. For only the second time in her life – and she remembered the first time had been when she'd thought Andrew dead – Bel was beside herself. Her eyes blazing, she advanced on her son, raising clenched fists as if to strike him. 'You lazy, contemptible little oaf,' she snarled. 'You parasite! You ingrate! Get out of my sight before I kill you!'

And then, too late, she understood, and her mind seemed to break, to fall in razor-edged shards of wisdom and bitterness. It had all been for nothing! There was no point to any of it, no meaning, no bright, victorious future to be lived in peace and plenty! They had fought and striven, sacrificed, wept; they'd plumbed the depths of their courage and energies only to die like rats in a freezing corner! Oh, who could blame the boy for wanting to sleep, to hide himself away?

Andrew shrugged and turned away, raising his hands in a

cynical show of submission. 'Think I'll go to bed,' he murmured. 'Goodnight . . . *Mother.*'

Shaking with reaction, Bel sat for a moment and stared hopelessly at her hands. She was aware that Jinny had tiptoed into the room, but didn't dare look at her, or at Miles. She had come close to madness many times before, but this was different: this was worse, far worse. Always, before, she'd had something – some hope – to set her back on her course. Always, before, she'd turned to God (who still looked exactly like the Archdeacon) and asked, 'Show me the way.'

But the Archdeacon had deceived her. God wasn't there. She had lived all her life for a lie.

'Mummy?' Jinny's voice was soft and anxious, calling, it seemed from a great distance. Poor, sad little girl. She, too, had lived all her life for a lie.

'Mummy! Mummy, please! Come here! Daddy's ill!'

The rest of that night passed like a black dream, a nightmare travelled on plodding feet, with all the demons of hell running behind. The doctor came. Groaning, sweating, crying with pain, Miles was rushed away to hospital. They wouldn't let Bel anywhere near him. For two days and two long nights she paced the echoing vaults of the hospital corridors, praying with all that was left of her strength to the God who wasn't there: 'Save him, save him, I can't live without him!'

At ten o'clock in the morning of the third day, they amputated his left leg. She saw him at last at four in the afternoon, his eyes sunken in the grey shell of his face, his flesh worn to the bone by long days of agony. He was alive. But that was all he was.

Chapter Twenty-Two

Felix was just driving away from his uncle Sol's farm when he saw Jinny hurrying along the lane towards it. The news of Miles's illness had run like wildfire through the valley and both Solomon and Leonard were mourning him as if he was already dead. Felix had refused to contemplate such an eventuality, but now it seemed they'd been right. There was no hope in Jinny's face. She looked beaten.

Yet Felix took hope, for as she looked up and recognised him, her expression changed. She blushed and lowered her eyes, and as he stopped the tractor and jumped down, she turned away, prodding the hedgebank with her toe.

'Jinny,' Felix murmured cautiously. 'What news of your father?'

She did not look up. Staring at her feet, she murmured bleakly, 'Gangrene. They've amputated his left leg.'

'Oh, my God.' Almost retching with horror, he covered his mouth with his hand, wondering what else he could possibly say. The usual wish, that Miles would 'get well soon', seemed inappropriate almost to the point of cruelty. For a man like Miles – so active, graceful and strong – death might have been the better alternative and Felix almost found himself wishing that he *had* died, for what had he to look forward to now?

The life of a cripple: useless and dependent. *Mutilated*. Felix would rather die than endure such a fate and he was certain that Miles would feel the same.

'I can't tell you how sorry I am, Jinny. Will he . . . be all right?'

'I don't know. No one tells me anything.' Her voice rose very slightly, ringing like a clear bell in the frosty air. 'I know he's lost his leg because I heard my mother telling Grandma. She's his mother, you know. *She* must be told. The rest of us must find out as best we can.'

'Oh, Jinny!' Shocked, he held out his hands to take hers, but she snatched them away, her grey eyes blazing in a face that had become livid with rage. 'I don't exist!' she said through her teeth. 'No one even knows who I am! But *I* do! I *do*! I'm his *daughter*!'

Then suddenly she crumpled. Her eyes filled with tears, her lip wobbled and she shook her head, slowly, like an angry bull, thwarted and confused by the violence of her own rage. 'I love him,' she whispered. 'I love him. And if he dies . . . without telling me . . .'

Felix took her in his arms and let her cry. When she failed to produce a handkerchief, he scrabbled in his pocket for his own: a tattered rag smeared with cow-dung and engine oil, which no child of Miles Huntley's should have been allowed to see, let alone use. But she blew her nose, scrubbed her eyes and then, noticing it, muttered, 'Thanks. Your mother's gone back to normal then, I see.'

He laughed. 'The cholera's winning this time. I hope you don't catch it.'

'Think I'd care?' She sighed and leaned her head on his shoulder, but Felix, although he wanted to go on holding her, hadn't the courage for it. Gently he set her away from him. There was something about her, something which confused him. She made his head spin so that he could scarcely think, and he mustn't – mustn't ever – forget again how young she was. He went back to the tractor to douse his feelings on the cold metal seat.

'Is there anything I can do to help?' he asked briskly. 'Tell Andrew to ring me if – '

'Andrew's gone.'

'*Gone*? Gone where? *When*? What d'you mean?'

Again she shook her head. 'He's gone. Gone away. I don't know where and I'm not sure when. But then,' she smiled stiffly. 'I'm only his sister. Why should anyone tell me?'

Felix could only stare. 'Then what – ? What will you do? How will you manage? Jim Brooks doesn't know his – er . . .'

' – from his elbow,' Jinny supplied coolly. 'I know. But I have no idea what we'll do.' She produced a bleak little smile. 'Go to pieces, I suppose.'

'Not if I can help it!' Felix put the tractor in gear, let his foot off the clutch and yelled, 'Tell your mother I'll be up this evening!'

He spent the rest of the day on pins of anxiety, knowing that, if Andrew really had gone, the situation at Home Farm would be desperate. Even with the capable Billy Chard as manager, Miles had still carried an enormous share of the work. But since Jim Brooks had taken over . . . He knew the farm like the back of his hand, but he couldn't organise the men, couldn't plan, couldn't delegate. Left alone for a few days, he'd be running round in circles, while everyone else stood and watched him, waiting to be told what to do.

Felix had to help. Miles had helped him through thick and thin the past few years – they couldn't have managed without him – but it was one thing to know you must help, quite another to know how. If it hadn't been for Jim Brooks, Felix could have simply taken a deep breath, tightened his belt and gone charging in, crying, 'God for Harry!' but Jim would regard anything like that as a threat to his authority, and then the Huntleys would have even more trouble on their hands.

He expected to find Bel frail and tearful, rendered as helpless by Miles's absence as by his ruin. But he found nothing of the sort. Although as gracious and courteous as usual when she showed him into the library, there was a light in her eyes and an edge to her voice that scared him witless. He had never seen a woman so angry. He had never seen anger so fiercely controlled. He had the feeling that she was poised on the edge of madness, and that if he said a single word out of place, she'd fall, foaming at the mouth, into a pit so deep that she would never climb out of it again.

'Oh,' she smiled when he asked what he could do to help, 'I'll manage, Felix, thank you.'

She snatched a cigarette from the silver box on Miles's desk, lit it and inhaled deeply, throwing up her chin to smile again. 'It's extraordinary,' she declared blithely, 'what one can do when one's back's to the wall. I've noticed it before, you know. Just when you think you've gone as far as you can go – ' She paced the floor, away from him and then back again until she stood before him, head up and shoulders back, like a soldier reporting for duty. 'You find,' she said, 'that you can go further and further; that your strength, which you'd thought had limits, in fact had no end. Wonderful, isn't it?'

Felix smiled stiffly, still certain that she was half-crazed, but then she laughed and bowed her head and suddenly was crying. 'Don't say it,' she whispered. 'Please don't. I know pride ever goeth before a fall, but I have to cope with this, Felix. If it's the last thing I do, I have to cope with this. Andrew's gone . . . and it's all my fault. Miles doesn't know. If he . . . lives . . .'

'How is he?'

'Ha!' She turned away to mop furtively at her eyes. 'How should I know? He's survived the operation. He's survived another night. But . . .' She stared at the wall, her mouth trembling. 'The pain doesn't go away, you know. They . . . they cut off your leg and you think it's still there, still driving you crazy with pain. I want to be with him! But they won't . . .' Her voice changed to a cynical whine: ' "Visiting on Wednesdays and Sundays, Mrs Huntley!" He could die! He could die, Felix, and never . . .'

'He won't die.' He spoke more harshly than he'd intended, for he took little comfort from the idea that Miles would live – perhaps for many years – as a helpless invalid. 'He won't die,' he said again. 'He'll live. And when he comes home he'll want to find you well, Mrs Huntley, not worked to the bone over responsibilities he never meant you to carry. I owe him – '

'*You* owe him?' She faced him again, her eyes blazing in the stone-white mask of her face. 'Don't *I* owe him?' Her lip curled with contempt. 'What's he done for you that he hasn't done for me a million times and taken only – ' She stopped herself and closed her eyes for a moment before adding softly, 'Forgive me, Felix. I'm not . . . Go home, my dear. Thank you for coming, but I can't . . .'

Felix turned to go. 'The offer still stands,' he said softly. 'Anything you want at any time, Mrs Huntley, just let me know.'

He closed the door and paused in the hall for a moment, wondering where Jinny was and whether he had the nerve to go and find her. But before he summoned the nerve, he heard Bel scream, 'Damn you!' and then the crash of something hard (and, sadly, brittle) hitting the inside of the library door.

He was halfway home before he stopped trembling.

It was the best part of an hour before Muriel came to pick Bel up off the floor. 'There,' she said dourly, 'fillin' better?'

'Oh,' Bel smiled, her lips sore and swollen with crying. 'Yes, indeed. Feeling fine. I'm frozen, I've got a crashing headache, I feel sick . . .'

'That'll wear off. I've ran a barf an' put a bottle in yer bed. A good long sleep, that's what you needs.' With a rough hand she stroked the wet hair from Bel's eyes. 'You'm wore out; that's what's wrong wiv you.'

Bel gazed blearily into Muriel's face, seeking a sign of the love, loyalty and intelligence she knew was there... somewhere. Muriel had stuck by her through thick and thin. She'd worked like a horse, never complained, never even made comment – until now – unless comment was invited. But even now her face was the same as it had always been. As blank, as shapeless and unlovely as a cold suet pudding.

'Come on. I'll give you a 'and upstairs.'

Her arm was hard and strong around Bel's waist. Her willpower an iron shield you could run against until hell froze over without making so much as a dent in it. Bel laughed. 'What keeps you going, Muriel? What's the secret? Tell me. I need some of it, whatever it is.'

'Nuffin,' Muriel replied shortly. 'Ain't got nuffin. Never 'ad nuffin.' She shrugged. 'Never shall 'ave nuffin, neiver. Firtyfree I am now, and I still got all I started out wiv. Born lucky, I were, Suntley. I never lost a fing.'

Torn between laughter and tears, Bel stared at her in amazement. Well, there was the intelligence, at any rate! She'd summed up Bel's disease *and* given her the cure in a single word! *Nuffin*!

'Thank you, Muriel,' Bel said softly. 'Thank you for everything.' Thank you for nuffin, she added silently as she sank gratefully into the bath. *Thirty-three I am now, and I've still got all I started out with. I never lost a thing.*

It was strange how such an idea could tip the balance between madness and sanity. Bel *had* been mad, and she could see now that she'd been going that way ever since Simon's death. Loss, loss. A terrible loss. But not as terrible as having nothing to lose. Should Muriel leave her now (and God grant that she never would!), she would leave as she'd arrived: with no more to carry than would fit in a carpet bag.

In spite of her many losses, Bel had much more than that. Her husband was very ill... (She pushed the thought from her mind, unable, yet, to confront it.) But he was still alive. Where there was life there was hope; she mustn't despair yet.

She had driven Andrew away. He'd gone, she supposed, almost as soon as she'd ... *Get out of my sight!* She turned scarlet and groaned, hiding her face in the bath sponge. While she'd fussed and wept over Miles, called the doctor, Andrew had quietly packed and quietly departed, leaving nothing to say where he'd gone. But he might come back. Tomorrow, next week, next month or next year. They would hear of him, at least. He wasn't lost so much as mislaid. She *mustn't* despair.

And she still had Stephen and Robin. She still had her home, the farm and the estate, money in the bank, countless friends. (Felix, white-faced and stiff with embarrassment, came to mind and she groaned again. Ring him tomorrow. Apologise.) But Muriel hadn't even a friend, poor thing.

The worst thing about a hot bath on a cold night was getting out, dripping wet, feeling that the water would freeze on her skin before she could get dry. Bel had been known, in such circumstances, to flee to her bed without doing the virtuous thing with the scouring rag, but tonight she felt that virtue was her only salvation. She would never do a wrong, selfish or stupid thing again. She would never view a single one of her blessings without appreciating it.

And there *was* a God. There was. There had to be, if only because she couldn't manage without Him ...

Jinny arrived, bringing a mug of cocoa, just as Bel climbed, shuddering, between the sheets. Bel drew a shawl around her shoulders, clamped her feet to the old-fashioned stone hot-water bottle that the blessed Muriel had supplied and sank back against her pillows, closing her eyes. Up at five tomorrow. See Jim Brooks. Get organised. Miles had talked enough, about the farm, to have given Bel a pretty clear idea of how things worked, and she was strong and capable. Clear-headed now, too, thanks to Muriel. Keep things ticking over, that was all that was necessary. Let Jim know he wasn't carrying the whole load on his own.

She heard a sigh and opened her eyes. Jinny was still there, staring bleakly at Miles's pillow, her eyes glittering with tears . . . and something else. Rage? Hatred?

'What's wrong?' Bel gasped. 'Jinny?'

Jinny's eyes widened. A strange, twisted little smile lifted one corner of her mouth. Then, leaning forward slightly as if to give Bel the best possible chance of understanding her, 'Nothing,' she said.

She was gone before Bel realised what she'd meant.

Nuffin. Nothing. How could the same word mean such completely different things? And how could Bel, who had so recently counted her blessings, have forgotten to include her own daughter? But Jinny had never been counted as a blessing. From the day of her conception, one way or another, Jinny had been a curse, a thorn in the flesh, something one suffered while trying to forget, until it became just . . .

'Heavens, Bel, how on earth did you get that horrid little thorn in your flesh?'

'What? Oh, that! I've had it for years. It's nothing.'

'God help me,' Bel whispered. 'Poor fool that I am.'

Jean was too busy, now, to work on the post full-time. The Tomkins's 'palace' wasn't as big as Drayfield, but there was far more in it (all of it beautiful) and it all had to be cleaned, waxed, buffed and huffed upon, boiled and blued and starched and pressed, arranged and sorted and placed just so. As soon as Fred Holmes had come back from the war (one of the first: more than half of the valley's servicemen were still awaiting demob), Jean had handed in her bicycle clips, donned her pinny and, almost slavering at the mouth with glee, cleaned her home as it had never been cleaned before.

She hadn't quite finished her first '*really thorough*' spring-clean when, towards the end of February, Fred went down with the first in a series of cider-related headaches and Jean was called upon to cover his tracks. She was quite glad of it, in a way. The thing she hadn't anticipated was that she'd miss the social side of her twice-daily round: seeing people, learning things about them, keeping an eye on the valley at large.

A half-hour's gossip in the bread queue didn't make up for that, and although the bread queue seemed to get longer by the day, Jean never learned enough to satisfy her. She'd realised, too, that Bert's beautiful home had its drawbacks. That secret, hidden away quality, which had so charmed her at first, now drove her crackers with frustration. Only two of the bedroom windows overlooked the square (and they were the cleanest windows in England), but there was a limit to how much time she could spend cleaning them. The rest of the time she felt quite shut away, so that sometimes she mourned her ripe lace curtains at Briar Cottage. Nothing had escaped her there. No one had put a foot out of doors without Jean knowing about it.

But oh, she'd lock herself away for ever, just as long as Bert was with her! He wasn't perfect. She hadn't expected him to be. But he was nearer to being perfect than any man she'd ever heard of. Patient, gentle, funny, generous. *Generous!* Generous was hardly the word for it, and she still hadn't got accustomed to having money left over at the end of the week. After pinching and scraping all her life, trying to make every shilling do the work of two, just having *enough* would have been a luxury. Having more than enough, having a home that was bought and paid for, not rented, having a sense of real security, was heaven indeed.

So was getting up with Bert to sort the post again. It was a freezing, foggy morning. They had to beat their arms and jump up and down to get warm. But Bert smiled sleepily and said, 'Cor, it's lovely to have you back, Jean. It's not the same with Fred.'

'I should hope not,' she giggled. 'He'd have you arrested!'

'Well . . . We didn't always have a cuddle in the middle of it, did we, Jean? We just used to talk, didn't we? Fascinating, that was, for me. I always wanted to know what made you tick. Fred never says anything, much. Had a hard war, I expect. It does things to people, war does... Even our Geoff's not the same as he was, and you can't really call working for BAC active service, can you?'

'You can, Bert. They were bombed left, right and centre. Machine-gunned. Terrified.'

'That's what I mean, love. If our Geoff went through all that on his own doorstep...' He sighed.

'Drop him a note,' Jean suggested softly. 'Ask him over for a few days. A breath of fresh country fog'll do him the world of good.'

Bert chuckled. 'P'raps I will. You won't mind? Really?'

No, Jean didn't mind. She hadn't seen much of Bert's son and his wife, but the little she'd seen she'd liked more than a little. She'd been prepared for a bit of jealousy, even a bit of resentment, but if Geoff had felt anything of the sort he hadn't shown it. 'Glad to see the old chap happy,' had been his attitude.

Old! Cheeky blighter! Bert wasn't old! But even the thought of his one day being old didn't scare Jean. He had a Post Office pension!

No one could accuse Jean of loving him for his money, yet if she was honest with herself, his money did make a difference. It made her twice as happy as if he'd been poor, if only because it made everything so easy. There'd been times, when she was on her own, when even if she'd had the coupons to buy new shoes for the kiddies, she hadn't the money to spare. And she'd been scared for the future, always scared. The life she'd lived then... Well, it seemed like a nightmare now. Not as bad a nightmare as when Jack had been alive, but a nightmare just the same. Fear, poverty, loneliness... Oh, it was amazing what a difference a few years had made.

The fog had lifted a bit before Jean set off for the first round of the day, but it was perishing cold and icy underfoot. Leaving her bike propped at the corner, she delivered around the square and along Church Lane, stamping her feet. She'd come out in the dark. Before she returned to her bike for the long ride to Drayfield a ghostly grey dawn had broken, although it was still not light, just a little less dark. She pulled a pair of Bert's old socks over her fingerless mittens (cycling, in weather like this, was murder to the hands) and, standing astride her bicycle, walked it into the muddy opening of Drayfield Lane.

For as long as she'd lived in the village, she'd never passed the gate at Home Farm without looking in, hoping for a glimpse of Miles Huntley. Funny... She'd been in love with him, in a way. In many ways. She'd seen in him her dream of the perfect man, the sort of man every woman dreamed of. Courteous and kind, hard-working and dignified. Handsome, elegant, clean. Wholesome. A lump came to her throat, for Miles Huntley was whole no more, poor man. He was still in hospital, what was left of him, and there was no knowing when he'd come home again, if at all. Was it her fault?

It wasn't, of course. Of course it wasn't. But it seemed she'd never get rid of the feeling... The feeling that perhaps it was. She ought really to confess to someone, get it out of her system. Go to see the Rector perhaps. Say, 'Remember what you were saying about curses? Well, I put a curse on someone (some two, three or a dozen) about ten years back, before the war, and your sermon made me think. Is there a way of taking it back? Is there a way...?'

Jean looked into the yard at Home Farm and saw no one. She sighed, spun her pedals and looked again, just as an old man she didn't recognise came out of the dairy, bearing an old-fashioned wooden yoke from which two large, slopping pails of water were suspended. Jean frowned. The daylight still deserved no such name and the air was still hung with freezing mists, but Jean knew everyone – she knew *everyone* in the valley! A mere gloom, a mere *fog* was no excuse! She could recognise people from half a mile off, just from the way they walked! But not this one . . .

He had on an ancient felt hat, rubber boots and a tattered ulster which reached almost to his ankles. His shoulders were bent (that could be the yoke, of course) his feet shuffling warily over the icy cobbles. In the split-second that this appraisal took, Jean also deduced that the old chap wasn't accustomed to farm work, for she'd never in her life seen a proper countryman moving so slowly. When a man set himself to get through a day's work, he went at it hell-for-leather, sure-footed and sure-handed, having enough confidence in his strength to avert any disaster the weather might have planned for him. So who was this?

There was one good way to find out. 'Morning!' Jean called out cheerfully. 'Warm enough for you?'

The bent head was raised. Wearily the 'old chap' turned his head and wearily smiled.

Without pausing for more, Jean pedalled off to Drayfield. *Old chap!* No wonder she hadn't recognised him! Oh, God, oh, God, what had brought Bel Huntley to this? She'd looked so old, so tired and frail . . . And that yoke! Jean had sometimes used a yoke to carry water out at Drayfield, especially in winter when the pipes froze and she'd had to fetch supplies from the well in the garden. But Jean was different! She'd been born to be a work-horse. She was just an ordinary woman, not a lady, like Bel!

She'd travelled scarcely one of the two miles to Drayfield when, blinded by tears, Jean stopped, leaned her arms on the handlebars and her face in her hands and sobbed as if her heart would break. Miles was ruined, Andrew gone, Simon dead. And now . . .

Bind her in the coils of thy might . . .

'No!' she wailed. 'Oh, no, please!'

Shocked and shivering, she rubbed the tears from her face and stared mutely into the freezing air, remembering . . . Bel in a lilac frock and silk stockings, as fresh as a summer day. Bel, smiling and warm, her voice like honey, lifting Shirley's pram on to the pavement as if it weighed nothing at all. Jean could see her now, as plain as plain: her lovely smile, her shining hair, a beautiful tweed jacket with a little gold brooch in the lapel . . .

Jean had spat on that brooch. She'd hurled it away. Since then, over the years, it was as if she and Bel had changed places. Jean was living in a palace with her dream of the perfect man (or as near as made no odds), while Bel was hefting water across a freezing farmyard . . . In the dark.

Chapter Twenty-Three

It wasn't until Felix began to advise Bel at Home Farm that he realised something strange had happened to him. He'd become a farmer. Not the kind of farmer his father was, nor even the kind Miles Huntley had been, but a farmer just the same. While he'd striven to feel the love of farming he'd known at the outset was wanting, it had escaped him. Yet as soon as he'd stopped looking for it . . .

Strange. He'd thought Alan's death had been the end of everything. Beyond that point he'd mentally lain himself down, like a dog on its master's grave, feeling certain that he would never again move from that spot. He *hadn't* moved. He'd settled there. But even over a grave the wind blows, the sun shines, the rain falls. And without being aware of anything except the grave beneath his feet, the dog sees and feels and suffers it all – and is changed. He no longer loves the man who lies in the grave. He loves the grave.

There were still a number of things Felix hated about farming, but these came into the 'nothing's perfect' category, providing as much stimulus and challenge as frustration and despair. There was virtually nothing in farming (except perhaps a tractor wheel) that could be changed overnight, and yet change had been so accelerated during the war years that Leonard and Solomon could scarcely credit the difference.

Before the war, their working methods, machinery and scientific knowledge had barely moved forward from the Middle Ages: in six hundred years they'd travelled that many inches. Yet in the past six years, they'd travelled that many miles. Electricity, internal combustion engines, artificial fertilisers and combine harvesters: these things alone had revolutionised agriculture, changing its face beyond all recognition. But that wasn't all. From being a combination of art, craft and hard, sweated labour, the nation's desperate need for food had turned farming into a modern science: an exciting, world-opening venture, as wonderful (and perhaps as devastating) as the invention of the aeroplane had been.

And Felix was in the vanguard of it all! One of the first truly modern farmers, a trail-blazer, a pioneer! This thought, among several others of a more contemplative nature, had made him happy with his lot as never before. He looked upon Drayfield now not with the simple affection of a man for his home, but with the passion of a man who had great achievements in view. It seemed almost magical to him that simply by staying put he'd found all the challenges he'd longed for when he'd dreamed of going away.

The only thing it hadn't done was to make him sociable. Beyond his own family and the men who worked at Drayfield, he rarely saw anyone now and he missed Miles's company more than he could say. Bel was no substitute. Although she'd made Felix a heart-warming apology for embarrassing him with her grief, he suspected she'd never really forgiven him for witnessing it.

She needed him to 'organise' her into organising Jim Brooks; she needed his help with the accounts and the eternal 'red tape'; she'd even asked him, on one occasion, to arrange some vital repairs to a terrace of cottages over at Church Molton. But she never looked him straight in the eye. She never engaged in small-talk. And if he ever mentioned anything personal (beyond the barest bones of day-to-day courtesy), she became very remote. Not cold. Bel was never cold. She just seemed to drift away. 'Hmm? Miles? Oh, better . . . He's much better, thank you, Felix. How kind you are . . .' (So kindly depart by the nearest exit.)

He often saw Jinny at Bishop's Court, but there was never a chance to talk to her and, in a way, she'd become almost as remote as her mother. She never failed to blush when she saw him (it was usually Jinny who opened the door) but then she'd stumble and dither, mutter something about finding 'Mummy', and then disappear – backwards, sideways and in ever-decreasing circles – into the dark passageway which led to the kitchen. 'Er – sorry. Er – do go into the er – library. She won't be a sec.'

She never said his name. Felix could have coped with all the blushing and dithering if only she'd said his *name*! The Huntleys had always been very good with names; it was a trick they had and a very charming one. Charming even in Robin, who had as few claims to charm as anyone could who'd always won their spitting contests out at Drayfield! Yet whenever they met, even if it was only to remark about the weather, Robin had usually managed to say, 'Felix,' three or four times. There was something affectionate about it, but also something respectful which recognised and emphasised one's identity. It said, 'You are important to me.'

Jinny, like her parents and her brothers, had always used Felix's name. Now that she failed to use it, was she saying she'd lost her respect for him? Was she saying he was no longer important?

God, he wished he'd never kissed her!

But he wished with all his heart he could kiss her again . . .

'Well?' Bel demanded incredulously. 'Aren't you going to open it?'

She'd been to visit Miles and was still wearing her best coat and hat. Her lipstick had worn off, but that aside she looked ten times better than when she'd gone out. Something good had happened and although Jinny guessed she'd find a clue to it in the scrappy grey envelope Bel had given her, she couldn't, somehow, bring herself to open it.

She recognised her father's handwriting, of course. He had terrible handwriting: sharp and angular with long, slashing sidestrokes which made it look as if he'd crossed it all out, but in fact were just the dottings of 'i's and the crossings of 't's.

'Miss Virginia Huntley. Bishop's Court.'

He'd never written to her before.

Wide-eyed and blushing, she looked at her mother and asked 'What's it about?'

'I don't know!' Bel laughed. 'Open it!'

Jinny opened it, her fingers shaking, her eyes blurring in the heat that scalded her skin. The envelope contained two sheets of paper, folded once. Jinny unfolded them as if expecting something with teeth to jump out at her. Then she shut her eyes, swallowing the first words to have caught her eye: 'Darling Jinny'.

He had never called her darling . . .

'Umm,' Bel prompted sarcastically. 'I think you'll make more sense of it if you *open* your eyes, darling.'

'Oh, don't be *mean*, Mummy!'

'Liv 'er be fruh minute,' Muriel advised roughly, and Bel, pulling a face, tiptoed away to report her husband's progress to his mother.

'Darling Jinny,' Jinny read again. 'Mummy tells me you've been worrying about me. Until very recently I'm afraid you had cause to be worried. The food here is quite shocking, you know. I spend hours of my time trying to decide what they do with it and, more to the point, why. When next Mummy serves her dreaded cottage pie, I strongly advise you to give thanks for it, remembering your father's words of wisdom: *Things could be worse.*

'I have to confess that in the weeks following my "little operation" I felt quite low-enough to think that things couldn't possibly be worse. Then, for my sins, my appetite returned and I thought I might just manage a little soup. They called it "Ox Tail"; quite appropriate as it turned out because it both looked and tasted like farmyard sweepings, complete with carbolic and a lavish seasoning of axle grease. Before I leave here I'll be doing my utmost to get the recipe for it. If I succeed, we'll patent it as a miracle cure and make a fortune. Just one spoonful of this extraordinary potion and I felt quite strong enough to hop all the way home.'

In the midst of tears Jinny giggled, then, plucking her lips with her fingertips, read on.

'They've given me an artificial leg. Even after my spoonful of miracle soup I wasn't convinced that I'd ever manage to control the confounded thing, but since then I've eaten steak and onion pie, apple crumble and custard, mince and carrots. Incredible as it must seem, they're all made to the self-same recipe! Now, as it says somewhere in the Good Book, I am "rejoicing as a strong man to run a race" and hoping to make my escape before you are very much older.

'I'm longing to see you again. Mummy says you are brooding too much, but she says this of me, too, and probably of Muriel, so you needn't tell *me* there's no truth in it. Muriel, brooding? That merry, vivacious little soul? There've been times, over the years, when I've thought myself as miserable as anyone could be, yet when I've come home to Muriel, I've never failed to think, "No. *Things could be worse.*"

'Remember this, darling. We've been through some hard and unhappy times which are not yet over, but while we can love and appreciate each other, while we still have Mummy's cooking and Muriel's smiling face to support us, we can survive and be glad.

'One day, quite soon, you will grow up, marry and have children of your own. Take my word for it, you will not live happily ever after. You'll live as we all live, on carbolic and axle grease, with only a few sweet moments to lighten the load. Cherish those moments, Jinny. Laugh, sing, dance and make merry whenever the opportunity arises, for otherwise, as I am doing now, you'll look back and say, "Well, hang it all, why did I never learn to polka?"

'It's almost time for Matron's round and I am shaking in my shoe. She's a frightful creature in a steel-grey uniform, with hair and beard to match. I shall never look at Nurse Stokes again without telling myself, "Things could be worse."

'Hoping to see you very soon, I remain (for the most part) your hungry and affectionate . . . Daddy.'

Jinny read the letter three times, analysing every word, every phrase, every joke; tasting and treasuring each mention of Miles's feelings for her. 'Darling' (twice!) and 'I'm longing to see you again', were the best bits. She'd remember them until she died. Yet at the same time she could appreciate that, even without them, the letter was an expression of love, a glimpse of Miles's personality which, until now, he'd kept hidden from her. His remarks about Muriel, Bel and Nurse Stokes were very typical of him: they identified him as the man she knew, the man who had hurt her so much when she was small. But when she was small (perhaps because she was small) she had never – never once – detected the warmth and humanity of the man who was her father.

She'd known that he was vulnerable. She'd known that he had feelings 'too deep for words', but it had seemed to her that she'd discovered these things too late. It was as if, over the years, he'd hurt her too much for any cure to be possible.

It went back to the time when she'd injured her leg and thought she would die before he noticed she was missing. Something had broken in her then. She'd heard it go, almost as clearly as she'd heard the ligaments snapping in her knee.

The ligaments had mended eventually. The other thing never had. No matter how kind he'd been to her afterwards, the part of her which had so longed for him to be kind wasn't there any more. She'd ceased to reach for him. She'd turned away. She'd given up hope.

How strange it was that when you'd given up hope, hope came back, like a kicked dog, asking you to stroke it again, feed it, give it a home. '*While we can love and appreciate each other . . .*'

Jinny smiled. Yes, she could do that now.

Bel came back, wearing the ragged breeches and darned jersey that was her 'lady-farmer' outfit. There'd been talk in the village that she'd been mucking out pig-sties and milking cows in Miles's absence, but all she'd really done were a few odd jobs to release one of the men for more important work. She fed the dogs, let the geese out (and shooed them home again) and cared for the horses. Before the war, the horses had been a full-time job, but now there were only five left and all, except Miles's hunter, were pensioners, left out to graze except in the hardest weather. It hadn't been easy, but neither had it been especially hard: no harder, at least, than digging the garden, which Bel had been doing for years without anyone saying it was 'a wicked shame'. People were funny . . .

Jinny slid Miles's letter back into its envelope and then pushed the envelope into her cardigan sleeve.

Bel laughed. 'Not going to share it, darling?'

'Share what?'

'Daddy's letter!'

'Oh . . . Yes, of course. He says he's dreading coming home to your cottage pie.'

'Ooh! You little fibber!'

'It's true. "Mummy's *dreaded* cottage pie," were his precise words. He also said you should let me go dancing.'

'He didn't! Show me!'

Laughing, Jinny jumped up from her chair and dodged

around the table, where Bel couldn't catch her. 'He says he wants me to learn to polka!'

Bel stood with her hands on her hips, trying to look outraged, but not trying too hard. She looked wonderful. Young and happy, bubbling with excitement. '*I'll* teach you to polka,' she threatened. 'Cheeky madam! What's wrong with my cottage pie, anyway?'

'Woss right wiv it?' Muriel groaned from her post at the sink. 'No meat, no gravy . . .'

'No carbolic,' Jinny giggled. 'No axle grease.'

'Axle grease? What on *earth* are you talking about? Muriel? What's she talking about?'

Muriel was peeling potatoes, leaning so far over the sink she looked as if she was doing it with her teeth. Without straightening up, she turned her head, stared at Jinny for a moment and . . . winked.

It was a wonderful moment. Jinny laughed. Bel laughed. They fell into each other's arms and laughed until they cried.

The letter had been Bel's idea. Miles had resisted it for a while; he'd been too depressed to care and, in a way, too angry, although even his anger had been of that miserable variety that sees reason in all things and hope in none. He'd been too turned in on himself to understand the significance of Bel's humble confessions.

'She says I treat her as if she doesn't exist. And I suppose it's true. But I hadn't realised it, Miles. I thought . . . I thought I loved Jinny *more* than I loved the boys, not less. I thought I understood her. And I suppose I did . . . in a way.'

It was the sort of revelation that, in happier times, Miles would have laughed at and demanded, 'say that again – in English.'

But he hadn't bothered. He hadn't cared, and after a few more hesitant attempts to explain herself, Bel had given up and talked about other things. Oddly, though, her words had stuck at the back of his mind, like a lump of wet clay thrown against a wall. About six weeks later it had dried out and dropped off, and between listening to the night nurses' footsteps squeaking up and down the ward, he'd thought it all over and realised something terrible. Bel hadn't loved Jinny as much as she should because he hadn't let her!

His fault? Was everything going to turn out to be *his* fault? He sighed. No, it was all Lord Kitchener's fault. Or Kaiser Bill's. In fact, if one could only fit all the historical pieces together, the fault would probably land in the lap of Julius Caesar. Swine . . . If his lot hadn't invaded Britain (barely fifteen hundred years ago) Jinny would have been very much happier. The whole course of history would have worked out differently. She'd have been . . . But no. For if history had been different, if there'd never been a Caesar or a Kaiser Bill, Miles would have gone on producing boys, Bel wouldn't have strayed and Jinny really *wouldn't* exist!

He liked that idea no more than Jinny did. He loved her. She intrigued him. She was like a closed box with a rusty lock. One knew that if one just fiddled with it a little it would fly open and reveal its mysteries for all to see. But there was a fear of breaking it beyond repair. And worse . . . a fear that it might prove to be empty.

In the end, it was a looking glass that prompted Miles to write to her. He'd taken his first 'long' walk (ten paces) to the bathroom and there met an emaciated, whey-faced old fellow who looked – if only vaguely – familiar. On the off-chance that he'd met him before, Miles nodded. The old fellow nodded. Miles said, 'Oh, my God,' and so did the other chap. Then both yelled for a nurse and collapsed, groaning in perfect harmony, into the same wheelchair.

The shock took some time to wear off. 'I was thirty-six when I set off for that walk,' he told Bel when she came to see him on Wednesday. 'And when I arrived in the bathroom I was eighty-six!'

Bel pressed her lips together. She was trying not to laugh.

'What's so funny?' Miles demanded irritably. 'I know I walk slowly, but I'm sure I didn't take fifty years to get there!'

They laughed then. Bel took his hand and squeezed it firmly. 'You just got your sums wrong,' she said. 'You were fifty-six when you set off, so in fact it took only thirty years.'

'Oh, thanks!' His grin faded. 'Do I really look . . . ?'

'No. You're very thin, but that's not irreversible; and you've lost your sun-tan, ditto. A few months at home and you'll be back to normal.' She smiled again. 'You'll even have the same limp.'

'Slightly worse, perhaps.'

'But in the end not as painful.'

'So they say . . .' He sighed. 'Odd, isn't it? I know I'm getting older; I can acknowledge the *number* of my years, but inside . . . Inside . . .' He closed his eyes. 'Jinny won't know me.'

'Did she ever?' Bel murmured softly.

Miles thought about this. No, except when she was tiny, Jinny had never been given a chance to know him. He'd been a face, a figure, a voice and a limited selection of attitudes. Save for one or two of the least pleasant attitudes, Jinny had no more insight into his character (in fact, rather less) than most of the residents of Bishop Molton could claim. Mrs Carter, for instance (Tomkins: he kept forgetting), had glimpsed him in most of his moods and, being a touch over-familiar, had caught him off his guard often enough to see that there was more to him than met the eye. Jinny had seen that, too, he supposed, although never through over-familiarity. Only once had she come close to him: that day in the office when he'd tried to break her heart. Instead she'd broken his. Broken *through* . . .

That was it! If he wanted to open the lock on Jinny's box, he had first to unlock his own! And of all the things she didn't know about 'Daddy', surely his sense of humour was the best of them?

Writing that letter was the best thing he'd done in years. Jinny's reply, which arrived the next day, was even better. 'Thank you for your letter. I've learned it by heart and can now recite it backwards. Muriel and I have had a long talk about your welcome home dinner. I said you should have roast chicken and she said, "In a pig's eye". It sounds delicious, doesn't it?'

During the next three weeks they exchanged letters on an almost daily basis and, for Miles at least, there were new revelations on every page. Jinny's style of writing was an enlightenment in itself. She'd always been good at composition and was capable of constructing quite lyrical passages entitled, 'A Walk in Winter', or 'The Secret Grotto'; but her letters had a different quality. The sentences were short, crisp and – seemingly – to the point, but there were messages written between the lines that spoke far louder than words. She was still holding back. She still couldn't trust him. Yet the love was there, reined in like a frisky horse which, given its head, might jump too high a fence and break poor Jinny's neck.

It was the middle of May when he went home at last. Jinny was at school – a blessing, because he wept all the way home and for the best part of an hour afterwards. The joy, oh, the joy of coming home! And the terror. It all looked so strange. And wickedly dangerous. There were corners everywhere, steps and stairs, chairs that were either too soft or too low (or both), dogs, cats and people all doing their utmost to knock him over. And nothing was as he'd left it.

'What the hell's happened to this wallpaper, Bel? It's filthy!'

'Filthy? Of course it's filthy! It's been there fifteen years!'

His mother had aged since he'd last seen her. 'You're looking as spry as ever,' he lied.

'Thank you,' she replied archly. 'I'd say the same for you if

I had as long to repent of my sins. Still, you don't look too dreadful. A touch pale, perhaps. How's the leg?'

'They've cut it off, Mother. Didn't Bel tell you?'

'I meant the peg-leg, you fool! You're walking better than I'd expected. Does it hurt?'

'Only in the ankle.'

'Hmph! Why can't they amputate sarcasm, I wonder?'

He grinned. 'And leave me *crippled*, Mother?'

Muriel stood at the far end of the hall, lurking like a footpad in the shadows. 'Struntley.'

'Oh, Muriel, I've missed you!'

'Ah. Well.' She shrugged and turned away. 'That'll wear off.'

She was right. It would all wear off. He'd get used to it all in a day or two. Even sleeping in the morning room would seem natural, although just at the moment he could scarcely bear the thought of it.

'How on earth did you get the bed downstairs?'

'Felix did it. He's been an angel – considering.'

'Considering what?'

'Oh . . . nothing.' She blushed.

'You've gone pink, darling.'

'I know. Silly, isn't it, at my age? I'm afraid I was rather rude to him at first. He came the day after your operation. Offered to help with the farm. I knew he was being kind, but I . . . Well, I suppose I wasn't quite up to it. I was tired. I thought I'd gone crazy. I imagine Felix thought so too, but I was just . . . tired.'

Miles looked at her sideways, reading between the lines. Crazy? How tired would Bel have to be to think she'd gone crazy? But then, they'd all been crazy: he with pain, Andrew with war-fatigue, Bel . . . Oh, poor, dear, brave little Bel! What the hell had she been through? Worse than he could imagine. More than he could ever thank her for. Better than he deserved.

'I'd like to hug you,' he said gently. 'But I'd fall over.'

She smiled. 'I can wait.'

He was trying to walk to the cloakroom when Jinny came home. He'd hoped to be seated when she saw him for the first time, but an artificial leg, inadequately schooled, makes no allowances for the urgent calls of nature. So when Jinny first saw him, he was doubled over his walking sticks and creeping through the hall like a snail.

'Hello, Daddy.'

'Jinny!' Mists of tears and embarrassment clouded his eyes, but when they cleared he saw no such mists in hers. He saw love. He saw laughter.

He saw his little girl.

Jean missed it, of course. She'd been making excuses all afternoon to 'just dash across the street', taking knitting patterns back to their owners, asking for recipes she didn't want, dashing into this shop or that and then 'forgetting' what she'd come for. It was like waiting for the King to pass by. But she missed it.

It was her own fault. If she'd had the sense, just for once, to leave the dinner dishes lying about for five minutes, she'd have caught him going right past her door. But no. She couldn't abide to see her beautiful kitchen splattered with gravy and bits of cabbage. Everything had to be washed and wiped and put away, the table scrubbed, the sink scoured, the floor swept. Then, tearing off her pinny and grabbing her purse (just in case), she fled out the door, only to meet a beaming Miss Bright, who said, 'You missed him!'

'Ohhh! No! *When*?'

'Five minutes ago. He waved at me! But oh, Mrs Tomkins, he looked dreadful! *Thin*? If he hadn't been sat right next to Mrs Huntley, I wouldn't have known him. Aw, the suffering that man's been through. Doesn't bear thinking about, does it? And his hair! *Snow white*. Snow white it is, as I'm standing here talking to you. Still curly as ever. But *snow white*.'

Jean let her breath out in a huge, deflating sigh. His hair had turned white (about time, too: he was pushing sixty after all) and she'd missed it. There were little groups of people standing all round the square, chatting nineteen to the dozen, comparing notes. Everyone must have seen him, except her! Never again, if she lived to be a hundred and moved house fifty times, would she live in a place that faced backwards!

There was, however, some (small) comfort to be had, for as she passed from group to group, gleaning as much news as she could, it turned out that in fact nearly everyone had missed it. Either that, or they'd just caught a glimpse from their front windows.

'Miss Bright says his hair's gone white, but if you believed everything *she* said, it could be sky-blue-pink and you'd never know the rights of it. I only caught a *glimpse*, mind, but his hair looked the same as ever to me. A bit greyer, p'raps. No, it was his *nose* struck me.'

'His nose?'

'Well, he've always had a big nose. I'm not saying he never. But it looked . . .'

'That's because he've gone so thin, though, Mrs Shilling. His flesh've dropped away. That'll always make a nose look bigger, see.'

'*Thin*? Like a skellyton, he was. Mind, I never seen much. I was putting the cat's food down, and they'd went by just as I stood up again.'

'Aw, but you should have seen Mrs Huntley's face. Proud as punch, she was, bringing him home safe an' sound after all these months. She deserves it, too. When you think what she was in the old days . . . Never done a hand's turn. Never even had to scratch her own nose if she didn't feel like it.'

'*No*, Edith. Don't forget the soup kitchen. She done that, didn't she? Cooking, cleaning, peeling spuds . . .'

'No, that was *after*! I was talking about *before*! Butlers, gardeners, bootboys, maids by the flippin' dozen!'

'A nanny for the kiddies!'

'Cor... Them was the days. The changes we've seen since our Roger was born! We used to think we was all... Well, that we was all like *fixed*, didn't we? In our proper places, like. But some've fell, and some've rose...'

Disappointment aside, Jean had already been feeling uncomfortable about the way the talk was going: she hated – absolutely hated – to be reminded of Bel Huntley at her best. But at the words, 'some've rose', everyone turned to look at her, lifting their eyebrows as if silently assessing her 'rise' and deciding she didn't deserve it.

She laughed. 'Well,' she said gaily. 'This won't do, will it? I must get on. I only came out to get the paper!'

She'd come out to see Miles Huntley, to check that he was all right, not thin as a skeleton and white as the driven snow! Oh, God...

Bert had the *Daily Express* and the *Evening Post* delivered but rather than be caught out in a lie, Jean bought the weekly *Guardian*, and heard Mrs Foggitt (another one who'd missed the homecoming) saying, 'Nah, we've seen the last of poor Mr Huntley. He've only come 'ome to die, I reckon.' Then, with a smile, she added brightly, 'Nice to do it in your own bed, though, that's what I always say.'

Jean was just creeping out of the shop when Felix Clare came in. They sidestepped each other a few times before Felix took charge. 'After you, Mrs Tomkins.'

He bowed and held the door open for her and, blushing a little, Jean thanked him and made her exit. She was acutely aware that the top of her head barely reached his shoulder, and even more aware that he'd grown in other ways, too. He'd lost the boyish innocence that had so touched her when he was walking out with Evelyn. He'd become harder, colder, more dignified. The way he carried his head, the way he walked, even the way he smiled gave him a 'touch-me-not' air which reminded her a bit of Miles Huntley.

Felix bought the *Guardian*, too. He came out of the shop before Jean had moved far from its door and, passing her with a smile, he strolled off down the street, reading the front page. He stopped. He snatched the fold open and read a little more. It could have been just the cricket results, but Jean didn't think so. He looked really shocked.

Frowning, she scanned the front page of her own paper. More rations cuts, ROVER TO THE RESCUE! (dog saves child from drowning), THE WEEK AT WESTMINSTER. No, nothing there. Then she saw it: a tiny article in the 'Westminster' column: DRAY RESERVOIR PLAN RESURRECTED.

'Oh, my God!' Jean clapped her hand to her mouth.

They were going to flood the valley!

Chapter Twenty-Four

Felix began to wake up at two o'clock every morning. After worrying himself silly for an hour or so, he'd then go back to sleep again, only to be wakened at five by the ringing of his alarm clock. He thought he was going mad. About a week later, when the noises began, he thought he'd *gone* mad.

None of the Clares had ever been superstitious. Felix had never touched wood, crossed fingers, thrown salt over his left shoulder, avoided walking under ladders or even (once he'd found out what it meant) said, 'Bless you,' when someone sneezed. He didn't believe in God, in the devil, in fairies, witches, ghosts or vampires. Consequently, when he'd heard the odd mention of Drayfield's 'lost room', he'd taken very little notice. Who needed it, anyway? Who cared? Even if a so-called witch *had* once been walled-up in it, it was too late to save her now.

But the noises came from the lost room, immediately next to his own. When he first heard it, it was just a faint scratching which could, at a push, have been mice. He told himself it was mice, convinced himself it was mice and was just drifting off to sleep when the scratching ceased and the knocking began. Faint, but very definite. Tap-tap-tap. It wasn't urgent. It seemed to be followed by a question mark: 'Tap-tap-tap? Anyone there?'

Woodpeckers! No . . . In the dark? In stone walls?

'Tap-tap-tap? Anyone listening?'

'No,' Felix muttered. 'Shut up and let me sleep.'

But he lay as stiff as a board, his eyes wide to the darkness, listening, listening. What the hell could it be?

Still, it kept him from worrying about the reservoir. In fact, the reservoir slipped his mind so completely that he began to drift away, his eyelids drooping, his mind floating . . . He saw Jinny standing on a hilltop, her hair flying in the wind, a thin white dress clinging softly to the contours of her body. Rounded breasts, flat belly, a smooth, deep vee where her thighs –

'Tap-tap-tap? *Tap?*'

He sat up, his heart thudding like a drum. He was wide awake again. He'd never sleep now!

Exhausted and furious, he dressed and went downstairs to put the kettle on, but even this proved difficult. The sink was piled so high with dirty dishes there wasn't even room to hold the kettle under the tap. In the dull yellow light that came from a single fly-specked electric bulb in the middle of the room, the kitchen looked like a sepia photograph of a city slum-dwelling. Penny had gone back to normal with a vengeance and although Felix was usually able to overlook the mess, this morning he couldn't. Cursing under his breath, he washed up, cleared the table, collected clothes, newspapers and bits of knitting into tidy heaps, carried out a huge pile of rubbish and, on his way back, stood in the grey light of dawn, staring at the bricked-up window of the lost room. There were no birds' nests under the eaves just there. Nothing to give a sensible explanation of the sounds he'd heard.

He shrugged and sighed. What did it matter? In a year or two, unless Parliament threw out the reservoir scheme, it would all be gone. The house, the land, the beautiful trees;

his work, Mike's and his father's, all drowned for evermore. And then what?

He couldn't see beyond that. He didn't want to move away, couldn't imagine giving his heart to another farm, another place. He wasn't certain he had a heart to give, any more. Drayfield had taken it and buried it somewhere and it, too, would be drowned unless . . .

Miles might do something, but unless Felix could speak to him there was no way of knowing. 'Give him a few weeks,' Bel had said. A few weeks! When every day would count against them!

Leonard seemed scarcely to care what happened. Since Alan's death, he'd largely lost interest in the farm and although he still worked, he worked as the other men did, turning to Felix for decisions. If Felix was in doubt, he might make a suggestion or volunteer advice, but he didn't really care. In fact, Felix had begun to wonder if Leonard would even bother to leave the valley if the Waterworks moved in. He gave the impression that earth, air and water were not significantly different. Cover him with any one of them. It wouldn't change a thing.

Felix woke at two o'clock the next morning. He'd forgotten the 'witch' and was busily (and expensively) pursuing a lawsuit against Bristol Waterworks when she reminded him of her presence.

'Tap . . . tap-tap-tap? Remember me?'

'Piss off,' Felix said, but his imagination didn't. It wasn't a witch; it was a German prisoner of war. He'd escaped from the camp over at Foreston, hidden in the lost room and couldn't get out again.

'Tap-tap-tap? Is the war over, yet?'

'Yes!' Felix snapped bitterly. 'And you lost it!'

'Tap-tap-tap? Let me out?'

Naked, shivering, raging, Felix leapt out of bed, grabbed

up one of his boots and hit the wall with the heel, once, twice, three times.

'There! What do you say to that?'

Nothing. No frantic messages in morse code: 'SOS. Have been walled up here for two hundred years. Getting hungry.'

Felix waited. And waited. Nothing.

He dived back into bed, pulled the covers over his head, curled himself into a ball and muttered, 'Sleep, sleep,' until, like a soft warm sea, sleep engulfed him and carried him away.

'*Tap-tap-tap*!'

'Oh, darling, do be careful!'

Penny stood at the foot of the ladder, holding on to it for grim death. Felix, at the top, was more aware of the distance between them than he cared to admit. 'Go indoors, Mother. What do you imagine you'll do if I fall? Catch me?'

'No, but at least you'll land on something soft.'

'That's true.'

'Hmm! I sometimes wonder why I love you.'

'Yes, it's a mystery, isn't it? *Aha*!' He'd found a tiny gap in the stonework, just above the lintel of the lost room's 'window'. It seemed scarcely big enough to admit a spider, but he'd seen mice disappearing through cracks no bigger, and although he was certain his 'witch' wasn't a mouse, where a mouse could go so could a few other creatures. And so, for that matter, could the rain. Was the tapping sound just dripping water?

'Wh-what the heh-heh-hell's he duh-doing?'

Felix sighed. He'd hoped Leonard would be elsewhere for a few minutes yet. He'd been scared of heights ever since Mike fell through the barn roof and even though Felix wasn't scared, he'd be delighted in more ways than one, when he could put this job behind him.

'It's all right, Dad. There's a hole here. I'll put some mortar in it later. I'll just check –'

He'd brought his penknife with him. Rather stupid, since he had to take both hands off the ladder to get the damn thing open.

'Oh, be *careful*,' his mother moaned.

'I'm *being* careful, Mother! D'you think I want to fall off?'

He prised the knife open. 'Right,' he said. 'You're surrounded. Come out with your hands up, or I'm coming in to get you!'

'Who-who's he t-talking to?'

Penny giggled nervously. 'The Drayfield witch. She's put a spell on him. If he doesn't let her out before midnight, she'll turn him into a frog.'

'Oh,' Leonard said dismally. 'Is th-that all?'

Felix slipped the knife-blade into the crack and slid it back and forth. Nothing happened, but the silence seemed somehow meaningful. Something was in there. Holding its breath.

'There's definitely a space behind here, but my knife's not long enough. I can't tell how far back it goes. Get the breadknife, will you, Mother?'

Penny, no doubt glad to be doing something more useful than holding the ladder, hurried off. Felix jiggled the penknife again and in the process dislodged another lump of mortar. From the large hole that resulted came a shriek and a clatter, and then something vast, black and stinking burst out into his face.

He screamed and leapt backwards, taking the ladder with him.

It was a long, long way to the ground.

The church was packed to the rafters. Jean and Bert had arrived early enough to find seats in the gallery, but there were more than a dozen mourners – even people from as far afield as Bristol and Frome – who had to stand in the churchyard until it was over.

Jean hadn't wanted to come. She'd known she would sob

from start to finish, and that wasn't right. It wasn't decent. The Clares were nothing to her – or thought they were nothing. Why should *she* weep for their dead? Oh, God... Three dead in so many years! And it was all her fault! It was all her fault!

She hadn't wanted to come, but Bert wouldn't hear of it. 'You must go to show respect, love. Everyone else is going. They'll think it funny if you don't. After all, you saw him every day, practically, all through the war. It's not as if you didn't know him.'

'But I'll cry!'

'We'll all cry, Jean. One look at poor Mrs Clare...' He shook his head. 'The grief that poor woman's been through. You wonder when it'll all end, don't you?'

It'll never end, Jean thought bleakly. Not until... *Until their line is ended and nothing that is theirs endures upon the earth.*

That was what she'd wished on them. And that was precisely how it was turning out. If the reservoir scheme went through, even Drayfield itself would be lost. *Nothing* that is theirs; not even a blade of grass!

The Huntleys were among the last to enter the church, dressed in black from head to heel and looking as if they'd both taken poison. Bel's head was up, her mouth down, her eyes blazing with rage and sorrow. But not once did she look at Miles.

Everyone else did. No one had held out much hope of ever seeing him again alive, let alone walking, but that the walk was crucifying him was written plain in every line of his face. He was very thin, but by no means a skeleton, and his hair wasn't white, just three shades paler than it had been before; but his beauty had gone. People stared at him as he approached and bowed their heads as he went by. Only Mary Winterson dared to give him a pitying smile, but he must have given her short shrift because she went as red as flannel straight after and started fumbling with her hymn book. No one patronised Miles Huntley and got away with it.

The coffin was borne in by Drayfield labourers: squat, bow-legged, apple-faced men, two of whom had worked for Jack and never mourned him for a minute. But Syd Leach, combed and spruce in a dark blue suit and polished boots, was openly weeping and old Martin Wheeler's lip was wobbling like a jelly.

Penny Clare, who followed behind, was like a queen carved in stone: proud and cold, straight and calm. And, for the first time since Jean had known her, she was beautiful.

'No make-up,' Jean whispered on a sob.

'Oh . . .' Bert sighed. 'Bless her.'

Jean wiped floods of tears from her face to stare, almost mesmerised with horror, at poor Felix, who crept at his mother's side like the ghost of a man who had died in agony. His face was gashed and badly swollen, his eyes bruised, his left arm cradled in a sling of old blackout curtain. Like Miles, he could barely walk, for he'd fallen the best part of twenty feet, and the only reason *he* wasn't dead was because he'd landed in a tree. Crashed straight through it with the ladder on top of him and then just hung there, helpless, watching his father die.

Heart attack, and who could blame him? Two sons gone and the third tumbling through the air like a bird full of shot . . .

It was a bird that had caused it. A starling, they said. Got in there somehow and couldn't get out again – until Felix had gone up there, looking for it. But starlings were like that. They'd driven Jean half-crazy at Briar Cottage. The damn things never slept! Running around on the rafters at dead of night, pecking holes in the mortar. Worse than rats for the damage they did . . . And now they'd killed Leonard Clare.

No. *Jean* had killed Leonard Clare.

Well, she'd had enough! As soon as this was over . . . Not

today, perhaps, but certainly tomorrow, she'd go straight to Rector Winterson and tell him what she'd done. No, she couldn't go tomorrow. Tomorrow was Saturday. She'd promised to take the girls out, and she couldn't possibly go on Sunday, his busiest day. Monday, then. *Definite*.

The day had been a scorcher and the evening wasn't significantly cooler. Jinny eyed the huge jug of cider with a lustful smile, even knowing that it had a kick like a mule and that she wouldn't be allowed a sip.

'I'll take it out, Mummy.'

'No, I will. Daddy and Felix are talking business and –'

'Please? I won't say anything. I'll just take it and leave it and creep away again. Please?'

'All right.' Bel sat at the kitchen table, holding up her hands in mock surrender. 'But – !'

'What?'

Bel's smile was wan. 'Don't expect too much, darling.'

The warning was unnecessary. Jinny had ceased to expect 'too much' from Felix a long time ago. She'd ceased to expect anything. But she hadn't ceased wanting him. She took him to bed with her every night and lay in his arms, safe and warm and softly laughing. She talked to him (but only in her mind: she wasn't *that* far gone) and heard him whisper, 'Jinny, oh, Jinny, I love you!'

He'd never said that, of course. But he'd said, more than once, that she was his 'special girl'. He'd said it in the manner of a grown-up handing out sweets to a baby, wanting only to keep it from crying. She knew it hadn't meant anything. But she couldn't let it go. *Couldn't*, not wouldn't, for in many ways Felix had become like a chain around her ankle, holding her down. She wanted to be free of him. Free of loving him. Yet at the same time, she wanted to go on loving him until she died.

The two men were on the terrace outside the morning

room. Violet had fallen asleep in her chair, her head lolling backwards, her mouth open. She'd been reading, and the book still lay on the rounded mount of her stomach, sliding stealthily downwards with every breath she took. Jinny had mixed feelings about her grandmother. She seemed incapable of opening her mouth without saying something spiteful, yet there was something very sad about her too. She looked so vulnerable when she was asleep: like a dozy rooster, with Jim Brooks sneaking up on it from behind. Also, she had a sore place on her leg which would hurt like blazes if the book fell on it...

Jinny set the tray on the table, crouched at her grandmother's feet and, very gently, lifted the book clear. Violet had once been a devotee of Hardy, Trollope and Dickens. Now she preferred cheap romances which had bigger print, shorter words and nothing too difficult to think about.

' "No, Reggie, no!"
"Oh, yes, yes, Sophronia! Don't fight it, my darling. We were meant for one another, you and I! The stars in their courses – " '

Jinny read that as, 'The stars in their corsets,' and bit her lip on a grin. But it made her wonder... Should *she* have said, 'No, Felix, no!'? She'd heard things, since then, about 'naughty girls' who either forgot, or didn't want to say, 'no'. She'd also learned what it was they were meant to be turning down, and it sounded rather unpleasant, nothing like Felix's hands on her body, his lips... Anyway, they didn't respect you if you didn't say no. So perhaps that was it. Perhaps that's what she'd done wrong, and he didn't respect her any more?

'So... If I understand you, Mr Huntley, you don't care what happens. They can flood the valley, take everything – '

'*Buy* everything, Felix. And it isn't a matter of not caring. We have no real options, you see, and there's nothing to be gained by pursuing a lost cause however greatly we might care about it. As I mentioned earlier, I took advice in '38 and was told – '

'But that was different! Farming was depressed then. No one wanted us! Now – '

'Yes, now. But the war's over, Felix. True, the country's still desperate for all the food we can produce, but that won't last. At a guess, I'd say we'll peak in 1950, or even sooner, and after that prices will begin to level out. Then they'll fall. And once they begin to fall, there's no knowing where – or even if – they'll hit bottom. If I were you – '

'You are not me, Mr Huntley.'

'No, Mr Clare, I am not.'

There was a smile in Miles's voice, but Jinny knew that smile and still, in spite of everything, feared it. Felix was playing with fire. He was angry, trying to push Miles into a course of action he wouldn't take, and if he went on pushing he'd lose not just Drayfield, but Miles's friendship, too.

With a laugh that belied her white face and trembling hands, Jinny hurried outside. 'Refreshments!' she gasped brightly. 'Sorry it took so long! Oh, hello, Felix! Gosh, isn't it *hot*?' The tray hit the stone table with a crash. 'Whoops! Sorry. Shall I pour, Daddy?'

Miles blinked and raised one eyebrow, viewing the pool of spilled cider which now filled the tray. 'Is there any left to pour?'

'Sorry,' she said. 'Two left feet.'

'Sit down, then, and get them untangled. You'll have a drink won't you, Felix?'

Felix had averted his head and was staring down the garden, the tendons in his neck standing out like rope. He didn't reply.

'Of course he will!' Jinny laughed. 'He must be dying of thirst. I certainly am, and *I* haven't walked up from Drayfield! Won't it be lovely, though, if it goes on like this? I adore hot weather, don't you, Felix?'

He sighed and, turning to Jinny, said flatly, 'The weather's never right for farmers, is it?'

His wounds had healed, but his face was still badly scarred.

One of the scars had gone very deep at the corner of his mouth, and although it hadn't pulled his lips out of shape, the scar itself went downwards, giving his smile a cynical twist which Jinny found rather daunting. He had changed so much. He was no longer the sweet, gentle boy she'd known so well and loved so dearly. He was a man now, as cool and remote as Miles had once been, his feelings a music which only he could hear. She ached to touch him, to be close to him again, but she meant nothing to him now. He'd grown up. Gone away.

'I'd better go,' she said. 'And let you talk.'

'No need,' Miles held out his hand as if to push her backwards into her seat. 'We've talked. Now it's your turn. Tell us about – '

'Sorry, I must go.' Felix drained his glass and stood up, darting his hand across the table to shake Miles's. 'Thanks for the drink, Mr Huntley. Jinny.' With a curt nod to each of them, he departed, leaving Miles with his eyes closed, chewing his lip on despair.

'Damn,' he said softly.

'Was it my fault, Daddy?' Jinny whispered. 'Did I come at the wrong moment?'

'No,' he sighed. 'It was a disaster from start to finish. He wants me to fight it, Jinny, and I can't. I won't. It wouldn't make sense. How can the interests of a handful of farmers compete with the needs of an entire city? We wouldn't have a hope.'

'But wouldn't it be worth trying just to comfort him? He's so sad, Daddy. He isn't – ' Tears filled her eyes. 'He's got nothing left!'

'He's got money in the bank, darling, and if the reservoir goes through – as I'm almost certain it will – he'll have a good deal more money. So shall I, of course. But if we start legal proceedings now, we'll spend every penny we have and *still* lose the valley. Where's the comfort in that?'

Miles reached under the table to bring out a roll of draughtsman's linen: the plan of the reservoir as it had been presented in 1938.

'Here. Look.' He unrolled the plan and held it down at the corners with the empty cider glasses. 'This is the northern boundary of the reservoir, with the villages well outside it. Can you see Drayfield?'

Jinny traced her finger over the map. 'Yes. The house is . . . here. Almost in the middle.'

'Quite. Now find Home Farm.'

Jinny found it. Except for a thin fillet of land on its southern edge, Home Farm was safe.

'Oh . . .' she breathed. 'So Felix will lose everything and you'll lose – ?'

'Nothing. I'll be paid for the sale of the valley as a whole, but I'll also keep my living, my home and my village properties. If I'd drawn up this plan myself, I couldn't have been better served.'

'But you didn't draw it up!'

'No. And Felix knows it.' He sighed again. 'But who can blame him for feeling as he does? He gave up everything for Drayfield, and now he's losing that, too. But I wouldn't go to law even if I stood to lose as much as he does, Jinny. It would be like putting my money on a blind horse. I couldn't win.'

He laid his chin on his fist and stared at the plan as if trying to move it sideways, leaving Drayfield free and clear. Since the weather had turned warm, he'd spent most of his time in the garden and now was as tanned and almost as fit as he'd ever been. But only when he was sitting down. His daily struggles with a pair of walking sticks had developed the muscles of his arms, shoulders and back, but in spite of all his efforts to 'get back to normal' he still couldn't do very much. His 'new' leg hurt him, as did the cumbersome harness that held it in place, and he was often depressed, always frustrated and wishing he could do more.

He blamed it on Nurse Stokes, who came every night to dress the sore places, calling him all the names under the sun for trying too hard. 'Now, look, you daft bugger, walking a hundred yards on this bloody thing's like walking twenty miles on your own two feet! Would you do that twice a day, putting blisters on blisters on bloody stupid blisters?'

'I would if I had to.'

'Hmm. I know. That's how you lost your leg in the first place, you silly great lummox. Learn from your mistakes, Cleversticks, or I'll wash my hands of you, once and for all!'

Jinny was appalled the first time she overheard one of these exchanges – she'd been sure he'd show Stokesy the door – but he hadn't seemed to mind. He said she was a wonderful nurse; but what a *pity* it was about the rest of her.

'Daddy?'

'Hmm?'

'What do the other farmers think about the reservoir?'

'They're a lot older than Felix, darling. They understand.' He sighed. 'Farmers become very cynical as they get older, you know. What Felix said about the weather never being right . . . It's true. Even when we get a hot spell for haymaking, it can be too hot, or too humid, or it lasts so long the grass won't grow back. It's almost *never* perfect. But after a while we realise that it makes no difference how we feel about it. We can't change it, therefore why fight it? We complain, of course, but not with any passion. Passion is for young men; and when they're as unfortunate as Felix has been, passion is *pain*, Jinny.'

Suddenly the corners of his mouth curved downwards and his eyes filled with tears. 'Poor boy . . .'

Jinny laid her hand on his arm and gently squeezed it.

'He reminds me of myself,' Miles sighed. 'He's lost too much. Too young.'

Chapter Twenty-Five

Mrs Shilling's daughter, Ivy, ran off with a Council workman in 1942 and wasn't seen again until 1947, when she ran back again, complete with two black eyes, a swollen lip and three little kiddies. Ivy was still only twenty-two. Her name was still Shilling.

Her mother didn't know where to put herself for the shame. If it hadn't been for the little ones, she'd have shown Ivy the door.

'I would, Mrs Tomkins. No, I mean it! I would! Oh, when I think how I brought her up: as respectable as . . . Well, *you* know, Mrs Tomkins. There was never *anything* like that on our side of the family! I set her as decent an example as . . . Clean sheets every Sat'dy, Sunday school reg'lar! You'd think . . . But no. Three kiddies wrong side of the blanket and every one of 'em alive with nits! I'll make her rue the day she brought this on me! How I'm supposed to keep 'em, that's what I'd like to know! Just as we was getting comfortable, seeing light at the end of the tunnel . . . And now this!'

Jean saw Mrs Shilling's point of view. Well, of course she did. She had girls of her own, and if any one of them . . . But it didn't bear thinking about and anyway it wouldn't happen. Evelyn was settled in a tidy little job in Bath and courting ever such a nice boy from over Clutton way. Lovely family. Very clean. You couldn't imagine people like that leading Evelyn astray, and even if they tried it, Evelyn had more sense than to be led. Jean had told her and told her. Told her until she was blue in the face: 'You can't trust a man until you've known him five years, and even then you'd best wait another five!'

But you couldn't tell the young. They wouldn't listen. They thought *they* knew best, thought *you* were the daft one, thought, in their innocence, that nothing bad could ever happen to them.

'Oh, Mum! It was all *different* in your day!'

Different, yes. But whatever times you lived in, turnips were the same, thistles were the same. Innocent babes and cruel bastards, they were the same.

But Evelyn had her head screwed on. Jean wasn't – really – worried about Evelyn. It was Ivy Shilling who preyed on her mind. She started dreaming about her, seeing those black eyes and bruises even in her dreams and waking up all of a sweat, needing Bert, turning to him in the dark, stroking his face to check that he really *was* Bert and not Jack, come back to haunt her.

Ivy had been such a *lovely* girl! Nice-natured. Very trusting and kind. But that had been her downfall, of course, as once it had been Jean's. Trusting. Believe anything. Father Christmas, fairies at the bottom of the garden, 'Oh, my darling, I'll make you so happy!'

Jean couldn't imagine a man who dug drains saying any such thing to poor Ivy, but whatever he'd said it amounted to the same thing: a handful of kiddies, a face full of bruises, a heart full of pain.

And it wasn't something you ever got over. When a man had despised her, a woman was like a china cup thrown against the wall. Oh, you could stick it together again, make it useful, make it pretty. But the cracks were always there. *Always* there.

'I feel so sorry for her, Bert! I know everyone says she only got what she asked for, but I feel sorry for her. She reminds me of me, Bert . . . After Jack died.'

'Nonsense, you were a respectable married woman, love. Not the same at all!'

'No, not the same, but as near as makes no odds. I had nothing. I didn't know where to turn. If it hadn't been for Mr Huntley . . .' She shook her head. 'Oh, Bert, I wish I could help Ivy the way Mr Huntley helped me!'

Bert slid his arms around her waist (which was getting a bit chubby again: Fred Holmes hadn't had one of his headaches just lately and she was missing the exercise). 'You're too good, love,' Bert said. 'People have to sort out their own problems. All right, the Huntleys gave you a hand when you needed it, but you were all alone, love. Ivy's got her mother.'

That was true. Cruel and vindictive though Mrs Shilling was, she was still Ivy's mother. And Jean wasn't. So that was the end of it.

But she still dreamed about her, night after night, and woke up crying for a girl called Ivy who looked like a girl called Jean. She'd been so young . . . Too young to be marked by so many hurts and sorrows, too young to be *blamed*!

'Hey,' Bert turned over in the dark and dropped a sleep-heavy arm across her belly. 'What's up?'

'Bad dream.'

He snuggled close. 'Sssh. Go to sleep. It's all over, now.'

There'd been a time when Jean had thought Bert was right about everything. Now . . . Now she only *wished* he was right.

The reservoir scheme was passed almost a year to the day after Leonard Clare's death. It would take a few more years for all the processes of law to run their course and perhaps another five years before the valley would disappear. But that was by the by. To all intents and purposes, Drayfield was no more.

'So!' Felix flung the *Western Daily* across the breakfast table. 'Consider yourself homeless, Mother.'

'Why, what have I done?'

In spite of himself, Felix smiled. She hadn't reacted to Leonard's death half as badly as he'd expected. She cried for him at night, but on the whole . . .

He didn't like to ask her what was going on in that extraordinary mind of hers. He had a suspicion she felt the same as he did: as much relieved as grieved, as much thankful as sorrowing. Some lives are better over. Some lives are too hard. Felix couldn't yet claim that his own life was too hard to be borne, but on the other hand . . .

'Why have we been so unlucky, Mother? Why does all our gold turn to dross?'

'I don't know. Perhaps we found it at the end of the rainbow, dear.' She'd taken off her glasses and was polishing them with the corner of her apron, her pale blue eyes narrowed to slits as she tried to see what she was doing. 'Either that, or we're swimming against the tide. Some people do that, you know, just to be different.' She put her glasses on again and gazed at him in pretended amazement. 'My God, you're a smart-looking chap! Have we met before?'

'Not since the last time you cleaned your specs, Mother. What d'you mean? Swimming against the tide?'

'Well, take me, for example. Good family, plenty of money, friends in high places. I could have married a duke if I'd wanted one. Or a prince. I danced with a prince once, you know. Where was it? Madrid, I think. Or was it Eastbourne? Lord, he was beautiful. I've never seen a man like him, before or since. *Beautiful*. I was a big, strapping gel in those days, but he made me dance like a fairy. My feet scarcely touched the ground.' She sucked in her breath and swallowed something which, judging from the expression on her face, tasted of milk and honey.

'What went wrong?'

'He couldn't speak English.'

Felix blinked. 'Neither could Dad when you met him.'

She smiled. 'Couldn't speak at all. But he understood what *I* was saying, and he wrote wonderful letters.' She rested her cheek in the palm of her hand. 'I fell in love with his letters. He wrote to me every day, you know, even after we were married. They grew shorter, of course. The last one he wrote – I remember every word – said, "Where the deuce have you hidden my best shirt?" The romance goes out of everything, given time.'

'Regrets, Mother?'

'*Regrets?* No. I've never regretted anything *I've* ever done. Never. But I've sometimes regretted things other people have done. For their sakes, mostly. Not everyone is blessed with my turn of mind, you see. Most people see their mistakes as endings, but life's a ball of string, Felix. You're given one end of it on the day you're born, and the other on the day you die. Everything in between is a continuation, part of a process of learning. If you decide you've reached the end before you're dead, you waste an awful lot of string.'

She smiled, gazing around her eternally messy kitchen as if it were heaped with jewels. 'I'm fifty-eight and feel as if I was born last week. I'm certain I've made the best of it, but I've barely scratched the surface. There's always so much more to *learn.*'

'About what?'

'Myself, of course! What else is there?'

Again Felix blinked. He rarely had a serious conversation with his mother without being knocked sideways and this one was proving more 'violent' than most! 'Well,' he said, trying to sound ironic but in fact sounding hurt, 'there's me. Don't I count for anything?'

Penny looked puzzled. 'You, darling?'

'Me! Felix! Your son! Remember?'

'Ohh.' She lifted her chin and murmured, 'Well, you're

really nothing to do with me, are you, darling? Trying to learn about another individual is like trying to read a closed book. If the title and the author's name are familiar you can make a fair *guess* at the contents, but you can't learn the truth of it without turning the pages. We're allowed only one book to read in its entirety, darling. Mine's called, "Penny Clare".'

'Isn't that . . . ? Isn't that . . . ? Isn't that incredibly *selfish*, Mother, or am I missing the point again?'

'You're missing the point. Our understanding of the world – including our relatives – can only be measured against the understanding we have of ourselves. If you don't know what's right for you, you can't know what's right for me. If you don't judge yourself fairly and honestly, you can't hope to judge anyone else.' She cast him a look over the top of her spectacles. 'Miles Huntley, for example. Do you judge him according to the things you know about yourself, or according to the things you can only guess about him?'

Felix reddened and looked away. He drummed his fingers on the table. 'He'll be a millionaire when he's finished selling us out, Mother. What more do I need to know?'

For a moment his mother was silent. Then, 'You can't read his book,' she said softly. 'Read your own.'

'Oh . . . Ooh-oh . . . Oh, my back!' Pressing her hand to the base of her spine, Bel tottered to a chair and gasped, 'Tea!'

She and Muriel had spent all day (between meals) whitewashing the kitchen. They'd also cooked the meals, cleaned the windows, scrubbed the floor, washed out brushes, pails and dust-sheets and were now allowing themselves a half-hour's rest before they began to cook supper.

Bel giggled weakly. 'You look as if you've been out in a snowstorm.'

'So do you,' Muriel complained. 'Reckon you got more on us than you got on the ceiling.'

'Still . . .' Bel looked around the spotless room. 'It's done.

Looks marvellous, doesn't it? God, what a relief!' She giggled again. 'Only twelve more rooms to do, and we'll be straight. Think you can face it?'

Muriel chewed her lip. 'Ah . . . I bin minnin ter mention that, Suntley.'

'Mention what?'

'Well, facin' it, like. An' I can't say I can, Suntley. Not any more. Enough's enough, like. F'you know what I means.'

Bel caught her breath. She could scarcely believe her ears, yet at the same time believed them all too well. Muriel had had enough! She was about to give notice, and who the hell could blame her? Had she been sold into slavery she couldn't have worked harder or complained less! Bel had tried very hard to be appreciative, but Muriel never seemed to like being appreciated and any show of affection or intimacy 'beyond the call of duty' embarrassed her half to death. Yet in spite of all that, Bel loved her. Loved her, trusted her, *needed* her! She couldn't imagine life without Muriel.

She tried to imagine it. It felt like falling into a quicksand, in the middle of a treeless moor, in the dark. Even sending Andrew away hadn't felt as bad, and she still had nightmares about that, about him. He was a treeless moor, too; one she walked and wandered, crying, 'Andrew! Come back! Where in hell's name are you?'

Losing Muriel was worse than that. She couldn't live without Muriel! But she mustn't say so. Not now. She must make it as easy as possible for the poor girl to say . . . To say she was leaving.

'Of course I know what you mean,' she said gently. 'You've been an absolute trooper and we couldn't have managed without you, but I *quite* understand how you feel, Muriel. And whatever you want to do . . .' She took a deep breath and fetched an understanding smile to a face that almost cracked under the strain. 'You must do with our blessing.'

'Eh?' Muriel demanded suspiciously. 'Worra bout Struntley? What'll 'e 'ave say about 'un?'

'He'll say precisely as I've said, Muriel. That you must do . . . Do exactly as you think best.'

Muriel's scowl deepened. 'She'm not thought too highly of, mind. Folk'll talk. But we needs the extra 'elp, an' Ivy needs the wages, so . . .'

As she registered Bel's sudden bewilderment, Muriel's eyes narrowed. 'Yer,' she said. 'What wuz *you* talkin' about?'

Bel smirked. She'd caught the gist at last, and now didn't understand why she hadn't thought of it for herself. *Months* ago! Or at least two days ago, before they'd spring-cleaned the blasted kitchen!

'Ivy Shilling, of course,' she said coolly. 'And you're quite right, Muriel. Enough is enough. It's high time we had a proper staff again.'

Muriel heaved a patient sigh. 'Nah,' she said. 'Them days is gorn, Suntley. Ivy can only come mornin's. But 'er'll do the rough. That's the main thing.'

While they prepared the supper, Bel wondered why on earth *she* hadn't thought of Ivy, and why on earth Muriel had.

'Is Ivy a friend of yours, Muriel?'

'Nah. She ain't nobody's friend. But 'er got friends 'er don't know about. It was that Mrs Tomkins put the notion in my 'ead.'

'*Jean*? But what – ? Now, why on earth should *she* – ?'

'Said she knows what it's like, bein' all alone, like Ivy. Said she knows what it's like . . .' She turned a questioning look in Bel's direction. 'Bein' despised.'

'*Despised*?' Bel felt her face reddening as an inexplicable guilt squeezed her heart. 'Well!' she gasped. '*I've* never despised her, Muriel! I did everything I could for her! As for Miles . . . Well, you know how *very* kind Miles . . . He even spoke for her about the postwoman's job when Fred Holmes was called up.

And look how well *that's* turned out! *Despised?* What on earth can she mean?'

Muriel turned back to the sink. 'I dunno,' she said dully. 'Free wise monkeys, I am. See nuffin', 'ear nuffin', say nuffin'. All I want's a bit of 'elp wiv the rough.'

See nothing, hear nothing . . . Say nothing. But it was amazing how much Muriel could say, and how very articulate she could be, 'between the lines'. For of course she had seen . . . And heard . . . She must know everything that had passed in this house over the years and at least have guessed what lay behind it. The long years of marital strife, Miles sleeping in the dressing room, his treatment of Jinny . . .

As for Bel despising Jean Tomkins . . . It was true. She wasn't sure why it was true, or even if 'despise' was the right word for it. Hatred might be nearer the mark, or perhaps . . . revulsion. Yes, that was the word. It was the same word that best explained Bel's fear of spiders. She knew spiders didn't bite, and that, among the vast number of creepy-crawlies that could invade a woman's home, spiders were virtually the only ones that served a useful purpose. Yet no matter how useful they might be, they were, for Bel, the very symbol of evil. Black, brooding evil, lurking in corners, laying traps for the unwary. It didn't describe Jean Tomkins . . . Yet for some reason, it described her all too well.

Bel avoided telling Miles about Ivy Shilling until they went to bed. He'd become a little 'crusty' since he'd lost his leg. Crusty enough to have driven his mother back to London, where she was now living in 'a modest hotel', and – according to Robin – having a whale of a time. Miles's crustiness extended even so far as to say that Violet had no business having a whale of a time at her time of life: 'Blasted woman! Why does *she* always end up having fun, while the rest of us –'

'Thank God she's not doing it at *our* expense, darling.'

'Yes . . . Well, there is that, I suppose.'

His sense of humour was still functioning. So, to Bel's

delight, was much of the rest of him. After long months of pain and frustration he could now walk very well, even to the extent of being able to climb the stairs, but his patience was limited and Bel had a creeping suspicion he wouldn't like the idea of employing the community's 'fallen woman', not so much because she'd 'fallen' as because . . .

'*What?*' he howled. 'Ivy Shilling? Are you mad? We'll have her damned mother and the kids moving in on us before we know where we are!'

'I knew you'd say that,' Bel murmured.

'Oh, you did? Then why the deuce did you agree to it without consulting me?'

'Because I thought . . .' (Bel sighed and decided that, in the circumstances, a small white lie wouldn't go amiss.) 'Because I *think* Muriel will resign if we don't get some extra help.'

'Resign? Don't be ridiculous!'

'She will. I'm sure she will. She's worked jolly hard, Miles, and she's had enough. "Enough is enough," were her very words. I thought she was going to give notice on the spot, so when she suggested Ivy . . .'

'Enough is enough?' Miles repeated incredulously. 'Nonsense. You're making it up. She can't possibly have said that. It's five syllables!'

He grinned suddenly. 'Oh, all right. I know when I'm beaten. Tell Ivy she can come. And tell her mother I'll set the dogs on her if she comes anywhere near us. The woman's a witch.'

Bel laughed with relief and then, to her utter amazement, burst into tears and cried like a child.

'Bel! What on earth is wrong? Was it something I said?'

'No!' Furious with herself, Bel blew her nose, laughed again. Cried again.

'You're tired.' He slid his arm around her shoulder. 'Coochie-cooch, byesie-byes . . .'

'You used to say that to Jinny,' Bel chuckled tearfully. Remember?'

'*I* remember. I wish Jinny did.'

Over the past few weeks, he and Jinny had been having 'words' about her future. She wanted to be a nurse. Miles wanted to send her to finishing school. It had been curious to see how they argued the point, hard to say who was most scared of whom. They tiptoed towards each other, backed off and tiptoed again. So far, they hadn't progressed much beyond the preliminaries and Bel had begun to fear that the decision, when the time came, would fall to her. In her heart she favoured nursing: a career, an independence, some experience of the 'real' world to support Jinny when reality, as it always did, made itself too evident to be avoided. On the other hand . . .

'Nursing,' Miles mused bitterly. 'It'll be like sending a rabbit into a lion's den. She's not the *type*, Bel. She's . . . Oh, damn. What is she? I'm no nearer to understanding her now than I've ever been. I sometimes wonder . . .'

They'd had this conversation before. Like the subject of Jinny's future, it never made much progress and Bel was tired. Very tired. Miles's voice was just a soft rumble, his words no more urgent than 'Coochie-cooch, byesie-byes'. A cradle song. The world slowly tipped and Bel slid off it, into the misty margins of sleep.

'I sometimes wonder if it's Jack Carter,' Miles murmured.

'What?' Bel was wide awake again.

'Would she be different, would I understand her better if . . . ? Sorry. Raking old ashes. But sometimes I think the bastard's haunting me through her. She was so sweet to me when I first came home. She was so . . . Oh, I don't know. Warm. Funny . . . Like you.' His arm tightened around her shoulders. He ran cool, gentle fingers over her face, tracing her lips.

'Mmm . . .'

'So I know there's someone there, Bel. Inside her, I mean. I know she has thoughts, feelings, ideas. But sometimes she seems . . . Sometimes I think she's living someone else's life, not her own. It's as if she's learned certain phrases, attitudes and mannerisms – ours, I suppose – and is just acting them out, like a part in a play. It isn't really *Jinny.*'

'Were you really Miles when you were fifteen?'

'No, I suppose not. But that's not the point. Not for me.'

'You mean you're still waiting for Jack to emerge?'

'No. No, I mean maybe she *is* Jack. Maybe this is all there is, Bel. Because I've realised . . . *He* didn't really exist, either. He was just acting a part – several parts – and was never his own man. I think that's what I most disliked about him: I could never be certain who he was. With most men, whatever their faults, you can say "his bark's worse than his bite", or "he means well", or "his heart's in the right place". But there was nothing of that with Jack. He was acting all the time. You never knew who the hell he was. And I've never known who Jinny is. Is she the girl I created when I . . . cast her off, or the girl *he* created when he . . . ? You know what I mean.'

Bel knew what he meant. And even though their marriage had survived 'what he meant', the reminder of it was still as painful as it had ever been. Stupidly painful. Childishly painful, for he was no longer accusing her, no longer blaming her, no longer rejecting Jinny. Quite the contrary . . . He'd spent years snarling, 'Keep her away from me!' and now seemed to be crying, 'Bring her closer!'

But it wasn't a thing Bel could do. Jinny was very much her own person: private, secret and remote. On the surface of things she was just an ordinary schoolgirl, complaining about teachers, homework and friends, leaving her room in a mess, always wanting something to eat and then (but not until she'd eaten it) worrying that she might run to fat or break out in pimples. Beyond that, she was a complete mystery. Her favourite answers to personal questions were, 'I don't know', 'Perhaps', and, 'Not necessarily'. That wasn't Jack. It wasn't even Bel, for even at her most evasive Bel always tried to *sound* positive! No. Jinny was her own person, and whoever that person was, she was keeping her under wraps.

'Why should she be either of those, Miles? Are you a perfect replica of your mother or your father? Or even half of each? Say for the sake of argument that your father had all the intelligence and your mother all the courage. Intelligence without courage makes one kind of person; courage without intelligence makes another. But if you inherit both intelligence *and* courage, you're bound to be different from either of them.'

'Mm . . .' Although it was too dark to see him, Bel could feel his head nodding in agreement. 'And when you add my separate experience to the mix . . .'

'You're on your own. Entirely unique. And that's what Jinny is, Miles. Unique. A unique iceberg, at that.'

'Iceberg?'

'Two-thirds under water. She's *young*, Miles. I don't know about you, but I hadn't a clue who I was when I was fifteen. So how can she know? How can *we* know?'

'You're right.' He sighed. 'Thanks, Bel. I love you.'

'Do you?' She smiled in the darkness. 'How much?'

'Ohh, the best part of a Miles. Minus a foot, of course.'

He nuzzled closer. His arm under her neck softened as sleep overcame him. But Bel lay awake for a long time, thinking of Jack.

Twelve years dead, and still he wasn't at rest. Twelve years dead, and he hadn't gone in silence. Jean knew. Jean knew. And that was why Bel hated her. She was like a spider, lurking in corners, spinning webs for the unwary . . .

The sins of the fathers will be visited upon the sons . . .

Like English grammar, the Bible used the masculine form to describe all humanity, but the meaning was clear enough. *The sins of the mothers will be visited upon the daughters unto the third and the fourth generations.*

And oh, it would kill Jinny to learn that she was not Miles's daughter!

'Finishing school,' she decided suddenly. (Send her away. Keep her safe.) 'Finishing school, Miles.'

'Mmm-uhh . . .' He was asleep.

Chapter Twenty-Six

There wasn't a place where one could overlook the Dray Valley and see it entire. Even from the heights of Dundry it looked not so much an area of farmland as a carefully thinned forest, with here and there a glimpse of ripening wheat or a glint of the river.

Yet as the valley's sentence of death by drowning drew ever closer, Felix had an increasing desire to see it all, to fix it in his memory as something complete, not just the sum of its parts. It seemed strange to him that the valley would be revealed only in the moment of destruction. He had an idea that it meant something, that it could teach him something that would be of value for the rest of his life; but he was blowed if he knew what it was. Uncover the mystery and you destroy the life? Yes, perhaps that. Where there's life there's hope, and what is hope if not a question, a mystery, a veil over the future?

Felix's future was still as heavily veiled by mystery as the valley was by trees. He could see glimpses of things as he might wish them to be: another farm with a smaller house, closer to the nearest village than Drayfield was to Bishop Molton. But with farming in such good heart, people weren't moving from the land as they'd done before the war. They were putting down roots, much as Felix had done here, and his chances of finding a tenancy this side of Yorkshire . . .

He'd grown accustomed to the idea of leaving Drayfield, of losing the valley. He'd been saying goodbye to it for more than three years now and, in many ways, would be glad when it was gone, for that would at least mean that he'd *have* to move on. But he didn't want to go. He felt much as he did when he sank in mud to the tops of his gumboots, knowing that even if he pulled himself clear the boots would stay behind.

It was a fine, watery evening in April. They'd had rain and high winds for the past two days, but now the wind had dropped, the sky had cleared and the air was warm and sweet. Penny was in the parlour, stretched out in an armchair with her eyes closed, listening to *The Magic Flute* on the wireless. In a perfect world, Felix would have liked to listen too, but it was not a perfect world. Penny was in silent raptures at the moment, but five minutes ago she'd been leaping about (still with her eyes closed) conducting the dratted thing, and although Felix found this funny, it also scared him a little. If anyone else saw her, she'd get locked up . . .

'I'm going out, Mother.'

Without opening her eyes, she waved.

'Might stop for a drink at the Boy and Badger.'

She waved again.

Felix had no head for alcohol and rarely went into any of the local pubs, but sometimes he was afflicted by the kind of thirst that only a cool glass of cider could relieve. It arose, he was sure, from loneliness. He'd mended his fences with Miles Huntley, but the reservoir still ached between them, no longer a matter of resentment but simply of different interests. Miles didn't need to uproot himself, leave all he loved behind and start again. Felix did, and for the first time since they'd known each other, Miles had no power to help him. He wasn't even Felix's landlord any more. The Waterworks was, at least for another year.

Studiously inspecting his fields as he went along, Felix walked out to Molton Draycott, skirting the boundaries of Joss Radnor's land. The sun was very low now, turning the western sky a pale rose pink. High overhead a wide band of mackerel cloud presaged yet more rain.

He looked down the hill and saw a woman walking towards him wearing a grey costume whose long flared skirt echoed the famous 'New Look' which, last year, had taken the world by storm. Even in the deep gloom of the hedge-bank that shaded her face, he knew she wasn't a local girl. There was an energy to her walk, a grace in the way she moved her hips and set her feet that marked her out as a 'townie'. Someone taking an Easter holiday, perhaps.

Felix hated meeting strangers. His heart began to thump uncomfortably and he found that he was wondering what to say (one had to say *something*), but the agonising choice between, 'Nice now,' and 'Lovely evening,' threatened to tie his tongue in knots before he could say anything at all. She'd think him an idiot. He wished he'd changed his jacket before he'd left home. He wished he'd put on a collar and tie. She'd think him a yokel.

Suddenly, when they were still some distance apart, she stopped walking and turned indecisively into the shadows, prodding the bank with her toe. He still couldn't see her face, but he recognised her now (no one could kick a bank the way Jinny did), yet instead of feeling better, Felix suddenly felt much worse: bad enough, almost, to turn tail and run home again. He hadn't seen her since Christmas and then only very briefly. She'd been away. 'Getting herself polished up,' Penny had said pityingly, 'for the marriage market.'

Perhaps owing to the streaming cold she'd been nursing, she hadn't looked very polished at Christmas. She'd had on two cardigans (both in holes), a wincey blouse with a frayed collar, a pair of her father's socks and Muriel's plaid woolly slippers. 'Polished up', he'd thought then, might have been better phrased, 'polished off'; but she looked very different now . . .

'Hello, Jinny,' he said softly.

'Felix.' He heard her sigh.

'Er . . . Out for a walk?'

'Mmm.' She turned, gave him a bright, impersonal smile and announced firmly, 'Lovely evening.'

She was either sixteen or seventeen. Felix had lost track of the difference between them and had to work it out. He was twenty-three, which meant . . . Seventeen. Oh, what an irony. Just as he was about to move on, the perishing kid grew up . . .

'How's school?'

She sighed again. 'Bloody.'

They drifted closer to each other and Felix saw that she'd been crying. Not very recently, but the signs were there: a fading flush of pink above her cheekbones, a gloss on her eyelids, a shine to her nose. 'How bloody?'

She smiled wanly. 'I *hate* it, Felix. If he makes me go back there for another term . . .'

'Come on. I'll walk back with you.'

'But weren't you – ?'

'No. Just wasting time. I'd much rather walk with you.'

'*Really?*' She laughed and caught his arm just as she'd done when she was little: hugging it against her ribs, like a miser clutching a bag of gold. They marched up the hill, she matching his stride until she was panting for breath. She laughed and let go, taking a few dance-steps to cross the lane. 'Oh, look at the sunset!'

Shyly he watched while she played her shy, girlish games, leaning on a gate to watch the sun go down, pointing out things they'd both seen a million times before. She was extraordinarily beautiful. The polishing process had been remarkably effective considering how 'bloody' it had been so far. Essentially of course she hadn't changed a bit, but her hair was fashionably styled, her jacket a perfect fit (this was probably the first time he'd seen her wearing anything that really fitted!), her nails shaped and buffed to a soft, pearly glow.

Felix, on the other hand, was wearing a white shirt without a collar, a tweed jacket his father had deemed 'done for' ten years ago, a pair of rough, cavalry twill breeches and hobnail boots which had cracked across the toes. Add to that a faint aroma of pig-swill, the light, wafting fragrance of cow manure and a day's growth of beard . . . He hadn't given Penny's 'marriage market' much thought until now, largely because he'd kept telling himself that Jinny would always be 'too young'. But now . . . 'What do you hate about it?' he asked softly.

'What? Oh, *school* . . .' She averted his face. 'Everything. I hate living away from home, I hate Town, I hate men.'

'Men?'

'Yes, men. They're on the curriculum, you know, like French, Art, Cookery and Deportment.'

'No . . .' He frowned.

'Well, no. But we are taken to places where there will be men. Gentlemen, you know, of stainless character – ho-ho – and impeccable pedigree. We're chaperoned to the hilt and forbidden to talk about anything but the balleh, the theatah and other desperately serious topics. I . . . I can't do it. They're all such dolts. They make me giggle. I've never in my life done anything really naughty, Felix, not *deliberately* naughty, but those . . . *men* . . .'

'*What*? What on earth do you mean?'

'They bring out the devil in me. I've become a little devil. And I rather enjoy it, but only because I'm so frantic to get away. It's like digging tunnels to get out of prison camp. Daddy says I'm being ridiculous but I'd rather die than marry a man like that. I don't care how rich he is, or who his father is, or – '

'Jinny?' He caught her elbow and turned her, very gently,

to face him. 'This is me, your old chum Felix, not some dolt you met at the balleh. What the hell are you talking about?'

'You go to a finishing school, Felix, to catch a husband. I didn't realise it at first. I thought it was just . . . Well, I don't know what I thought.' She sighed. 'Actually, I thought they were just trying to get rid of me for a year because I was being difficult.'

'Difficult? *You?*'

'Mmm. I wanted to be a nurse and they wouldn't hear of it. Everyone says they're not snobs, but they are, Felix. They can put it aside when duty calls, with the war and all that, but now they want to get back to normal and do everything as it should be done. Chaps in the Forces or at the bar, gels presented at Court and then married off to the highest bidder. Well, Andrew's thwarted them on the side of the chaps and now, come hell or high water, I'm going to thwart them, too. I will not go back, I will *not* go back!'

She thumped her fist on the top bar of the gate and Felix saw that she was trembling, helplessly raging as he'd seen her do once before, when Miles was ill. 'Come on.' He slipped his arm around her shoulders and quickly let go again, remembering that he still smelled of pig-swill. 'It'll be dark soon. Let's go.'

They walked in silence for more than a mile, separated by the width of the lane and by a growing tension which scared Felix rigid. He had a terrible feeling that this was the last time he'd see her, that she *would* go back to school, *would* knuckle under and do all the things her parents wanted of her. She always had. Her parents were powerful people. Jinny was not.

'Any news of Andrew?'

'Hmm? No. Not news, exactly. Stephen knows where he is, but he's not at liberty to say. Fraternal loyalty, you know. All he's said is that Andrew was chummy with an American chap at prison camp, so we think we're meant to suppose he's gone to America. God, it's a good thing he didn't tell *me* where he was going: they'd have wrung it out of me in no time flat.' She burst into tears. 'I'm so bloody pathetic, Felix! I hate myself so much, it *hurts*!'

'I know the feeling.'

'*Do* you?' She turned to face him, her eyes swimming with a touching combination of tears and hope. 'Honest?'

He grinned. 'Honest.'

'So you can't tell me how to get out of it?'

'Hating yourself?'

'Mmm.' She nodded.

'Well, first, you have to know *why* you hate yourself. You can't solve any problem until you know what causes it.'

'Oh, well, I do know. It's because I'm so feeble! Pathetic, weak, stupid –'

'Why are you feeble? In what way?'

Jinny walked on, her mouth grimly set. After a while she said, 'It's Daddy. If he told me to jump off a cliff, I'd do it. It might take a while, but I'd do it in the end.'

'Why? What can he do to you that would be worse than jumping off a cliff?'

'Hate me,' she whispered.

'Nonsense. He'd hate you if you *did* jump. But even if he loved you for it, what good would it do? You'd be dead. You wouldn't know. And apart from all that, it's a mistake to think that your parents count for anything beyond a certain point in your life. Say you marry one of your dolts – '

'I won't!'

'If you can jump off a cliff, you can marry a dolt.'

'Oh, I know, I know! That's what I'm so scared of!'

'Our parents die, Jinny. Sooner . . . or later. They go away and leave us. If we live our lives only to please them – whether by jumping off cliffs or marrying dolts – what are we left with? The only way you can hope to be happy is to live for yourself. Not selfishly, but . . . Well, if you don't live *for* yourself and stick up for what you think is right, how can you live *with* yourself? What's that thing in the Bible? Something about gaining the world and losing your own soul? It's your own soul that matters, Jinny. Not your father's. His soul is *his* business.'

They paused at Draycott Bridge to look at the moon, bright and full against a clear aquamarine sky. The silver-gilt disc reflected in the river, the river in Jinny's eyes. Felix forgot his rags and his reeks and rested his hand on her shoulder, stroking the nape of her neck with gentle fingers.

She sighed. 'I wish I could be a little girl again.'

'*I* don't.'

'You never were a little girl.' She turned into him and rested her head on his shoulder.

'No, but I deeply resented *your* being one.' His heart was pounding. 'One isn't allowed to kiss little girls. But I did, and I've hated myself for that, you know. I didn't mean to scare you. I just . . . forgot.'

She held her breath. 'Forgot what?'

'That you were too young.'

Her breath escaped in a slow, shuddering sigh. Her fingers strayed softly over his lapel, his neck, his bristly cheek, his mouth.

'I'm not too young now,' she whispered.

Miles paused in the letter he was writing and gazed at his reflection in the uncurtained window. He liked window-reflections of himself. They fuzzed over the more unfortunate details – crow's feet and the like – and told him that he was still a reasonably good-looking man. He'd done well. He'd done very well. Even Nurse Stokes, who kept her compliments in a strong-box under the floorboards, had said he'd amazed her.

He hadn't amazed himself. Except for one or two lapses into hopeless depression, he'd never expected to spend the rest of his life as a cripple. Life was short and life was brutal, but there was no sense at all in making it more brutal than it need be.

'Miles, it's almost dark!'

'Hmm?' He jumped. 'Almost dark? Yes . . . ?'

'Well, where is she? She's been gone almost three hours!'

'Oh . . .' He sighed. He hadn't forgotten Jinny. Just tried to. She'd stormed out of the house in rather a state; in fact in tears, although Miles wasn't absolutely certain what had upset her. She didn't speak the language the way most people did. She disguised it, somehow, disguised her feelings to the very point at which they broke her and then made a sudden exit, leaving everyone asking, 'What the hell's got into *her*?'

Something to do with that wretched school, he supposed. He wished now he'd never dreamed up the idea of sending her there. It was costing an absolute mint and if she thought he'd let her do the Season next year she had another think coming! Thanks mostly to the reservoir, he was better placed financially than he'd been for many years, but he still felt sick when he wrote a cheque for more than twenty pounds and the Season would cost hundreds. No . . . *thousands*. Anyway, Bel wasn't up to it. She'd been very nervy just lately – something to do with her age, apparently – even quite little things could reduce her to tears, or temper, or both. Ask her to arrange a ball for three hundred guests and she'd go off like a ruddy buzz-bomb.

'Well, if you don't care where she's got to, I do! She's only got that little jacket on. She'll be frozen. And what if she's – ?'

'All right, all right.' He hauled himself to his feet. 'Don't panic. I'll go along to the square, see if there's any sign of her. She's probably just called in on Stokesy.'

'She hasn't. I've just rung her.'

Miles sighed and reached for his walking stick. It was far more a moral prop now than a physical one, but he never went far without it. 'Get my raincoat, will you, darling?'

'Ohh . . .' She threw back her head and closed her eyes. 'No. You're tired. *I'll* go.'

'No. Really. I feel like a walk.'

Actually, he didn't. He'd had quite an energetic day, one way and another, and was feeling a little weary, but he didn't quite trust Bel to go and meet Jinny. The sheer relief of finding her safe (as she was sure to be: it wasn't entirely dark, even now) would probably set her 'nerves' off again, and they'd had enough tears for one day. If *he* met Jinny, on the other hand, he could perhaps find a diplomatic way of asking what was wrong and what, if anything, he could do to help.

It was a lovely evening. Full moon. Not really cold at all. Bel's new gardener had ripped out most of the shrubs by the path and planted hundreds of little blue things which gave off a faint, but quite delicious, scent. He really must ask what they were called. He liked flowers; especially the fragrant ones, yet still could scarcely tell an iris from an aspidistra. Roses; he knew roses. Daffodils, tulips, primroses. And lilies and hyacinths for their scent.

He scowled. How could a man get to be sixty without knowing the names of more than a dozen flowers? He was a disgrace to the uniform.

He walked along the street to the corner of Drayfield Lane. No sign of her down there. He walked through the square but by the time he reached Briar Cottage he'd had enough. Hell, it was only nine o'clock and Jinny was seventeen! If she couldn't take care of herself now, she'd *never* learn.

As he walked past the Post Office on the way back, he felt the hairs on the back of his neck creeping erect and looked up to see the net curtain in one of the bedroom windows twitch swiftly back into place. Damn that woman! You couldn't scratch your own nose without Jean Tomkins knowing all about it!

'How's your nose now, Mr Huntley? Stopped itching, has it?'

God only knew what she'd make of his wandering up and down the High Street at dead of night! Think Bel had thrown him out, probably . . .

As he passed the top of Drayfield Lane he glanced down it, saw nothing and walked on. He had to step off the pavement just where the High Street became the Bristol Road and hesitated for a moment, trying to remember which leg should go first. It took him this way when he was tired and aching. Didn't even think about it when he was fresh; but there was a touch of rheumatism in his right knee, and sometimes he didn't know which was worse: the pain in the leg that *was* there, or the pain in the leg that wasn't.

Just as he made his decision he hesitated again, having seen something move in the main gateway to Home Farm. He thought at first it was an owl stooping to an unwary mouse, but as it moved again more slowly, he recognised it as someone's hand. Sweethearts, no doubt, kissing in the shadows of the wall.

He stepped off the pavement, walked on and stopped again. Jinny was seventeen. He'd tended to think this roughly the same as being seven, but taller, and of course it wasn't. Bel had been seventeen when he'd first met her; only eighteen when he'd *married* her, damn it. That could be Jinny, kissing someone . . . Some country lout laying his greasy paws on her . . . The thought infuriated him.

It is hard to tiptoe on an artificial leg. Bearing this in mind, Miles walked a little further towards home then crossed the road and walked back along the grass verge. It suddenly crossed his mind that it probably wasn't Jinny, and that his sudden appearance might scare another couple of lovers out of their wits. Lifting his eyebrows despairingly, Miles coughed a warning.

There was no mistaking Felix Clare for 'some country lout'. Later, when he had time to think it over, Miles wondered why this should be, for there'd been no *distinguishing* Felix from a lout if you judged him only by appearances. But he had something else: some kind of presence which Miles could only suppose amounted to good breeding. His mother was the same. Whatever she had on, whatever she said or did, you could never mistake her for anything less than the lady she was and had always been. It was bred in her bones. It was like an aura she carried with her. And she'd given it to her son, clearly labelled 'gentleman'.

They *had* been kissing. The truth (an agony of embarrassment) was written all over Jinny's face. But Felix was calm. His face, clearly illuminated by the street light on the corner, was quiet, dignified and rather sad. He caught Jinny's hand as she edged away from him and drew her gently back to his side, murmuring, 'Sssh,' as if to a nervous young colt. Then he smiled and nodded, leaving Miles with nothing to do but smile and nod in return, as if this sort of thing happened every night and was nothing at all to remark upon.

'Have I been missing something?' Miles asked cautiously.

'No,' Felix said. 'This is the beginning.'

Tears flooded Miles's eyes. He didn't know why, and even later . . . No, he didn't know why, except perhaps that he'd realised he was losing Jinny again, without . . . Without ever really knowing her. But he couldn't proceed, didn't know where to go after that. He swallowed. He reached out his hand to Jinny. 'Mummy's been worrying about you,' he said softly. 'Time to go home.'

Jinny said nothing as they walked back to Bishop's Court and Miles was content to leave it that way. He was shocked. Confused. The future – as he had seen it before and as it might now turn out to be – flashed before his eyes like loose snapshots falling from an album, making no sense at all.

But as he opened the door to show Jinny inside, she looked at him as she hadn't looked at him for years, with her soul in her eyes, begging him not to hurt her.

He felt sick.

'Don't say anything now,' he whispered. 'Here's Mummy.'

Mummy cross and Mummy anxious; Mummy bursting with whats, whys and wherefores. But Jinny needed time. *Miles* needed time.

Pretending an irritation he didn't feel, Miles took off his raincoat, using it as a guard for Jinny's face while she pulled herself together. 'I don't know what you were fussing about,' he said crossly. 'She's perfectly all right. Felix walked home with her.'

'Oh . . .' Bel stopped in her tracks and grimaced an apology. 'Sorry, darling.'

'I should think so. Sending me off on wild-goose chases at my time of life. You're a disgrace to the – Oh, that reminds me; what are those little blue flowers beside the path?'

When Jinny had scooted upstairs and Bel had gone to make coffee, Miles went back to his desk to stare grimly at the letter he'd been writing earlier. It was an arrangement to view a three-hundred acre dairy farm in South Somerset. A farm for Felix.

Baring his teeth, Miles tore it across and threw it into the heart of the fire.

Chapter Twenty-Seven

Jean was cleaning the front bedroom windows when she saw the new Rector walk by. Probert, his name was: Jonathan Probert. He was married, with two little kiddies, although if you didn't know it you'd *never* guess to look at him. He looked barely a day older than twenty: tall and slender with a shock of corn-gold hair, the exact colour of Bel Huntley's before she'd gone grey around the edges. If it wasn't for his cassock, you'd be more likely to think him a film star than a clergyman, or a young lion, preening himself in the sun.

Jean didn't like him. Every time she saw him she felt like crying, not so much for his own sake as because ... Well, because she'd never quite screwed up the courage to go and see Rector Winterson about her little problem. She'd meant to. And she'd *tried*, really tried! She'd actually arrived on the Rectory doorstep twice, shaking like a leaf, going over it in her mind to make sure she began with the right words. But the first time the dratted man had been out and the second time she'd lost her nerve and asked Mary Winterson if she wanted some cabbage plants Bert had had going spare. After that, she couldn't face it. She'd needed time to screw herself up for it again. Then the Wintersons had moved to Wells and her chance had gone.

Mr Probert was better than Mr Winterson had been in the pulpit. He had a lovely speaking voice: strong and compelling, like the newsreaders on the wireless. You couldn't help listening to him. But talk to him? No! Well, how could a woman of forty-odd confess something like that to a mere *boy*? She couldn't. He'd think she was crazy. He'd think she was on the change!

It didn't matter, of course. It wasn't so much that Jean really *believed* in the curse as that she couldn't . . . She couldn't quite *not* believe in it. She couldn't quite *forget* it. Things kept happening to remind her, to make her wonder. Just last week, for instance, she'd popped down Drayfield Lane to buy a couple of ducks' eggs from Miss Bright and met Penny Clare coming up the other way. She'd looked all right. She'd sounded all right. But when they'd come level with Home Farm on the way back, Penny had said, 'Goodness, are those roses? In April?'

No, they weren't roses. They were splotches of red-lead paint on Home Farm's rainwater tank. If you narrowed your eyes until everything was a blur you could, if you tried, 'see' them as roses; but how blind did you have to be (with your glasses on, too!) to make a mistake like that? Blind as a bat, that's how blind. Jean had watched Penny afterwards: feeling the side of the road with her foot to find the kerbstone, feeling along the grocer's window to find the door. She did it very cleverly. You'd need to have been warned, as Jean had been warned, before you'd even notice.

And bring her ever unto darkness . . .

For what? Oh, dear God, for *what*? For a cold, echoing, spooky old house that Jean had loved just because . . . Well, just because it had seemed to love *her*. It had given her something when all else was taken away: the shine on the windows, the gloss on the stairs . . .

She could clearly remember how she'd felt about being evicted from Drayfield. It hadn't been just a matter of being rendered homeless, of no longer having a roof over the kiddies' heads. It was more as if she was leaving a lover behind, someone who . . . No, not a lover. *A mother*. Someone who comforted you when you cried and healed you when you were wounded. Someone who, with a few stern words, could drag you from the brink of despair and put you on your road again. 'Yes, well, if you're going to kill yourself, Jean, you'd better get that larder scrubbed out first, hadn't you?'

Yet when you came right down to it, she hadn't had a day's happiness in that house. Not only that, but she hadn't even missed it when she'd moved out! Briar Cottage had been better in so many ways (barring the starlings in the roof): warmer, brighter, easier to keep nice, cheaper to run. And smack-bang in the middle of the village, where even her loneliness had been softened by the passing of neighbours' feet. Oh, what a treat that had been, for when she'd heard footsteps at Drayfield they'd nearly always been Jack's, heralding misery. . . . No, she hadn't missed Drayfield a bit. It hadn't even been *worth* cursing!

It would be a good thing when they knocked it down and drowned it! But . . . no, it wouldn't, for she hadn't cursed only the house. She'd cursed the woman who'd moved into it, never guessing how nice she'd be, how little deserving of . . . bereavement, blindness, ruin.

But you had to be sensible. The Clares weren't the only people in the valley to have suffered and Jean hadn't cursed *them*; she hadn't even *looked* at them a bit comical. There was little Johnny Daniels, crippled by polio, young David Bright (one of Miss Bright's many nephews) who'd taken a head wound during the Normandy landings and wasn't at all 'bright' any more. There was poor, poor little Arthur Skinner from Molton Draycott, who'd spent three years in a prison camp in the Far East, starved, tortured and beaten out of all recognition. She hadn't cursed them. They'd just been unlucky. So had the Clares. So had the Huntleys. It wasn't *anything* to do with Jean.

It began to rain. Mr Probert disappeared into the tobacconist's just as Jinny Huntley came running down the road, holding both hands over her head to keep the rain off. She'd been riding, by the look of her, and Jean frowned, wondering how in heaven's name people like the Huntleys always managed to dress so well. You'd think to look at them they'd never heard of clothing coupons! White breeches, polished boots, tweed jacket . . .

Bel had had a jacket like that (it might even be the same one!), a little tweed jacket with a gold brooch . . .

No, she'd been through all that. Forget it. *Forget* it. But Jinny looked so like her mother, it was almost like seeing a ghost of Bel as she'd been in the old days: so tall, neat and slender. And just look at the belly on that girl! Flat as a plank!

Jean laid both hands against her own abdomen and pressed it in for all she was worth. Talk about spare tyres! She was getting fat again. Bert hadn't seemed to notice, but Jean was beginning to have nightmares about it, terrified that he'd start calling her . . . No, he wouldn't. Not Bert. He wasn't the sort. He was never unkind. But, like Jack, he'd married someone an awful lot daintier than he was married to now, and you couldn't blame him if he decided he didn't like it. He had an eye for beautiful things . . .

She'd go on a diet. She'd do all the exercises in Bert's 'Universal Home Doctor' book. Yes, she'd go on a diet and get thin again. *Definite*.

Straight after lunch.

'I want you to be there, Bel, but I'd rather you didn't say anything. At least, not until . . . Not until it looks as if we're *getting* somewhere. You know what she's like. One wrong word – '

Bel felt her face burning, half with temper and half with

shame. No, perhaps only a third of each and a third of nature's own. Since she'd begun having hot flushes it was hard to tell which was which. 'Huh!' she said. 'And you naturally assume that *I'll* be the one to say the wrong word!'

'No . . . But you do seem to have some fixed ideas about – '

'Why shouldn't I have ideas for her? She's my daughter! Aren't I entitled to want the best for her?'

'Yes. Yes, of course. But the best we can give anyone, Bel, is a chance to be happy. We can't give Jinny that chance simply by pushing her along the course we think best, without properly considering the things she wants for herself.'

'She wanted to be a nurse!'

He sighed. 'If she still wants that, she can have it, Bel. She was too young to make that decision a year ago. Now . . .'

'But she doesn't want it! She wants to marry Felix!'

For the second time that morning (and it was still only half-past ten) Bel dissolved into tears. She knew it wasn't sensible. She knew it wasn't wise. She just couldn't *help* it. She could cry for much more trivial things than this. She'd cried yesterday just because the heel had come off one of her gardening shoes.

'We don't *know* if that's what she wants, Bel. We don't even know if Felix wants it. They were necking, darling, not plighting their blasted troth!'

'Necking,' Bel muttered bitterly. 'My daughter, necking in the street, like a – '

'Like a perfectly normal young girl,' Miles sighed. 'Just remember that we were young once, Bel, and *we* didn't do it quite by the book, did we? One lamp-post is much the same as another, whether it's in Bishop Molton or the ruddy Strand.' He shrugged and grinned. 'Well, ours are a bit nearer the ground perhaps, but that's as much as I'll concede. Now, dry your eyes and . . . and smile. Come on. The end of the world is *not* yet nigh.'

With deep reluctance Bel smiled. 'It's all right for you,' she muttered. 'You don't have hot flushes.'

'Oh, I know.' He pulled his face into a parody of deepest sympathy, à la Jean Tomkins at her mawkish worst.

They laughed. Bel threw a cushion at him and found herself blushing again. Blushing all over. It was like being soaked in petrol and set alight.

'She'll be home soon,' Miles said. 'I'll go and tell Ivy to rustle up some coffee. . . .' He stared down at his badly inflamed wife. 'Why don't you go and stand out in the rain, darling? That'll cool you off.'

'Why don't you go and sit in the oven and see how *you* like it?'

It was all such a strain. Merely staying calm enough to put the kettle on, pick daffodils, read a book . . . It was all such a *strain*.

So how the dickens was she to cope with Jinny's latest antics? Felix Clare! Of all the ridiculous, impractical, terrifying . . . For one thing, he was virtually homeless. He might even be penniless for all Miles knew. God, how could she even *think* – ? It was the most stupid, unsuitable, outrageous . . .

She took several deep breaths, fanned her face with the newspaper and by force of will . . . relaxed. Think. Think.

But she'd already thought. She'd lain awake half the night, doing nothing else but think, and she knew what was at the root of it all. She'd known for a long time that Jinny had a soft spot for Felix and, during recent years, she'd known precisely why. It had first struck her on the night – three years ago now – when Felix had caught her on the hop with his offer to help with Home Farm. On the hop? On the loose! Even now the very memory of it could make her stomach lurch with embarrassment.

It had taken her a long while to think it over and be sure, but she was quite sure now. Felix was Miles all over again. It had been that which had driven her crazy that night. One husband lying half dead in that wretched hospital, and another – whole, strong and miraculously rejuvenated – standing within grabbing distance of her arms. Oh, and she'd wanted him, *wanted* him. Mostly for comfort, it was true, but also . . . If he'd touched her, if only with the tip of one of his fingers, she'd have been lost for ever. *God*!

In fact, Felix didn't really *look* like Miles. His eyes were blue and he had a similarly large, ugly nose. He was built along the same lines, too: very large across the shoulders and scraggy at the hips, as if God had run out of human bones at that point and used two lamb chops instead. But Felix was dark where Miles was fair. He had a different face (especially since he'd fallen through that thorn tree), a different smile, a very different mind. Where Miles was emotionally linked with a rhinoceros, 'just charge on regardless', Felix was more like a large, hunting cat: shy, fierce and watchful, with acutely sensitive whiskers.

But essentially they were the same. Gentlemen born, with rods of iron where ordinary men had spines. They were too strong to employ their strength for anything more violent than hard work, too sure of themselves to quarrel (you either did as you were told or went to Halifax) and too . . . too . . . What was the word? Aloof? Remote? Whatever; they lived on a higher plane than the rest of the world and had become very lonely up there. They didn't expect anyone to match them, join them, share with them anything more taxing than afternoon tea. They were on their own.

Even for a woman of ordinary strength, living her life with such a man was a challenge fit to break her. The years had informed Bel that she was a woman of (just marginally) more than ordinary strength, but Jinny wasn't. Jinny was flawed, both by her birth and her upbringing, and whichever one of them counted for most, the result was still the same. She was about as strong as a heap of stewed macaroni, and as easy to push around.

Marry Felix Clare? Over Bel's dead body!

* *

Jinny had barely closed the kitchen door when Miles began to speak to her: his voice quiet and urgent, his smile restrained to a mere, 'This is serious' quirk.

Jinny took just one glance at his face before freezing inside. Outside, she calmly brushed the rain from her shoulders, took off her jacket and poured herself some coffee from the pot on the table. 'Ugh,' she murmured. 'It's Camp. Have we run out of fresh again?'

'Will you answer me, please? And no beating about the bush this time. Mummy's in one of her frets.'

'Sorry. I didn't quite catch the question.'

'Then catch it this time. When Felix said, "This is the beginning," he was making a declaration of his intent. Was he speaking for you?'

'No.' She wandered away to the sink, still clutching her cup, and behind her Miles breathed a sigh which sounded ominously like relief. Her mouth hardening, her eyes directed firmly at the plughole, where lurked a soggy triangle of potato peel, she said quietly, 'I've loved him for as long as I can remember. It isn't the beginning for me.'

'A child's love and a woman's are very different, Jinny. A boy's and a man's even more so. Are you sure you know the difference?'

Jinny didn't believe there was a difference. When she'd been as young as seven or eight Felix's hands on her hair, her shoulders, her arm, had made her soul leap towards him like a bird trying to break from a cage. When she was thirteen it had broken free for a little while before being wounded and caged up again. But last night it had flown away . . .

'Yes,' she said. 'I know.'

He sighed again. 'I want few things,' he said sadly, 'more than I want your happiness, Jinny. If your happiness lies with Felix, I'll do what I can to help you. But your mother's happiness comes first with me – '

'And the boys', of course,' Jinny murmured.

'What?'

Jinny's heart was racing, and, as usual, she was sorry she'd spoken. But Felix had spoken, too, and his words had made sense: If you can't fight for yourself, you can't live with yourself. You can't even live except as a vehicle for other people's ideas and decisions. A puppet . . .

Felix had said he loved her. She wasn't certain she believed him. It was too good to be true, like a dream that, although it seems to last a lifetime, leaves you barely a minute older, exactly as you were before, aching for all the things you couldn't have because you were too damn feeble to grab them, hold them.

She whirled on her heel and faced Miles out, her eyes wide and blazing, her entire body shaking with rage.

'You said Mummy's happiness comes first. And I said, the boys' happiness, too. And Grandma's, and Muriel's, and probably even Ivy's. Everyone's happiness comes before mine. I don't matter! You don't care what happens to me! You never have!'

Miles said nothing. He just pressed his lips together and looked at the floor.

Jinny turned back to the sink, closing her eyes, knowing that unless he threw something at her pretty soon, she'd have nothing to do but cry and run away. And drown herself.

'Well said,' Miles murmured softly at last. 'It isn't true, Jinny, but it was very well said. You so rarely say what you mean. You speak in riddles or not at all. Even in your letters, lovely though they are, you say nothing of importance. A night at the ballet was never so funny as when you wrote about it. Mummy laughed so much she almost fell off her chair. So *we* enjoyed it hugely, but did you? You didn't say.'

Jinny stopped trembling and stared at him in bewilderment. He was right. About that letter, at least. And perhaps one or two others. It was so much easier to be funny than to complain. After all, if they'd gone to the trouble and expense of sending her to the blasted school (not to mention giving her most of their clothing coupons), they weren't likely to be pleased if . . .

His soul is his business.

'I'm afraid of you,' she whispered. 'How can I say what I mean, when I'm . . .'

'You're being very brave now, Jinny, and what has happened? What have I done to you? Have I roared at you, slapped you, done anything to frighten you? Are you really afraid of me? Or of yourself?'

He was speaking very gently, very kindly, but Jinny felt as if he'd knifed her through the heart. Or of yourself? Or of yourself? Or of *yourself*?

She was done for. She couldn't go on with this, and she knew very well how to get out of it. A shrug, a smile, a joke: Well, you have to admit I *am* pretty terrifying, Daddy.

He *could* be diverted. It needn't go on. But how could you crack jokes when your eyes were running with tears? How could you crack jokes when you were dying? He was right! He was right; it was all her fault, not his! He'd never done anything to –

Suddenly an image flashed into her mind, one she'd almost forgotten, yet as clear to her now as it had ever been. Miles in a tweed coat, a grey hat dripping with rain. Miles, his teeth bared with rage, throwing her aside.

'*You threw me against the wall!*' It was a scream, tearing out of her like a train from a tunnel, whistling, roaring, running her down. Then she sobbed. And sobbed. But even while she sobbed, even knowing that Miles would deny it, even knowing that she'd started something she could never stop, she felt at peace with herself for the first time in her life.

Bel arrived, crashing the door back on its hinges to gasp, 'Miles! Jinny! Miles, what on earth's happened? What have you done to her?'

'Umm,' he said. 'Well,' he said. 'Er . . . I – er.'

Jinny felt Bel's arms around her shoulders, felt her hand

pushing under her chin to make room for the motherly handkerchief. 'Here, darling, here. No, don't cry any more. It's all right, Jinny, really. Daddy shouldn't have . . . But don't cry. Please don't cry any more, darling. You'll start *me* off again and then we'll never get anywhere!'

Jinny laughed tearfully. She blew her nose, wiped her eyes, and subjected her hands to a long, trance-like inspection, heaving the occasional sigh until she felt calm again. Bel, having found the coffee pot almost cold, was buzzing around the kitchen, filling the kettle, searching for cups and saucers.

'I've *set* the tray, darling . . .' Miles sounded very distant and dreamy, as if he was talking in his sleep. Jinny glanced at him under her eyelashes. He was sitting at the table with his chin in his hand, gazing at her with as much bewilderment as if she'd painted her face with purple polka-dots. He pointed to his chest and mouthed, 'Me?'

'It was when I was very little,' she said.

'What was?' Bel turned from the stove, her smile a little too bright, her gaze a little too steady to be true.

Jinny ignored her. 'I didn't know what I'd done. I've never known. And I suppose . . . Just because you never did it again – '

'Did what? What's she *talking* about, Miles?'

'I've always supposed I'd done something terrible. You never seemed to like me much afterwards and I . . . I blamed myself, but I didn't know *why*. I didn't know what I'd done. I was only four; five at the very most. So what had I done to make . . . ?'

'Jinny!' Bel's voice was sharp and urgent, which made it seem rather strange when she laughed suddenly, slapped the coffee pot on the table and cried merrily, 'Coffee! Now, come along, cheer up, everyone! I'm afraid it's only Camp, but it's just what we all need at a moment like this! *I* certainly need it, anyway!' She laughed again. 'Heavens, where on earth is Muriel? It's gone eleven! Now, how was your ride, darling?

Did Joker behave himself? Did you get wet on the way home?' She darted a fascinated smile at the window. 'Look at it! Emptying down again, and it's Good Friday tomorrow! Isn't that typical?'

Even taking the state of her nerves into account, this outburst, in Jinny's view, was a bit extreme to say the least. For one thing, Bel didn't know what Jinny was talking about, so why wasn't she asking the usual questions? 'Well, Miles, what had she done? Put the poor girl out of her misery; then perhaps we'll *all* know what's going on!'

That was the typical Bel. Twittering about coffee and Muriel, rain and Good Friday . . . That *wasn't* Bel.

'What are you trying to say, Mummy?' Jinny teased wryly. Her eyes narrowed with sudden suspicion. 'Or was it something *I* said?'

In a moment Bel's complexion turned from its normal hue to the colour of raspberry jam. In another moment she'd buried her face in her hands and was wailing, 'Oh, God, what's happening to me? What are you *doing* to me? What's going *on*? Miles, Miles! For God's sake, *stop* her!'

'Stop me *what*?'

In contrast to his raspberry coloured wife, Miles was as white as the wall. He clambered to his feet, put his arms around Bel's shoulders and murmured, 'Ssh, ssh, it's all right. It's all right . . .' Then, after glaring at Jinny and laying a finger to his lips, he added smoothly, 'Mummy's a little worried about your friendship with Felix, darling. But we'll talk about it later, shall we?' He took a deep breath and blew it out through pursed lips. 'When we're all a little calmer.'

'Felix?'

(Why didn't she believe that? They hadn't even *mentioned* Felix after Bel had joined them!)

'*Later*,' Miles said grimly.

Dismissed, Jinny stood up and departed, but she departed

slowly and very quietly, pulling the door closed behind her. But not quite shutting it. Then she stood. And listened.

Bel was twittering again, but so softly, and with so many tearful hiccups, that Jinny heard only a few words of it: ' – if she ever finds out! That's why I wanted her to – '

'*Hush!*' Miles hissed. 'Hush, Bel,' he added more gently. 'She won't find out. Leave her to me.'

Chapter Twenty-Eight

The truth was that Miles had absolutely no recollection of 'throwing Jinny against the wall'. The lie was that he had no idea why he should have done such a thing and, when he found an opportunity to speak to her in private (Bel was having her hair done), he worked that lie for all it was worth.

'You were four, and I picked you up and – ?'

'No! You pushed me. Like this!' She stood up, laid her right arm across her body and then swept it back, with force, at the approximate height of a child's shoulders. There was a passion in her face which Miles recognised as his own: the passion of pain, rage and bewilderment which came back to him now as if it had only just happened. He couldn't remember the incident Jinny was describing, but he had no doubt at all that it was true and that it had stuck in her mind like a burr from that day to this. He had similar memories of his own childhood. They *did* stick. And hurt like hell.

'I don't doubt you, Jinny, but I doubt the importance you've placed on it. If you were four – '

'I'm not certain how old I was, but I know I was very young. I might have been five, or even six, but – '

'That's not important. Even if you'd been seven or eight, you couldn't have done anything so bad that I would have *punished* you in such a fashion. It was far more likely an accident, darling. You say my hat was dripping with rain. That probably means I was soaked through, and if you'd been running to me, perhaps in your nightgown, I might have pushed you away to keep you from getting wet. It's very easy for a man to mistake his strength in such circumstances. I probably pushed you harder than I intended.'

'No! You were angry!'

'But not necessarily with you. I might have been angry at something that had happened while I was out. I might even have been angry because I was wet through. And then having you come hurling yourself at me . . . But I'm certain, I'm *quite* certain, that whatever it was was *not* your fault.' (And that much, at least, was true.)

She didn't believe him. She didn't say anything, but 'Liar' was written all over her face, with not even a flicker to show that he was beginning to convince her.

'I'm not saying you were perfect,' he smiled. 'You were very naughty at times. If you'd been told not to do something, that was precisely what you did. Teetering at the edge of the pool to watch the fish, climbing in the rafters in the summerhouse. You used to scare the daylights out of me.'

'Scare you? Why?'

'Isn't that obvious? I was afraid you'd hurt yourself. And I didn't know how to deal with you: I'd never had a daughter before. When the boys were naughty, I knew what to do because *I'd* been a boy; I knew how they'd respond to a clip around the ear – or whatever. But girls are more sensitive, more vulnerable. A man has to be very careful with his daughter's feelings.'

Shame griped in his guts and dried out his mouth like vinegar, but he *had* to convince her; not just for her own sake, but for Bel's. He leaned forward suddenly, laying his palms on his knees in an attitude of helpless apology.

'I was careful, Jinny. You were my first daughter, my only daughter, more precious to me than gold.'

Jinny blushed and lowered her eyes. Encouraged, Miles went on softly, 'Before you were born I'd had tremendous money worries. After you were born I was no richer; but I wasn't worried about it any more. It didn't matter because I had *you*. I wouldn't have hurt you for the world, Jinny. I never smacked you when you were naughty. I never shouted at you. I used to hold you between my knees and say, "Now, look here, young lady," and you'd pout and open your eyes very wide and make me feel as guilty as if I'd whacked you over the head with a mallet.'

Jinny smiled. He'd won. Now to press his victory home.

'How do you suppose I feel now,' he demanded gently, 'knowing that after all the care I took I ended up hurting you by *accident*?'

They were sitting in the morning room, in opposite armchairs. Miles had chosen the room. The armchairs were a bonus, revealing Jinny's physical language when she failed to speak. She was very still now. Thinking. Remembering. Putting two and two together. He hoped the answer she arrived at would be five.

'You loved me?' she whispered.

'Isn't that what I've been telling you? Yes, *yes*. I loved you. You were all the world to me.'

'And now I've spoiled it?'

Five!

He laughed. 'No Jinny. When you were small your mother always said you had me jumping through hoops, and I can assure you, with my hand on my heart, that I'm still jumping. I want you to be happy. I can't, however, put your happiness *before* Mummy's. On that, some kind of compromise must be reached. And so we come to Felix. Have you seen him again?'

She shook her head. 'No. He said . . . He said he'd telephone you in a few days. He said he wanted me to think about it. But I don't need to, Daddy! I *know*!'

'Hmm. That's what we all say when it's all in the future, Jinny. I don't doubt that you love him, but there's more to life than love. There are also errors and . . . accidents, things we *can't* know or even guess at, which change the whole course of our lives. Practicalities matter too, very much, and on the practical side Felix is not the most eligible bachelor you could have chosen. He has very little to offer at the moment. No home. No living. No plans. This is partly what's upsetting your mother, of course. I keep telling her . . . But it's no use, just now. All I can say is that until we know what Felix is going to do with his life, we will *not* give him our blessing.'

'Daddy, he hasn't *asked* me to marry him! He's only – '

'Jinny, if you love him as you say you do, he has the power to break your heart. We don't want that to happen. We'll do everything we can to prevent it.' He smiled and tapped the side of his nose with his finger. 'We will proceed with *caution*, Jinny.'

'And when he phones? What . . . will you say?'

'I don't know. Much depends on what *he* says. If he's thinking of making an elopement of it, I'll lock you up in the cellar and throw away the key. If he merely wants to take you dancing – ' He shrugged and raised a considering eyebrow. 'I might be open to persuasion.'

It was worth all the lies to see her face then. She looked as she'd looked when she was tiny and he was threatening to tickle her: half fear, half delight, half tears, half laughter.

'Ohh, *thank* you!'

(The tears won, damn it.)

With only six months to go before his departure from Drayfield, Felix found a farm within a half-hour's drive of Bishop Molton. It wasn't, in practical terms, an especially good farm. The land was well enough, but laid out piecemeal all over the village: fifty acres here, sixty acres there, with an L-shaped ninety acres surrounding the house and buildings. Until the early years of the century the village had been a coal-mining community and there were three large, cone-shaped slag heaps and a ramshackle collection of ruined mine buildings to mar the landscape. But it was a farm. A living. It had a decent house with well-kept gardens. And it *was* within a half-hour's drive of Jinny.

Their 'romance' so far had not gone as smoothly as Felix could have hoped. Bel seemed to be resisting it for all she was worth, and Miles . . . Felix couldn't be sure about Miles. He'd been very kind, but also evasive in a way that Felix could only describe as 'peculiar', as if he had something up his sleeve, some secret plan. Felix found this rather frightening. He'd never forgotten Jinny's telling him that her parents were snobs, wanting more than anything else to do things according to their status. And Felix didn't fit those requirements. He wasn't 'right'. He had a nasty feeling that Miles would think him even less right when he saw his little farm among the slag heaps, and wished with all his heart that he had not promised to consult him before making a final decision.

He consulted. He drew plans, reported on the state of the house and buildings, power and water supplies, labour (four men and a boy) and the condition of the stock, grass and grain. Miles didn't say very much. He nodded a good deal, thought a good deal, remarked that Felix would have to drive three miles a day just to inspect everything and perhaps five times that when he was muck-spreading and harvesting. He also said, even less cheerfully, that the place was only two-thirds the size of Drayfield.

'Still, if you're sure it's what you want, Felix . . . How about taking me over there before you decide? Would tomorrow night suit you?'

It was the last thing Felix wanted, but since he could scarcely refuse . . .

'Can Jinny come too?'

'Jinny's staying in Bristol, I believe. Is Jinny staying in Bristol tomorrow, Bel?'

'Mmm. Going to the theatre, darling.'

'Well, that's all to the good,' Miles said. 'We can stop for a drink on the way home, perhaps. Talk things over.'

It was settled. But as Felix drove home to Drayfield, 'settled' was the very last thing he felt. He was certain Miles wouldn't approve of the farm, but at the same time he was just as certain that he wouldn't say so. He was a powerful man. The kind who didn't so much fight his enemy as give him enough rope to hang himself.

Enemy? Did Miles see Felix as his enemy? It was beginning to look that way. And all because of Jinny . . .

She *had* completed her year at finishing school. Now she was taking a secretarial course in Bristol, often staying with friends of her parents when 'social engagements' required. But Jinny's social engagements, like everything else, were mostly of her parents' making. They wanted her to 'have fun', as if spending an evening in *his* company was too dreary for words!

He *had* become rather too serious, he supposed. And he couldn't have done the jitterbug had his life depended on it. But that wasn't really the point. Without saying a word against him, he was almost certain the Huntleys were hoping (perhaps even praying) that Jinny would meet someone else.

Depressed beyond bearing, he told Penny about the farm, deliberately emphasising all its worst points, almost as if he hoped *she* would give it the kiss of death before Miles could. But Penny just said, 'Oh, slag heaps! Splendid. So dramatic aren't they? Like little volcanoes. I adore volcanoes.'

'The house is quite small, Mother.'

'Good. Easier to manage.'

'There probably won't be room for your piano.'

'I'll get an upright.'

'I don't think Miles will like it, Mother.'

'Nonsense. He's a farmer. If the land is good, he won't care about anything else.'

Penny was now so nearly blind she couldn't recognise him even with her glasses on, but it seemed to have made very little difference to her state of mind. She could still play her music, still see bright colours. She could also, as she was fond of saying, see roses where other people saw only splotches of red paint. Typical of her. Felix wished he could be more like her in that respect. He'd thought he was. Now he was beginning to feel more like Leonard, seeing the black side of every damn thing.

'Mother? Do you suppose . . . ?'

'What?'

'Do you suppose Miles thinks I'm not good enough for Jinny?'

'Not good enough? Well, he might, I suppose, but he'd be daft if he did, and Miles Huntley *isn't* daft, darling. Bel might be. But that's just her age. She'll grow out of it. Even *I* was a bit cuckoo when I was fifty.'

Felix bit his lip on a grin. 'Oh,' he murmured. 'I didn't notice.'

'Cheeky brat. I was cuckoo when I was fifty. Now I'm just barmy. There's a subtle difference, I'll have you know.'

'Yes, Mother.' He thought about it. 'What were you when you were forty?'

'Mildly eccentric, dear. And, before you ask, at twenty I was as cracked as I am now, but since it's frightfully jolly to be cracked when you're young, nobody noticed. Jinny's very young, you know. Look at it from Bel's point of view, darling, and keep *me* in your mind's eye. I'm blind, I'm batty, I spill my food. Before very much longer, I'll probably be wetting my drawers, too. Would you wish *me* on your only daughter? Or are you planning to send me to the Workhouse before you get married?'

'Jinny adores you,' Felix said softly. 'You know that.'

'Yes, I do. And the feeling's mutual. But that's not the point, Felix. I'm not likely to improve with age, and the Huntleys are well aware of the fact. They have to think of *Jinny's* best interests, not yours and mine.'

'It's not snobbery, then?'

'Puh! No. When it comes to the revolution, Felix, you'll go off in the tumbrils before they do. Your blood's bluer than theirs by *several* shades of purple.'

'Yes, and my bank balance is redder than theirs by several shades of pink, Mother. Do you suppose that's why they've sent Jinny on this dreary secretarial course? So that she can support herself if I go broke?'

'Does Jinny think it dreary?'

'No,' Felix sighed. 'She seems to be enjoying it.'

'But you're scared she'll meet someone else?'

'I think that's what her parents are hoping will happen.'

Penny was silent for a long time. Then, 'Read your own book,' she said at last. 'Do what's best for you, Felix. Love's wonderful, of course, but self-respect lasts longer.'

They sat in the tiny, smoke-blackened snug bar of a pub called The Jolly Farmer, an irony to beat all since they were its only patrons and had said nothing more jolly than, 'Cheers,' and, 'Good health,' since they'd first crossed its threshold. Felix was trying to look relaxed and unconcerned, trying not to look at Miles who was staring, as if in a trance, at a knot in the floorboards. Their tour of Felix's 'rolling acres' had tired him. He hadn't seemed too critical at the time, but now . . .

'I take it you weren't impressed,' Felix said quietly at last.

'Hmm?' Miles widened his eyes. 'Oh . . . Oh, yes, Felix, it's a good farm. You could go a lot further and do very much worse.'

He scratched his eyebrow, sipped at his cider, rubbed his leg. 'The retiring chap – Ransome, was it? Good man. Charming man. Very prosperous, too. That's the bench mark, Felix.

He's done well out of it, which means . . .' He frowned. He rubbed his leg again. 'I can't advise you against it,' he said.

'But – ?'

Miles smiled and shrugged. 'No buts. It's a good farm. Smaller than Drayfield, but that doesn't matter. Ransome's bought up odd pieces over the years, and there'll probably be opportunities for you to do the same. It's just . . .' He turned away, sucking his teeth.

'Just – ' Felix prompted nervously, ' – Jinny?'

'What? Oh! No . . . No. It's just that I've had some news since I saw you yesterday and I'm not sure what to do about it.' He bit his thumb. He nodded. 'It's a good farm. Good house and buildings. Well equipped, well maintained.'

He attacked his cider again, this time half draining the glass. 'Mm,' he said, and nodded. 'Very good man. I had a spot of difficulty sympathising with him about his sons, though.'

'Sons? I thought he didn't have – '

'He hasn't. That's what I mean. He's giving up his farm because he had three daughters, and here's me . . .' He sighed and directed a despairing scowl at the ceiling, from which was suspended a roll of yellow fly-paper, stuck all over with horrid little black corpses. 'I had four sons. One dead, one AWOL and the other two as fond of farming as I am of the bloody jitterbug.'

Felix choked back a laugh. Even with the full complement of working limbs, Miles had *never* been the jitterbugging type.

'And now Jim Brooks has decided to leave me,' Miles went on drearily. 'Just as I'd got him where I wanted him.'

'Jim? Leaving?' Felix was astounded. 'Why? Where's he going?'

'Down south somewhere. Found himself a dairy farm. Three hundred acres. A bit run-down from what I can make out, but he'll soon put that to rights. I don't blame him. But it leaves me up a gum tree, Felix. *I* can't work the place any more and none of the other men is up to managing it.'

Felix's heart clenched with dismay. If this was a subtle way of asking him to manage Home Farm, Miles had another think coming! Felix could no more work for another man now than he could fly. He had his own ideas, and they weren't (as Miles's occasionally were) rooted in the feudal system! Still, if Miles could be subtle, so could Felix, and the most subtle thing to do in a situation like this was to keep his mouth shut. *Tight*.

Miles slanted him a tired smile. 'You think I did all right out of the reservoir, don't you, Felix? But I'd have given my teeth – and that's saying a lot – to have had Home Farm taken off my shoulders. I'm . . . no longer young. And I'm by no means able-bodied. If they'd bought me out I could have put my feet up, bought in a few cases of decent port, taken Bel – ' He grinned suddenly. 'To Butlins, and had a whale of a time.'

'Jitterbugging,' Felix volunteered dryly.

'Mm. Oh . . . *Ugh*! Still, it takes all sorts, I suppose. Another drink?'

He wouldn't let Felix fetch them, which was just as well because Felix needed time to think. Miles . . . In many ways he'd been like a father to Felix and if things worked out he might eventually be his father-in-law. But this was asking too much!

He turned cold suddenly, realising how very, *very* subtle Miles was being. For if he had doubts about Jinny marrying a poor tenant farmer, how much more doubtful would he be (not to mention Bel!) about letting her marry an even poorer manager? No, no. Never!

Read your own book, Felix. Hmm, that was all very well, but if you didn't take an occasional glance at the other man's book, he'd take you for a sucker before you could blink!

Love's wonderful, but self-respect lasts longer.

Felix felt that he would love Jinny for ever, but what did it matter? If he took Slag-Heap Farm, he might very well lose her; and he had no other choices. Time was running out. If he didn't decide now he and his mother would be homeless.

He was wondering how the devil Jim Brooks had found a farm when there were so few up for let. Felix had been scouring the relevant papers, journals and land agents for the best part of a year without finding even a 'run-down' dairy farm worth considering.

'Where's this place Jim's going?' he asked casually as Miles crept across the floor with their drinks.

'Hmm? Oh . . . south, somewhere. Somerton way, I think, though he's being rather close about it. Didn't even tell his wife until the last minute and she's not entirely pleased. Women hate being uprooted, don't they?'

'Oh.' Felix was turning cold again. He *had* seen a dairy farm going down that way. The farmer had died very suddenly as he recalled. Something like that. But the farm had been for *sale*, not to let, and Jim Brooks didn't have that kind of money. He'd thought he was rich when he'd taken the manager's job and his wages went up by ten bob a week! Had *Miles* bought it? And if he had, *why* had he?

While Felix was still running all this through his mind, Miles jumped: so suddenly and so swiftly that Felix almost panicked. 'Well, Felix? How about it? Good as Ransome's place is, Home Farm is better, bigger. Good house, too.' He smiled. 'Plenty of room for the piano.'

Felix felt sick. He couldn't say no! Not just 'No', as if Miles meant nothing to him! And even if the bloody man was robbing him blind, he'd never cheated in the past. He'd been . . . He still was the finest man Felix had ever known. And what was he doing, after all? Looking after Jinny. You couldn't blame him for that!

Self-respect, his mother whispered, about six miles west of his left ear. And Felix sighed, smiled and was calm again. Lead into it gently. Make out he'd misunderstood, that he thought Miles was offering him a tenancy, not a measly *job*.

'I couldn't afford the rent on eight hundred acres.'

'No, not at first, but I've thought of that.'

You can manage the place.

'If you take on the tenancy you'll be getting me out of a deep hole, Felix, and I'd be less than appreciative not to give you the first two years at the rent you'd be paying for Ransome's place. Oh, and if you're afraid I'll interfere, I can reassure you on that point, too. I've had enough, Felix. I want to retire.'

His head spinning with shock, his ears ringing with his mother's, 'Read your *own* book, *fool*', Felix stared, open-mouthed, into his glass of cider and murmured dizzily, 'Good stuff, this. Are you sure you want me to drive you home?'

'Answer me, damn you.' Miles was grinning.

But Felix couldn't speak. He just nodded. And nodded.

He nodded again.

Miles laughed. 'Could you put that in writing? I didn't quite catch it.'

'And . . . Jinny?' Felix whispered.

For a moment Miles was silent. 'I can't give you Jinny,' he said, softly at last. 'Jinny's her own person; not mine to give. All I can give is my blessing, and you have that, Felix, with all my heart.'

Felix sighed. Felix smiled. 'Could you put that in writing?' he said.

You could miss your own funeral in a house that faced backwards. And Bert wouldn't tell you anything. He must have heard that Jim Brooks was going from Home Farm, but the first Jean knew of it was when she saw Oslook's furniture van backed up into the yard. This was remarkable enough (no one seemed to know where he was going) but when she asked the other onlookers who was taking *Jim's* job . . .

'No,' Jean said firmly. 'No, you're wrong there. He wouldn't, you see, and if you'd ever been a farmer's wife, you'd *know* he wouldn't.

Once a man's worked for himself, he'd have to be desperate to work for – '

'Well, p'raps he *is* desperate, Mrs Tomkins! I know I would be, with no home to go to and a blind mother to – '

'She's not blind!' Jean snapped. 'She can see colours, she can walk up here on her own! If she was blind – '

'Huh. There's none so blind as them that won't see, Mrs Tomkins, and if you'm sin her walking up here this past year, it's more than any of the rest of us has done! Last April you keep saying t'was, but t'wasn't. T'were April last *year*: these sempteen months gone! Still, bless her, she can still play her pianner. That's the main thing, when all's said and done.'

'What a tragedy, though . . .' Miss Bright shook her head. 'Remember when they first came here? Such a lovely family. *Quality.* You could see it, couldn't you? Even in the boys.' She chuckled sadly. 'Young devils. But there was never any bad in 'em. They never deserved all that came – '

Jean hurried away without hearing the rest. Oh, poor Felix! Five quid a week and the house thrown in. *Managing* for Miles Huntley!

But it was none of her business. You couldn't spend your life worrying about other people, not when you had any *sense*, you couldn't. And Jean had plenty of sense. Sense enough to count her own blessings, even if she couldn't count anyone else's. Her girls were all respectably settled; she had a lovely home, a decent husband, a secure future. And Bert – bless him – had actually bought a car! It was only an old one and it had at least one puncture every time they went out in it, but oh, it was fun! They'd run down to Weston in it last Sunday, and they'd motored over to Filton twice already to see Geoff and the kiddies. Bert was a lovely grandad. He'd been a lovely step-father, too. He was a lovely *man*. He'd be retiring the year after next, and was planning all sorts of things for them to do: holidays by the seaside, hikes in the mountains . . .

Just as this rather daunting thought crossed her mind, Jean caught sight of her own reflection in the draper's shop window. The glass wasn't quite flat. It didn't reflect quite true. But there was no arguing with the evidence it presented. She looked like a short stack of tractor tyres: wide, squat and lumpy, with a shocked little face sticking out of the hole in the top. She must go on a diet. She must, she must! Try walking up a mountain in this state and she'd fall flat on her face and roll all the way down again!

She'd start today. She wouldn't eat a thing! But she'd been saying that for years and had almost always lost her willpower around about teatime. Six weeks was as long as she'd lasted, and that was only in desperation to look nice at Shirley's wedding. Then she'd made a pig of herself on wedding cake and trifle and three weeks later been just as fat as before! What was the matter with her? The one thing that was really, truly wrong with her was something she might *do* something about if she really put her mind to it. So why didn't she? Why *couldn't* she?

As she walked into her bright, immaculate kitchen, she was overwhelmed by the steamy aroma of the steak and kidney pudding she'd left simmering on the hob. Her mouth watered. Her stomach griped with pangs of hunger so painful it was as though she hadn't eaten for a week. Yet she'd had an enormous breakfast: porridge (with treacle), sausage (with fried bread), three slices of toast (with marmalade) and two cups of tea.

She sat at the table and burst into tears. She couldn't do it! She couldn't do it! She was *starving*!

She was still sitting there ten minutes later when Bert came in for his dinner. 'Hey, hey, hey! What's all this? What's happened? What's wrong?'

'Oh, nothing.' Jean laughed and pulled herself together. 'Just me being soppy again. Felix Clare's taking the manager's job at Home Farm and I feel sorry for him, Bert, that's all.'

'Manager's job? He's not, then! He's taking the place on.

Tenant, not manager! He's going *up* in the world, not *down*, love!'

Jean closed her eyes and breathed a huge sigh of relief. 'Ohh,' she whispered. 'Oh, thank God.'

'Dinner nearly ready?'

'Mmm,' Jean smirked, realising with astonishment that she wasn't hungry any more. 'But *I'm* not having any,' she announced proudly. '*I'm* going on a diet.'

Chapter Twenty-Nine

The valley was empty. Even in the radiant light of a fresh October morning, Jinny felt as if she walked through a dream, seeing ghosts. Solomon and Mrs Hicks had moved to a bungalow on the Bristol Road and their cosy old farmhouse looked lonely without them, its boarded-up windows sill-high in weeds. No horses in the paddock, no cows in the byre, no murmuring hens scratching up titbits from the yard. No dogs . . .

Jinny had begun her valedictory walk through the valley more in the spirit of duty than of pleasure; but, like most duties, it gave satisfaction as well as pain. Was satisfaction the word? Probably not, but she couldn't think of another that would do. It was like reaching the end of a difficult school essay, knowing you'd get only five out of ten for your efforts, but knowing also that it was the best you could do. That you'd tried . . . Oh, and *tried*! And still ended up only halfway there.

The death of the valley marked the end of Jinny's childhood as no counting of years could ever do. Nineteen or thirty, while the valley lived she'd still have been a child, finding solace for her hurts in the lanes and the trees, seeking comfort in Prissie's parlour, Penny's kitchen, or in the weight of Felix's arm around her shoulders.

'Who's my special girl?'

'Me,' Jinny murmured wistfully.

But she hadn't believed it then. She didn't believe it now. She'd tried. Oh, she'd *tried*! And still ended up only halfway there.

It was like a story you read on a cold winter evening, living every word, believing every line, turning pages with frantic, snatching fingers to see what happened next. It was another world, another life. You ceased to be yourself and became a princess or a pirate or King Arthur as a boy. Then, just a few pages before the end, your father said, 'Jinny, it's time you were in bed. Leave your book behind.'

So you didn't know how it turned out. You never really knew, because although you could read the last few pages the next day, it wasn't quite the same. Last night you'd been a princess, a pirate, or King Arthur as a boy. Today you were just Jinny, reading the end of a book and not really believing it any more. 'And they all lived happily ever after.'

Loving Felix had been like reading the story at night: a world apart, an escape from herself. She still loved him with all her heart, but now it was morning. She wasn't a fantasy child any more; she was Jinny: the real thing, a creature who ate Force Flakes for breakfast and knew ... And knew that there was more to love than 'happy ever after'. She was afraid she wouldn't be equal to it. She was afraid she would never be equal to Felix. She was afraid ... of *him*.

Or of yourself? A knife-thrust, an answer, a truth. But not the whole truth. She was certain Miles hadn't told her the whole truth, perhaps because she hadn't dared to ask him the whole question. 'You threw me against the wall,' was only a part of it; the least part, because of course she couldn't have done anything very bad when she was four. It couldn't have been as important as it had seemed. It *could* have been an accident. No, the whole question was about what happened *after* that. He hadn't loved her.

He loved her now. He loved her softly, intently, watching her every move, listening to her every word, sometimes hearing even the words she couldn't say: *I don't believe it! It's too good to be true!* But there were other words unsaid which he didn't hear, couldn't hear. 'Quick, send me to bed! I don't want to read the last page!'

She won't find out.

She didn't want to. She didn't want to know.

Yet how could she marry Felix *without* knowing?

She walked along the river bank for a while, acutely aware of her appearance: the young lady of the manor out for a country stroll. Sturdy brown brogues polished to a conker-like glow; thick stockings, tweed skirt, matching twin-set and a single row of pearls. For a properly 'finished' girl there were rules for everything: even for walking in the country, and Jinny had always obeyed the rules when she could, always tried to be good, always been . . .

'Bloody stupid!' she hissed suddenly. 'That's what you've always been, Jinny Huntley!' and she plonked herself down on the muddy river bank, tore off her shoes (Rules for disrobing: never remove your shoes without properly unfastening them), unclipped her suspenders, dragged off her stockings and plunged her feet in the river. The cold water made her gasp. The red, silty mud oozed up between her toes and floated away on the current. She grinned. She stood up and, hitching her skirt to her thighs, paddled into midstream, searching for pretty pebbles, looking for minnows. Green waterweed caught at her ankles with a caress like feathers. Oh, this was more like it! This was fun! And what was wrong in finding pleasure in something so simple? Nothing at all. What was seriously wrong with any of the things she did, or the things she thought, or the things she wanted? Nothing, or at worst very little. She'd never, to her knowledge, done anything very bad. Most of her failings (and it was true she had plenty of them) were things that happened in spite of her efforts to control them, not because she didn't care, didn't try; and who was without such failings? Who was perfect? Even Penny Clare wasn't perfect!

No. When you came down to it, you were what you were: good, bad, and indifferent, like everyone else. Just being yourself was the important thing and as long as that didn't include theft, murder and 'malice-aforethought' it wouldn't hurt anyone to accept you, *exactly* as you were. Whatever you were.

She returned to the bank, dried her feet on her hanky, and put on her stockings and shoes. The sun was warm on her face, the breeze cool on her neck. She hugged her knees and stared smiling into the water, and suddenly there was a flash of blue as the kingfisher dived into the stream, rocketed out again and sat on a willow branch, barely twelve feet away. He shook himself – an explosion of iridescent blue, rust red and bright river water – and then darted away downstream and was gone. The whole thing had taken barely five seconds, but Jinny had never seen anything like it before. When she'd seen the kingfisher before it was like seeing a shooting star: a flash across the sky, beyond one's grasp or understanding. It was as if he'd been saying goodbye.

She wandered towards Drayfield, past the bridge where Felix had . . . Where Jinny had kissed him. 'I'm not too young now.'

No, she was not too young now. She wanted him. She wanted him. And there was no sense in waiting any longer. He loved her, whoever she was, and if 'whoever she was' was good enough for him, he might as well marry her (whoever she was) and put them both out of their misery!

Felix had moved out of Drayfield within days of his deadline and, perhaps because of that, no one had bothered to board up the windows. The house looked as beautiful as it had ever done, seeming to emanate waves of serenity as tangible as Penny's music had been as it tiptoed softly from the open windows. The windows were closed now, but glittering brightly as if (by a miracle) Penny had thought to have them cleaned before she'd moved out. Even the window over the front door, with its tiny leaded panes . . .

Jinny jumped, blinked and, with pounding heart, looked again. Tiny leaded *panes*? But it was bricked up! It was *still* bricked up, so how could she have seen . . . ?

She shrugged and turned away. Trick of the light. And on a morning like this, with the air as clear as crystal, the light did play tricks, filtering down through the rusty leaves of the elm, oak and sycamore trees which hemmed in the yard on every side.

On Monday the foresters would move in, the valley would be closed to everyone who loved it, and within a month or two not a tree would be left standing: trees that had stood for hundreds of years . . . Gone to make tables, rafters and doors. Gone for ever.

There was nothing wrong with tables, rafters and doors. In their way they too were alive, or at least life-giving. Trees, just like these, had made the rafters and doors of Drayfield and Bishop's Court, and had given shelter to men and women for at least as long as, in their previous life, they'd given shelter to squirrels and birds.

The end, then, wasn't the end. The end was just the beginning.

'Goodbye, Drayfield,' she said aloud. 'Goodbye, Dray. Goodbye, Jinny Huntley.' She smiled and waved, yet even smiling was blinded by tears. 'Hello, Virginia Clare,' she whispered.

But she ran home just as she'd run as a child, snatching blackberries from the hedges, zig-zagging back and forth, flapping her arms like a butterfly until she rounded the last bend and came in sight of the village.

Then she grew up.

Joss Radnor had moved to a farm on the Somerset Levels, leaving his housekeeper behind. Mrs Cooper had four sons and a daughter sprinkled around the locality and she wouldn't move more than a sixpenny bus-ride away from any of them. Felix had engaged her, 'just for a month or two' to help him move out of Drayfield, and although Mrs Cooper had been quite old enough to retire, she'd decided she liked Penny too much to want to leave her. They were much of an age, and although they came from vastly different backgrounds, they hit it off like nobody's business, chatting nineteen-to-the-dozen from morning to night. Mrs Cooper was musical. She played the organ for the Methodists and could sing like an angel: hymns, anthems, old love songs. Penny was too fond of Mozart to abandon him entirely, but now she and Mrs Cooper (and sometimes Felix and Jinny) had an old-fashioned sing-song around the piano, in a house that smelled of lavender and beeswax and clean white linen still hot from the iron.

Penny was happy. Felix was almost happy. The only remaining fly in the ointment was Bel, who seemed to think letting her daughter get married was roughly the equivalent of selling her into slavery. She had all manner of unpleasant things planned for Felix to do: go bankrupt, run away with a barmaid, drop dead just as their fifth child was born.

Felix could see her point: there was no knowing what might happen in a world that contained both Joe Stalin *and* the Atom Bomb; but Bel was taking it to extremes. First Jinny had had to train as a secretary, 'You have to know how to take care of yourself if the worst happens', and then she had to get a job, 'So you know what it's like to work for your living'. Next thing you knew she'd be making Jinny join the Civil Defence Corps, 'so you'll know what to do if the Bomb drops', and learning do-it-yourself midwifery, 'in case the car breaks down and you can't get to hospital in time'. Then, when she knew how to shoot rabbits with a bow and arrow and cure their skins to make clothes for the babies, *then* (if they weren't too old by then to care) Bel just *might* let them announce their engagement.

Where Miles stood in all this, Felix still wasn't sure. He'd given them his blessing; but on the other hand, he never spoke up in their favour. 'Weddings are women's work,' he'd said benignly. 'Let them get on with it, Felix.'

Huh! For how long? Felix was going out of his mind with frustration. He wouldn't touch Jinny until she was his for the taking (if anything went wrong, Bel would be making clothes for the baby out of *his* skin!) but sometimes... And Jinny didn't help. Every time he kissed her she went all to pieces, melting in his arms like butter on a hot plate, so that sometimes he felt he'd die with the effort of pushing her away. 'Jinny! Hey, Jinny, Jinny, Jinny, for God's sake, *behave* yourself!'

He was turning into a wild man. If they kept him waiting much longer, he'd just drag her off by the hair and... But that way lay madness. Better to keep his teeth gritted and think of England.

But England, for Felix, was the valley, which was being raped and battered beyond all recognition. He hadn't minded too much when the largest trees had been felled and carried out by the lorry-load, like bundles of enormous matchsticks. There was use in good timber, especially now, with the government putting its vast post-war rebuilding scheme into action. But when the big trees had gone, there were still thousands upon thousands of smaller ones; and they drove through those with their bulldozers, snapping them off so that the remains stood like broken teeth in a vast mouth full of blood-coloured mud. The hedgerows went the same way. The banks of the river were flattened and torn. It looked like a battlefield where millions had died. Felix could scarcely bear to look at it.

They'd demolished Solomon's farm and Joss Radnor's (but not yet, for some reason, Drayfield), and done it as carelessly as they'd knocked down the trees: leaving odd corners of buildings standing, as if cruelly to remind people of things as they'd once been.

* *

Even in a house that faced backwards, you saw things, heard things. At first Jean had told herself that her eyes and her ears were deceiving her; that Felix and Jinny couldn't be courting; that it was all a mistake, or at worst a flash in the pan which would soon fade away. They weren't suitable for each other! Felix, for all his brains and his good looks, was just an ordinary farmer, while Jinny was . . . Well, she'd been to finishing school, hadn't she? She was the squire's only daughter. She had a polish and a glamour that should have been bestowed on a man of wealth and breeding, someone who'd take her round the world in his yacht and cover her with mink and diamonds, not flour and home-made jam!

'P'raps that's what she wants,' Bert said reasonably. 'She've seen a bit, love. Been to London, met all the nobs. Maybe she likes home best. Anyway, if it's breeding you're on about, wasn't Mrs Clare's dad some kind of lord? Viscount, wasn't it? Something of that sort?'

'No! He was something high up, I know, but not that high up, Bert! He couldn't have been, could he? If he had been, Mrs Clare wouldn't be Mrs Clare, would she? She'd be a Lady Something!'

'Well, as to that, I believe she *is* a Lady Something, underneath. But doesn't a woman lose a title when she marries someone ordinary? It's either that or Mrs Clare wouldn't use it once she'd got married. That'd be typical. No show, no fuss, just take her as you find her.' He smiled sadly. 'Lovely woman, Mrs Clare. I've never met a better.'

He forgot to say, 'present company excepted', and although Jean felt it, she was glad of it, too. God, if he ever found out how much worse she was than Penny Clare – or even Miss Bright! – he'd hate her until the day he died.

And now, if it was true about Jinny and Felix . . . Not that the curse had anything to do with anything; she knew it hadn't; she was certain it hadn't . . . But if it had, poor things, they'd be double-damned, and if any more harm came to those sweet young people . . .

'Still,' she said with affected brightness. 'I still don't believe they'll get married, Bert. I'll believe it when I see it, and not before.'

She believed it when she and Bert were invited to the engagement party. She believed it when she saw Jinny's beautiful diamond and sapphire ring. She believed it when she saw the happy couple dancing together, their eyes shining with love, their bodies moving as if they were one. She believed it utterly, yet still tried to pretend it wasn't true. She talked endlessly, ate everything she could lay her hands on, drank and was merry until her knees began to wobble and she had to sit down and pull herself together.

Double-damned . . .

She scarcely noticed when Miles Huntley came to sit beside her, and he'd been talking for some time before she began to hear what he was saying. ' – private people, all minding our own business, getting on with our lives as if no one else mattered. But it isn't really like that, is it? We're like beads on a necklace: separate beads caught together on the same string.'

'Mm?'

'Community, Mrs Tomkins. The best kind of family.' He chuckled pensively. 'Remember those dreadful telegrams you brought us? How you cried? I didn't understand it at the time. Now I do.'

'You . . . do?' Jean whispered.

'Yes. For if one bead is lost the whole necklace is broken. Our griefs are not suffered alone. Thank you for sharing our griefs, Mrs Tomkins. And thank you for sharing our joy with us tonight.' He grinned suddenly as Felix and Jinny collapsed in gales of laughter on the far side of the room. 'They make a handsome couple, don't they? Made for each other, wouldn't you say?'

Jean felt sick. She felt very, very sick.
Double-damned.

Violet Huntley died that January and was brought home to be buried beside her husband in the churchyard at Bishop Molton. The turn-out for her funeral was almost as good as it had been for Leonard Clare's: people from London, people from Bath (all very posh, too), people from Bristol by the car load. But it wasn't the attendance of these people that was so surprising. It was that of the people from the village: some so old, so ill and so frail, they hadn't stuck their noses out of doors since the winter set in. But they came to Violet Huntley's funeral, and one of them, old Archie Weaver, stayed weeping in the churchyard when everyone else had gone.

It was Jean who found him there, quite by accident. Nurse Stokes had left her purse in the Post Office and on the return journey from taking it back Jean just happened to look over towards the church, and there he was. Doubled up, poor old chap, like a question mark, and wiping his eyes on his muffler. There was a perishing wind with a bit of snow in it, so Jean couldn't just be tactful and leave him there.

'You've got a long walk home, Archie,' she called cheerily. 'Why don't you pop in to us for a cup of tea before you go?'

'Ah . . .' He sighed as he detached his frozen feet from the path. ''Er was a fine, fine 'ooman, that 'un, Mrs Tongkunz. Priddy's a zummer dawn when virzt I led eyes on 'er, and as good, as koind . . .'

This didn't seem a bit like the catty old harridan Jean had known, but Archie was sad and bitterly lonely. You had to humour him, poor old soul, even if his memories were a bit mixed up.

'Ah, but life treated her cruel,' he went on mournfully. 'Widdered s'young, zee. An' then 'er boys, 'er beloved zons . . . Three on 'em took, and scarce space for 'er to weep betwixt one death an' the next. 'Er were nivver the zame again, Mrs Tongkunz. Nivver.' He shook his head, very slowly. 'Well, now 'er's at rest. Now 'er's with 'em all agin and in 'eaven, Gawd bless 'er zweet zoul.'

He faltered. He stood quite still, staring at the ground. Jean stood too, looking helplessly at his wizened old neck in its motheaten scarf, and saw his tears hit the path like sudden rain. 'Ohh, I wishes . . .' he said softly. 'I wishes I could go with 'er, Mrs Tongkunz. Me days zits 'eavy on me shoulders now and I do wish every one of 'em could be me last.'

'Cup of tea,' Jean said firmly. 'Come on.'

Archie died two days later, and was buried in the midst of a brief, but cruel, snowstorm. Barely a dozen mourners turned out to see him off (Miles Huntley was one of them), but the rumour of Archie's death began another rumour, which kept Jean awake at night, seething with a dreadful anxiety.

'Who'll be next, I wonder?'

'Bound to be another, see, Mrs Tomkins. They always goes off in threes. Specially this time of year, see. It's the cold what does it. Remember '47? Three in a *week* in the January, three in the February . . .'

That would have been bad enough, but some people were never satisfied with 'bad enough'; they had to go for worse.

'Miles Huntley's bad in bed, I hear. Stood out in all that snow, seeing Archie off, gone on his chest something terrible. And *he's* not as young as he was, see. Mrs Huntley's worried *sick*. You can see it in her. Worried *sick*, she is.'

So was Jean. She spent the best part of two weeks worrying about him, praying for him, remembering all the kindness he'd shown her over the years, and all the terrible things she'd done to him.

Then, on January the twenty-eighth, she met Miles in the square, looking as fit as a fiddle and scarcely a day over forty.

'Oh, Mr Huntley! Am I glad to see *you*! How's your chest? Have you still got it?'

He blinked. He looked down at his chest and gently tapped it. 'Y-es,' he smiled. 'Still there, Mrs Tomkins. It was my leg that went missing, you know.'

Jean laughed, one of the hysterical high-pitched yelps that still caught her out now and then, when she was upset about something. 'Ooh-heeh-ya! No! It was your cough, I meant, Mr Huntley! I heard you had a bad cough!'

'Oh, that,' he said. 'Quite better, thank you. I'd forgotten all about it.'

She slept like a baby that night, warm and contented, untroubled even by dreams.

Robin Huntley was killed in a road accident in London on the last day of January. And that made three.

Jean went to see the new Rector three times before Drayfield was demolished. On the first occasion she told him she'd lost her cat (she hadn't), and asked if he could keep an eye out for her on his travels. The second time she told him that Evelyn, who was expecting her first, wanted it to be christened at Bishop Molton (she didn't), and asked if that would be all right when the time came. The third time, stuck for any other excuse, she said she wanted to be included on the church-cleaning rota (she didn't) and he thanked her and said he wished everyone could be as good.

Then they demolished Drayfield and the lost room spilled out. Books, books and more books: most of them ancient, many of them valuable. All about witchcraft.

It was a sensation to beat all. Newspaper reporters everywhere you turned, photographers, book dealers, professors from the university!

A nosey-parker to her bones, Jean felt like a child at a fairground who'd lost her sixpence. All the gossip and the hoo-ha meant nothing to her. It was as if she saw it through thunderclouds and heard it through thunder. She was sick, she was dying. She wanted to die.

The reporters were terrible. 'Did you ever feel there was anything wrong with the house? Any funny noises? Cold draughts? A feeling of anything wrong? Were you happy there?'

She said 'no' to everything, and didn't notice how pleased they were with the last one.

'And Mr Tomkins? Did he ever feel –?'

'I wasn't married to him then. My first husband died . . .'

'In the house?'

'No. In the river.'

She wasn't thinking very clearly. Everything felt a bit fuzzy, a bit strange. It never occurred to her that they'd be asking the same questions of everyone else in the village, putting two and two together, making four. But when the papers came the next day, with 'The Drayfield Curse' plastered all over them . . .

They knew everything that had happened to the Huntleys, everything that had happened to the Clares. They'd even found out Jack's full name (John Gerald), and his age (32) at the time of his death. But they'd blamed the 'curse' on the witch, and Jean knew it had nothing to do with the witch. The worst thing that had happened to the people who'd been there before (what had their name been? Morris? Ford? Austin?) had been Bel's disapproval of their taste in pictures! And they'd been there ten years! They'd had three healthy children! Nothing bad had happened to them at all!

She spent most of that morning on a switchback of decision and indecision, satisfaction and terror. If they were blaming the witch, everything would be all right. It was over. She was free!

But it *wasn't* the witch.

It was all *her* fault, *her* fault! And it *wasn't* over yet. It wasn't *over*!

It was when she started counting up how far it still had to run that the thunderclouds began to strike lightning. Miles,

Bel, Penny. Stephen and Andrew (if he was still alive), Jinny and Felix . . .

Until their line is ended and nothing that is theirs endures upon the earth.

She closed her eyes, and heard John Winterson's voice speaking close against her ear. 'Evil works are the devil's works and the men who help him in that work are his victims, his slaves, more to be pitied than blamed . . .'

'Oh, yes,' she whispered brokenly.

Conjure the devil.

She had conjured the devil and become his slave!

Suddenly she was running, gasping with terror, and she didn't stop running until she was at the Rectory door, pounding at it with both fists, her teeth bared, her voice, thin and starved, crying, 'Help me, help me! For God's sake, help me!'

It was the Rector's wife who opened the door (a mousey little thing whom Jean had always thought of as the lamb that lay down with the lion), but Jean was past caring by that time. 'Where is he?' she shrieked. 'Quick! Quick! I've got to see him! I've got to see him *now*!'

Just as Felix was sitting down to lunch the phone rang. He groaned and got up to answer it, frowning in bewilderment when a soft voice murmured, 'Jon Probert here, Mr Clare. I've . . .'

'Who?'

'Probert!' It was a frantic hiss. 'The bloody rector! Listen!'

His eyes popping with amazement (*bloody* rector?), Felix listened.

'I've a woman here in trouble of a very strange sort. It involves you and several other people whose welfare concerns you. I think you should get over here. Now.' The phone clicked. Probert had rung off.

'Oh! Stick it in the oven,' Felix shouted angrily. 'I'm going out!'

* *

Jon Probert didn't look half so pleased with himself in the cold light of dawn, and he swore more than once as he and Felix slithered through the sticky red mud that was almost all that was left of the valley.

'This is so ridiculous,' Felix said. 'I can't believe I'm doing it. I suppose you know we'll get arrested if anyone – '

'At five o'clock in the morning?'

'We're trespassing! We've climbed over three "Keep Out" notices already!'

'God will protect us,' the Rector said smugly. 'Where are we?'

Felix didn't know. He knew they were at Drayfield because Drayfield had been the only farm at this end of the valley; but it had been flattened. All the landmarks had gone. He couldn't get his bearings. 'Hang on,' he said. 'Where's east?'

'Directly opposite west,' Mr Probert muttered sarcastically.

'This was your idea, Rector,' Felix reminded him coolly. 'If you'd rather go home, just mention it, will you?'

'Sorry. So where's this house of yours?'

'Over here. At least . . .'

Just bits of it. Bits of wall, bits of floor, heaps of mud, heaps of rubble. Felix nodded grimly. 'And we're looking for a little *brooch*? You're crazy, Mr Probert, and that's an understatement, phrased more for kindness than accuracy. I think you'd better start praying.'

They'd brought two spades, two pick-axes, a lump hammer and a garden fork. Mr Probert wasn't competent with any of them, and it was some time before even Felix could work out a system. Each one of the kitchen flagstones weighed the best part of a ton and they'd intended to be there until hell froze over. Felix managed to change their minds; but only just. Lift them on one side, look, drop; lift the other side, look, drop. An hour passed. The sun rose in a blaze of rose and gold.

'I hope you're doing plenty of praying,' Felix muttered angrily. 'Because I'm doing most of the digging!'

He hadn't really meant it. It had just been something to say in a situation which, however much he tried to believe it, defied all belief. Mrs Tomkins had put a curse on an inch-long brooch, seventeen *years* ago, and the Rector was hoping to *find* it?

Clenching his jaw with frustration, Felix lifted another flagstone and was just about to drop it again when the ascending sun, directed in a thin beam between his elbow and his ribs, picked out a tiny glint of gold among the mud.

'*Gotcha*!'

'Ahhh! The power of prayer works many miracles, Mr Clare.'

'Oh, does it, Mr Probert? I'd say it was more the power of human muscle. *Mine*. Pick the damn thing up before my back breaks!'

Yet as Mr Probert (his life for a moment depending very much on the power of human muscle) crawled beneath the stone and prised the brooch out, Felix really did begin to believe in miracles. For the glint he had seen – and would not have seen had the sun not picked it out – was just the tiniest part of the brooch, the point of the pin. Everything else was caked in thick, compacted slime.

They didn't speak again until they were safely back on Felix's own land, when the Rector stopped to wash the brooch in a puddle and reveal it – quite undamaged – in all its mysterious complexity. 'Look,' he whispered as he turned it in his palm. 'The serpent of old . . .'

'Oh, come on!' Felix scoffed. 'This is the twentieth century! You don't really believe – '

'It's not a matter of believing, Mr Clare. It's a matter of fact. Mrs Tomkins cursed this brooch and has been driven nearly mad by her conscience ever since. Is that good, or is it evil?'

'Perhaps it's justice,' Felix suggested curtly.

'Ah . . . But if you call it justice, you must think she did wrong, Mr Clare. And what was it she did? Muttered a few naughty words in a naughty little temper. Haven't *you* ever done that?'

'Not those particular words, no.'

'And if you'd known those particular words, instead of the ones you used instead, would you have said them?'

The answer was no, but Felix didn't say so. He didn't say anything. He just stared at the ground, remembering. Remembering that the Rector hadn't let Mrs Tomkins say the words aloud. He'd made her write them down, as if to allow them to be spoken again would contaminate the air... *I conjure thee, O serpent of old, servant of the wise and begetter of all the wisdom of the earth, take my enemy from me. Bind him in the coils of thy might and bring him ever unto darkness.*

The Rector was right. There was a power in those words which rendered more everyday curses about as potent as a nursery rhyme. But the power was in the *words*, not their meaning! It was the power of *poetry*, not evil!

'Words,' he said flatly, 'don't kill people.'

'Depends whose words they are,' the Rector murmured. 'You might try remembering a few of Hitler's if you doubt their power to kill.'

'Hitler and Mrs Tomkins were hardly playing in the same league, Mr Probert.'

'No. But they were playing the same game, Mr Clare. And for the same captain.'

More words. But they sent a shiver through Felix's spine just the same.

Chapter Thirty

The post had never been the same since Jean Tomkins had 'retired'. Whatever else her faults, she'd been good at her job, taken a pride in it, done it *properly*. Bel wished she could say the same for Fred Holmes, who didn't even ride his bike up the drive as Jean had done, let alone use the letter box! He just nipped in through the side gate, opened the scullery door, shouted, 'Post!' and dropped the letters on the lid of the boiler.

During the war, when there'd been excuses for such behaviour, Bel wouldn't have minded so much; but it seemed to matter more now. A great many unimportant things seemed to matter so much more than they should, making her angry, making her cry. She wanted everything to be as it had been in the old days. The best silver on the table, three courses at lunch and six at dinner... Robin wiping his hands on his jersey. Simon complaining about his haircut, Andrew burbling on about cricket as if it was the most important thing in the world...

'Why didn't you get fat, Mummy?'

'I beg your pardon?'

'You said four courses for lunch – '

'Three. Six at dinner.'

'Small courses,' Miles murmured. 'An inch of soup, a few flakes of fish – '

'It was rather more than that!' Bel snapped. 'And just look at us now! Call this a decent breakfast? A bowl of Force Flakes and a measly little sausage, stuffed with sawdust!'

'Are you hungry, darling?' Miles frowned at his plate, apparently considering handing over the remains of his own lump of sawdust.

'No,' Bel said wearily. 'I was just . . . Oh, never mind. I was just being silly.' She fixed a smile to her face and turned to Jinny. 'Any more news of Felix, darling? Have you found out what he's up to at the Rectory?'

'*No*. And it's driving Penny crazy. She says she doesn't actually *mind* if he turns religious, but she'd like to know *why*. So would I. It can't be anything to do with the wedding, can it, Daddy?'

Miles shook his head. 'Blowed if I know, darling. But I don't see how it can be. The wedding's our pigeon, not his. All he has to do is wait at the altar.'

'The thing *I* can't make out,' Jinny said, 'is why it's so important! He's been there at least twice this week, right in the middle of harvest! He can barely find the time to see *me*, let alone the – '

'Post!'

The scullery door slammed shut and Bel, narrowing her eyes, muttered, 'I'll kill him,' and ran through to the scullery with precisely that intention in view. But something in the pile of letters caught her eye before she could get any further. A little edging of red-white-and-blue, looking for all the world like V-E Day bunting . . .

'Andrew?' she whispered, and then, snatching the Air Mail envelope from the heap, 'Andrew!'

Eight months had passed since Robin's death, and she'd prayed and prayed that Andrew would hear of it somehow and write to her. 'Somewhere in America,' was such a small comfort when you needed so much more. But this was his handwriting! 'Oh, God, oh, God,' she gasped frantically. 'Let him be coming home!'

'Bel?'

Wide-eyed and trembling, barely able to stand for the shock, she passed the letter over. 'Andrew,' she croaked. 'I – I – Oh, Miles! Open it!'

'Come on,' he said gently. 'Let's sit down. Before we fall down.'

They went to the library and sat on the couch, trying to read it together, every word.

'My dearest Mother and Father and Jinny, I must ask your forgiveness for a thousand things, not least of them my tardiness in writing this letter. I've written many others over the years, all of which have hit the dust before they could hit the mailbox. I wanted to explain, to justify myself, to put myself in the right; and it's only since Steve wrote me the dreadful news about Robin that I've understood how little it all matters – and therefore how wrong I was, all along.'

Miles rubbed his thumb across his eyes. Bel wept. Jinny, muttering something about coffee, tiptoed from the room and left them to it.

It was a long letter, full of extraordinary news (he was married!), and although Bel read every word of it at least ten times over, she'd have been content with the fewest words, the smallest and the best: 'I love you,' and, 'I'm coming home.'

Jean had never thought much of Mr Probert. He laughed too much; he talked too much. And his hands were like women's hands, soft and white, with frail blue veins shining through skin as thin and as smooth as paper. But when they touched her, when his beautiful voice murmured the words of benediction in her ear, Jean felt the strength of him like a brisk March wind, blowing all the dust away, making everything clean again.

'Say your prayers now,' he said kindly. 'And go in peace.'

Jean had never known how to pray. In all the years she'd been going to church (on and off, ever since Jack died) she'd never quite got the hang of talking to someone she wasn't certain was there. She'd always, when she thought of Him, seen someone young and strong, fierce and unforgiving; someone who knew her conscience like the back of His hand – and hated her for it. 'Dirty little hypocrite,' He'd sneered. 'Coming here, pretending you're a Christian! Well, I know better! I know what you've been up to! You don't fool me!'

So she'd tried very hard not to think of Him. She'd sung the hymns and said the Creed, even recited the General Confession, like a child parroting the six times table, vaguely aware that there was some meaning in the pattern but not greatly caring what it was.

'One six is six, two sixes are twelve . . .'

'Our Father which art in heaven . . .'

Now she could pray. She could thank Him with all her heart, not for forgiving her (*He'd* never blamed her), but for letting her forgive herself. The curse hadn't been real. It hadn't 'worked' except in her heart, turning everything back on herself, so that, in the end, only she had been harmed by it.

'For what is evil,' Mr Probert had asked, 'except our own frailty? What is goodness, except our own love?'

'But I *did* love them!' Jean had wept. 'The Huntleys, the Clares! I did love them! I *do*!'

'And who do you hate, Mrs Tomkins?'

'*Myself.*'

'But for what? For losing your baby? For bearing four lovely daughters when your husband wanted sons? For suffering grief, loneliness, poverty and fear? My dear Mrs Tomkins, if this were the story of another woman's life, would you hate *her*?'

'No. Oh, no . . .'

Ivy Shilling was married now, still working mornings at Bishop's Court, but only for the extras: little luxuries for the house, little treats for the kiddies. She'd done far worse than Jean had ever done (three babies wrong side of the blanket!), but no, Jean had never hated her. Pitied her, cared about her; even loved her in a way. But hated her? Oh, no.

And now, after that sweet young man's blessing, she didn't hate herself, either. True, she was fat and silly and getting on in years, but so what? Bert still loved her, bless him; so what else mattered?

'And thank you, *thank you*, for Bert,' she concluded sweetly. 'Amen.'

Felix was well aware that if Mr Probert had stood a chance of finding that brooch on his own, he'd have kept it a secret from everyone. Even now, with all things blessed which could be blessed and Mrs Tomkins shriven of her guilt, a great many things were still a secret. The Huntleys didn't know, Bert Tomkins didn't know, Penny didn't know. Even Felix knew no more than the Rector had deemed necessary: that Mrs Tomkins had laid a curse on Drayfield – and burned in her own personal hell for it ever since.

Felix knew about 'personal hell'; personal heaven, too; but he still didn't believe in the other sorts, beyond the world. Hell was just a lack of understanding of one's own needs and motives, trying to live according to one's assumptions about other people instead of one's knowledge of oneself. His own self-knowledge was still very slight (as Penny had said, the book took a lifetime to read all through), but that didn't matter. As long as he kept faith with what was written – his own feelings, his own ideas, his own understanding of right and wrong – hellfire kept its distance and heaven was in view. And what, after all, was heaven? Self-respect, respect of others . . . And peace. Peace of mind.

But his peace of mind took a bit of a shaking when, on his

next visit to Mr Probert, he saw that tiny gold brooch lying in solitary state on the Rector's immaculate desk.

'Ummm!' Mr Probert said. 'Now we have a problem, Mr Clare. What do we do with this?'

Felix was rather irritated. He'd been called away from his end-of-year accounts this time, and the answer to Probert's question seemed so obvious as to verge on the ridiculous.

'Give it back to Mrs Tomkins,' he said. 'Or, if she doesn't want it – '

'But it isn't hers, Mr Clare. That's my difficulty, you see. It belongs to Mrs Huntley, and I'm not entirely sure that she'll want to see it again.'

'Oh?' Felix looked at him sideways.

'Hmm . . .' Mr Probert grinned. 'I can't answer that, so don't ask it, Mr Clare.' He took the brooch between forefinger and thumb and turned it to the light. 'It's a beautiful thing, and most unusual. It might be very valuable for all I know, and there's always a chance that Mrs Huntley would be delighted to have it back. *But* . . .'

He curled the brooch into his palm and thought about it for a while. 'I have a feeling,' he murmured.

Felix sat down, mentally abandoning his end-of-year accounts for yet another day.

'As you've said on numerous occasions, Mr Clare, it's just a little scrap of gold. No evil in it now and no good either. Yet I think it has . . . a purpose.'

'Oh, Lord,' Felix said dismally.

'No, I don't really mean that. I mean only that I'm loath to get rid of it in *case* it has a purpose.' He smiled. 'And since you're so certain that it hasn't, Mr Clare, and since you know the Huntleys as well as anyone can, I give it to you, to do as you choose with it. Take it back to Drayfield, throw it in the midden, keep it for your grandchildren, give it to the poor. Or . . . return it to its owner. Up to you.'

As convinced as he still was of the complete uselessness of

the brooch – it was just a *brooch*, for heaven's sake, nothing more! – Felix felt that he'd been given a burden, more equal in size and weight to one of the Drayfield flagstones than to the bauble he'd found beneath them.

'Now, hang on,' he said as the brooch fell into his palm. 'If this belongs to Bel Huntley, how did Mrs Tomkins – ?'

'Sorry. I can't tell you. I wouldn't have involved you at all had Mrs Tomkins not been so anxious to find it and have it blessed. You don't believe in this sort of thing, of course; but if it's any help . . . It *has* been blessed, Mr Clare. It won't burn a hole in your pocket.'

And he was right. It didn't. Felix dropped it into the pocket of his waistcoat and completely forgot it was there.

Andrew and Oriel, his wife, were coming over in March for a six-month visit which would cover Jinny's wedding in April, the Queen's Coronation in June and as many other delights as Bel could organise for their pleasure. She kept saying, 'How about Henley? How about a Test Match? Oooh, and Wimbledon! Oh, and how about – ?'

'How about a few quiet weeks at home?' Miles was inclined to mutter tetchily. But Bel took no notice. There was so much to do!

The wedding was at the forefront of her mind: not merely because it was only six months distant (with absolutely *nothing* done), but because Jinny was taking no interest in it at all.

'I'm getting married, Mummy, not crowned. It doesn't have to be a state occasion, you know. If it weren't for Felix turning religious – ' (his mysterious visits to the Rectory were still not explained) ' – I'd be perfectly happy to do it in a register office and blow all the fuss.'

'Don't be so ridiculous,' Bel sighed. 'You are a Christian, even if Felix isn't, and your marriage will be consecrated in the proper – '

'Okay. Consecrate it. Do as you think best. But don't expect me to get excited about it, Mummy. I'm not interested.'

'You aren't *interested*? In your own *wedding*?'

'Nope.'

'Ooh, I wish you wouldn't say that! It's so slangy!'

'*No*, then. I'm *not* interested in my wedding: I'm interested in my *marriage*, which will last a good deal longer and matter a great deal more.'

Bel knew she was right, but at the same time it seemed all *wrong*. Entirely too post-war, too frugal, too sensible, too... *drab*. A small part of her mind (a sharp fingernail of conscience) told her that she wasn't thinking so much of Felix and Jinny as of Andrew and his wife. She wanted to give them a wonderful time, to make everything perfect, to make everything *right*, to prove herself...

'Your mother's a wonderful woman, Andrew!'

'Mmm? Why yes, now you come to mention it, darling, I suppose she is!'

Wrong. Quite wrong. On Jinny's wedding day, if on no other, Jinny must come first. But what the hell? She'd said 'do as you think best,' hadn't she? And that was just what Bel was going to do! It was high time they all had some fun!

She settled down, that evening, to arrange all the fun, consulting Miles at every stage and getting no help at all.

'How about St Mary Redcliffe for the ceremony, darling?'

'*What*? Why the deuce – ? What's wrong with our own church, for heaven's sake?'

'Too far from the Grand Spa. I thought we'd have the reception in the Grand Spa, and the – '

'*Grand Spa*? I thought Jinny wanted to keep it simple!'

'Oh, shush! Weddings are women's work, remember? How much do you think you could run to for the dress?'

'With the reception at the Grand Spa? About a fiver, I should think.'

'You might try being more helpful, Miles. I'm thinking of Norman Hartnell. Something – ' She fluttered her hands around her hips in an expansive gesture which seemed to imply, 'forty yards of silk organza'.

'Norman Hartnell,' Miles repeated softly. 'Fine. Fine. I should be able to raise that amount, darling. I've never liked this house, anyway. We'll be much happier in a bungalow, just the two of us.' He sighed. 'It's poor Muriel I feel sorry for. There won't be room for her, of course. But there.' He sighed, again. 'Norman Hartnell it is. Take Jinny to Town for a few weeks, darling. Stay at the Dorchester. Spare no expense. *Ruin us.*'

Bel was still wondering whether to laugh or throw something at him when Jinny came in: flushed (as she usually was after a night out with Felix) and smiling a rather strange, secretive little smile which, in Bel's opinion, had 'Nope' written all over it.

'*What?*' she asked suspiciously.

'What what?' Jinny smirked.

'What are you up to?'

'Nothing. I've got something for you.'

'Ohhh? What?'

Whatever it was, it was very small: small enough to be hidden in Jinny's closed fist. And whatever it was . . . But what did that smile mean? It was so strange, so . . . mischievous. But more than that . . . *Worse* than that.

Bel laughed nervously. 'If it's a spider – '

'No. It's something pretty. Something precious.' Her eyes glinted, and still she smiled, stretching out her hand, holding it over the desk, within easy reach of Bel's hand. But Bel was afraid.

'Look,' Jinny whispered. 'Recognise it?'

She opened her fingers very suddenly. Bel felt the blood draining from her face, the sense draining from her mind. The briar rose . . .

'Miles,' she whispered. 'Miles . . .'

Jinny seemed not to have noticed anything amiss, for she went on brightly, 'Remember it, Mummy? You lost it out at Drayfield, a long time ago. Felix had it in his pocket. It fell out when he was looking for his keys. I thought it was a present for me, but he said it was yours. Mrs Tomkins gave it to him.'

Jean Tomkins . . . The spider.

Bel's teeth were chattering. She jammed her finger between them and bit down until the pain . . .

'Miles!' she wailed. 'Miles! Help me!'

'*What?* What the devil's wrong?' It seemed to take hours while he prised himself out of his chair and limped to her side. And he seemed to stare at the brooch for hours before he spoke.

'Well,' he said softly at last. 'So the wanderer returns. How much do you know, Jinny?'

She laid the brooch down and turned away. 'I've known for a long time there was something you didn't want me to know. Something bad. Something painful. And I didn't *want* to know. But now I do.'

Miles sat down and rested his head in his hands. 'Pandora's box,' he said. 'Why does someone always have to open the bloody thing?'

'Daddy, I'm getting married. If there's something wrong with me, something Felix doesn't know –!'

'Wrong with you? There's nothing wrong with you!'

'Isn't it wrong to be incomplete, Daddy? Isn't it wrong to give yourself to a man without even knowing what it is you're *giving*? Tell me! I don't care how much it hurts. I just want to *know*!'

'But it won't hurt just *you*, darling. Your mother –'

Suddenly Bel took his hand and squeezed it firmly. 'It's all right,' she said softly. 'You . . . forgave me. God didn't. And

I . . . never can until – ' Her voice fell to a mere breath. 'Tell her, Miles. Tell her . . . the truth.'

Miles took a cigarette from the box on the table. He lit it. He inhaled. Then, after a lengthy pause for thought, 'It was entirely my fault,' he began gently. 'Or perhaps Julius Caesar's.'

He exhaled. The smoke stung Bel's eyes and she smiled, she wept. And her tears fell unheeded to her notepad and washed Norman Hartnell away.

The tale was ended. Miles, Bel and Jinny sat like statues in a room full of smoke, where the clock ticked and the embers sighed, and the moon, peering between a gap in the curtains, smiled the benign smile of the old Archdeacon and whispered, 'It's over.'

At last Jinny spoke. 'Is that all?' she asked incredulously.

Miles scratched his cheek. 'It's all I know,' he said. 'If anyone joined the circus too, I was left in ignorance of it. What do you mean, child? Is that *all*? What more do you want? I've exposed my soul and your mother's. I've smoked myself sick, talked myself hoarse – '

'Yes, but . . . It was just . . .'

'Just what?'

She shrugged. 'I just thought it must be something terrible, and it wasn't. After all, you couldn't help it, could you? It was the war's fault, not yours. And Mummy . . . I quite understand Mummy. She thought you didn't love her, you see, and that hurts . . . so much.'

Bel stared at her, amazed. Perhaps it hadn't sunk in yet. Perhaps Jinny hadn't realised what it all meant: that she wasn't Miles's daughter.

'So all that time when you were cross with *me* – ' Jinny was waving her finger back and forth, as if trying to paint in a picture.

'You *weren't* cross with me. You were just cross with Mummy, because – '

'Because she'd taken you away from me,' Miles said gently. 'At least, I thought she had. But we're each of us the architects of our own doom, Jinny. I loved you with all my heart and tried to deny it and when, in my slow, lumbering fashion, I realised that such things *can't* be denied, it was too late. I'd driven you away. To Felix.'

Jinny shrugged again. 'Oh, well,' she said casually. 'I think I'd have loved him anyway.' She looked at her hands for a moment and then, grinning like the cat that got the cream, 'Hand on heart, Daddy.'

He obeyed.

'You really loved me?'

'Oh, yes.'

'Even though I wasn't yours?'

'Even though.'

She slumped in her chair, letting her hands droop over the arms. 'Wow,' she breathed. And she laughed.

Bel covered her mouth with shaking fingers. She couldn't believe it. She couldn't believe it! It didn't hurt any more! And it hadn't hurt Jinny! But –

'What about Jack?' she asked incredulously. 'Don't you . . . care?'

'No. Why should I? He was nothing to you. He's nothing to me. All I ever wanted – ' She smiled and opened her arms as if to embrace the whole world. 'All I ever wanted was to *understand*!'

They had never been a demonstrative family. Expressions of affection had been trained out of Bel, first by a houseful of watchful servants, then by the lack of the necessary affection and at last by force of habit. But they ended that night (at three in the morning) in a circle of arms, kisses and tears. And laughter and love. And forgiveness.

'How's this wedding coming on, Mummy?' Jinny asked sleepily at last.

Bel smiled. 'I thought we'd keep it simple, darling. A simple frock. A simple posy . . . And a wreath of wild roses in your hair.'

Bel strolled along the banks of the Dray Valley Lake, feeling the sun hot on her face, watching it glint on the water. Swans and mallards swam nearby, looking for crumbs from her picnic and a trio of sailing dinghies sped out towards Drayfield, reminding her . . .

She turned and tiptoed back to the car, kneeling to pack up the remains of their little feast: a thermos of tea and some cake. Richard adored the lake. He adored picnics. He adored ducks. And he adored his Grandpapa.

They were asleep now. Miles in a camp chair with his panama over his eyes; Richard sprawled on his grandfather's knee, with his thumb in his mouth. He was two: the most beautiful child Bel had ever seen, with his mother's red-gold hair, his father's slate-blue eyes and his grandfather's . . .

Frowning, Bel adjusted her thoughts, forcing herself to remember that Miles *wasn't* Richard's grandfather and that therefore . . .

She put the picnic basket in the car and, forgetting that she was trying not to wake the sleeping beauties (she'd forget her own head if it wasn't screwed on) she slammed the boot-lid closed. Miles woke and Richard woke. They smiled simultaneously.

'Hello, Gamama. Feeda ducks?'

'Hmm?' Bel turned her head, first one way and then another. She narrowed her eyes, staring at them both in utter perplexity. The same wide mouth, giving exactly the same impression of having too many teeth . . . Yes, she'd thought it before without daring to believe it: minus only the curls, Richard was the image of Robin when he'd been tiny. And Robin had been the image of *Miles*!

'Boat, Gampapa! Boat!'

With Miles holding Richard's reins and Bel holding Miles's

arm, they strolled down to the water's edge to watch the boats sail by.

'Time *we* tried that,' Miles said.

'You'd never manage it. What about your leg?'

'Mm. I was thinking of something a little larger. The Queen Mary, perhaps. It's high time we took a look at our American grandchildren – if only to see how many more of the little bastards have turned out like me.'

'Bartard!' Richard repeated happily.

'No,' Miles said firmly. '*Not* bartard, darling. *Outboard*. See? On the back of the boat? Outboard motor.'

'Owbord! Owbord motor!'

'So Jinny *isn't* one?' Bel demanded incredulously.

'Good Lord, no. Don't be so ridiculous, Bel. Jinny doesn't even resemble an outboard motor. Whatever made you think she did?'

As they drove back to Bishop's Court, they passed Jean and Bert Tomkins, who were strolling along the lakeside in the opposite direction, hand in hand. 'They look happy, don't they?' Bel murmured, and Miles, glancing first in the rear-view mirror and then lovingly at his wife, said softly, 'You know something? They're saying exactly the same thing about us.'